SEP 2 7 2012

STORMDANCER

STORMDANCER

Jay Kristoff

THOMAS DUNNE BOOKS ⚐ ST. MARTIN'S PRESS NEW YORK

This is a work of fiction. All of the characters, organizations, and events portrayed in this novel are either products of the author's imagination or are used fictitiously.

THOMAS DUNNE BOOKS.
An imprint of St. Martin's Press.

www.thomasdunnebooks.com
www.stmartins.com

Map artwork © David Atkinson: handmademaps.com

Kanji designs: Araki Miho: ebisudesign.com
Clan logo design: James Orr

ISBN 978-1-250-00140-5 (hardcover)
ISBN 978-1-250-01791-8 (e-book)

First published in Great Britain by Tor, an imprint of Pan Macmillan, a division of Macmillan Publishers Limited

First U.S. Edition: September 2012

10 9 8 7 6 5 4 3 2 1

For Amanda,
My love, my life, my first and only reason

MONS OF THE SHIMA IMPERIUM

TIGER CLAN (TORA)

FOX CLAN (KITSUNE)

DRAGON CLAN (RYU)

PHOENIX CLAN (FUSHICHO)

THE LOTUS GUILD

THE SHIMA ISLES

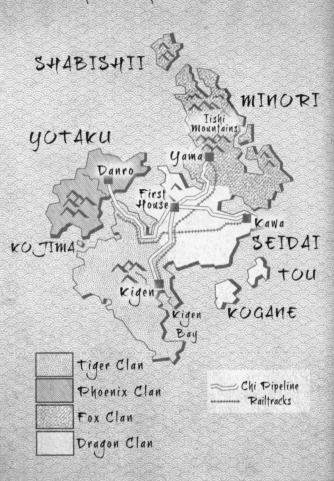

SHABISHII

MINORI

Tishi Mountains

YOTAKU

Yama

Danro

First House

KOJIMA

Kawa

SEIDAI

TOU

Kigen

KOGANE

Kigen Bay

Tiger Clan

Phoenix Clan

Fox Clan

Dragon Clan

Chi Pipeline

Railtracks

CITY

UPSIDE

DOCKTOWN

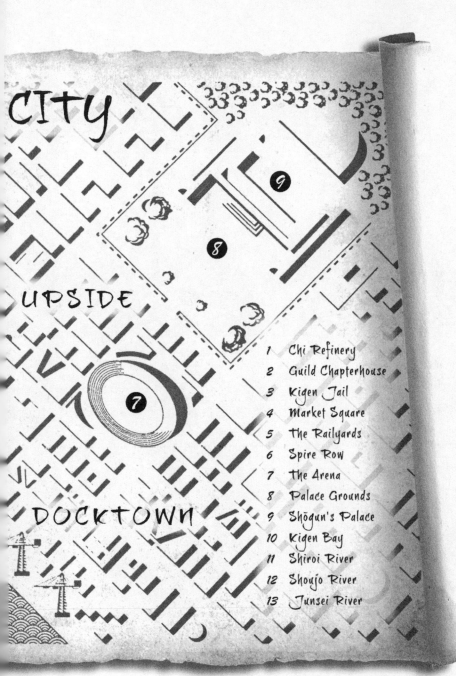

PART 1
FIRE

Our prelude was Void.
The vast possibility, before life drew breath.
Unto none came two; shining Lord Izanagi, Maker and Father,
His beloved bride; great Lady Izanami, Mother of All Things,
And from wedded bliss, eight children drew precious life:
The Isles of Shima.

The Book of Ten Thousand Days

1

YUKIKO

As the iron war club scythed toward her head, Yukiko couldn't help wishing she'd listened to her father.

She rolled aside as her cover was smashed to kindling, azalea petals drifting over the oni's shoulders like perfumed snowflakes. The demon loomed above her, twelve feet high, all iron-tipped tusks and long, jagged fingernails. Stinking of open graves and burning hair, skin of polished midnight blue, eyes like funeral candles bathing the forest with guttering light. The club in its hands was twice as long as Yukiko was tall. One direct hit, and she would never see the samurai with the sea-green eyes again.

"Well, that's clever," she chided herself, "thinking about boys at a time like this."

A spit-soaked roar pushed her hard in the chest, scattering a cloud of sparrows from the temple ruins at her back. Lightning licked the clouds, bathing the whole scene in fleeting, brilliant white: the endless wilds, the stranded sixteen-year-old girl, and the pit demon poised to cave in her skull.

Yukiko turned and ran.

Trees stretched in every direction, a steaming snarl of roots and undergrowth, stinking of green rot. Branches whipped her face and tore her clothes, rain and sweat slicked her skin. She touched the fox tattoo sleeving her right arm, tracing its nine tails in prayer. The demon behind her bellowed as she slipped away, over root and under branch, deeper into the suffocating heat.

She screamed for her father. For Kasumi or Akihito. For anybody.

And nobody came.

The trees erupted and toppled in front of her, cleft to the heartwood by an enormous ten-span sword. Another oni appeared through the shower of falling

3

green, tombstone mask for a face, lips pierced with rusted iron rings. Yukiko dived sideways as the great sword swept overhead, clipping her braid. Strands of long, black hair drifted down to the dead leaves.

She was rolling to her feet when the oni snatched her up, quicker than flies, its awful grip making her cry out. She could read the blasphemous kanji symbols carved on its necklace, feel the heat gleaming from its flesh. The first oni arrived, bellowing in delight. Her captor opened its jaws, a black maggot tongue lolling between its teeth.

She drew her tantō and stabbed the demon's hand, burying six inches of folded steel to the hilt. Blood sprayed, black and boiling where it touched her skin. The oni roared and hurled her against a nearby cedar. Her skull cracked against the trunk and she crashed earthward, rag-doll limp, the bloody knife skittering from her grip. Darkness reached up to smother her and she desperately clawed it away.

Not like this.

The first demon's laughter reminded her of screaming children, burning on Guild pyres in the Market Square. Its wounded comrade growled in a dark, backward tongue, stalking forward and raising its sword to end her. Lightning glinted on the blade's edge, time slowing to a crawl as the blow began to fall. Yukiko thought of her father again, wishing for all the world she'd done what she'd been told for just once in her life.

Thunder cracked overhead. A white shape burst from the undergrowth and landed on the oni's back; a flurry of razors, broken blue sparks and beating wings. The demon shrieked as the beast tore into its shoulders, ripping mouthfuls of flesh with a blood-slick beak.

The first oni growled, swinging its war club in a broad, hissing arc. Their attacker sprang into the air, tiny whirlwinds of falling leaves and snow-white petals dancing in time to the thrashing of its wings. The demon's tetsubo slammed across its comrade's shoulders. Bone splintered under the war club's impact, the oni's spine shattering like dark, wet glass. It crumpled to the ground, its last breath spattered in steaming black across Yukiko's terrified face.

The beast landed off-balance, digging bloodstained claws into the earth.

The oni glanced at its companion's corpse, shifting the war club from one hand to the other. Howling a challenge, it lifted the weapon and charged. The pair collided, beast and demon, crashing earthward and tumbling about in a flurry of feathers, petals and screams.

Yukiko wiped at the sticky black in her eyes, tried to blink away her concussion. She could make out blurry shapes rolling in the fallen leaves, dark splashes staining the white azalea blossoms. She heard a crunch, a choking gurgle, and then a vast, empty silence.

She blinked into the gloom, pulse throbbing behind her eyes.

The beast emerged from the shadows, feathers stained black with blood. It stalked toward her and lowered its head, growl building in its throat. Yukiko groped toward her tantō, pawing through the muck and sodden leaves for the blade as her eyesight dimmed. The darkness beckoned, arms open wide, promising an end to all of her fear. To be with her brother again. To leave this dying island and its poisoned sky behind. To lie down and finally sleep after a decade of hiding who and what she was.

She closed her eyes and wished she were safe and warm at home, nestled in her blankets, the air tinged blue-black with the smoke from her father's pipe. The beast opened its beak and roared, a hurricane scream swallowing the light and memories.

Darkness fell completely.

2

HACHIMAN'S CHOSEN

It was on a sweltering morning two weeks earlier when Yoritomo-no-miya, Seii Taishōgun of the Shima Isles, emerged from his bedchamber, yawned and declared that he wanted a griffin.

His elderly major-domo, Tora Hideo, fell perfectly still. His calligraphy brush hovered over the arrest warrants piled on the table in front of him. Blood lotus smoke curled up from the bone pipe in his left hand, and Hideo squinted through the haze at his master. Even after seven years as Yoritomo's chief minister, there were still days when he found his Shōgun impossible to read. To laugh, or not to laugh? That was the question.

"My Lord?" he finally ventured.

"You heard. A griffin."

"My Lord refers to a statue of some kind? A monument, perhaps, to celebrate the bicentennial of the glorious Kazumitsu Dynasty?"

"No. A real one."

One traitorous eyebrow rose toward Hideo's hairline.

"But, my Lord . . ." The old man cleared his throat. "Thunder tigers are extinct."

Dirty opalescent light filtered through the sitting room's tall bay doors. A vast garden stretched out in the palace grounds below, its trees stunted and sickly despite the multitude of servants who toiled beneath them every day. Faint birdsong drifted from the greenery like mist; the mournful cries of a legion of sparrows. The birds were imported monthly from the north at the Shōgun's request, their wings kept clipped so they couldn't flee the reek.

The sky hung heavy with a pall of fumes, sealing in the day's already oppressive heat. As the Ninth Shōgun of the Kazumitsu Dynasty stalked to the balcony and looked out over his capital, a sky-ship rose from Kigen harbor and started its long trek north, trailing a suffocating plume of blue-black exhaust.

"The cloudwalkers say otherwise," he declared.

Hideo sighed inwardly, placed his calligraphy brush aside with care. Smoke curled up from his pipe to the ceiling; a vast dome of obsidian and pearl reminiscent of the once-clear night sky. The silken sokutai robe he wore was abominably heavy, layer upon layer of gold and scarlet, and he cursed again at having to wear the confounded thing in this heat. The old man's knees creaked as he rose. He inhaled another lungful of lotus and stared at his Lord's back.

Yoritomo had changed much in the seven years since his father, Shōgun Kaneda, had passed on to his heavenly reward. Now in his twentieth summer, his shoulders were broad, jaw chiseled, long black hair tied up in the style of manhood. As was custom among all the great bloodlines of Shima, he had been adorned with beautiful tattoos on his thirteenth birthday: the fierce tiger prowling down his right arm venerating the guardian spirit of his clan, and the imperial sun over a field of blood lotus flowers down his left declaring him Shōgun of the Four Thrones of the Shima Empire. As the major-domo watched, the tiger tattoo blinked, flexing claws as sharp as katana across his master's skin. The totem seemed to stare right at him.

Hideo squinted at the pipe in his hand, deciding he'd smoked enough for one morning.

"These cloudwalkers were men of the Kitsune clan, hai?" He exhaled a plume of narcotic midnight blue. "The wise man never trusts the fox, great Lord."

"You have heard the rumor, then."

"Nothing escapes my spies, great Lord. Our web is spun across the entire Shōgunate." The old man moved his arm in a broad arc. "Fox, Dragon, Phoenix or Tiger, there is no clan and no secret that—"

"You did not think to report it to me?"

Hideo's arm fell to his side, the faintest shadow of a frown creasing his brow. "Forgive me, my Lord. I had no desire to trouble you with the superstitious babbling of peasant folk. If I roused you every time the taverns or brothels crawled with some fancy about flying tigers or giant sea serpents or other yōkai—"

"Tell me what you know."

A long silence fell, punctuated by the calls of choking sparrows. Hideo heard the soft footfalls of a servant roaming distant hallways, ringing ten notes upon an iron bell and announcing in a clear, high voice that the Hour of the Crane had begun.

"A fantasy, great Lord." Hideo finally shrugged, "A crew of cloudwalkers arrived in port three days ago, saying that monsoon winds drove their sky-ship off course beyond the cursed Iishi Mountains. While praying that their inflatable would not be burned to a cinder by the Thunder God Raijin, several of the men claimed to have seen the silhouette of an arashitora among the clouds."

"An arashitora," Yoritomo repeated. "A thunder tiger, Hideo. Just imagine it."

The minister shook his head.

"Sailors are fond of their tall tales, my Lord. Those who sail the skies most of all. Any man who spends every minute of his day breathing lotus exhaust sooner or later finds himself possessed of an addled mind. I heard of one crew who swore they saw the blessed Maker God Izanagi walking among the clouds. Another group claim to have found the entrance to the Yomi underworld, and the boulder great Lord Izanagi used to seal it closed. Are we to believe their demented fictions also?"

"This is no fiction, Hideo-san."

"My Lord, what—"

"I have dreamed it." Yoritomo turned to face Hideo, his eyes alight. "I have seen myself riding among the thunderclaps astride a great arashitora, leading my armies to war overseas against the round-eye gaijin hordes. Like the Storm-dancers of legend. A vision sent from mighty Hachiman, the God of War himself."

Hideo covered his mouth and gave a small cough.

"Great Lord, equal of heaven—"

"Spare me."

". . . Shōgun, there has not been a confirmed sighting of a thunder tiger since the days of your great-grandfather. The lotus fumes that claimed the sea dragons have claimed them also. The great yōkai beasts are gone forever, back to the spirit realms that once bore them." Hideo stroked his beard. "Or to the realms of the dead."

The Shōgun turned from the window and folded his arms. The tiger tattoo paced around his bicep, crystalline eyes glittering, pausing to roar silently at the now sweating minister. Hideo fidgeted with his pipe.

"The beast will be captured, Hideo-san," the Shōgun glared. "You will visit my hunt master and send him forth with this decree: he will bring me back this thunder tiger, alive, or I will send him and his men to dine with dread Lady Izanami, Mother of Death, and the thousand and one oni demons birthed from her black womb."

"But Lord, your navy . . . all of your ships are either engaged in the glorious war or have been allocated to the lotus farms. The Guild will—"

"Will what? Deny their Shōgun? Hideo-san, the only *will* you should be concerned with at this moment is my own."

The silence gleamed like an executioner's blade.

". . . Hai, great Lord. It shall be so."

"Good," Yoritomo nodded, turned back to the window. "I will feast before breakfast. Send in three geisha."

Hideo bowed as low as his old back would allow, the tip of his thin beard sweeping the polished boards. Retreating a respectful distance from his Shōgun, he turned and hurried away, closing the elegantly decorated rice-paper doors behind him. His sandals beat a rapid pace along the nightingale floor, boards chirping brightly beneath him as he scurried through the sleeping quarters. The thin walls were adorned with long paper amulets the color of blood, scribed with protective mantra in broad, black strokes. Spring-driven ceiling fans were affixed to the exposed beams overhead, fighting a futile battle against the scorching heat. At each doorway loomed a granite statue of the Tora clan's totem; great and proud Tiger, fiercest of all the kami spirits, his claws raised and fangs bared.

Next to each statue stood two members of the Shōgun's personal guard, the Kazumitsu Elite. The samurai were clad in golden jin-haori tabards that reached almost to the floor, their armored hands clasping the hilts of chainsaw katana. The guards watched Hideo depart, as motionless and silent as the statues they stood vigil beside.

Hideo mopped his brow with the long sleeves of his robe as he shuffled out of the royal wing, his trail marked by the blue-black smoke still drifting from his bone pipe. He wheezed, his walking stick tapping a crisp beat across the boards. His stomach was busy turning somersaults.

"So now he's receiving visions from the gods," he muttered. "Heavens preserve us."

3

RED SAKÉ

Masaru squinted through the pall of greasy smoke at the cards in front of him. The dealer watched him through half-closed lids, a blue-black wreath coiled in the air around his head. Masaru lifted his pipe and inhaled another lungful of lotus.

"Don't let the dragon steer the ship, my friend," whispered Akihito. It was the traditional warning for a lotus smoker about to make a very bad decision.

Masaru exhaled, tendrils of smoke wafting up through his graying mustache, past bloodshot eyes. He took a sip of red saké and turned to his friend, eyebrow cocked.

Akihito was a mountain carved out of solid teak, harder than a seven-pipe hangover. His hair was drawn back in diagonal cornrows across his scalp, blond streaks bleached through the black. Four jagged scars ran along his chest, cutting across the beautiful phoenix tattoo on his right arm. The big man was handsome in a rugged, weather-beaten kind of way, dark, clear eyes regarding his friend with concern.

"You worry too much," Masaru smiled.

Six men sat in a semi-circle around the low table of the gambling house, their cushions torn from some abandoned motor-rickshaw. The walls were ricepaper, painted with figures of exotic women and even more exotic animals: fat pandas, fierce leopards and other extinct beasts. Low light flickered in the overhead globes. A sound box sat above the bar; crafted out of dull, gray tin, its speaker cans connected to the main unit with frayed spools of copper wiring. Guild-approved music spilled from its innards; the thin wavering notes of shakuhachi flutes, accompanied by the clicking beat of wooden percussion. The growl of a struggling generator could be heard somewhere downstairs. Fat, black lo-tusflies swarmed among the rafters.

Each man had stripped to his waist in the sweltering heat, displaying a myriad of irezumi—tattoos—in all colors of the rainbow. A few of the players were Tiger clansmen, sporting ink from the hands of minor artisans that marked them as men of moderate means. Two others at the table had no kami spirits marked on their flesh at all, just simple patterns of koi fish, geisha girls and wildflowers that singled them out as lowborn. Known as Burakumin, these clanless types lurked at the bottom rung of Shima's caste system, with little hope of ascending. Unable to afford elaborate ink-work, a straight razor and a smudged handful of cuttlefish ink was the closest any of them had come to a real tattoo parlor.

The intricate imperial suns radiating across Akihito and Masaru's left up-per arms had been noted by everybody in the room, and not for the fact that the irezumi marked the pair as the Shōgun's men. There was no shortage of desperate folk in the streets of Downside, some perhaps even desperate enough to risk Yoritomo-no-miya's wrath, and the simple fact was that the more elabo-rate a man's ink, the fatter his purse was likely to be.

Hushed conversations could be heard from the thugs and lowlifes skulking at other tables. Rumors of last week's refinery fire, news of the war against the round-eyes overseas and whispers about the latest attack of the Kagé rebels on the northern lotus fields all drifted in the air with the smoke.

Masaru cracked his neck and touched the exquisite nine-tailed fox design sleeving his right arm, whispering a prayer to Kitsune. Fox was not as fierce as Tiger, brave as Dragon, nor as visionary as Phoenix. His people were not great warriors or explorers, nor lauded artisans; among the clan kami spirits, he was the easiest to discount. But Fox was cunning and quick, silent as shadows, and in long-forgotten days when the kami still walked Shima with earthly feet, Fox had imbued his people with his most precious gift. The gift of a desperate, un-canny luck.

Masaru rolled a kouka coin between stained fingers; a two-inch rectangu-lar braid of dull gray iron stamped with the seal of the imperial mint. The game was *oicho-kabu*, a pastime older than the Empire itself. It was Masaru's turn as first player; he would determine how many cards were dealt to each of the four fields in front of them. He pointed at the second field on the table, asking for another card, and left the others alone. The assembled gamblers glanced at each other and muttered, each bidding his stake a reluctant goodbye.

The dealer was a blubbery slug of a man, his fat, shaved head gleaming in the dirty light. The serpentine design spiraling down his right arm declared him a member of Ryu, the Dragon zaibatsu; once a clan of seafarers and raiders in the dark, uncivilized days before the unification of the Empire and the rise of the Lotus Guild. Irezumi across his left arm heralded his allegiance to the Sasori-kai; a gang that ran the illicit card dens across the toxic portside slums of Kigen city. To find a blooded clansman among the yakuza gangs was a rarity, but from the quality of the dealer's ink, the syndicate of cutthroats, pimps and extortionists was doing very well for itself.

The man-slug placed Masaru's declared card on the unfinished wood, and taking the fourth card from the deck, he added it to his own hand. A gap-toothed grin spread behind his braided mustache, and he turned over a maple and chrysanthemum. The gamblers scowled and sipped their drinks. One gave Masaru an unappreciative shove.

Masaru held up a hand, tapped his cards with his forefinger.

"What's the point?" moaned Akihito. "He has nine, dealer wins ties."

"Fox looks after his own." Masaru brushed a lotusfly away. "Turn them."

The dealer shrugged and turned the first field: pine and silver grass for a total of nine. The second field revealed three cherry blossoms, also for nine. The gamblers perked up through the lotus haze; if the third field also flipped a nine, every man would receive triple his bet.

The field already held five points. Akihito prayed aloud, promising to perform several implausibly acrobatic feats on the Lady Luck's nether regions if she delivered. The dealer turned the final card. Everyone in the room caught their breath. It was a card sent from Uzume herself. A wisteria bloom. A blessed, miraculous four.

The gamblers erupted in a deafening cheer.

"You magnificent bastard!" Akihito clasped Masaru's face with a pair of meaty hands, planting a kiss squarely on his lips. Masaru grinned and pushed his friend away, holding up his hands for mercy as the other players slapped him repeatedly across his back. He hoisted his saké cup and roared.

"To Kitsune! Fox looks after his own!"

A broad hand slapped the cup away, and it smashed into glittering fragments against the opposite wall. The dealer rose, flushed with anger, hand on the studded wooden club at his belt. Masaru's new friends began studying the bottoms of their glasses and the fixtures in the ceiling. The serving girl gathered up the tip bowl without a sound and sank behind the bar.

"Damned Kitsune," spat the dealer. "Cheaters, one and all."

Akihito sighed.

Masaru's eyes widened and he swayed to his feet, flipping the table over and

STORMDANCER

sending the cards and coins flying. His skin had the pale gray hue of all lotus addicts, but his body was lean and hard, muscles coiled tightly across long, sharp lines. He wrapped his fist around the polished nunchaku in his belt and glared with red, weeping eyes.

"Typical Ryu," he growled. "Why do you Dragons always squeal like corpse-rats when you start to lose?"

"Bastard Foxes . . ."

"You cut the godsdamned deck. Another insult to clan Kitsune, and I'll do the same to my face."

The dealer raised an eyebrow.

". . . I mean *your* face." Masaru blinked, stumbling slightly.

"You can barely stand, old man," the thug sneered, glancing down at the nunchaku. "You really think you can swing a pair of those?"

Masaru paused for a moment, eyes roaming the dirty ceiling.

"Good point," he nodded, and introduced his fist to the dealer's nose.

Yukiko walked up to the entrance of the gambling den, took a determined expression from the rack and slapped it on her face. She paused to frown up at the noonday sun, its sickly red glare reflected on her goggles. A sky-ship sputtered through the perpetual haze of lotus exhaust fumes overhead, dull light glinting off its filthy, smoke-stained hull.

She wore an outfit of sturdy gray cloth, unadorned save for a small fox em-broidered on the breast, cut simply for the sake of utility. An uwagi tunic cov-ered her from neck to mid-thigh, open at the throat, long, loose sleeves with folded cuffs rippling in the feeble breeze. An obi sash of black silk was wrapped tight around her waist, six inches wide, tied in a simple bow at the small of her back. A billowing pair of hakama trousers trailed down to her feet, which were covered by a pair of split-toed tabi socks. Long hair flowed around her shoul-ders, midnight black against pale, smooth skin. A gray kerchief was tied over her mouth, polarized glass lenses trimmed with thin brass and black rubber covering her eyes.

The cobbles around her were awash with people, a tumbling din of voices and the occasional growl of a motor-rickshaw swelling amidst a sea of sweating flesh and colored silk. A chattering flock of neo-chōnin merchants and their stern, silent bodyguards were gathered nearby, haggling with a junk dealer about the price of scrap iron. Gloved hands pawed through ledgers and fingered purses full of coins; Upside men skimming the surface of Downside streets. The entire group wore face-length breathing apparatus to protect themselves from the burning glare of the sun and the exhaust fumes hanging over the city like a shroud. The masks were sculpted of smooth brass, corrugated rubber and twisting filter pipes, the round glass windows covering their eyes filmed in a fine layer of soot and lotus ash. Like Yukiko, most of the grubby crowd around them made do with kerchiefs tied over their faces, goggles crafted from rat leather and cheap, polarized lenses, or perhaps an umbrella of colored rice-paper.

Yukiko heard glassware smashing, loud cursing. A man crashed through the doorway in a rain of splinters, nearly knocking her over. He landed face first in the dust and started bleeding the road red, broken fingers twitching. The crowd ignored him, most skirting around without a glance. The gaggle of neo-chōnin merchants stepped over him on their way to whatever it was they considered important.

"Not again," she sighed, and stepped inside.

She screwed up her nose at the reek of lotus and sweat and red saké. Pulling her goggles and kerchief down around her throat, she squinted into the gloom. She recognized the shape of a giant, sweat-slicked Akihito. Two yakuza were in headlocks under his arms. His headbutt smeared a third gangster's nose all over his cheeks. Masaru was being held in an armlock by a fat, bloody-nosed bald man. A rat-faced fellow was punching him repeatedly in the stomach to the brittle tune of a shakuhachi flute. Masaru's salt-and-pepper hair had come loose from his topknot, splayed across his face in dark tendrils wet with blood. As she watched, he craned his head around and sank his teeth into his captor's forearm.

The bald man howled, released his grip, and Masaru kicked the rat-faced man square between his legs. The fellow let out a high-pitched squeal and sank to his knees. Masaru dropped a hook across the bald man's jaw, sending him backward into the bar to land on a pile of broken beach glass. He was picking up a table to clobber the rat-man when Yukiko's voice rang out over the chaos.

"A little early in the morning, isn't it, father?"

Masaru paused, squinting bleary-eyed in her direction. He brightened when he recognized her, and took one unsteady step forward, a grin breaking out on his face.

"Daughter! Just in—"

A saké bottle sailed into the back of his head and he crashed across the up-turned gaming tables, out cold. The bald man picked up his war club from the wreckage and stalked toward Masaru, wiping his bleeding nose on the back of one fat, greasy paw.

Yukiko stepped forward and held up her hand.

"Sama, please. Enough for one day, hai?"

"Not nearly," he growled. "Get out of my way, girl."

Yukiko's hand drifted to the tantō hidden at the small of her back, fingers slipping around the knife's lacquered hilt. With her other hand, she pulled up the loose gray cotton of her uwagi's left sleeve. Even in the guttering tungsten light, the elaborate imperial sun inked across her bicep was plainly visible. Her long, shady eyes glanced down to the identical tattoo on her father's arm, then back up to the face of the advancing yakuza.

"Please, sama," she repeated, the barest flicker of warning in her voice, "if this insignificant servant of Yoritomo-no-miya, Ninth Shōgun of the Kazumitsu Dynasty, has caused your house offense, we humbly beg forgiveness."

The fat man paused, breathing heavily, drool and blood dripping down through his goatee to spatter on the floorboards. He surveyed the wreckage of the room: the unconscious bodies, broken furniture and braided iron kouka coins scattered across the floor. The serving girl peeked over the bar, squeaked and dropped back into hiding.

The fat man pouted, brow creased in thought.

"We keep his winnings," he finally grunted, motioning to her father with the business end of his tetsubo. "Call it even."

"That is more than fair." Yukiko gave a small bow, releasing her grip on the knife. "Amaterasu bless your kindness, sama."

She turned to Akihito, paused mid-brawl, his arms still locked around the necks of the two smaller, rapidly suffocating men.

"Akihito, give me a hand please?"

The giant raised an eyebrow, looked back and forth between the purple faces stuffed into his armpits. Shrugging, he clobbered the men's heads together and tossed them over the bar. The crash of shattering glass and the sound box's tune were drowned out by the serving girl's shriek.

Akihito stooped down and hefted Masaru over one shoulder, flashing Yukiko a broad grin. She frowned in return.

"I asked you to watch him."

Though he towered a good foot and a half over the girl, the big man looked slightly abashed. "He's still in one piece, isn't he?"

She scowled and rolled her eyes. "Barely."

"So where to, little fox?"

"The harbor." She stalked over the broken furniture and out the door.

"Harbor?"

Akihito frowned and stumbled after her. Emerging into the blast-furnace heat, he tugged his goggles up over his eyes with his spare hand. People swarmed about them in the street, lotusflies swarmed about the people, all buzzing to and fro beneath the glare of that burning scarlet sun.

The big man pulled a gray kerchief up over his mouth, a conical straw hat onto his head.

"What the hells are we going to the harbor for?"

In answer, Yukiko produced a scroll from the inner breast pocket of her uwagi and slapped it into the big man's palm. Akihito shifted Masaru's bulk across his shoulders. The rice-paper made a sound like brittle bird wings as he unfurled it, scowling over the symbols painted on the page. The kanji were written in a thin, spidery hand, difficult to read through the film of grime and ash covering his goggles. It took a few seconds for the color to start draining from the big man's face.

"This is an imperial seal," he said.

"So it is."

Akihito was pale as old bones by the time he finished reading the orders. He drew a deep breath, stared at Yukiko for a long, silent moment, then screwed the scroll up in his fist. Blotches of color bloomed at his cheeks.

"The Shōgun is sending us after an arashitora? A godsdamned thunder tiger?"

A trio of passing sararīmen shot them curious glances as the big man's temper flared. Yukiko took the crumpled scroll from his hand, rolled it up as best she could and tucked it back inside her breast pocket. Akihito scowled around the street, lowered his voice to a furious whisper.

"Why is he doing this? Is he angry with us?"

A shrug.

"He wants a thunder tiger, Akihito."

"Well, I want a woman who can touch her ears with her ankles, cook a decent meal and keep her opinions to herself. But they don't fucking exist either!"

Masaru groaned as Akihito shifted him to his other shoulder.

"Do you feel better now?" Yukiko folded her arms. "Got it all out of your system?"

"We can't hunt what doesn't exist, Yukiko."

"You don't think I know that?"

"And what do you think is going to happen if we fail Yoritomo-no-miya?" The big man punctuated his questions with his free hand. "What do you think will be waiting for us when we come back empty-handed? Orders for Masaru to commit seppuku, for starters. You want to watch as your father is forced to disembowel himself? Who knows what they'll do to the rest of us . . ."

"Maybe you could tell the Shōgun how you feel. I'm sure he'd understand."

Akihito drew breath to retort, blinked and swallowed his words. He gritted his teeth and ran one hand across the back of his neck as he glanced about. The streets around them overflowed with people; layers of the social strata heaped one on another, brick upon cracking brick. Neo-chōnin merchants with fat bellies and fatter purses; sararīman wageslaves with their modest lives and honest coin; sweating farmers with half-empty wagons; gomimen with their salvage carts and recycled wares; traveling peddlers with their lives and livelihoods stacked on their backs; beggars in the gutters, fighting with the rats for the tablescraps the rest had left behind. Countless figures jostling in the oily haze, none of them paying anyone else the slightest heed.

Yukiko's expression softened, and she reached up to lay a gentle hand on the big man's arm.

"Every word you're saying is true. But what choice do we have?" She pulled her goggles on and shrugged. "Try to deliver the impossible, or defy the Shōgun and just die right here and now. Which would you prefer?"

Akihito exhaled, shoulders slumping like a flower wilting in the scorching heat.

"Come on, let's go." Yukiko turned and began walking toward the docks.

Akihito remained motionless as the girl slipped away into the throng. Screwing his eyes shut and juggling his unconscious friend, the giant pinched himself on the arm hard enough to leave a bruise. He waited a long moment, then opened one eye, glancing around the street. Against all hope, the world remained exactly as he'd left it.

"Izanagi's balls," he muttered, and hurried after the girl.

4

PURITY

Kigen city was awash with sight and sound; a thrumming, sweltering hive peopled by two-legged insects in rainbow colors. A pall of lotus fumes hung in the air, bubbling in dozens upon dozens of oily black streams from the exhaust pipes of the sky-ships floating above.

Cigar-shaped canvas balloons with rusted metal exoskeletons filled the sky. Their inflatables were under-slung with the long hulls of wooden junks, their holds full of gaijin prisoners of war, trade goods and precious blood lotus transported from the clan fields. Each balloon was painted with the totem spirit of the zaibatsu that owned it, and the skies seemed full of clashing tigers (Tora), snarling dragons (Ryu), blazing phoenix (Fushicho) and even the occasional nine-tailed fox (Kitsune). Each hull also wore the distinctive kanji symbols of the Lotus Guild, painted in broad brush strokes along the keel. Shima's roads were not made of brick or dirt, but of red, choking cloud.

The clans of the Tiger, Phoenix, Dragon and Fox had once stood among two dozen extended families, scattered across the Eight Isles, all subjects of the great Shima Imperium. Yet when the first Shōgun of the Tiger clan, great Tora Kazumitsu I, rose in rebellion against the corrupt Tenma emperors, he had rewarded his three loyal captains with vast tracts of land, and stewardship over all the clans within. And thus, two dozen slowly became four, the great zaibatsu conglomerates gradually consuming the clans of the Falcon, the Serpent, the Ox and their fellows, their kami spirits fading from thought and memory, until all that remained were a few scattered tattoos and footnotes in the great, dusty scrolls of history.

Exotic scents and rippling heat drifted up from the distant marketplace, always overshadowed by sputtering motors and lotus exhaust spilling from the engines of the sky-ships, the motor-rickshaws, the rail yards, the vast, smoking chi refinery. Yukiko found herself gagging whenever she was down here; the myriad smells and colors mixed with that oily stench were enough to make her stomach turn.

She pushed through the crowds, keeping one hand on the purse hidden in the obi sash around her waist. Knowing her father, he had already spent his pay on drink and smoke, and the few coins she possessed would be all they had to eat with this month. The gutters of Kigen had birthed a thousand pickpockets with ten thousand sticky, oil-stained fingers, each more hungry and desperate than the last. Here in Downside, the fool who only found himself parted from his money was having a good day.

The crowd was a mix of grimy skin and painted, pristine flesh, dirty rags and luxuriant silk, pressed together in the flyblown throng. There was scarcely a bare face in sight: common folk wore polarized goggles and kerchiefs tied over their mouths, people of wealth and standing had expensive mechanized breathers slung around their faces. It was as if the entire populace had something to hide. Without facial expressions to serve as a guide, social interaction on Kigen streets was mostly measured in flesh; deference gauged in the depth of the other man's bow, hand gestures serving in place of a smile, an aggressive stance adopted to showcase a frown. A language spoken by the body as well as the mouth.

The buildings of Downside were a multi-storied, ramshackle affair, piled on top of one another without forethought or planning; a constantly swelling blister of cracking clay and bleached wood. The Upside architecture across the river was just as decrepit, but the compositions at least held something close to symmetry. The city's broad cypress-bark roofs were desiccated and gray, stripped of paint by the merciless sun and polluted black rains that fell in Shima's winter months. Windows of clouded beach glass or rice-paper stared out with blind, vacant expressions onto the churning crush of flesh on the cobbles below. At each twisted intersection crouched a small stone shrine to Fūjin, the God of Wind and Ways. Temples to the Lady of the Sun, blessed Amaterasu, and her father, Lord Izanagi, the great Maker God, stood shoulder to shoulder with towering brothels, gambling pits and the smoke-filled, tar-stained walls of lotus dens. Each north-facing window was scattered with a small handful of rice; an offering to appease the hunger of the Dark Mother, dread Lady Izanami, the Earth Goddess corrupted by the Yomi underworld after the birth of Shima.

Three rivers clawed sluggish paths through the city's bowels, their waters as black as tar. Kigen jail sat hunched on the crumbling banks of the Shoujo, glowering at the rusted metal skeleton of the rail yards across the way. Chapterhouse

Kigen loomed at the black, foaming collision of the Shiroi and Junsei, a five-sided fist of yellow stone, punching skyward through broken cobbles. It stretched four stories into the reeking air, pentagonal, windowless walls set with five rusted iron gates around the base, throwing a dark shadow over Kigen's pockmarked face. The vast, charred chimney stacks of the refinery to the south retched their filth into the sky, black fingers of greasy stink and acrid taste worming their way down the throats of the seething masses. The din of metal upon metal, thousands of hungry voices, the squeal of rutting corpse-rats. High, pitched roofs thrust their peaks at the red skies above, lending the smoking city skyline a jagged, saw-toothed shape.

Shouldering her way through a mob of rickshaw runners on a smoke break, Yukiko caught sight of the barometric apparatus of a weatherpriest bobbing through the crowd. The whirling, multi-armed periscope disappeared through the door of a noodle store and her stomach growled, reminding her that she hadn't eaten today.

"You want some breakfast?" She looked back at Akihito, still wading through the masked mob a good distance behind.

"I thought we were hunting thunder tigers?" he yelled.

"You want to do that on an empty stomach?" Yukiko smiled, stepping into the crowded bar and pulling down her kerchief.

A short boy with a pimpled face and a small tiger tattoo asked her desire, and was soon scooping spoonfuls of thin black crab and tofu into rice-cracker bowls. The air boiled, thick with steam. Yukiko glanced around the store as she waited, listening to the sound box reporting on the day's crop yield (bountiful, all praise the Shōgun), the war with the gaijin overseas (after twenty years of glorious battle, inevitable victory would soon be at hand) and last week's refinery fire (an accidental fuel leak being the cause). A greasy film coated the army recruitment posters plastered over every inch of wall. Illustrations of stern-faced boys shouted silent slogans against a backdrop of imperial suns.

> "Be all you can be."
> "The best and brightest."
> "For Bushido! For honor!"

Yukiko watched the weatherpriest, a wizened little man in a rubber suit of buckles and straps. Small arcs of red current danced up the apparatus on his back as he shook his divining rod at the posters and cackled. His sort were an uncommon sight in the clan metropolises—most weatherpriests spent their time in the rural provinces, bilking superstitious farmers from their hard-earned kouka in exchange for prayers and invocations to Susano-ō, God of Storms.

"Bring the rain," they would cry. "Stop the rain," they would pray. The clouds would come and go exactly as they pleased, the weatherpriests would enjoy the blessings of serendipity or shake their heads and speak of "unfavorable portents," and the farmers would stand a few coins lighter either way.

Nodding her thanks and paying the lad behind the counter with a few braided copper kouka, Yukiko stepped back into the babbling street and handed a bowl to Akihito. The big man was busy slapping away the hands of a rag-swathed pickpocket. A sharp boot to the backside sent the boy running off into the crowd, shouting colorful criticisms of Akihito's sexual prowess.

"None for Masaru?" The giant swiped at the sea of flies around his head.

"He can buy his own."

"You gave all his winnings to the yak'," Akihito made a face. "Mine too, I should add."

Yukiko smiled sweetly, "That's why I'm buying you breakfast."

"What about Kasumi?"

Yukiko's smile disappeared. "What about her?"

"Well, has she eaten, or . . ."

"If Kasumi wants to eat, I'm sure she's taken care of herself. She's never had trouble with getting what she wants before."

The giant pouted and shouldered his way through the crowd, sipping the piping-hot noodles with care. Masaru groaned on Akihito's shoulder.

"I think he's coming round."

Yukiko shrugged.

"Knock him out again if you like."

The crowd in front of them parted, stepping out of the path of an iron motor-rickshaw marked with the kanji symbols of the Lotus Guild. Yukiko stayed in the street as the sputtering metal beast rolled toward her on thick rubber tires, bulbous headlights aglow, spewing blue-black fumes into the air behind. It creaked to a stop a few inches short of colliding with her shins. The driver sounded the horn, but Yukiko refused to step aside.

The driver blasted the horn again, waving at her to get out of the road. His profanities were muffled behind the beach glass windshield, but Yukiko could still make out the best of them. She plucked a noodle from her bowl, popped it between her lips and chewed slowly.

"Come on." Akihito grabbed her by the arm and dragged her out of the way.

The rickshaw driver stomped on the accelerator. The machine belched a cloud of fumes into the already choking haze of street-level exhaust and began rolling again. Yukiko could see the silhouette of a Lotus Guildsman in the rear seat.

Like all its brethren, the Lotusman was encased head to foot in a brass atmos-suit, studded with fixtures and gears and spinning clockwork, shielding it from the pollution the rest of the populace breathed daily. Its helmet was insectoid, all smooth lines and sharp curves. A cluster of metallic tentacles spilled from its mouth, plugged via bayonet fixtures into the various contraptions riveted to its outer shell: breather bellows, fuel tanks and the mechabacus that every Guildsman wore on its chest. The device resembled an abacus that had been dipped in glue and rolled around in a bucket of capacitors, transistors and vacuum tubes, and the Lotusman clicked a few beads across its surface, staring at Yukiko with red, faceted eyes as the vehicle cruised past. Although the rank-and-file members of the Guild were referred to as "Lotusmen," their gender was actually impossible to determine.

She blew it a kiss anyway.

When the motor-rickshaw was a good distance away, Akihito released his grip on Yukiko's arm and sighed. "Why do you always get in their way?"

"Why do you always move?"

"Because life out here is better than life in Kigen jail, that's why."

Yukiko scowled, and turned away.

They walked on, past the pentagonal walls of the Guild chapterhouse, passing in silence over wide stone archways bridging the slime-smeared banks of the Shoujo and Shiroi. Yukiko glanced over the railing at the black river water below, saw a dead fish floating in the choking muck, two beggars wading out through the filth toward it. A street minstrel was bent over his instrument in the shade on the other side of the bridge, singing an out-of-tune song about the spring wind, the threadbare rug before him scattered with a few meager copper bits. The crowd grew thicker, street volume rising, hundreds of voices joined together to form a constant, rolling hum.

Yukiko and Akihito squeezed through the mob and out into the broad, bustling expanse of the Market Square. The plaza stretched one city block on each side; a vast, crowded space lined with store facades of every variation under the sun. Spice merchants hocked their wares alongside flesh pedlars and textilemen. Food stalls and clothiers and herbalists, holy men from various temples selling blessings for copper bits next to street courtesans and thugs for hire. Dozens of performers amazing the crowds while cutpurses weaved among the flesh with sharp, smiling faces. Goggle vendors everywhere, selling mass-produced lenses from wooden boxes slung around their necks. Beggars in the gutters, swaying before their alms bowls, the flint-eyed stares of grubby children with growling bellies and shanks of sharpened iron hidden in their rags. The scarlet jin-haori tabards of the city soldiers were everywhere amidst the mob; red sharks cruising for wounded meat.

In the center of the market lay a large mall of gray brick, sunk one or two feet below street level. Four columns of scorched stone rose out of the ground, one at each cardinal point, towering above the milling crowds. Each one stood ten feet high, studded with pairs of charred iron manacles. The official name for the mall was the "Altar of Purity." Locals called them the "Burning Stones."

Four Lotus Guildsmen were stacking bundles of dry tinder around the northern pillar, eyes glowing the color of blood, red light gleaming on the sleek surfaces of their mechanized atmos-suits. Segmented pipes connected the blackened fixtures at their wrists to large tanks mounted on their backs. Yukiko stared at the white jin-haori tabards they wore over their metal shells, the kanji symbols that denoted their sect within the Guild.

"Purifiers," she spat.

She caught a glimpse of color on the steps leading down to the Burning Stones; a small freestanding slab of polished flint, no more than four inches high. It was an ihai—a spirit tablet laid to mark the passing of a loved one. Real flowers were impossible to find in the streets of Kigen, so the mourner had arranged a delicate circle of rice-paper blooms at its base. Yukiko couldn't make out the name carved into the stone. As she craned her neck to get a better look, one of the Purifiers clomped up the stairs, stamped on the tablet and scattered the flowers with its boot.

Yukiko stared at the ashes beneath the blackened columns, at the crushed paper petals blowing in the wind, gnawing at her lip. Her heart was pounding in her chest.

Akihito kept his voice low, shook his head.

"The Guild must have caught another one."

A crowd was gathering around the edges of the mall; a mix of the morbidly curious and the genuinely fanatical, young and old, men and women and children. Their heads turned as a wail rang out across the market, an anguished cry, threadbare with fear. Yukiko saw a small figure being dragged through the square by two more Purifiers, a girl only a few years younger than her. Kicking and thrashing as she came, dressed in black, hair tangled about her face. Her eyes were wide with terror as she struggled against that cold, mechanized grip; a child's fist against a mountainside. She stumbled, knees dragged bloody across the cobbles as the Purifiers hauled her to her feet again.

"Impure!" A cry went up from a few of the zealots among the mob, echoed across the square. "Impure!"

The girl was dragged down the steps, screaming and sobbing all the way. The Guildsmen hauled her onto the tinder, pressed her back against the northern Burning Stone. As two Purifiers closed a pair of manacles about the girl's wrists, a third stepped forward and spoke in a mechanical rasp, a voice that sounded like the song of a hundred angry lotusflies. The words flowed as if known by rote; a snatch of scripture from the Book of Ten Thousand Days.

> *"Soiled by Yomi's filth,*
> *The taint of the Underworld,*
> *Izanagi wept.*
> *Seeking Purity,*
> *The Way of the Cleansing Rite,*
> *The Maker God bathed.*
> *And from these waters,*
> *Were begat Sun, Moon and Storm.*
> *Walk Purity's Way."*

Another Purifier stepped forward, lit twin pilot flames at the blackened fixtures on its wrists and held them aloft to the crowd.

"Walk Purity's Way!" it bellowed.

Approving cries rang out across the Burning Stones, the voices of fanatics among the mob drowning out the uneasy murmurs of the remainder. Akihito clenched his teeth and turned his back on the grim spectacle.

"Let's get out of here."

Yukiko tried to tell herself it was rage that turned her stomach to water, made her legs shake and stole the spit from her mouth.

She tried to tell herself that, but she knew better.

She looked up at Akihito, her face a mask, drawn and bloodless. Her voice trembled as she spoke.

"And you ask why I get in their way."

5

BLACKENING

The heat was blistering.

Yukiko and Akihito made their way through the squeezeways, over the refuse-choked gutters, past the grasping hands of a dozen blacklung beggars and down into Docktown; a cramped and weeping growth of low-rent tenements and rusting warehouses slumped in the shadow of the sky-ships. A broad wooden boardwalk stretched out over the black waters of the bay, hundreds of people shoving and weaving their way across the bleached timbers. The docking spires were thin metal towers, corroded by black rain. Hissing pipes and cables pumped hydrogen and the volatile lotus fuel, simply called "chi," up to the waiting sky-ships. The towers swayed in the wind, creaking ominously whenever a ship docked or put out to the red again. Lotusmen swarmed in the air about them like brass corpseflies, the pipes coiled on their backs spitting out bright plumes of blue-white flame.

Steam whistles shrieked in the distance; breakfast break for the workers slaving in Kigen's sprawling nest of chi refineries. It was a well-known truth that most of the wretches sweating inside those walls were expected to die there. If the toxic fumes or heavy machinery didn't end them, working twenty-hour shifts for barely more than a beggar's salary probably would. The laborers were known as "karōshimen"—literally, men who kill themselves through overwork. It was ironic, given that many of them were little more than children. Flitting among grinding cogs and crunching gears that could snag and chew a stray lock of hair or an unwary hand without skipping a beat, soft flesh withering in the shadow of hard metal and blue-black smoke. Children turned old and feeble before they ever had a chance to be young.

"Vwuch vwyy?" Akihito asked.

Yukiko sipped her broth and found she'd completely lost her appetite.

"Don't talk with your mouth full," she murmured.

The giant stuffed the last of his cracker bowl into his mouth. Yukiko pointed in the direction of the eastern docks, furthest away from the cloud of smog and ash and reeking exhaust fumes.

"Is that . . . crab I smell?" The voice was weak, muffled against Akihito's ribs.

"He lives!" The big man grinned, slinging his friend down off his shoulders and planting him in the street. Masaru squinted, eye swelling shut, long pepper-gray hair a bedraggled mess. His face was smeared with blood.

"Izanagi's balls, my head." He winced, rubbing the back of his skull. "What hit me?"

Akihito shrugged.

"Saké."

"We didn't drink *that* much . . ."

"Here, eat." Yukiko offered her father the remainder of her breakfast. Grabbing the bowl, Masaru gulped it down as the crowd seethed around them. He swayed on his feet, looking for a moment as if the crab might make a break for freedom, then patted his stomach and belched.

"What the hells are we doing down here?" Masaru glared around the docks, one hand aloft to shield his eyes from the hothouse light while he fished out his goggles.

"We've been summoned," Yukiko said.

"Summoned to what? Breakfast?"

Akihito snickered.

"A hunt." Yukiko frowned at the big man.

"A hunt?" Masaru scoffed, checking to see if his ribs were cracked. "For the Shōgun's slippers?"

"I thought you'd be at least a little happy about it." Yukiko looked back and forth between the pair. "It'll give you both something to do besides smoking your money away in card houses all day."

Akihito frowned. "I don't smoke . . ."

"There's nothing left out there that's worth hunting." Masaru rubbed at the saké bottle-imprint on the back of his head. "The Shōgun should just bloody dismiss us and be done with it."

"He's sending us after an arashitora," Akihito muttered.

Masaru scowled up at the big man.

"I thought you just said you didn't smoke. Did you start when I wasn't looking? Bloody fool, it's a filthy habit, I'll not—"

"The scroll arrived last night, father," Yukiko said. "Set with the seal of the

Shōgun himself. A thunder tiger has been spotted by cloudwalkers past the Iishi Mountains."

"Damned cloudwalkers," Masaru shook his head. "Drunk on chi exhaust twenty-four hours a day. They'd say they saw the cursed fruit of Lady Izanami's black loins, the thousand and one oni dancing naked in the lotus fields, if they thought it'd get them a free meal or into some harlot's bed . . ."

Masaru caught himself and pressed his lips shut, cheeks reddening.

"We're commanded to bring it back alive." Yukiko steered the subject away from sex as fast as she could. She was still occasionally woken by nightmares about the day her father had tried to sit her down for "the talk."

"And how are we supposed to do that?" Masaru asked. "They're extinct!"

"That would be your bloody problem, wouldn't it? Or was someone else appointed Black Fox of Shima and Master of Hunters when I wasn't looking?"

"Don't swear," Masaru scowled.

Yukiko rolled her eyes behind her goggles. She wiped the lotus ash from the polarized lenses with her kerchief, then tied the cloth around her face to filter out the stench. With a flick of her long dark hair, she turned and walked toward the eastern docks, hands stuffed into the black obi about her waist.

Her father watched her, still rubbing the back of his head, a pained expression on his face.

"May you live a hundred years and never have daughters, my friend," he warned Akihito.

The giant sighed and clapped him on the back, and the pair followed her into the mob.

Kasumi loaded the last pack onto the elevator, then straightened her back and sighed. She wiped her brow and re-tied her ponytail, catching up the dark strands of hair clinging to her face. At a signal from the dockman, the elevator ascended the docking spire, wheels and pulleys shrieking in protest. High above her, the *Thunder Child* clanked against its couplings, cloudwalkers calling from her rigging like lost birds.

Kigen Bay stretched out to the south; an undulating carpet of bobbing filth and flaming refuse. Lotusmen had lit a fire on the black waters three days ago to burn off some of the accumulated chi-sludge, and parts of it were still ablaze, trailing dark columns of smoke up into the curtain of exhaust overhead. A gull with threadbare feathers cried a mournful song from atop the charred remains of a capsized fishing boat. It caught sight of movement in the muck, and readied itself for the plunge.

Pulling on a conical straw hat, Kasumi cast her eyes over the sky-ship above. She allowed herself a grudging smile; at least they were being sent on their fool's errand in style. The ship was gleaming black, highlighted with blood-red, the long serpentine coils of a green dragon painted down the flanks of her inflatable. Her skin and fixtures were still unscarred by corrosion or toxin bleaching, telling Kasumi that the *Child* couldn't have been commissioned more than a season or two ago. Nothing stayed beautiful under Shima's black rain for long.

Kasumi was dressed in loose gray cloth. The short sleeves of her uwagi revealed beautiful tattoos; the imperial sun on her left shoulder and upper arm, a ferocious tiger stalking down her right, marking her as a member of the Tora clan. The geisha at Shōgun Yoritomo's court whispered that she was well past the age when she should have found a husband, but she still possessed a sharp, feral kind of beauty. Deeply lidded eyes, skin turned nut brown by a life spent beneath Shima's sweltering red sun. Black hair ran in rivers down her spine, pierced by jade combs carved to resemble prowling tigers. There was a hardness to her, calluses and lean muscles, a glint of ferocity in her movements: a big cat, pacing a cage as wide as the world.

Several of the *Child*'s crew nodded as they filed past her to climb the spire. They were cleaner than the average cloudwalker, meaning that you could probably toss one into the black "water" of Kigen Bay and have him emerge dirtier than when he went in. But their skin was still coated in a greasy film of dragon smoke, their eyes the perpetual red of a lotus-fiend's.

The *Child*'s captain emerged from the small office at the spire's base, slapping the back of the fat customs man inside.

"The lotus must bloom," he said, nodding farewell.

"The lotus must bloom," the fat man replied.

The captain sauntered over to Kasumi, muttering under his breath. He stuffed some paperwork into his obi as he scowled up at the *Child*. He was around ten years younger than her, twenty-four or twenty-five if she was forced to guess, with a long plaited mustache descending from a handsome, if slightly overfed face. His gaudy, short-sleeved tunic proudly displayed his elaborate dragon tattoo and the single lotus bloom of a Guild-approved contractor. Custom Shigisen goggles and a fantastically expensive breather were slung around his neck.

"Son of a ronin's whore," he said. "I should've been born a Lotusman. These bribes get worse every trip."

"Bribes?" Kasumi frowned, tilted her head in question.

The captain gestured to the paperwork in his belt.

"We have to fly over three clan territories to get to the Iishi Mountains. Tiger, Dragon, then Fox. That's three different permits, and three different officials who need their palms greased to make sure my paperwork doesn't get 'misplaced.' Plus we'll need to refuel in Yama city before we fly back, and the Kitsune just bumped their docking fees another three percent."

"I'm sorry to hear that, Yamagata-san," Kasumi said. "Perhaps you should tell your customs man that you fly at the Shōgun's command."

"Wouldn't matter." He scowled, shook his head. "Any discount I haggle would only get added to my next flight. He has his own bribes to pay, and lotus contracts don't come cheap. The Guild always get their coin, one way or the other. Even the Shōgun knows that."

Yamagata fell silent as a Lotusman clanked past, cogs of its atmos-suit whirring. Red sunlight glittered in its eyes as it gazed up at the *Thunder Child*'s hull. It clicked a few beads across the mechabacus on its chest, whispered something distorted, then launched itself into the sky. The pipes on its back spat out bright plumes of blue-white flame. It flitted about the *Child*'s underside, spewing smoke and clicking more beads from one side of its chest to the other.

"Always like you to know they're watching, eh?" Kasumi murmured.

"Comes with the territory," Yamagata shrugged. "Every ship that hauls lotus has a Guildsman living on board. You get used to them looking over your shoulder."

"Nice to be trusted."

"It's worse since last week. Two of them burned to death when the refinery caught fire." Yamagata shook his head. "They locked down the whole complex for three days. Nothing coming in or out. You know what that does to the bottom line of a man like me?"

"Didn't the radio say the fire was an accident?" Kasumi raised an eyebrow. "Seems a lot of fuss over bad luck."

"What, and that surprises you? When was the last time you heard about a Guildsman getting killed, accident or no?"

"Guildsmen are flesh and blood under those suits, just like everyone else." Kasumi shrugged. "All men get their day before the Judge of the Nine Hells; Guildsman, beggar or Shōgun. It makes no difference to him."

Yamagata sniffed.

"True enough, I suppose."

Kasumi touched her brow, then her lips, muttering beneath her breath, "Great Enma-ō, judge us fair."

The Lotusman descended from the skies in a rolling cloud of chi exhaust, landing forty feet down the boardwalk. Peasant folk hurried out of the way, knocking each other over in their haste. The Guildsman clomped away over timber and cobbles without a backward glance.

"Is all your gear aboard?" Yamagata asked.

"Hai." Kasumi nodded, ran her hand across her brow. "The others should be here soon."

"Good. I want to get off before the day grows still. Wind at our backs."

"Minister Hideo commanded we were to wait until he'd arrived."

"Yomi's gates, I didn't know he was coming down here." The captain sighed. "Bad enough that my ship is being sent north to chase a smoke vision in the middle of monsoon season. Worse that I have to sit on my hands waiting for some bureaucrat to kiss me good-bye. My Guild rep is a son of a whore, wasting my time on chaff like this."

"Well, someone in the Guild obviously thinks this is important, or they wouldn't have assigned their best captain to the task, no?"

Yamagata scowled. "The Lotusmen might be happy wasting the finest ship in the fleet on the Shōgun's pride, but kissing my ass isn't going to make me turn cartwheels about it, Hunter."

"If it's so foolish, why waste the finest ship in the fleet on it?"

"You know that as well as I do." Yamagata spat onto the wooden decking. "Politics. The Shōgun controls the army, but only the Guild know the secret behind chi production. Both sides need to keep the other happy or the whole shithouse goes up in flames. I'm just a commoner who gets paid to lug their product from place to place. If I want to keep my contract, I go where I'm bloody told."

"Oh, I know the workings of court politics, Yamagata-san," Kasumi smiled. "I've hunted with the Black Fox under the reign of two different Shōgun now—long enough to become well acquainted with the mating habits of vipers."

"Then why interrogate a lowly cloudwalker about it? What the hells would I know that you don't?"

"Well, between the lines, I was asking who you'd angered to land this errand?" Kasumi brushed a stray hair from her eyes. "It must have been someone important."

The captain glanced at her sidelong, a slow, grudging smile forming on his lips. "I don't kiss and tell, Lady."

"Ah, so." She smiled back. "The *wife* of someone important, then."

"Daughter, actually. But it all ends the same. An empty hold, a wasted trip and me cursing the bastard responsible for both."

"I hope she was worth it."

Yamagata closed his eyes and gave a delighted little shiver. "You have no idea."

Kasumi laughed. "Just keep your hands off any daughters you might meet on this trip, Yamagata-san. Master Masaru isn't as forgiving as some neo-chōnin merchant with a fat purse and a few Guild contacts."

"No fear. I'd sooner put my wedding tackle in the mouth of a hungry sea dragon than anger the Black Fox of Shima, Lady."

Yamagata grinned and gave a small bow, one fist covered by the palm of his other hand. Kasumi returned the bow and watched him begin his long climb up the spire. The man swung on the corroded rungs, deft hands on rusting iron, up toward his ship above. The *Thunder Child*'s captain seemed a decent sort, and Kasumi breathed a small sigh of relief. The Dragon and Fox zaibatsu had been fighting border skirmishes for decades, and there was little love lost between the two clans. Although not every Ryu or Kitsune took the long-standing grudge to heart, she had been worried Yamagata might not appreciate having the Black Fox or his daughter aboard.

Kasumi turned her eyes to the crowd, leaning on her bo-staff—a six-foot length of ironwood capped with burnished steel. The mob milled around her: cloudwalkers fresh off their ships, sararīmen rubbing shoulders with the clockwork suits of the Lotusmen, young boys handing out sticky printed newssheets and singing tales of barbarian atrocities against Shima colonists overseas. She even noticed a few gaijin traders among the mob, short blond hair and pale, smog-stained skin, clothed in dyed wool of a strange cut, animal furs draped over their shoulders despite the crushing heat. They were surrounded by wooden crates and looming piles of genuine leather, negotiating the price on a dozen rolls of tanned cowhide with a swarming gang of neo-chōnin.

For the past twenty years, the round-eyes had worn the label of "enemy"; painted in the newssheets as treacherous blood-drinkers who stole the spirits of beasts and wore their skins. They had wasted the last two decades fighting a futile resistance against the Shōgunate invasion, when it would have been easier for everyone if they simply rolled belly-up and allowed themselves to be civilized. Kasumi marveled that even in the midst of all-out warfare, there were men who sought profit in the beds of their would-be conquerors. Yet here they were: gaijin merchantmen trekking across the seas in their lightning-powered freighters, each one with an elaborate residency permit inked on their wrists. They stood on the boardwalk under the narrowed stares of the city guards, selling their leather goods at exorbitant prices in a country where hide made from anything other than corpse-rat was now virtually impossible to find. They haggled and traded and counted their coin, pale blue eyes hidden behind polarized glass, watching war prisoners arrive by the shipload. But if the Docktown gaijin had misgivings about the treatment of their countrymen, they also had no wish to join their fellows on their march up to the chapterhouse. And so they kept their heads down, and their opinions to themselves.

After a spell, Kasumi caught sight of Akihito, standing a head taller than most of the mob. The big man appeared as if he was treading water in a sea of dirty straw hats and paper umbrellas.

She waved, and the trio shoved their way through the throng until they were face to face.

"You found them, I see." Kasumi smiled at Yukiko. "And in one piece."

The girl grimaced, pulled her goggles down around her throat. "One smelly piece."

"Masaru-sama." Kasumi bowed to Yukiko's father. She tried not to notice when the girl rolled her eyes.

Masaru returned the bow, still looking quite ragged about the edges. An ugly purple bruise was forming under one eye, spilling out from under the lens of his goggles.

"How are you, you big lump?" Kasumi looked Akihito up and down. "Excited?"

"No, I'm hungry."

"You just ate!" Yukiko shook her head.

"Oh, cheer up." Kasumi slapped the big man on the arm. "Don't tell me your blood doesn't quicken at the thought of hunting a thunder tiger, you grumpy sod. It's been years since we went after something like this."

"Something like what?" Akihito folded his arms, clearly unimpressed. "The figment of a smoke-fiend's imagination?"

"We should get moving," Masaru interrupted the pair, squinting through the haze at the sky-ship above. "Is all the gear aboard? Extra Kobiashis and blacksleep?"

"Hai, Masaru-sama," Kasumi nodded. "It cost me a few extra kouka to get the cage down here on short notice, but I needn't have rushed. Minister Hideo said we were to wait until he arrived."

"Aiya," Masaru sighed, lying down across a stack of crates and rubbing the back of his head. "That could take all day. Someone kick me when he gets here."

"You got anything to eat?" Akihito raised a hopeful eyebrow.

Yukiko snorted over Kasumi's laughter. Reaching into a pouch at her belt, the older woman tossed the giant a rehydrated rice cake, and the pair sat down in the shade to wait.

A dozen beggars were huddled across the way from the *Thunder Child*'s berth, wrapped in dirty rags, fingers outstretched and trembling. One was a young girl around Yukiko's age. She was a pretty thing: deep, moist eyes and creamy skin. Her mother sat beside her, rocking back and forth, the dark, tell-tale marks of blacklung smudged around her lips.

Kasumi touched the kerchief tied around her own face, wondered for the thousandth time if it would be enough to protect her from that dreaded stain. Blacklung had reached epidemic proportions in the last decade, and the final stages of the disease were terrible enough to make its victims envy the dead. She'd feel safer with more than prayers and a grubby rag over her mouth to protect her.

Perhaps if this fool's errand bore fruit, the Shōgun would reward them with enough kouka to afford their own mechanized breathers . . .

Kasumi scowled, shook her head at the thought.

And perhaps the Shōgun will sprout wings and have no need of a thunder tiger at all.

She watched as Yukiko wandered across the street, knelt down beside the beggars in the dust. They spoke, Yukiko and the girl, a few minutes together under the red sun. Kasumi couldn't hear what they said. She saw Yukiko glance back at her slumbering father, then up to the sky-ship that would be their home for the next few weeks. The beggar girl followed her gaze. The mother began coughing, shoulders hunched, face twisted in pain, knuckles pressed hard over her mouth. When she drew her hand away, it was smeared with dark fluid.

The girl wrapped her fingers in her mother's, greasy black smudged between their skin. Yukiko looked up from those stained hands into the girl's eyes. Reaching into her obi, she tugged out her coin purse and handed it over. Then she stood and walked away.

Kasumi smiled, pretended not to notice.

The sun climbed higher in the sky. The stone around them became the walls of a kiln, sweat trickling across their dusty skin. The crowd milled about amidst the fumes and flies and oppressive heat, a seething ocean of flesh and bone and metal beneath a burning sky.

"An arashitora, Kas'," Akihito muttered. "Gods help us."

Kasumi sighed and turned her eyes to the horizon.

High above them, the lone gull called into the choking wind and received no answer.

6

A BOY WITH SEA-GREEN EYES

It was mid-afternoon when the sound of singing roused Yukiko from her stupor. Akihito stood and tilted his straw hat away from his eyes, frowning into the distance.

"Here he comes," the big man muttered.

Yukiko and Kasumi rose to stand beside him. Masaru still snored on his bed of packing crates. Through the shimmering heat, they could see a procession winding down the broad cobbled boulevard from the imperial palace.

Long red banners adorned with the imperial sun were caught high in the dirty breeze, whipping about like headless serpents. The figures of nine huge Iron Samurai led the cohort, another nine bringing up the rear. The men stood almost seven feet tall, golden tabards marking them as members of the Shōgun's personal guard; the Kazumitsu Elite. They were encased in great suits of mechanized armor known as "ō-yoroi." The piston-driven iron was lacquered with black enamel, awash with the color of old blood beneath the scorching red sun. Chainsaw katana and wakizashi were sheathed at their waists. To inspire terror in their enemies, the mempō faceguards of the samurai's helms were crafted into the likenesses of snarling oni: the demon spawn of the black Yomi underworld. The spaulders protecting their shoulders were broad and flat, like the great eaves of the imperial palace. The gleaming cloth of their jin-haori tabards was embroidered with the kami totem of the Tora clan: a proud, snarling tiger. Tall golden banners marked with the same symbol fluttered above the combustion engine mounted on each samurai's back, their exhaust pipes spewing chi smoke into the already greasy breeze. They marched with one thick gauntlet wrapped tight around the scabbard of their katana, right hand grasping the hilt, as if ready to draw the weapons at a moment's notice. The armored suits made a din like iron bolts being dropped into a meat grinder.

A cadre of infantrymen followed behind the Iron Samurai, naginata spears clutched in their gauntlets. The weapons were nine feet tall, curved blades as long as katana mounted at the end of thick hafts, a glittering thicket of folded steel. Each man was clad in the banded iron breastplate, scarlet tabard and flanged helmet of a soldier in the Shima Army. Fierce, grim faces were hidden behind polarized lenses and blood-red kerchiefs. Known as "bushimen," each of these common-born warriors was sworn to the same code as the samurai nobility: the Way of Bushido.

Loyalty. Sacrifice. Death before dishonor. These were the principles that beat within the living chests of the Shōgun's war-machine. Bushido was the glue that held the military together, a code of conduct that the very first samurai of the nation had lived and died by. More than a simple philosophy; Bushido was a way of life that defined every facet of a soldier's existence, a dedication to martial prowess, honor and servitude. Encased in a lumbering shell of deadly clockwork or a simple breastplate of black iron, to die gloriously in service to their Lord and Shōgun was the greatest honor any of these men could hope for.

Three motor-rickshaws trundled along in the soldiers' wake. Geisha girls with bone-white faces and black goggles sat atop the vehicles, wrapped in long flowing kimonos of scarlet silk. Waving and laughing behind their breathers, they threw tiny bags of lotus buds into the vast crowds lining the streets. A small legion of children marched around the bushimen, filling the air with bright voices; a hymn to the glory and majesty of his resplendent highness, Ninth Shōgun of the Four Thrones of Shima, firstborn son of Kaneda the Nagaraja Slayer, Yoritomo the Mighty.

"The Mighty?" Akihito frowned. "I thought he was 'the Fearless.'"

"That's no ministerial procession." The toxic glare refracted on Yukiko's goggles. "It's too big."

"You're right," Kasumi nodded. "Yoritomo must be coming to see us off personally."

"Izanagi's balls, I haven't had a bath in three days." Akihito gave his armpit an experimental sniff.

Yukiko kicked her father, who started up from his sleep and tumbled backward off the crates. He rolled up into a crouch, hand on his nunchaku, glaring about like a startled cat.

"The Shōgun is coming," she hissed.

"Aiya," Masaru groaned. "My head feels like an oni took a shit in it . . ."

The quartet set about making themselves presentable. Masaru scratched at the dried blood on his face while Yukiko tried to run her fingers through her hair. Countless knots and tangles snagged her hands and entwined among her knuckles. Kasumi noticed the girl's struggles and slipped one of the combs from her ponytail, held it out in her palm with a smile. Yukiko eyed the jade tiger as if it might bite her. Her voice was cool as the sea breeze.

"No thank you."

Kasumi's smile faded. She slipped the comb back into her hair without a word.

The procession snaked down Palace Way, past the looming walls of the arena and the clamor of the Market Square, into the wide central street of Docktown. The soldiers fanned out to press back the common folk, gathered en masse to catch a glimpse of their Lord and a handful of his generosity. The children's song drifted on the poison wind, growing louder as the group approached the sky-spires. Captain Yamagata arrived via the spire's elevator, hair slicked back, face freshly scrubbed. The cocksure cloudwalker looked distinctly uncomfortable at the thought of meeting the supreme overlord of the Empire.

The hunters lined up in a row and dropped to their knees, eyes averted as the procession made its way up Spire Row, finally grinding to a halt before the *Thunder Child*'s berth. The children were clad in snow-white furisode robes, their long sleeves dragging across filthy cobbles. They gathered in a knot before the centermost of the three elegant motor-rickshaws and continued singing, a full five minutes passing before their choir mistress rang a small brass gong to command silence.

The motor-rickshaws were low-slung, made of iridescent metal that reminded Yukiko of the dragonflies she'd seen as a child. Their lines were sharp and semi-organic, each retching a great plume of lotus smoke behind it as the engine idled. One of the children stifled a cough, receiving a stinging rebuke from the back of his choir mistress's hand.

The door of the foremost rickshaw unfurled, and a paunchy man in a flowing kimono of cream and scarlet stepped out from the velvet interior. He wore an elaborate breather over his face, an embossed iron breastplate and a pair of beautifully crafted neo-daishō at his belt: the chainkatana and wakizashi that marked him as one of the landed military class.

Yukiko stole a quick glance and recognized the man as Tora Tanaka, herald of the Shōgun. Downside rumor had it that the Tiger lord had tested his new swords on the necks of no fewer than thirteen Burakumin peasants before he declared them to be of acceptable quality.

Tanaka unfurled a scroll, raising his voice over the scrabbling wind. He touched a button at his throat, and his voice emerged from the breather as a loud metallic rasp, amplified by the speakers nestled among the filter coils around his mouth. He proceeded to recount a full list of Yoritomo's titles, a litany that seemed to take an eon beneath the scorching afternoon sun. The hunters kept their foreheads pressed into the dust as the herald's voice droned over their heads, the monotonous white noise of a broken sound box.

Tanaka finished his list and glared around the assembled multitude from behind lenses of smooth polarized glass. The throng dropped to their knees as if someone had flipped a switch; only the Iron Samurai and Lotusmen remained on their feet, bowing from the waist. The door to the central rickshaw bloomed.

A young man emerged, dressed in a banded golden breastplate and red silk kimono. A magnificent pair of old-fashioned daishō swords was crossed at his obi, alongside the snub-nosed barrel of a chi-combustion iron-thrower—a recent Guild invention that hurled small metal balls with enough force to kill an armored man at a hundred feet. His hair was a black ribbon flowing in the fetid breeze, head held high and proud. The lenses of his goggles glittered like metal. An elegant mechanical breather was affixed to the lower half of his face with dark leather straps and gleaming buckles. The device was lacquered with the same golden finish as his breastplate, crafted to resemble a tiger's maw, fangs bared and grinning in a jagged, razorblade smile.

The Shōgun of Shima surveyed the people around him, a casual grip on the crisscrossed bindings of his katana's hilt. He then reached into the rickshaw and offered his hand.

Pale fingers dipped in gleaming red enamel took his. A beautiful painted woman dripped out of the door, wrapped head to foot in an exquisite red jûni-hitoe gown embroidered with golden tigers. Her face was caked in pearl white. Deep slashes of kohl rode around the goggles covering her eyes, a vertical wet stripe of scarlet glistened on her lips, bright as fresh blood. A small black and white terrier wriggled in her arms, struggling to free itself.

"Lady Tora Aisha, beloved sister of Shōgun Tora Yoritomo-no-miya, first daughter of Shima!" the herald cried.

Yukiko stole another glance. A small army of serving girls were fussing about their Lady as Aisha drew a delicate breather from within her sleeve. The device was crafted to resemble a fan, and she unfurled it in front of her face, still struggling to keep the puppy in her embrace.

It had been years since Yukiko had seen a dog in the city; the combination of toxic lotus exhaust and the growling bellies of Kigen's populace had put paid to the notion of household pets long ago. Funny how quickly man's best friend became man's next meal when there were no more cows or pigs left to slaughter.

Funny how tasty the idea of roasted tomcat could sound after three days of eating nothing but dust and choking, blue-black smoke.

Aisha's puppy was worth more money than the average sararīman could hope to earn in a lifetime. Yukiko couldn't imagine what the gown and breather must have cost. Enough to clothe every child in the city, most likely. Enough to feed a hundred blacklung beggar girls for a month. Even though the wealth on display between the imperial siblings was probably meant to inspire awe in their subjects, Yukiko looked at the filthy, starving faces around her and felt only a vague disquiet. After seven years of living at the periphery of Yoritomo's court, the opulence she found there had begun to raise unanswered questions in her mind. The kind of questions that were bad for your health. The kind that ended with an arrest warrant scribed with Chief Minister Hideo's signature and a quiet death by starvation in the stinking bowels of Kigen jail.

Yukiko pressed her forehead back into the ground.

Shōgun Yoritomo released his sister's hand and took three strides forward, split-toed boots crunching in the gravel at the boardwalk's edge. His cool gaze swept over the prostrate hunters, one hand still on his katana.

"Masaru-san, my Black Fox." His voice was honey-smooth, tinged with a hint of metal from the respirator's depths. "Rise."

Masaru snapped to his feet, eyes still fixed on the ground, delivering a waist-deep bow. The Shōgun returned the bow with a slight nod, covering one fist with his palm. He unclasped the buckles behind his head and removed his goggles and breather with a wet, sucking sound, offering a small, tight smile as he put his hands on his hips. His face was fierce, handsome, smooth and cold as ice. There was an undeniable aura of authority about him despite his youth; a regal bearing that had reduced many of his older ministers to quivering heaps, and courtly women to wistful sighs.

"You are well, Masaru-san?"

"Hai, great Lord." Masaru's voice was deadpan neutral.

"And you know what I command of you?"

"Hai, great Lord."

"I have no doubt of your success. The man who stood beside my father as he slew the last nagaraja of Shima will not be troubled by a simple thunder tiger, hai?"

"You honor me, great Lord."

The Shōgun took the older man by the arm; a shocking display of familiarity that sent whispers rippling through the throng. Yoritomo ushered Masaru aside and spoke in a low voice, intended for the hunt master's ears only.

"Hachiman, almighty God of War has sent me a vision of this beast, Masaru-san. I ride it at the head of a great army, subjugating the gaijin barbarians across the seas to my will. I will be as the great Stormdancers of old: Kazuhiko the Red, Kitsune no Akira, and Tora Takehiko." His grip was painful, eyes bright with mania. "Bring me this prize, and you shall be the richest man in all of Shima."

Masaru cleared his throat. "And . . . if no such beast exists, great Lord?"

The Shōgun stopped short, eyes narrowing to slits. His mouth opened, but whether it was to reply or rebuke remained a mystery. At that precise moment, the terrier in Aisha's arms growled and sank puppy-sharp teeth into his Lady's finger. She cried out and dropped him. He scrabbled up in the dust and ran straight to Yukiko, yapping and wagging his tail. Aisha sucked her bitten finger as opened-mouthed horror washed through the crowd. Most people averted their eyes to spare their mistress further loss of face, and themselves the Shōgun's inevitable wrath.

Yoritomo's face grew dark, eyes narrowed with rage. He snapped his fingers at a nearby Iron Samurai and pointed at the pup bouncing around Yukiko's head.

"Destroy that mongrel."

"Hai!"

The warrior's bark rang out through the iron covering his face. He stalked toward the pup, his armor making a din like fighting vipers. Yukiko climbed to her feet, cradling the dog in her arms. The samurai stepped close, lotus smoke rising from his power unit, glaring from beneath his helm. His oni faceplate was horrifying to look at; sharp metal tusks protruding from a freakshow grin, twin horns sprouting from his forehead. Towering over the girl, he held out a hand encased in embossed black iron, silently demanding the frightened terrier.

"Yoritomo!" Lady Aisha cried. "Please!"

Yukiko glanced from the Lady Aisha to the chubby pup, who licked her nose with a bright pink tongue. She blinked and looked into his eyes as the wind played in her hair and the earth fell away from her feet. The sun glinted on his pupils, red pinholes in a curtain of night, and she fell into brightness as dazzling as a newborn rainbow.

"Yukiko!" barked her father.

She started from her reverie.

"But . . ."

"Daughter, give him the dog!"

"But he didn't mean to hurt her!" Yukiko felt a stab of dread as the words tumbled from her mouth. "The Lady's perfume burns his eyes! He just wanted to get away from it!"

With an impatient hiss, the samurai tore his chainkatana from its sheath and thumbed the ignition. The internal motor roared to life, the serrated chain-saw teeth skirting the weapon's edge blurring in time with each squeeze of the throttle. The samurai reached out toward the dog, iron fingers curled into claws.

"Hold." Yoritomo's command was flint on steel.

The samurai froze. Silence descended over the street, blue-black and full of menace, broken only by the idling of the chainkatana's motor. The Shōgun walked slowly toward Yukiko, head tilted to one side. The girl lowered her eyes, uncertain where to look, gaze flitting from the ground to the growling blade in the samurai's hand. The assembled crowd held its breath, most thinking they would have the pleasure of witnessing an unscheduled execution.

"What is your name, girl?"

"Kitsune Yukiko." Masaru blurted her name before she could speak. "My daughter, great Lord. Forgive her, I beg you."

The Shōgun's stare was cool, one finger on his lips.

"Ah, Fox's daughter. I remember." He held out his arms expectantly. "Give me the dog, Kitsune Yukiko."

Yukiko obeyed, handing over the puppy before dropping to her knees and pressing her forehead into the dust.

"Forgive your humble servant, great Lord."

Yoritomo held the puppy up by its scruff. A spotted pink and brown belly swelled above a rapidly wagging tail. The Shōgun glared, scowling as the puppy licked his nose. One of the choirboys clapped his hands over his mouth, trying to stifle the giggle spilling out between his fingers. His mistress raised her hand for a slap, but abruptly fell still. She turned, eyes wide, and looked at her sovereign Lord in amazement.

Yoritomo-no-miya, Ninth Shōgun of the Kazumitsu Dynasty, was laughing.

Ripples of amusement spilled through the crowd, and soon many were covering their mouths and laughing aloud. A bright chorus of children's laughter wafted on the noxious wind, the tinkling of a hundred silver bells. Mirth bounced off the pitted warehouse walls, refracting in the eyes of stoic Lotusmen as the Iron Samurai looked to each other in confusion. Yoritomo tucked the puppy under his arm and ruffled its ears, turning his stare back to Yukiko.

"Rise, daughter of foxes." The command was given with a smile, as if she hadn't been a breath away from decapitation moments before. "You have work to do."

The Shōgun turned back to Masaru, a dangerous glint in his eye. "A daughter with courage is a blessing to her father's house."

"Thank you, great Lord." Masaru dropped to his knees again and bowed.

"Do not fail me, Black Fox. I have no wish to take more from you than I already have."

". . . No, Lord. Of course not."

"Then good hunting, Masaru-san. Bring me back my arashitora."

He gave a cursory nod to Captain Yamagata, then spun on his heel and strode back to his rickshaw, scruffing the puppy's ears.

"The lotus must bloom," he added, almost as an afterthought.

Yukiko rose on trembling legs beneath the Iron Samurai's gaze. She met his stare as he unclasped his oni mask and swung the faceplate aside. He was terribly young for a samurai; barely seventeen, if she had to guess. High cheekbones and a strong jaw, tipped with a small pointed goatee, smooth skin the color of polished bronze. His eyes were a dazzling green, deep and sparkling like paintings of the great northern seas. He was smiling at her.

"That was very brave, Lady."

Yukiko stared, her tongue somewhere in her sandals.

Gods, he's gorgeous . . .

The samurai pulled off his gauntlet and ran his thumb across the now silent blades of his sword, leaving behind a thin smear of red on the patterned steel. He wiped the blood on his golden tabard, then slid the katana into its enameled sheath with the sound of a cicada's wings.

"Once drawn, it must taste blood." His eyes sparkled like creamy jade. "I am glad it was not yours, daughter of foxes."

He bowed, slipped his gauntlet on and lumbered back to his place in line. At a signal from the choir mistress, the children took up their song again, and the entire procession rolled out, kicking up clouds of acrid dust. Roiling plumes of blue-black smoke spewed from the motor-rickshaws and spattered the goggles of the assembled mob. The footsteps of the bushimen were a thundering percussion beneath the vibrance of the choir, accompanied by a lotus engine growl.

As the entourage departed, many of the crowd turned curious eyes on Yukiko, their murmurs filling the air like cricket song.

Akihito stood, wiped dirty sweat from his brow. "Beards of the hungry dead. Are you mad, little fox? They could've—"

"Not now." Kasumi gave the big man a shove. "Let's just get aboard."

"Hai." Yamagata cast a wary glance among the hunters. "Time we were away."

The trio climbed aboard the elevator, platform creaking in its corroded couplings. Yamagata lifted the hydraulic control from its rusted hook, looked at Masaru expectantly.

"Are you coming, Hunt Master?"

Yukiko's gaze was focused on the boot prints at her feet. She dared a glance up at her father and was met with a furious stare, unblinking, bloodshot eyes. His hands were fists by his side, muscles over-clocked, shaking with anger.

"Masaru-sama . . ." Kasumi's tone was gentle.

"We're coming," he growled, breaking the stare and stalking toward the elevator.

Yukiko joined him on the gantry, hands clasped and gaze downturned. She could feel her father's eyes on the back of her neck, a thin trickle of sweat running down her spine.

She watched the Shōgun's silk parade stomp off into the haze.

Stupid, stupid, stupid.

7

THUNDER CHILD

Yukiko and Satoru had always been close, even for twins. Each seemed to know what the other was thinking without ever saying a word. They loved to sit together on nights when their father was home, listening to his tales as the wind whispered through the bamboo and the cedar logs crackled and the fire filled their little house with comforting, ruddy warmth.

With a soft, sad voice, he would tell the legends of the henge and yōkai spirit beasts; the great sea dragons and thunder tigers now long gone from the world. He would speak of the gods and the creation of Shima; when great Lord Izanagi had stirred the endless oceans with the tip of his spear, and his bride Izanami had died giving birth to the islands beneath them, forever lost to her husband in Yomi; the blackest hell in the underworld. He spoke of heroes, of the Stormdancers who rode on the backs of arashitora in the days when myths walked the land with earthly feet. He spoke of the great hunts, of how he and Aunt Kasumi and Uncle Akihito and the great Hunt Master Rikkimaru had been tasked by the Shōgun to rid Shima of the last of the Black Yōkai, the demons and monsters of the old world. And Yukiko and Satoru would sit at his feet and marvel, and wonder if any children in all the world had a father as brave as theirs.

Their mother would sometimes sing to them in a voice as bright as the sun, and their father would look up from sharpening his blades or crafting his snares and stare, as if she were some magical thing he'd caught in his nets that might turn and escape at any moment. And then he would smile at her, and say that the Heavens should have been named Naomi.

Their mother would smile at his flattery, and kiss his lips even as she chided him for his blasphemy. She was old-blooded Kitsune, a true daughter of foxes.

Hair of raven black, skin of smooth alabaster, the kami spirits of the Iishi Mountains flowing in her veins.

The same spirits that flowed in the blood of her children.

Yukiko had discovered it first, playing with their old scent-hound Buruu by the stream when they were six years old. She had stared into the dog's eyes and felt the world falling away beneath her feet. And suddenly she was inside him, could hear the feelings and colors in his head, sense the overload of scent: wild azaleas and sakura-cherries, the moist earth, her own fresh sweat on her skin. She felt his simple joy at being with her, knowing he was hers and she was his, rollicking with her brother on the bank, tail wagging.

My pack. My boy. My girl. Love.

He barked at her, tongue lolling from his mouth.

Happy.

She closed her eyes and pushed her thoughts into his mind: that she was happy too, that she would love him always. He padded up to her and stared into her eyes, then slobbered around her face with his big pink tongue. She laughed and rolled onto her back, Buruu nuzzling her with his cold, wet nose as she giggled, throwing her arms around his neck. She sat on the grass beside Satoru and showed him how, holding his hand and reaching out with their minds to touch the hound's, and Buruu barked and ran in circles, his tail a blur for his joy as his thoughts sang in their minds.

Happy.

The twins laughed and ran their hands along his flanks.

Love you. Love you both.

Their father had been fearful, angry that the gods had touched his children with the strange gift. He was afraid of what others would do if they knew. His children were fox-touched—yōkai-kin—and even here in Kitsune lands, suspicion and fear of the unknown had risen in the wake of the Guildsmen and their campaign against "impurity."

The taint of the spirit world must be purged from Shima, or so spoke the Guild Purifiers. Lord Izanagi had cleansed himself of the underworld's stain, and from the waters he bathed in were birthed three children: Amaterasu, Goddess of the Sun, Tsukiyomi, God of the Moon and Susano-ō, God of Storms. So too would the islands of Shima transcend if its people were to purify the taint that infected their collective bloodstream. The elemental kami spirits, the yōkai beasts, these were things of the Otherworld. Not the province of men. An infection to be carved out. A withered limb to be amputated and cauterized by blessed flame.

"You must keep it secret," Masaru urged his children. "It is a gift, *hai*, but it is *not one to be squandered, nor extinguished on some fanatic's pyre. Tell nobody. Not even the wind himself."*

Their mother was less afraid, encouraging them to learn, to walk in the forest and listen to the minds of the birds and beasts. The twins would take Buruu with them, stalking silently, feeling ahead with the Kenning for the faint flutters of life, the rapid, shallow thoughts of the small warmbloods fleeing at their approach, their numbers dwindling every day.

Together. Their pack. Her brothers by her side, swimming in each other's minds among the brilliant green, wishing it would be that way forever, that it would never, ever end.

But of course, it did.

The *Thunder Child* plowed north through fields of burgundy clouds, buffeted by the gentle hands of the summer breeze. Its propellers hummed, gears and pistons singing a metallic dirge as it vomited streams of poison into the Shima skies. The stink of burning chi was ever present; no matter where Yukiko sought refuge topside, it followed her like a reeking shadow. Below deck, the stench made her want to puke.

Standing at the bow seemed to offer the most relief, so she crouched against the wooden railing, kerchief tied around her face, goggles over her eyes, as unobtrusive as possible. Captain Yamagata stood beside her, one boot on the prow, breather strapped on tight, mirrored lenses reflecting the horizon.

Kasumi and Akihito were seated close by, triple checking the gear: vast hemp lines looped beneath the barrels of gas-driven net-throwers, vials of blacksleep loaded into the hollow centers of hypodermic bolts. The big man was sharpening the curved edges of four elegant nagamaki—two-handed swords with hafts as long as their blades. The weapons were crafted from folded steel, dark patterns rippling on the metal like the grain in polished wood, the long hilts wrapped in cord of deep scarlet. Each blade bore the mark of the master Phoenix artisan, Fushicho Hatori, reputedly the finest swordsmith of the late Shōgun's court.

"Only the Shōgun and his samurai are permitted to carry blades longer than a knife." Yamagata lifted his goggles long enough to raise an eyebrow at Akihito. "Does the thought of death by slow dismemberment hold some appeal for you, Hunter?"

"They were a gift." Akihito didn't look up. "From Shōgun Kaneda himself."

"Presented to the Black Fox and his fellows after the grand hunt, Yamagata-san," Kasumi said. "The day we and the Shōgun stalked the last nagaraja of Shima through the Renshi swamps, and laid her to rest."

"The Mother to All Vipers." Yamagata stroked his goatee. "Last of the Black Yōkai. What was she like?"

"Twenty feet long. Woman from her waist up, serpent from her waist down. A mane of living snakes, skin like pale jade, eyes in which a hundred men had drowned. She was beautiful." Kasumi shook her head. "Beautiful and terrible."

Akihito nodded and recited,

> *"Serpents in her hair,*
> *A dark grace, midnight's beauty.*
> *I weep at her fall."*

"You'll have to forgive him, Yamagata-san," Kasumi smiled. "Our Akihito fancies himself a poet."

"It's in the blood." The big man patted the phoenix tattoo on his right arm.

"Maybe you were adopted?"

Akihito made a face, threw his whetstone at Kasumi's head. She snatched it from the air, tossed it back with a laugh.

"I have heard the tale sung in taverns from here to Danro," Yamagata said. "How Shōgun Kaneda and the Black Fox slew the only great evil of the Yomi underworld yet loose in the world. But I did not know you were there also." The captain covered his fist and bowed. "Respect, Hunters."

Akihito smiled at the memory, touched the scars on his chest. Yamagata seemed satisfied, and Kasumi began filling another hypo with blacksleep. The dark, viscous liquid was a potent toxin. A few drops would send the average man dreaming for several hours. Much more than a mouthful, he might sleep forever. The poison was derived from the black roots of the lotus plant, and each vial was adorned with a red paper amulet marked with Guild kanji.

"Are you all right up there?" Yamagata peered at Yukiko, crouched by the bow. "You're missing the view."

"I've seen it." Yukiko lifted her kerchief, scratched at her nose. "Chi pipelines, deadlands and blood lotus as far as the eye can see."

"Ah, lotus." Yamagata looked out over the swaying fields below. "Who would have thought that iron could grow on trees, eh? Lord Izanagi be praised."

Akihito glanced up at the captain. "Business is good, then."

"What do you think?" Yamagata grinned behind his breather. "A third of the country is hooked on bud smoke, and the rest drink lotus leaf tea. That plant is a blessing from the Maker God to anyone with eyes to see." Yamagata started counting off on his fingers. "Anesthetics from its sap, toxins from its roots, rope and canvas from its rind. And from its seeds? The lifeblood of the whole damn country, my friend."

He patted the *Thunder Child*'s rail.

"Fuel for sky-ships, ō-yoroi, motor-rickshaw, chainkatana and memory machines." He laughed. "Anything the Guild Artificers can dream up. Without chi, we'd still be a mob of farmer clans feuding in the mud. Instead, we're an Empire. Exploring the seas and conquering the skies. The most powerful nation in the history of the world."

"Everything comes with a price," Kasumi muttered. "You'll see."

Yamagata stared silently as she continued filling the hypos.

"She's beautiful now, Captain-san. But in a few years this ship of yours is going to melt under the black rain. And though you're probably safe with that breather, the chi fumes will see most of your crew in the gutters with the other blacklung beggars." She sighed. "Even walking among the clouds, you must notice the weather growing hotter by the year? Or that the sun is bright enough to burn you blind if you look at it with your naked eye? Did you know the skies used to be blue once, Yamagata-san? Brilliant blue, like a gaijin's eyes. And now?" Kasumi shook her head. "Red as your lotus. Red as blood."

Yamagata looked at her sideways. "Not that it's my business, but some might call that dangerous talk, Hunter."

"Perhaps. But no more dangerous than ignoring what lotus is doing to this land."

Yukiko peered over the *Thunder Child*'s railing, down through the filthy skies to the lotus farms stretched out below. The fields were an endless interlocking series of rectangular paddies, shrouded by choking scarlet pollen. A vast orange serpent stretched away into the distance; a hulking pipeline of corroded metal connecting the Kigen city refineries to a central collection hub in the midlands known as "First House." Though the refineries in each capital city kept a measure of the chi they processed on hand, the vast majority of it was flushed via rusted arteries to the seat of Guild power in Shima; a tithe to the masters of the fuel and technology that pumped the iron Shōgunate's heart.

Alongside the pipeline ran lengths of rusting metal and sleepers of bleached wood; tracks for Shima's combustion-driven railway. The snub-nosed hulk of a goods train was thundering away beneath them, retching a black, smoking trail from its snout as it wound its way back toward Kigen city. Before the advent of the sky-ships, rail had been the highway on which Shima's most vital commerce sped. Foodstuffs, trade goods and common folk still rolled back and forth along the corroded lines every day, but for cargo as important as blood lotus or gaijin slaves, the sky was now the only way to travel.

The chi pipeline and railway lines were weeping scabs, crusted across the sweeping vista of lotus fields. But in some places, the landscape of swaying red and green was also pockmarked by dark stains; broad tracts of smoking, ashen soil, utterly devoid of life. Yukiko had been nine years old when she'd first seen the blackened scars from the air, the great swathes of land they covered. She had asked her mother where they came from.

Her mother had explained that lotus roots gave off a toxic discharge that rendered the soil around it barren in just a few short years. Like cancer in a blacklung victim, the blood lotus flower crept across Shima's plains and valleys, dead earth in its wake, choking everything before it. Wildlife fled to the forests, only to have their sanctuaries cleared by the buzzing blades of the shreddermen, sent forth from the Guild's assembly lines in their screaming, smoking saw-machines. The plant grew on Shima's face like red mold across a rotting fruit.

"The deadlands were a problem in the past." Yamagata conceded the point with a shrug. "But the Guild gives the farmers inochi by the barrelful. The fertilizer is more than enough to stave off the soil death. The paddymen just need to use the bloody stuff."

"Gives?" Akihito scoffed. "You means *sells* them inochi, don't you? How in the hells can they use it if they can't afford to buy it?"

"I didn't expect you to be an idealist, Hunter," the captain smiled. "Don't you kill things for a living?"

"Have you been into the countryside lately, Yamagata-san? What the hells is left to kill? The only animals thriving are corpse-eaters: lotusflies and rats. Ask the average farmer's son if he knows what a deer looks like, if he's ever seen a bamboo bear that wasn't painted on a drinking house wall. There are only three tigers left on this entire island, all sickly curs, prowling the Shōgun's gardens and refusing to breed. And this is an animal with a *godsdamned zaibatsu* named after it. I can't remember the last time I saw a real fox. And as for dragons or phoenix?" The big man's laughter was short and bitter. "My father was a hunter, Yamagata-san. And his father before him. But my sons?" Akihito spat onto his whetstone. "They'll be factory workers."

"They can still hunt yōkai." Yamagata waved at the choking red sky. "Isn't that why you're here? To capture a spirit-beast?"

Akihito snorted. "The last official sighting of a sea dragon was a century ago. The last arashitora died during Shōgun Tatsuya's reign. The great yōkai beasts are legends now; bedtime stories to tell your children between coughing fits."

Akihito aimed a polarized stare at Kasumi. "And we're supposed to be out here catching one."

Yukiko stabbed her tantō into the deck and sighed. Everything Akihito said was true. Her father was right; the Shōgun should just release them from his service and be done with it. A few starving wolves were hardly worth the expense of their upkeep. There was no need for a Master of Hunters any more.

"Ah, well, you know what they say." Yamagata shrugged—the feigned helplessness of a man who profits from the status quo. He adjusted the breather on his face, stuffed his hands into his obi and wandered off in the direction of his cabin. "The lotus must bloom."

As if on cue, Yukiko heard the heavy tread of iron-shod feet. She looked up and saw the *Child*'s Guildsman emerging from below decks to peer at the balloon above.

Gods knew how many more dwelled in the chapterhouses, but Yukiko had seen three different kinds of Guildsmen in her life: three variations of the same metallic, insectoid theme. The first were the garden-variety Lotusmen who stalked Kigen streets and swarmed about its sky-docks like flies on dung. The second were the terrible Purifiers, reciting thousand-year-old scripture and lighting the pyres under children's feet at the Burning Stones. And lastly, there were the Artificers. If the Lotusmen were the Guild's troops, and the Purifiers their priests, the Artificers were its mechanics; a sect of engineers and technicians responsible for the creation of every machine and marvel the Guild had yet gifted to Shima's populace.

The *Thunder Child*'s Guildsman was one of these Artificers. Its brass suit was the product of a back-alley coupling between a regular atmos-suit and a chi-powered toolbox. Arcane apparatus were bolted across every surface: drills, torque wrenches, cutting torches and circular saws, its backpack replete with a small loading crane and acetylene tanks. Unlike the faceted eyes of the Purifiers or regular Lotusmen, the Artificers instead had a single rectangular slab of glowing red light in the middle of their empty faces. A series of switches and dials were arrayed on its chest, alongside the click-clack of the ever-turning mechabacus. As Yukiko watched, the Guildsman began pushing beads back and forth along the device's rungs, a series of complex, intricate movements, like a musician's fingers dancing across taut strings. Although most people assumed mechabacii were some form of counting machine, the truth was nobody but the Guildsmen knew what the hells they were actually for.

She glanced down at the knife waiting in the wood in front of her. Akihito nudged Kasumi, and the pair fell still, watching the Guildsman in its clanking brass suit approach across the varnished deck. It stepped up beside Yukiko and stared out over the railing, the geometry of the fields below refracted on its single, glowing eye. There was a small hiss as a discharge of oily smoke issued from its pack.

The hunters cast wary glances at each other.

The Guildsman turned and looked down at the vial of blacksleep in Kasumi's hand.

"Class six toxin." Its voice was a swarm of flies. "Purpose?"

"You know why we're here," Yukiko muttered.

"Permit." It extended one gauntleted hand to punctuate the demand.

"Of course, Guildsman," said Kasumi, doing her best to glare at the girl from behind her goggles. She reached into a pack and produced several scrolls, each set with the Shōgun's seal. The Artificer took them with care, scanning the kanji before returning the paperwork with a nod. The bellows on its pack pumped up and down to the sawing of hollow, mechanical breath.

"Thank you, citizen," it buzzed.

"You work on this ship?" Yukiko tilted her head at the Guildsman.

It turned to regard the girl with its strange, glittering eye. Yukiko wondered what it looked like beneath the metal shell, whether it missed the touch of the sun on its skin. If it heard the screams of burning children when it closed its eyes at night. The stare was blank and featureless, like looking into a mirror and finding no one staring back at you.

"Hai," it said.

Yukiko stared back hard, ignoring Akihito's not-so-subtle gestures for silence. "Why? No lotus is being hauled on this trip."

"Every sky-ship leaving port is required to have an Artificer on board."

"To spy on the crew, right? Make sure they aren't taking their own cut of the shipments?"

"To maintain the engines. Citizen."

Yukiko licked her lips and remained mute as the deck rocked beneath them. The Guildsman peered at her for a heavy, silent moment, then with seemingly nothing left to do, it turned to leave.

"The lotus must bloom," it rasped, clanking back toward the cabin.

Akihito waited until it was out of sight before turning on Yukiko. "What the hells were you speaking to it for?" he hissed. "Why are you always pushing those bastards?"

Kasumi's voice was gentle. "Yukiko, you should be more careful . . ."

"You're not my mother," Yukiko glared at the older woman. "Don't you dare try to lecture me."

She scowled down at the deck, stabbing her tantō into the wood again. Kasumi watched her for a moment, worry written in the set of her shoulders, the tilt of her head. Then with a meaningful glance at Akihito, she returned to her work. The big man sighed, spat on his whetstone again and resumed grinding it across the edge of one razor-sharp blade.

Almost everyone Yukiko knew distrusted and feared the Guild, but their Artificers built the technical marvels on which the Empire now depended to expand. She knew there must have been a time before all this, before the five-sided chapterhouses grew in the heart of Shima's cities, choking the streets with exhaust fumes and the skies with toxins. But if there was such a day, it lay too far back in history now for anyone she knew to remember it. If asked where the Guild had come from, or how they had come to control the fuel that drove the Shōgunate, the average citizen would most likely cast a wary glance over his shoulder and quickly turn his talk to other things.

What did it matter where they came from, or when? They were here now, brass fingers entwined in every zaibatsu court, lurking beside Yoritomo's throne like clockwork spiders, as vital to the Shōgunate as oxygen to a drowning man.

For their part, the Guild's Communications Ministry was always careful to downplay the citizenry's fears. They provided entertainments to distract the masses from their troubling thoughts about mass extinctions or spreading black-lung: the soapstar plays and traditional operas transmitted across the wondrous new wireless system, the bloody arena games using the seemingly endless stream of gaijin slaves from the wars overseas. Cheap liquor and processed lotus buds to intoxicate and befuddle; a grand, churning machine of misdirection and distraction that kept the factories grinding and the forges burning.

There was far too much at stake to allow a few missing pandas to get in the way of production quotas. The Guild had a world to conquer.

The rigging creaked above Yukiko's head. Sharp calls rang out across the crimson sky as a cloudwalker spotted a crane in the distance; a lonely silhouette against a backdrop of burning red. The sailors called to the bird, hands outstretched, asking for good fortune. To see a crane in the sky these days was a rarity. Surely Lord Izanagi had sent it as a sign of his blessing to the Black Fox's venture?

Masaru and Yamagata emerged from below deck, deep in conversation. Yukiko watched as the pair parted ways, the captain barking at his crew to put their backs into it. Masaru turned and stalked up to the bow.

"Kasumi," he rasped, "I want spotlights set up on either side of the pilot's deck. Ask Yamagata's permission before you drill any railings. Akihito, start assembling the cage. I'll be along in a moment."

Kasumi and Akihito exchanged a quick glance, packed up their gear and moved off without a word. Yukiko pretended not to notice the look that passed between her father and Kasumi, the way his eyes lingered on hers for just a fraction too long. She gritted her teeth, fixed her stare on the deck.

Masaru watched the pair descend into the cargo hold, then folded his arms and turned on his daughter. Yukiko glanced up at her father. He'd changed into his sleeveless hunting haori, loose-fitting hakama covering his legs. His arms were beaded with sweat, tattoos gleaming in the red light. He looked haggard, shadows under his goggles, face drawn and gray. An angry bruise had set up camp beneath his left eye and was sending out exploratory forces across his cheek.

"You look terrible," Yukiko murmured. "You should get some sleep."

"Do you want to tell me what the hells you thought you were doing today?" Masaru growled.

Yukiko pulled her knife free from the deck and stabbed it into the wood again. "I don't know what you mean."

"Don't play games with me, girl. Kenning in front of the Shōgun?"

"Was I supposed to let them kill it? Because some idiot girl wants to smell pretty and—"

"It was a damned dog, Yukiko!"

"There are a lot fewer dogs left on this island than there are people."

"It's not worth risking your neck over! The Guildsmen are burning Impure every bloody month. What were you thinking?"

"Probably the same thing you were thinking this morning when you risked *your* neck over a game of cards. That yak' almost killed you."

"Akihito was there," Masaru scoffed. "Nothing would have happened."

"You were so smoke-drunk, *anything* could have happened."

"Dammit, girl, this isn't about me! Kenning in public? What would your mother say?"

"What would she say about you?" Yukiko snapped, rising to her feet. "An old drunk so blinded by the dragon you could barely stand? Gambling and fighting and smoking yourself legless every godsdamned day? No wonder she left you!"

Masaru recoiled as if she'd slapped him, mouth agape, skin turning a paler shade of gray. Yukiko turned her back and stared out over the bow, loose strands of hair whipping about her face. She hugged herself and shivered despite the heat, great seas of swaying red and green flying away beneath her feet.

"Ichigo, I . . ."

"Just leave me alone," she sighed.

"Ichigo" was the pet name he'd given her when she was little. "Strawberry."

It seemed trite to her now; a remnant from days that were long gone, and never coming back.

She could feel him lingering behind her, silent and hurt. Remorse began bubbling up inside her, but she pushed it down into her toes, remembering all the nights she'd dragged him to bed reeking of smoke, unable even to undress himself. The months of watching every single coin while he pissed his pay away in smoke houses and drinking pits. The shame when he slurred or stumbled or got into fistfights.

She was sixteen years old. *He* was supposed to be looking after *her*.

The truth was she missed her father. She missed the strong proud man who had put her and her brother on his shoulders as he stalked through the bamboo forest. She missed sitting by the fire on her mother's knee, listening to him tell stories of the great hunts, his quick, dark eyes alight with life and flame. She missed the days before they had moved to Kigen city; those brief, wonderful years when they had all been together and happy.

It was all gone now. Forest, brother, mother, life. All of it disappearing in a puff of blue-black smoke.

You never even let me say goodbye to her.

She heard his boots scrape on the deck, soft footsteps retreating into the distance.

She was alone.

8

KIN

Yukiko awoke in the deep of night, staring at the hammock above her. Her father snored, swaying with the tilt and roll of the ship as it trekked northward. The room stank of lotus smoke, a half-empty pipe still clutched in Masaru's hand. She sighed, sitting upright and swinging her legs to the deck, her toes searching unsuccessfully for her sandals.

She stood and rubbed her eyes, steadying herself against the wall. The room was cramped but private, a round portal of cloudy beach glass staring out into the dark beyond. She had dreamed of the Iron Samurai with the sea-green eyes; a silly, girlish fancy of flowers and longing stares and happy-ever-afters that left her stomach fluttering with a hundred butterfly wings. She shook her head, pushed the thoughts from her mind. Nobility didn't mix with the common-born, even if she was a blooded clansman. Yōkai kin didn't mix with folk who would gladly see them burn on Guild pyres, either. The muck she stood in was deep enough already without starting to entertain childish fantasies.

The little room felt stifling, closing about her with wooden, smoke-stained fists. She opened the door and slipped out onto the deck.

The engines droned their metallic song through the still night. The cloud-walkers on watch were huddled in a small knot on the starboard side, passing a pipe back and forth and muttering over a game of dice. The sound of bones rolling across wood masked her soft footsteps, and she passed by without being noticed. The balloon above her creaked; the swollen bladder of some great, prehistoric beast. The wood was smooth and warm beneath her toes.

The *Thunder Child* measured one hundred and twenty feet from the dragon figurehead carved at her bow to her square, towering stern. Yukiko padded across the deck, hands stuffed into her obi. She headed up toward the front of the ship, as far from the engines as she could be, hoping for a moment's relief from the stink of burning fuel. Stepping up onto the foredeck, she felt a rush of cool wind in her face, whispering fingers running through her hair. A dozen barrels of chi were packed at the bow, and she leaned on them with both hands, looked out into the blackness with wide, dark eyes.

The moon was a smear of pink across a hazy sky. It cast a sullen light on the land below, enough to make out the lotus fields, the serpentine shadow of the iron pipeline, the gleam of a little river snaking down from the mountains on the horizon. They must be close to the lands of the Dragon clan by now, and the ship would soon have to turn northeast to avoid the no-fly zone around First House. Small pinpricks of light were dotted about the landscape, and in the distance she could see a tiny bright cluster in the foothills of the eastern mountain range: the great Ryu metropolis of Kawa.

She sighed and watched the night, trying not to think about a boy with an oni's face and a pair of dazzling, sea-green eyes.

"What do you see?" A soft voice. Behind her.

She whirled about, hand on the tantō at the small of her back. There was a boy in front of her, perhaps a little older than she, knife-bright eyes staring from a tired, fragile face. He was plain looking, unstained by soot or smoke; neat as freshly washed sheets or an unopened book. Clean gray linen was loosely draped over his lean body, hair cropped close to his scalp. He raised his hands and took half a step back, ready to ward off a blow.

"Hold, Lady."

"You shouldn't sneak up on people like that!" Yukiko snapped.

"I am sorry that I startled you." He bowed, hand covering fist.

Yukiko glanced back at the huddle of cloudwalkers at the other end of the deck. She heard a snatch of laughter, the sound of dice. She narrowed her eyes and turned away, cool breeze kissing her face. Annoyance had replaced her sudden fear, and she wished the boy would be on his way.

"What do you see?" The question came again, just as soft.

"Who are you?" she frowned, half turning. She thought she had already met most of the crew. He was too old to be a cabin boy. Perhaps a galley worker?

"My name is Kin." He bowed again.

"Your clan?"

"I have none, Lady."

"And why do you bother me, Burakumin Kin?"

"I did not say I was lowborn, Lady."

Yukiko fell silent. She turned her back fully to the stranger, indicating that she wished him to leave. Though she was not nobility, nor possessed of their notions about what was "proper" for a young, unwed lady, she was still uncertain if she should be up here alone with this strange boy. Her father definitely wouldn't approve.

The deck trembled beneath them as the helmsman adjusted course. Stars tried to twinkle in the skies above; faded jewels strewn across a blanket of dusty black velvet.

"I often come here at night to enjoy the breeze on my face," Kin continued. "The solitude is pleasant, hai?"

". . . I suppose so."

"You are Kitsune Yukiko, daughter of the great Masaru-sama."

She snorted, but said nothing.

"What brings you out here?"

"I couldn't sleep, if it is any of your concern."

"Bad dreams?"

Yukiko turned to look at him, a frown on her face. This was no galley boy. She peered at the ghost-pale chest between the folds of his robe, what little she could see of his arms. There was no sign of irezumi anywhere, which meant he couldn't be a blooded clansman, let alone one of the nobility. But he was far too clean and too well spoken . . .

Who is he?

"I have bad dreams too." He shrugged, eyes twinkling in smudged hollows.

"Are you . . . kami? A spirit?"

He laughed then, deep and rich, full of genuine mirth. Yukiko's cheeks burned for embarrassment, but soon she found herself caught up in his laughter, stifling a smirk behind one hand before chuckling along with the boy.

"I'm sorry, that was foolish." She smiled, smoothing her hair behind her ears.

"Not at all," he shook his head. "I am no spirit, Yukiko-chan."

"Then what are you?"

"Alone." He shrugged again. "Like you."

The boy gave a deep bow, lowering his eyes to the varnished floor. He straightened with a frail smile, nodded his head, then turned and wandered away. He stayed out of the guttering tungsten lamplight, sticking to the shadows as if he belonged inside them. The cloudwalkers were too intent on their dice to mark his passing.

Yukiko watched him disappear down the stairs, loose strands of hair caught in the wind and flailing at her eyes.

Well, that was odd . . .

You realize this is all bloody pointless."

Akihito wiped sweat from his brow as he muttered. He grunted and lifted another iron bar, sliding it into position on the heavy, soldered base. After almost two days of work, the cage was nearly complete.

Kasumi shrugged and fastened another bolt, shaking the bars to ensure the thread was tight. She stood and coughed, slightly out of breath in the thin air. Damp hair hung about her goggles, sticking to the glass. She lifted her kerchief to wipe away the sweat painting her lips.

"Well, service to Yoritomo the Mighty isn't all fancy women and cheap liquor," she sighed.

"The Shōgun is going to be disappointed if we come back empty-handed, Kas'. Yoritomo doesn't take disappointment well. Remember when General Yatsuma failed to break the gaijin siege at Iron Ridge?"

"I remember. His children were less than five years old."

"And Yatsuma was noble-born. An Iron Samurai. So how do you think he's—"

"Well, what option do we have?"

"Talk to Yamagata. He'll be in as much strife as us when this whole farce goes belly up. We could get him to drop us off in Yama city, maybe?"

"They'd hunt us down like dogs." Kasumi shook her head. "Just because Fox lands are a little provincial doesn't mean the Kitsune Daimyo won't dance if his Shōgun commands it. Yoritomo would have us hunted by every magistrate in Shima if we disobeyed him, it wouldn't matter how far away we ran. Besides, Masaru wouldn't hear of it. It would dishonor us all to leave. Our families would be disgraced."

"Well, what do you suggest? Because we sure as hells aren't coming home with an arashitora in this thing. Better for everyone aboard to just commit seppuku right now and save the damned chi."

He kicked the side of the cage, and a dull metallic thud rang out in response. Kasumi looked around at the multitude of cloudwalkers. They were mostly young men: crawling along the balloon's flanks, manning propellers and engines, adjusting altitude and course in response to the shifting wind. The stink of burning chi was making her throat hurt, her head feel uncomfortably light.

"You shouldn't be talking about this here," she muttered.

Akihito scowled, but as if to prove Kasumi's point, the Artificer emerged from below deck and began clanking toward them. Akihito bit his tongue, pretending to check the moorings of each bar as the Guildsman hissed to a stop close by.

"Very large cage." Its voice was that of an angry lotusfly.

The comment was an understatement. The boundaries of the enclosure stretched almost the width of the ship, a good twenty feet wide and deep. The slimmer cloudwalkers had got into the habit of slipping between the bars as they went about their duties. Larger ones were forced to hang out over the *Child*'s railings to navigate their way around it.

"We don't know what size this beast will be." Kasumi flashed a false smile. "Better the cage is too big than too small."

"Why do you not drug it?" Scorching sunlight refracted on the Artificer's single, glowing eye. "Make it sleep until Kigen?"

"We may not have enough blacksleep. Besides, it'd be foolish to rely on drugs alone."

"Stick to what you do best, Guildsman," Akihito growled. "Leave the hunting to us."

"Do you believe you will find one?" The Artificer turned its glittering eye on the big man, an insectoid curiosity flitting between each word. "A beast extinct for generations?"

"The Shōgun seems to think so," Akihito answered carefully.

"Does he really?"

"Fire!"

The cry rang out from the rigging, making Akihito start. Color drained from Kasumi's face. A fire on board a sky-ship could mean only two things: a desperate dash to the safety of the aft lifeboat, or a flaming death on the earth hundreds of feet below.

"Gods above," swore Akihito. "You get Yukiko, I'll g—"

"Not aboard." Faint amusement buzzed in the Guildsman's voice. "There."

It reached out with one metal hand, pointing across the bow. Akihito followed the gesture to the mountainous northwest horizon. Far past the rolling plains of the Ryu clan below, deep inside distant Kitsune territory, a bright pinprick of flame glowed against a backdrop of dark stone. It was almost too small to see through the haze; a tiny orange flare, a thin plume of smoke twisting into the sky and off into nothingness. Given how far they were from Fox lands, the fire must have been enormous for them to see it at all.

Several of the crew were gathering at the railing to stare. Kasumi and Akihito joined them, squinting into the distance. The cloudwalkers muttered and shot each other dark, knowing glances, several swearing so profanely that even Akihito seemed impressed. Kasumi turned to one of the sky folk, and saw the anger in his eyes.

"What's going on?"

From her nest between the chi barrels, Yukiko watched the sailors mill about on the deck, still too surly to wonder what the fuss was about. She'd been sulking around the bow for two days, avoiding her father, barely muttering a handful of words to Kasumi. Even Akihito's attempts to jolly her out of her funk were met with grumpy silence, and she'd outright refused their usual morning sparring sessions. She had not seen the strange, pale boy again.

She saw Captain Yamagata emerge from his cabin and stalk up to the bow, a mechanical spyglass in one calloused hand. Planting his boot on the railing, he pressed a button and watched the device extend, small motors and springs humming. He squinted through it toward the fire, hissing through clenched teeth and shaking his head. The spyglass whirred and clicked, extending its length, lenses within it shifting as they searched for focus on the wall of flames.

"Kagé," he whispered.

"Shadows?" Yukiko asked, perking up.

The captain flinched at the sound of her voice. He looked uneasy, casting a glance over his shoulder in the direction of the Artificer, then back to Yukiko's quizzical expression.

"Raijin's drums." A sheepish grin. "I didn't see you there."

"I'm Kitsune," she reminded him. "What was that you said about the Kagé?"

"You weren't supposed to hear that." Yamagata ran one hand over the back of his neck. "Don't be telling anyone I mentioned that word, Lady. It could see me in hot water."

"Why?" Yukiko lowered her tone to conspiratorial levels, keeping a close watch on the Guildsman. Yamagata was obviously worried about it overhearing.

"We're not supposed to talk about the Kagé. Officially, they don't exist."

"But they've been attacking lotus fields up north for years."

"How do you know that? It's never reported on the wireless."

"They operate in Kitsune country," Yukiko shrugged. "We lived there when I was a little girl. Whenever a field went up, the village wives would whisper about the Kagé and make the warding sign against evil. Mothers there even frighten their children with them. They say the Kagé come in the night and drag disobedient sons and daughters into the hells." Her eyes sparkled with the memory.

"Well, don't go spreading that kind of foolishness, do you hear?" Yamagata said. "Especially not when Old Kioshi's around."

"Old Kioshi?"

"Our Guildsman." Yamagata gave a subtle nod in the direction of the Artificer.

"He's an old man?"

"Been in the Guild longer than I've been breathing, if rumor is true. Hard to tell beneath the suit, I know."

Yukiko twisted to her feet and peered over the railing, one hand blotting out the sinking sun. Mountains loomed among a growling monsoon on the far horizon: the enormous spine of storm-tossed rock stretching across the north of Shima known as the Iishi ranges. Black spires rose up out of a carpet of scarlet, spear points tipped in white, dazzling snow. The Iishi were the last true stretch of wilderness in all Shima; haunted, if the tales were true, by the restless dead and demons from the deep hells. It was said in the old legends that when the Maker God, Lord Izanagi, had sought the Yomi underworld to reclaim his dead bride, he'd found the gateway in the Iishi. The lands of Yukiko's birth lay in the western foothills: the once lush and beautiful countryside of the Kitsune zaibatsu, now reduced to a vast lotus field scarred by stretches of smoking, dead earth.

She squinted, barely making out the fire blazing at the jagged feet of one of the mightiest eastern crags. Pulling off her goggles, she frowned at the layer of grime and smoke smudged across the lenses.

"The official story is always the same," Yamagata said. "Natural fire, nothing unusual about it. Certainly not started by human hands. To even suggest it is to invite trouble."

"So the Guild lies." She spat onto the glass, rubbing with the hem of her uwagi.

"You can't blame them." Yamagata scowled over his spyglass. "If they acknowledge that an organized group is incinerating lotus fields, they'd be admitting that they're incapable of protecting their own property—a show of weakness. A loss of face."

"But that's just stupid! Everyone up there knows the Kagé exist."

"People up there don't matter."

Yukiko blinked at him, taken aback.

"Farmers. Peasants." Yamagata waved his hand dismissively. "The Guildsmen don't care about their whispers, their lives. They care about the Shōgun, the Kazumitsu Elite and their grip over the army. They care about face. Weakness is not something most will admit to. Least of all them. So much rides on perception, the power in appearances. The Guild and the Shōgun's forces are like an old, bitter couple, locked together in a marriage they detest. If either side ever thought they could seize power entirely for themselves, well . . ." The captain shrugged. "And in the meantime, the radio broadcasts mention nothing of the Kagé, and more and more crops get burned."

"The old village women used to say the Kagé were wicked kami who delighted in fire. But you speak of them like they're men."

"Oh, they're men," Yamagata snorted. "Flesh and blood, no fear of that. Who knows why the bastards do it? Disenfranchised farmers out for revenge. Lunatics with nothing better to do. I heard one rumor that they're a group of gaijin trying to destabilize the Guild, weaken the war effort. White ants, chewing at the country's foundations. Damn savages."

"Then the fire at the refinery last week . . ."

"You heard the wireless. The Guild investigators said it was an accident. Believe that if you like." The captain lowered his spyglass, offered it to the girl as he replaced his goggles. "All I know is that they're costing the Guild a lot of money. Rumor has it they've started transmitting their own radio broadcasts now. Alternating frequencies, every weeksend. A pirate signal the Guild can't control."

Yukiko closed one eye and peered through the whirring glass, storm clouds and mountains leaping into focus and swaying with the motion of the ship. Steadying herself with one hand against the railing, she focused on a large field of lotus. Seething tongues of fire were spreading out among the swaying fronds, scarlet blooms blackening in the heat. The tiny figures of desperate farmers were running to and fro, spraying black water with hand pumps in a vain attempt to save the crop. The blaze stretched forth greedy hands, spurred onward by the scorching summer heat. She could see the terror and anguish; men risking their lives for the sake of a poisonous weed, stubbornly trying to hold their ground as Fūjin, God of Winds, drove the flames like terrified horses before the whip. It was obvious that the men could do nothing. The fire would run its course. Yet still they fought, watching their livelihoods go up in smoke before tear-filled eyes.

Yukiko lowered the telescope, feeling a terrible weight in her breast. She thought of the lives ruined, the children who would go unclothed and unfed because their parents had lost everything. Joining the faceless mob in one of the great cities, eking out a living in squalor and dust, choking on chi fumes as their lips slowly turned black.

"Whoever they are, they're cruel and wicked," Yukiko frowned. "Those poor people . . ."

"Aye. Wretches without the courage to face the enemy with a sword in their hands." Yamagata spat onto the deck. "Bastard cowards."

They stood together and watched the fields burn.

9
SMOKE ON A STARLESS SKY

The propellers hummed their monotone lullaby, but the dreams still dragged Yukiko from her sleep. The hammock above her was empty, a slack tangle of pale, knotted cord, bereft of father and the stink of lotus smoke. A moment's panic gripped her as she realized he was gone, but she clenched her teeth and shoved it away. She peered out of the window to the starless sky, tried to guess what time it was. A long way from dawn, she figured. A longer way from home.

Slipping from the room, she stole toward the stairwell, the wood beneath her feet vibrating with the constant hum of the engines. She was becoming numbed to the chi-stink, the lightness of head and shortness of breath that altitude carried in its arms, but still, it was the promise of a few moments of fresh air that drew her out onto the deck. Not the thought that her father might have stumbled up there, drunk on smoke. Not the knowledge that it would take one clumsy step to send him over the side and down into the dark. Not at all.

She found him keeping company with the watchmen in a puddle of lantern light, sitting cross-legged on a looped pile of thick hemp rope, and her momentary relief evaporated as the familiar smell of lotus smoke crept into her nostrils. Three others sat with him, passing a wooden pipe back and forth. A young man in a dirty straw hat, another man around her father's age, and a young boy not more than eleven or twelve.

The younger man wore no clan irezumi on his shoulder, just a collection of koi fish and geisha girls that marked him as lowborn Burakumin. The boy wasn't yet old enough to be considered an adult and sported no ink, so Yukiko could only guess at where he came from. His skin was pale, but not pale enough to be Kitsune. Phoenix, if she had to guess.

Yukiko crept forward and stood in the dancing shadows beside them, listening to the rough jests and gutter-talk and snatches of hoarse laughter. It was a few minutes before the cloudwalker in the straw hat finally noticed she was there. He blinked with bloodshot eyes, taking a few seconds to focus on her face. Dragging deeply from the pipe, he passed it to the young cabin boy sitting next to him.

"Young miss?" His voice sounded thick and raw, smoke drifting from his lips with each word he spoke. "Can I get you something?"

The others looked up from the circle, Masaru last of all. A quick glance was all she got, but it was enough to see the shame in him.

"I want for nothing, thank you, sama." Yukiko gave a small, polite bow, eyeing the lotus pipe with distaste. "Just seeking to clear my head with the fresh air."

"Precious little of that to be found up here," the young boy said, passing the pipe along to Masaru with a grimace.

The older cloudwalker clipped the back of the boy's head, fast as a jade adder. He wore a three-day growth of beard, graying at the chin, a simple dragon tattoo on his right shoulder etched by some Docktown artiste.

"Mind your tongue in the presence of ladies, Kigoro." He held a single, stained finger up in front of the boy's nose. "There's plenty of fresh air waiting over the starboard side for those who dishonor this ship."

The cloudwalker in the straw hat chuckled, the young boy mumbling apologies and turning a bright shade of red. For a moment, the only sound was the bass rattle of the *Thunder Child*'s bones, the hypnotic drone of the great propellers, the iron growl of the engines in her belly. Yukiko stared at her father, who steadfastly refused to meet her gaze.

"Forgiveness, please." The older cloudwalker covered his fist and nodded to her. "My name is Ryu Saito. This is Benjiro." The younger cloudwalker bowed in his straw hat. "The little one with the large mouth is Fushicho Kigoro."

The young boy rubbed the back of his head, bowed to her.

Phoenix, then. I was right.

"I am Kitsune Yukiko . . ."

"We know who you are, Lady." Saito held up a hand in apology. "The tale precedes you in the telling. You are daughter of the Black Fox, Masaru-sama," he thumped her father on the shoulder, "come to hunt the thunder tiger at the command of Shōgun Tora Yoritomo."

"Next Stormdancer of Shima," the boy added.

Saito frowned and took back the pipe. The wad of lotus resin inside the bowl glowed red-hot as he sucked on the stem.

"Is that what you think, young Kigoro?" Saito held the smoke in his lungs as he spoke. "Yoritomo-no-miya will be a Stormdancer?"

The boy blinked.

"It is what they say."

" 'They?' " Saito exhaled and waved his hand about. "Who are 'they?' The air kami?"

"People," the boy shrugged. "Around Docktown."

"Aiya." Saito shook his head, passed the pipe along. "How comes it that children today speak so much yet know so little?" He fixed the boy in a squint-eyed stare. "A Stormdancer is more than the beast he rides. It takes more than the shoulders of a thunder tiger to stand as tall as heroes like Kitsune no Akira."

"All praise." Benjiro raised the pipe in a toast, exhaling a long trail of smoke that was snatched away by the wind.

"All praise," Saito nodded.

"Why?" Kigoro looked back and forth between the men. "What did he do?"

Cries of dismay split the night, and the two cloudwalkers clipped Kigoro over the back of his head in turn. Feeling sorry for the boy, Yukiko raised her voice over the clamor.

"He slew Boukyaku, young sama. The sea dragon who consumed the island of Takaiyama."

"Ahhhh." Benjiro pointed at Yukiko and bowed, obviously a little the worse for smoke. "See, Saito-san? Not all youngsters are ignorant of this island's great history. The Black Fox at least teaches his daughter the lessons of the past." He gave another unsteady bow to Masaru. "Honor to you, great sama."

"There's no such thing as sea dragons," the cabin boy pouted, glaring about at his fellows. "And there's no island called Takaiyama, either. You're making fun of me."

"There are no dragons now," Yukiko agreed. "But long ago, before the oceans turned red, they swam in the waters around Shima. They have a skeleton hanging in the great museum in the Kitsune capital."

"You've seen it?"

"Once." She fixed her eyes on the deck. "With my mother and brother. Long ago."

"What did they look like?"

"Fearsome. Spines of poison and teeth as long and sharp as katana."

". . . and there was none more fearsome than mighty Boukyaku, the Dragon of Forgetting."

Yukiko glanced up as her father spoke. His eyes were fixed somewhere in the dark over the railing, far away in the deep of the night, his voice tinged with the rasp of smoke. He ran his finger down through his graying mustache and licked his lips. And as he began to speak, for just a fleeting moment, she was a little girl again, curled up by the fire with Satoru and Buruu, listening to tales of wonder.

"They say his tail was as broad as the walls of the imperial palace. And when he lashed it in anger, tsunami as tall as sky-spires rose in his wake. He could swallow a ship and all her crew with one snap of his jaws, suck entire schools of deep tuna down his gullet with one breath. He grew fat and huge on the plunder of the eastern ocean, and the fishermen of the island of Takaiyama—for such was its name, young sama—were close to starvation. So they prayed to great Susano-ō, God of Storms, asking him to drive Boukyaku from their waters."

Saito leaned forward with his hands on his knees, and Benjiro stared at Masaru as if hypnotized. The drone of the engines and the song of the propellers seemed to fade away, and the sound of his voice was as flame to dazzled moths.

"But the great sea dragon overheard the islanders' pleas." The lotus pipe hung forgotten in Masaru's hand, trailing a thin wisp of smoke. "And in his terrible rage, Boukyaku opened his maw and consumed the island and everyone on it: man, woman, child and beast. And this is why the holy Book of Ten Thousand Days speaks of eight islands of Shima, when now there are only seven."

Saito leaned back, stroking his graying beard and looking at the young cabin boy. "And why ignorant pups like you have never heard the name of Takaiyama."

"Was Boukyaku one of the Black Yōkai?" The boy looked to Masaru.

"No," the Hunt Master shook his head. "Not black."

"But he was evil."

"There are three kinds of yōkai, young sama." Masaru counted off on his fingers. "The white, such as great phoenix. Pure and fierce." A second finger. "The black, spawned in the Yomi underworld; oni, nagaraja and the like. Creatures of evil." A third digit. "But most breeds of spirit beasts are simply gray. They are elemental, unconstrained. They can be noble like the great thunder tiger, who answers the call of the Stormdancer. But like the sea dragons, they can seem cruel to us, just as a rip-tide will seem cruel to a drowning man."

The boy appeared unconvinced. "So what does Kitsune no Akira have to do with all this, then?"

The cloudwalkers looked to Masaru. He stared down at the pipe in his hand for a long moment, and then continued to speak.

"One man survived the destruction of Takaiyama. A simple fisherman, who returned from the deep sea to find nothing left of his home. He traveled long and hard roads for one hundred and one days, arriving at the court of Emperor Tenma Chitose just before the grand festival of Lord Izanagi's feast day.

"His clothes were rags, and he was mad with grief, and the Emperor's guards refused him entry to the palace, for the celebration feast was already underway. Yet great Kitsune no Akira, who was in Kigen at the Emperor's invitation, heard of the man's plight through the whispers of the swallows in the Emperor's garden. With the humility of a true samurai, the Stormdancer covered the fisherman with his robe, and bid him sit in his place at the Emperor's table and eat in his stead. Then Kitsune no Akira leaped astride his thunder tiger, the mighty Raikou, whose voice was a storm, wings crackling with Raijin song. And they flew faster than the wind to the lair where great Boukyaku lay."

The boy blinked.

"What is Raijin song, sama?"

"Arashitora are the children of the Thunder God, Raijin, young sama." A gentle smile. "It is the sound of their wings you hear when the clouds clash and the storms roll."

Saito took the pipe from Masaru's hand, fished a small leather pouch from inside his uwagi and repacked the bowl with a fresh blob of resin. Yukiko looked at the smudges on the tips of the lotus-fiend's gray fingers; the same blue-black hue that stained her father's.

Saito lit the pipe on the lantern's flame, and the fire swelled in Masaru's bloodshot eyes, setting them ablaze.

"The battle was as fierce as any the world had seen. Thunder cracked the sky, and great waves crashed on the mainland's shores, sweeping away entire villages as if they were twig and tinder. The people held their breath, for as great a warrior as Kitsune no Akira was, never had there been a foe as deadly as Boukyaku. His teeth were swords, and his roar, an earthquake.

"But at last, the Stormdancer returned, his armor broken and his flesh torn by poisoned fangs, and the mighty thunder tiger Raikou carried the bleeding heart of Boukyaku in his claws. Kitsune no Akira returned to the Emperor's feast, and presented the heart to the fisherman with a low bow. When asked by the Emperor what he required in thanks for his mighty deed, Kitsune no Akira told the entire feast that they should always remember the name of Takaiyama, so that the Dragon of Forgetting would remain forever defeated. Then he knelt in his appointed place at table, toasted the Emperor's health, and fell dead of the dragon poison in his veins."

"All praise." Benjiro covered his fist and bowed, then reached for the lotus pipe.

"All praise," Saito nodded, sucking down one more lungful before passing it over.

The cabin boy blinked, looked at Yukiko. "Is all that true?"

"It's what they say." Her eyes were still fixed on her father. "But who knows whether or not he really existed."

Masaru looked up, finally met her stare. "Of course he existed."

Yukiko kept speaking to the cabin boy, as if her father had not made a sound. "It could have been an earthquake that sucked Takaiyama below the waves. Men blaming dragons or gods for their own misfortune, as they often do, even when the fault lies at their own two feet." She glanced at Masaru's toes. "Kitsune no Akira could just be a parable. A warning for us to give honor to the dead by remembering their names." She shrugged at the boy. "Who knows?"

"I know." Masaru squinted at her with bleary, bloodshot eyes. "*I* know."

Yukiko stared back at him. Slurred words and a soft stare, that stupefied, slack-jawed look slinking over his face and turning his skin to gray. An anesthetic, numbing the pain of well-deserved loss.

A crutch for a weak and broken man.

She licked her lips, stood slowly to her feet.

"I'll tell you what *I* know." She looked back and forth between the cloud-walkers. "I know you shouldn't be offering the pipe to a twelve-year-old boy. I know you shouldn't mock him for being ignorant, while you sit there sucking that filth into your lungs." She fixed her father in her stare. "And I know all lotus-fiends are liars."

She covered her fist, gave a small bow to the cabin boy.

"Goodnight, young sama."

She turned her back and went in search of sleep.

The sun had barely raised its weary head before Yukiko awoke the next day. Her father was sprawled in his hammock, one foot dangling over the side, snoring like a shredderman's buzzsaw beneath his kerchief. His clothes reeked of lotus, his fingers stained with sticky, blue-black resin. She made as much noise as she could while washing and dressing, but he stirred not an inch. Cursing under her breath, she stalked from the room.

The deck was already alive with cloudwalkers, the rigging above crawled with at least a dozen men, double-checking knot and cable as they drew ever closer to the oncoming monsoon. Captain Yamagata stood at the helm, both hands on the broad, spoked wheel, shouting orders to his men and cursing up a storm. The *Thunder Child* had trekked deep into the territory of the Dragon zaibatsu, and a quick glance over the side revealed the Iishi Mountains looming like a dark, jagged stain on the far northern horizon. Soon they would be flying over Kitsune territory; a scarred and smoking landscape she hadn't seen up-close in almost eight years.

A thick tangle of hair blew across her face, and she tucked it back behind her ears, feeling too sullen to even tie it up. She sat on the chi barrels lashed at the *Thunder Child*'s bow and watched the red countryside blur and roll beneath her feet. The dawn wind was cool, but the sun's heat was already growing fierce, and she pulled her goggles up over her eyes to guard them from the piercing glare. She could see the brown stain of a chi pipeline, stabbing westward across the lotus fields; a rusted artery running through diseased flesh. Following the shape to a distant cluster of mountains on the port side, she squinted at the tiny specks of sky-ships floating around a dark smudge of dirt and smog; the mountain bastion of First House. The Guild stronghold was a pentagonal hulk of yellowed stone, squatting high among black clouds on its impregnable perch.

A short wooden practice sword clattered onto the deck between her feet, the blunt blade nicked and dented in a dozen places, hilt wrapped in worn, criss-crossed cord. She stared down at the bokken, then glanced over her shoulder at the person who'd thrown it. Kasumi stood behind her, another short bokken in her hands, long hair tied back in a thick braid.

"Spar?" The woman's voice was slightly muffled behind her kerchief.

"No." Yukiko turned her eyes back to the horizon. "Thank you."

"It's been days since you practiced."

"Four days off in seven years." Yukiko tried to keep the scowl from her voice. "I think I'll live."

"I'll go easy on you, if you're feeling air-sick."

Yukiko felt her hackles rise at the smile in Kasumi's voice. She glanced over her shoulder again. "You couldn't goad a rabid wolf with talk that weak. You want to try harder?"

"No, you're right." Kasumi flipped the bokken from one hand to the other. "I should probably just leave you up here to sulk like a six-year-old."

Yukiko turned to face her. "I'm not sulking."

"Of course you're not." Kasumi knelt and picked up the bokken she'd thrown, pointed at the floor between Yukiko's feet. "Mind you don't trip over your bottom lip when you decide to get off your backside."

Yukiko snatched the practice sword from the older woman's hand.

"Fine. Have it your way."

The foredeck was large enough for a decent scrap without getting in any of the sky folk's way. Yukiko felt a few curious eyes on her as she stood and tied her hair back in a braid, knotting it at the end. Kasumi took up position on the starboard side, flourishing the bokken sword in her hand, a sweeping spiral over her head and around her hip that turned the dented wood into a whistling blur. Yukiko walked to the port side, flipped the practice sword end over end. She took up her stance, stared at the older woman.

"You shouldn't be so hard on him," Kasumi said.

Yukiko dashed across the deck, swung the bokken right at Kasumi's throat. The older woman fell back, deflecting the blow with ease. Yukiko pressed, aimed three quick stabs at face, chest, gut, spinning down into a sweeping arc toward Kasumi's knees. The sharp crack of wood upon wood rang out across the ship, the thump of bare feet on the decking, the short, shapeless cries that punctuated each swing of Yukiko's sword.

She locked up Kasumi's blade, forced the older woman back against the starboard railing. Hundreds of feet of empty air yawned between them and the swaying lotus fronds below.

"Don't lecture me," Yukiko spat. "You're not my godsdamned mother."

"So you keep reminding me."

Kasumi hooked her leg behind Yukiko's and pushed her away. The girl tumbled backward and up into a crouch, parrying the blow falling toward her head. Kasumi kicked her hard in the chest and sent her rolling further across the deck, breath spilling from her lips in a spray of spittle. Yukiko barely flipped up onto her feet in time to ward off the next rain of blows: two diagonal slashes at her chest and a flurry of stabs at her face. She retreated back across the foredeck, trying to regain balance.

"Don't defend him," Yukiko hissed. "You know what he's like. Sucking down that godsdamned weed every day of his life. Drinking himself blind. Maybe you should be on his back instead of riding mine every chance you get."

"I do it because I care about you." Kasumi parried a clumsy blow, cracked Yukiko across her left shin. "And I see what you do to him."

Yukiko lashed out with her foot, leaped up and over the chi barrels to gain some breathing room, leveling the bokken at Kasumi's head. She was panting, strands of black hair plastered to the film of sweat on her skin.

"My father gets everything he deserves."

"He loves you, Yukiko."

"He loves his drink." She clawed the hair from the corners of her mouth. "He loves that godsdamned pipe. More than he loves me. And more than he loves you."

Kasumi stopped short, chest heaving. The sword wavered in her hand.

"Believe it, Kasumi." Yukiko pulled down her goggles so the older woman could see her eyes. "Believe it if you believe nothing else."

She tossed the bokken down onto the deck. It rolled across the polished boards, came to rest at Kasumi's feet, marking the end of the sparring session. Yukiko wiped the sweat from her brow on the sleeve of her uwagi, heart pounding, mouth dry as dust.

Kasumi's voice was soft, almost a whisper. "Maybe you don't know everything, Yukiko."

"Maybe not."

She shouldered past the older woman as she walked away.

"But I know enough."

10

ALIVE AND BREATHING

The rain started at the end of the sixth day, vast black curtains swaying across their path and hissing on the deck. The wood became slippery, and the stink of burned chi layered over melting varnish saw Yukiko's nausea return with a vengeance. Huddled in an oilskin among the barrels, she prayed the journey would end, sucking down gulps of fresh air and dreading the monsoon ahead.

Yamagata emerged from his cabin wearing a thick oilskin to protect him from the black rain. Masaru stood on the port side, leaning out into the abyss and staring at the clouds fuming on the horizon. The *Child* plowed through the toxic air, heading toward the tempest, the first foothills of the Iishi sailing away below them. Through the downpour, they could see the glow of Yama city flickering like a ghostlight in an ocean of growing gloom.

Akihito and Kasumi gathered at the railing beside Masaru, all clad in thick ponchos of protective rubber, the big man keeping one massive paw wrapped around the bars of the cage for balance. Yukiko drifted down from her nest at the prow to listen to their hushed voices.

"We're heading *into* the storm?" Akihito ran one hand over his braids.

"Where else do you think we're going to find a thunder tiger?" Masaru scowled.

"The sky folk are uneasy," Kasumi kept her voice low. "Being so near to the Iishi is bad enough. They say that sailing this close to the entrance of Yomi will tempt the Judges of the Hells, not to mention angering the Dark Mother. They whisper Yamagata is insane to lead them into the clutches of the Thunder God. They blame us, Masaru-sama. They say we're mad."

"They're right." Akihito shook his head. "Risking the whole damn ship and everyone aboard chasing a beast that doesn't even exist. We don't even know where to start looking." He turned to his friend. "We should go to Yama, Masaru. Abandon this fool's quest and the insane bastard who commands—"

Masaru spun, quick as a viper, wrapping his fist in the collar of the big man's uwagi.

"We are the Shōgun's men," he hissed, teeth bared. "Sworn to his service, our lives pledged to his house. Would you dishonor that vow and yourself for fear of a little lightning?"

Akihito slapped Masaru's hand away. "I might not rate a mention in the tavern songs, but I stood beside you when you slew the last nagaraja, brother. You think I'm afraid?" He puffed out his chest, long scars cutting across his flesh. "I know in truth what kind of man Shōgun Kaneda was. I know what kind of son he raised. This is a madman's errand. We risk all for nothing! This ship. These men. Your daughter . . ."

"And what do you think we risk if we run?"

Masaru's face was inches from Akihito's, eyes flashing.

"Masaru-sama, Akihito, peace." Kasumi shouldered between them, one hand on each man. "You are brothers in blood. Your anger dishonors you both."

The men stared at each other, eyes as narrow as knife-edges, wind shrieking across the gap between them. Akihito was the first to relent, turning with a growl and stalking away. Masaru watched him go, fists unclenching, drawing the back of his hand across his mouth.

"Whether we find this thing or not means nothing." His voice was flat, cold. "We are servants. Our Lord commands and we obey. That's all there is."

"As you say," Kasumi nodded, avoiding his stare.

She turned and began inspecting gear she'd checked a dozen times already. Masaru lifted his hand, fingers hovering a breath away from her skin. Looking up, he finally noticed his daughter's presence.

Bloodshot eyes stared across the gulf between now and the days when she was a little girl, small enough to ride on his shoulders through forests of tall bamboo. She and her brother, little fingers wrapped in their father's fists, laughing bright and clear as they danced in the dappled light.

Too long ago—the memory faded and blurred like an old lithograph, colors muted over time until all that was left was an impression; a half-image on yellowed, curling paper.

He turned and walked away without a word.

*D*irty gray snow lay in a blanket on the ground, crunching beneath their hessian-wrapped feet and crouching in thick drifts across bare branches. Ywukiko and Satoru darted through the bamboo, Buruu barking with joy, sending the few winter larks that remained in the valley spiraling up into the falling snowflakes.

Their father had been home for a few days, gifting them both with small compasses before he disappeared again. Tiny wheels whirled soundlessly beneath the glass, tracking the path of the hidden sun overhead. They would run into the wilds, straying further each day, finding their way back unerringly before dusk. Then they would sit by the fire, Buruu lying across their feet, listening to their mother sing and dreaming of their father's return.

Happy.

Buruu would wag his tail at them, fire reflected in his eyes, tongue lolling.

Love you both.

They were on the northern ridge that day, high above the bamboo valley, looking down on the frozen stream, the tiny waterfall of icicles spilling over snow-capped rock. Black, naked trees stood tall on a blanket of bleached gray, sleeping in the chill and dreaming of the beauty that would arrive with spring. The children called out their names and heard the mountain kami call them back, fading away into the distance like the last notes of their mother's songs.

The wolf was hungry, lean, ribs showing through its coat, legs like sticks. A rogue descending from the mountains with a growling belly and a jagged mind alight with their scent. Buruu caught the smell of it on the breeze, hackles rising, ears flat against his head as he growled. Satoru reached out and touched its mind, feeling only bloodlust, terrible and complete, pounding with a rhythm like a pulse. The wolf circled to the left and the children began to back away, urging Buruu to be calm. Satoru leaned down to grasp a small club of wet wood.

It moved in a blur, savage, sleek, hunger propelling it at Yukiko's throat. She held out her hand and screamed, pushing it away with the Kenning as Buruu launched himself like an arrow. The wolf and the dog fell on each other, all teeth and claws and awful screaming sounds. Buruu fought bravely, but his bones were old and the wolf was fierce, driven by desperate hunger to spend its last strength in this final, bloody gambit. She felt Buruu's pain as the wolf's jaws closed around his throat, tearing away crimson mouthfuls, spattering on the bed of gray snow in long bright ribbons.

She screamed in anger, in hatred, pushing her mind into the wolf's, feeling for its life, the source of its spark. She felt Satoru in there beside her, his rage fiercer than her own, and together they pressed down on the heat, snuffing it out like a candle, smothering it with their rage. Blood spilled from their noses as the pressure flooded their brains, warm and salty on their lips. They wrapped their hands *together and strangled until nothing remained, darkness fading away into a whimper as the wolf folded down inside itself and ended upon the frost.*

They sat beside poor old Buruu, lay on his wet, heaving flanks as the ashen snow turned red around him. Tears rolled down their cheeks as they felt him slipping. Not afraid, but sad. Sad to leave them, to let them wander in the world alone. They were his pack, they were his everything, and he licked their hands and wheezed, wishing he did not have to go.

Love you. Love you both.

As the darkness took him, they held him close, safe and warm, and whispered that they loved him too. That they would love him always. That they would remember.

He was too heavy for them to carry. And so they stood, hand in hand, watching the snow bury him. One flake at a time, falling from the poisoned skies and covering him like a shroud. Their friend. Their brother. Lying in a pool of dark red, brown fur spattered and torn, black and empty inside his mind.

When there was only gray again, they turned and walked away.

T he edges of the storm had come on them days ago, like thieves in the smothered light of dusk. Fingers of lightning stretched down into the sunset silhouettes of the nearby mountains. The wind buffeted the *Child* as if it truly were an infant, tossed about in the grip of a cruel, thoughtless giant. Days and nights were spent in fruitless search, the mood of the cloudwalkers growing ever darker as they sailed further and further into the Iishi ranges. The mountains loomed all around them, towering spires of dark stone and pale snow, the echoes of the thunder rolling down their flanks and rumbling among the black valleys at their feet.

How many days are we going to spend up here, hunting ghosts?

Rigging lashed against the balloon above Yukiko's head with the sound of bullwhips. After half a day of the deafening barrage, she had been forced to abandon her haven among the chi barrels and seek shelter inside. Black rain sluiced on the deck, rushing over the rails into the nothingness beyond, reeking of lotus toxin. Cloudwalkers shrugged on protective oilskins and perched trembling in their lookout posts, peering ahead into the darkness. Lightning arced down in blinding, brilliant strokes, hurled from the hands of the Thunder God.

Below decks in the tropical heat, the sky folk burned offerings to Susano-ō, praying for mercy day after day. Though the Storm God was considered a benevolent force, his firstborn son, Raijin, God of Thunder and Lightning, was renowned for his cruelty, his delight in the terror of men. Prayer and offerings seldom held interest for him, nor did the lives of those who sailed in his skies. It was chaos he loved above all, above the mewling of monkey-children in their fragile little boats, the wooden coins they burned in his father's name. And so the cloudwalkers knelt, prayer beads rubbed between calloused fingers, begging Susano-ō to stay his son's hand. Begging for their lives.

And still, Yamagata urged them onward.

Yukiko could see the tips of the Iishi Mountains beneath them, peering out through the porthole as the lightning turned night to day. She wondered whether the helmsman could even see in the dark, whether he would drive them into the black crags and end all of them in a bright blossom of super-heated hydrogen. Fear uncoiled inside her gut, and she thought of the boy in her dreams, the boy with the sea-green eyes. She did not want to die.

For three days the motors whined with the strain, Yamagata tacking back and forth across the face of the wind. The stench of burning chi was overpowering. The hunters' meals boiled inside their bellies and threatened to pay the air a second visit after every sitting. Masaru and Yamagata spent long hours in his cabin, poring over charts and plotting their course through the treacherous currents of wind howling between the saw-toothed peaks. They had the sense to keep the door closed when their arguments grew fiercest, but the volume was still enough to travel through the walls. The cloudwalkers muttered among themselves, wondering if this would be the last hunt of the great Black Fox. Whether Shōgun Yoritomo's command was leading all of them to their doom.

Yukiko lay as she had done for the past three nights: curled up tight, trying to hold in her dinner as her hammock swayed back and forth. Her father hung above her, swathed in a lotus stupor, empty pipe still clutched in one stained hand. She envied him for a moment, envied the peace he could find in that awful little weed. The voices of memory and loss smothered beneath a veil of sticky, blue-black smoke; the howl of the tempest around him nothing but a distant breeze.

Her stomach churned again, dinner surging against her ribs. Admitting defeat, she lurched up and stumbled for the door as the floor undulated beneath her.

Snatching up an oilskin, she burst out onto the deck, almost falling as the wood pitched away from her feet. She staggered to the railing and vomited, a rancid stream of yellow and brown splashing out into the blackness. The rain pelted down, plastering her hair to her skin. Tangles clung about her face in thick black fingers, as if they wished to cover her eyes. She gasped for breath, shrugging on the poncho and blinking around the deck.

She saw him on the prow, a white silhouette against the black, hands out-stretched. Clawing her way along the railing, not daring to look down, she swore she could hear him laughing over the sound of the roaring wind. He moved with the pitch and roll of the ship, head thrown back, howling like a sea dragon.

"Kin-san?" she yelled over the din.

He turned, surprised, and his face lit up in a wide grin. His clothing clung to him like a second skin, and she could see how thin he was, how frail. And yet he stood like a rock, legs planted among the tightly lashed chi barrels, turn-ing back and screaming at the storm. He wasn't wearing an oilskin.

"What the hells are you doing out here?" Yukiko yelled.

"Being alive!" he shouted over the rolling thunder. "Alive and breathing!"

"You're a madman!"

"And yet, you stand here with me!"

"What about the rain? It will burn you!"

She staggered as the deck rolled, a white-knuckle grip on the rails. One slip and she would sail off into the darkness, scream unheard over the thunder's roar.

"Come here!" he called. "Stand up here with me!"

"Not for all the iron in Shima!"

He beckoned with one hand, the other gripping the rope lashing the barrels together. It was as if the ship was an untamed stallion and he sat astride it, fin-gers wrapped in its mane. She pushed her fear away, grabbed his hand and hooked her legs among the barrels.

"Can you taste it?" he cried.

"Taste what?"

"The rain!" He opened his mouth to the sky. "No lotus!"

Yukiko realized that he was right; the water streaming down her face was clean and pure, translucent as glass. She remembered the mountain streams of her youth, she and Satoru lying beside them with Buruu in the long summer grass, drinking deeply from the liquid crystal. She licked her lips, eyes gleam-ing with joy, then opened her mouth and let the rain wash down her throat.

"Now close your eyes!" he yelled, rain whipping his face. "Close your eyes and breathe!"

He threw out his hands again, face upturned to the storm. She watched him for a moment, his expression like a child's, unburdened by any sense of fear or loss. He was so strange. So unlike anyone she had ever met before.

But then she tasted the rain on her lips, felt the wind in her hair, heard the roar of the storm around them. And so she closed her eyes, threw her head back and inhaled. She could see the lightning flashing against the bloodwarm blackness behind her eyelids, feel the wind buffeting the ship beneath them. The rain was a balm, washing away the fear. She breathed, cool air filling her lungs, warm blood pumping below her skin. Kin screamed beside her, a whooping holler as the deck rolled like a storm-tossed ocean beneath them.

"We are alive, Yukiko-chan! We are free!"

She laughed, calling out shapeless words into the storm. It was as if she were a little girl again, running with her brother through the rippling bamboo, strong and bright, wet earth beneath her feet. She could feel the lives she swam among, the hundred tiny sparks rising like cinders from a bonfire, catching her up and filling her with warmth. No fear. No pain. No loss. Before any and all of it had come in from the dark, when the simple act of being was enough.

She stretched out her senses into the tempest, mind uncoiling between the raindrops, engulfed by the beauty and ferocity around her.

A flicker of warmth.

Wait . . .

A heartbeat.

. . . What is that?

"Arashitora!" came the cry, followed by the sharp whine of a siren. "Arashi-tora!"

Yukiko opened her eyes, blinking in the blackness. She saw the helmsman leaning over the starboard side, pointing, yelling at the top of his lungs. The navigator was cranking a siren handle up on the pilot's deck, its shrill, grinding cry piercing the din. She looked to where the helmsman was pointing but could see nothing, a vast expanse of seething blackness beyond the *Child*'s deck lamps. Lightning flashed, a flare of white-hot magnesium across the clouds, the sun rising for a split second to cast off the blanket of night.

And then she saw it. A momentary flash, the green flare left behind on your eyelid after you stare too long at the sun. The impression of vast, white wings, feathers as long as her arm, broad as her thigh. Black stripes, rippling muscle, a proud, sleek head tipped with a razor-sharp beak. Eyes like midnight, black and bottomless.

"Izanagi's breath," she whispered, squinting into the black. "There it is."

Lightning flashed again, illuminating the beast before her wondering eyes.

The impossible.

The unthinkable.

A thunder tiger.

11
ARASHITORA

The smoke held him down with warm, soft hands, head underwater, the noise of the storm and siren and running feet all a distant murmur beneath the screams of dying beasts. Eyelashes fluttered against his cheeks, bloodshot eyes rolled back in his skull, trying to keep waking at bay. But finally the din became too much, too loud to ignore, a grating sliver of steel caught beneath an eyelid and dragging him up through the greasy chemical dream into waking.

"Aiya," Masaru frowned, rubbing at his head. "What the hells is—"

His cabin door smashed open. Kasumi stood in the doorway, the spring-loaded serpent of a net-thrower clutched in her hands. Her hair was loose, floating in the breeze around her face like black silk, a faint blush of excitement in her cheeks.

Beautiful.

"Masaru," she breathed. "Arashitora."

She dashed away without another word. Adrenaline kicked Masaru in the gut, peeling the lotus cobwebs from his eyes. He was alert, awake, veins thrumming with heat that tingled into his fingers and danced in his chest. He leaped down from the hammock and scrambled after her.

Up on deck, the cloudwalkers were gathered by the rails, pointing and babbling. Akihito was already on the starboard floodlight, kicking it into life as the wind whipped in his braids. The globe flickered and came alive, a curling spiral of brilliance in a cradle of gleaming mirrors. The light reached out into the clouds, turning bottomless black to rolling gray. The big man swung the spotlight in long smooth arcs, blinding rain frozen for split seconds in the beam, cutting through the darkness like a razor. The generator behind him growled, spitting chi fumes and mainlining power into the halogen bulb, reaching almost a hundred feet into the gloom; a finger of lightning, bright as the sun.

"Have you seen it?" Masaru roared over the wind.

"Hai!" The big man was elated. "Huge bastard. White as snow. Magnificent!"

The ship lurched beneath their feet; Masaru grabbed the rail to avoid a fall. "Hold it steady, Yamagata!"

The captain stood at the helm, swinging the great wheel hard to compensate for the wind. He blinked the rain from his eyes, clad in a blood-red oilskin. "Raijin wants our asses!" he cried. "We're lucky to still be flying, let alone flying straight!"

There was a loud cry as a great white shape flashed by the starboard side. Masaru caught the impression of jagged black stripes on white fur, wings broader than a man was tall, thrashing louder than thunder. Akihito swung the spotlight to follow its path.

Masaru stumbled to the gear cache and snatched up the Kobiashi needle-thrower, a black tube with a telescoping sight fixed to the top of the barrel. The base of the tube was connected to an iron bottle of pressurized gas that served as a shoulder stock. He slammed a magazine of hypodermics into the receiver, locked it in place and released the pressure valve. Slinging the other magazines over his shoulder, he climbed up to join Kasumi. She lay coiled in the rigging, feet twisted in the rope ladders leading up to the *Child*'s balloon. Net-thrower loaded, a second on standby across her back, thick coils of lotus hemp leading down to the winches bolted to the *Child*'s railing. Her eyes were fixed over the 'thrower's sights, following the spotlight arcing through the clouds. Rain ran in rivulets down her face, gathering in her long lashes and falling like tears.

"Are you ready?" Masaru shouted, twisting his feet among the rigging.

She nodded once, eyes never leaving the spotlight.

"Give the blacksleep a few seconds to kick in, or it could break its wings in the net."

The wind wailed; a screeching oni, all the fury of the Nine Hells breaking loose from its throat. The *Child* swung like a pendulum in the howling storm, thunder echoing down her spine. The cloudwalkers watched the dark, eyes and faces alight with anticipation.

"There!" cried one, pointing into the black. Akihito's spotlight cut through the rain, fell across a blur of white. They heard a tremendous cry, an animal roar akin to grating thunder, the beating of mighty wings. The ship was knocked hard to port by the storm, nose dipping toward the ground as lightning flashed nearby, and suddenly they had it; picked out neatly in blinding halogen, easily the most magnificent sight Masaru had seen in his life.

It was power personified. The storm made flesh, carved from the clouds by Raijin's hands, his children let loose to rollick in ozone-flecked chaos. The old tales said their wings made the sound of the thunder. The lightning was the sparks from their claws as they did battle across the heavens. The rain was Susano-ō's tears, the Storm God overcome with the beauty and ferocity of his grandchildren. Thunder tiger. Arashitora.

"Beautiful," Kasumi breathed.

The hindquarters of a white tiger, rippling muscle bound tight beneath snow-white fur, slashed with thick bands of ebony. The broad wings, forelegs and head of a white eagle, proud and fierce; lightning reflected in amber irises and pupils of darkest black. It roared again, shaking the ship, cutting through the air like a katana in a swordsaint's hands. Masaru shook his head, blinked hard. The rain whipping his face, the wind chilling his blood; it all told him he wasn't dreaming. And still, he doubted.

The beast was immense, a wingspan of nearly twenty-five feet, claws like sabers, eyes as big as Akihito's fist. Iron hard, sleek and growling, an engine of muscle and beak and claw. He wondered how much blacksleep it would take to bring it down.

"Where the hells did it come from?" yelled Kasumi.

"Let me get two volleys into it!" he cried. "It's too big!"

Kasumi nodded, eyes narrowed, jaw clenched. The cloudwalkers pointed in slack-jawed wonder as the beast wheeled overhead. It was obviously as fascinated with them as they were with it, screaming a piercing note of challenge, wondering who these interlopers were that dared to brave its sky.

Masaru pressed the trigger on the needle-thrower, the device spitting out a chattering, angry hiss as he emptied the entire magazine in a single burst. Two-dozen hypo shafts sailed through the dark, at least four sinking into the beast's hindquarters. The arashitora snapped left and swooped under the keel, shaking the *Child* with its bellow of rage. The sky folk ran across to the port side, saw the silhouette rise up over the railings and tear a great gouge through the hull. The impact was explosive, wood spraying in foot-long spears, the ship rocking on its haunches amidst the groan of breaking rope. One of the cloudwalkers lost his footing and plummeted over the side with a wavering scream. Another almost followed, saved only by the hands of his comrades.

"You pissed it off, Masaru!" Akihito's face split in a wide grin. He swung the floodlight around, listening for the sound of pinions over the tempest's din.

"Strap in!" roared Yamagata to his men. "Or get below deck!"

The crew lashed lengths of hemp around their obi and scattered to their posts, several climbing up into the rigging to secure broken cables. A scream split the air, the smell of ozone, rumbling thunder. A white shape plummeted from above and crashed into the portside engine, tearing it away with the shriek of tortured metal. The *Child* dropped thirty feet out of the sky, spitting a bright trail of flame.

Cloudwalkers cried out in terror as the inferno reached up toward the inflatable, burning tongues licking at the balloon's flank. Fire and water kissed, giving birth to great clouds of choking, black smoke, a haze that flooded over the deck and cut visibility down to a handful of feet. One sailor fell screaming from the rigging, landing on the timbers with a sodden crunch, his clothes and hair ablaze. Smothering sheets of rain beat the flames back from the balloon, leaving a trail of long black scorch-marks on the canvas.

Masaru gritted his teeth and emptied his second magazine as the fleeting shape disappeared underneath them again, needle-thrower hissing, bolts sailing harmlessly into the black. He cursed the smoke beneath his breath, blinking the blinding rain from his eyes.

The crunch of tortured gears spilled from the flaming tear in the *Child*'s flank, and the entire vessel was rocked with another explosion as a secondary fuel tank ignited. Flames vomited from the torn and smoking hull. The ship bucked beneath them and listed sideways, the thrust of the remaining engine threatening to tilt the entire vessel onto its wounded side. Yamagata bellowed at his men, demanding that someone find Old Kioshi and get the Guildsman below deck to shut off the port fuel lines. He clung to the wheel with a white-knuckle grip, breath heaving in his lungs, teeth drawn back from his lips as he roared at Masaru.

"The bastard's tearing us to pieces!"

A crag of rock loomed out of the darkness dead ahead and Yamagata cried a warning, leaning into the wheel with all his weight. The *Thunder Child* swung hard to port as the captain poured on the burn, the single propeller shrieking in dissent and spewing exhaust into the rain. Rivets popped along the engine housing as the ship rolled almost ninety degrees, showing her belly to the tempest. Cloudwalkers fell screaming from the rigging, those who'd had time to strap themselves in were jerked to a bone-jarring halt at the ends of their lines, watching their less-fortunate comrades plummet off into the mouth of the storm.

Masaru clung to the rigging and scanned the darkness, looking for a flash of white, listening for the sound of rushing wings over the crackling flames and rolling thunder and screams of dying sailors.

"Four darts' worth of blacksleep," he growled. "Hasn't even slowed him down."

Yukiko was crouched up near the bow, her arms wrapped around the chi barrels, Kin beside her. The boy looked frantic, almost petrified, his eyes fixed on the cloudwalkers gathered on deck. He hunched down below the level of the barrels, jaw clenched, face drawn and bloodless. He winced as the fuel tank exploded, the light of the roaring flames reflected in terrified eyes. Yukiko meantime was transfixed by the sight of the thunder tiger, mouth slack with awe, eyes shining and bright.

"Do you see it?" she breathed. "Gods above, it's beautiful."

Closing her eyes, she reached out through the storm, feeling the world fall away beneath her feet. She pawed through the blackness, a blind girl in search of the sun. And then she touched it, searing hot, fury coiled among the soporific gravity of the poison, clouded and dark. She felt the need to destroy. To rend. Animal rage layered over ferocious intelligence, indignant that it had been challenged by this wooden insect, this slug with no wings, dragging itself through the sky and reeking of dead, burning flowers.

And then it felt her. Confusion. Aggression. Curiosity. Its voice bounced around the inside of her skull, as deafening as the peals of thunder crashing through the skies around her.

WHO ARE YOU?

Yukiko.

Intrigue overcame anger, wheeling closer, and in that moment it returned her touch. A ghost of a whisper, the strength of a steel spring coiled behind it, waiting to be unleashed.

WHAT ARE YOU?

The wind rushed beneath them, the raging storm nothing but a summer breeze, electricity tingling on their flesh as the lightning flashed. And then they felt pain, a series of deep thuds into their belly, piercing, venomous. Sleep curled out along their veins, and rage rose to challenge it, a scream building in their throats and spilling forth to fill the skies.

You got him!" Akihito cried, swinging the blinding light overhead.

The creature roared again, a faint tremor of fatigue underscoring the anger. Kasumi leaned over her sights, braced the net-thrower against her shoulder.

"Now!" Masaru yelled.

A sharp burst of compressed air. Sixty feet of tightly bound lotus hemp spilled out into the night, gossamer threads as strong as steel, a choir of locusts buzzing in their ears. The line spooled out from beneath the weapon's belly, weighted strands engulfing the bellowing thunder tiger like a spider web. Masaru was already leaping down to the deck, sending the motorized winch spinning. Kasumi fired the second net-thrower, another volley of lines closing over the beating wings, pressing them tight against flanks now heaving with fear, fight giving way to flight.

But too late. Too late.

The beast plummeted from the sky, blacksleep pounding in its veins and knocking it senseless. It dropped away below the starboard railing, falling down into the dark. The *Child* lurched sideways, dragged down by the colossal weight as the winch lines snapped taut, motors screaming in protest. Cloudwalkers cried out in panic as the remaining engine strained to recover, Yamagata pouring on the fuel and pressing down on the wheel with the aid of his navigator. The storm battered the ship, as if Raijin himself were furious at their attack on his offspring. Several crew disappeared over the side, dangling by their lifelines over the whistling drop to the ground hundreds of feet below. But stubbornly, gradually, the sky-ship righted itself, limping back onto an even keel.

"Get him up on deck, he'll tip us over!" Yamagata bellowed.

The winches groaned and began reeling in the weight, lines smoking, engines spitting fumes into the rain. The cloudwalkers hauled their stricken brethren back on deck and then pitched in to help with the thunder tiger, reaching down with gaff hooks to catch hold of the nets. Gradually the shape came into view, curled tight in strands of black swaddling, narrowed eyes staring at the men with toxin-clouded hatred.

Sweating and heaving under the weight, the crew eventually employed the *Child*'s motorized cargo crane to heft the beast onto the deck. Rain sluiced down in waves, freezing cold and relentless. Lightning arced dangerously close, their ears splitting with the peals of thunder.

It took twenty men to drag the beast into the cage. Masaru urged caution, warning the crew to be careful with the tiger's wings. Akihito was foremost among them, muscles stretched and humming, joy plainly written on his face. Kasumi stood to one side, needle-thrower in her hands, watching for any sign of awakening. She radiated a quiet pride, lips pressed into a tight smile.

When the beast was locked behind bars, the bedraggled men gathered around and cheered, slapping each other's backs and saluting the brave hunters and their grim captain, still hanging onto the wheel of his wounded ship.

Yamagata saluted back, managed a weary grin. Masaru beamed like a proud father, eyes aglow, disbelief still etched plainly on his face.

They had hunted an arashitora. A beast of legend, only a dream. And they had bested it.

Only Yukiko hung back from the throng, sorrow welling in her eyes. She watched the men dance and caper around the beast, feeling for its mind amidst the blacksleep haze. Only the barest whisper of it remained beneath a blanket of thick sleep, a smoldering cinder, a spark of blinding rage that burned her mind when she strayed too close.

Indignity. Disbelief. Fury.

KILL YOU.

She could feel it fighting off the poison, fueled by a purity of intent. A promise to itself, to her, which bore it up slowly out of the blackness on a wind of hate and rage. Not yet.

Not yet. But soon.

KILL YOU ALL.

T he celebrations were short-lived.

The mournful whine of the *Child*'s remaining engine dragged the cloudwalkers from their moment of joy. Many of them glanced at the torn rigging or at the smoking hole in the *Child*'s flank, fear plain in their eyes. The storm pounded their ship without mercy; a child's toy adrift on a raging ocean. The portside engine was gone, severed fuel lines still spitting blood-red chi into the abyss below as the sailors struggled to shut down the valves. Even with the starboard motor at full burn, Yamagata couldn't maintain course. The *Child* plunged deeper into the tempest, compass spinning, silhouettes of black crags looming out of the darkness.

Masaru clambered up to the pilot's deck, pushed the rain-soaked hair from his eyes.

"Is it bad?"

"It's a far cry from bloody good!" Yamagata shouted, leaning into the wheel, his face as grim and pale as a hungry ghost's. "I can't see a godsdamned thing!" He turned to his navigator. "Toshi, get on that floodlight on the port side, and get somebody up here to take the starboard. We're too low. We could fly right into one of these bastard mountains and wouldn't even know it until we're dead. Where the bloody hells is Kioshi?"

The navigator stumbled away toward the ladder, yelling for one of the crew.

Masaru leaned in closer to Yamagata, shouting to be heard over the snarling wind.

"Can you get us out of the storm?"

"No chance!" The captain staggered as the *Child* bucked beneath them, wiped his eyes on his sleeve and spat on the deck. "We're at the mercy of the wind with only one motor. Even if we had a spare port engine, we couldn't fix it in this shit."

"Can you take her up?"

"I'm trying, godsdammit! We're carrying a lot of extra weight."

As if it could read their minds, the arashitora reared up in its cage, letting loose a groggy roar. The rain pooling across the deck danced skyward amidst the subsonic vibrations. Cloudwalkers backed away from the cage as the beast tried to gain its feet, tearing at the netting with claws and beak, steel-strong lotus fibers snapping like rotten wool.

"Izanagi's balls," Masaru breathed, shaking his head. "I put enough black-sleep into it to kill a dozen men."

"How much do you have left?"

"Not nearly enough for the trip home."

The sound of shearing cord rang out under the rumbling thunder and howling wind. The creature bellowed in answer to the clouds, the hairs on Masaru's arms standing rigid, air charged with static electricity. The beast shook itself, remnants of the net sloughing off its wings. Its claws dug great furrows into the deck beneath its feet, the planks cracking like dry leaves.

Kasumi called his name, and Akihito's face appeared at the top of the ladder to the pilot's deck moments later. The former quarrel between the men was forgotten, the big man still charged with the elation of their victory.

"It's waking up, Masaru! Seven darts and it's on its feet! Have you ever seen the like?"

There was a sound like thunder, close and deafening, splitting the air in two and rolling down their spines. Loud as the crack of an iron-thrower, a bullwhip snapping in the air. The ship rocked as if it had been uppercut, thrashing back on it haunches, cables groaning. A scream of pain rang out from below. Several cloudwalkers were rolling on the wood, covering bleeding ears with trembling hands.

The air split again, Masaru wincing as the ship bucked beneath his feet. He blinked through the rain at the beast, watching as it tried to rear up on its hind legs in the confines of the cage. The mighty wings flapped again, a burst of blue electricity arcing along its flight feathers, accompanied by that same, deafening

thunderclap. The ship dropped a good twenty feet in altitude, Masaru's stomach staying behind to admire the view.

"Gods above, what is that?" Yamagata cried.

"Raijin song," breathed Masaru.

Truth be told, he had thought it was a mere tall story. Gaudy trimming on the tales of the Stormdancers, one more magical power to elevate them from bedtime stories to legends. The old tales spoke of the song of an arashitora's wings, the deafening thunderclap that sounded as they wheeled in the storms above, sending the front lines of enemy armies scattering or curled in fetal distress on the battlefield. A gift from their father, the Thunder God himself, the stories said, to mark his children as his own. But it was only an old wives' tale.

As if in answer, the thunder tiger cracked its wings again, making the same head-splitting noise. Arcs of raw current seethed down the iron cage, bright, impossibly blue. The ship bucked again, rivets groaning, ropes unravelling one thread at a time.

"She can't take this!" cried Yamagata.

Masaru's thoughts were quiet. The faint trace of lotus smoke left in his system brought a strange calm, even when all hells were breaking loose around him. He narrowed his eyes, watching the beast as it flailed: the cruel beak, the proud glare in its eye. It beat its wings against the cage, tiny arcs of lightning racing along its blood quills and out into the span of its flight feathers.

Don't think of it as a living legend. Think of it as a beast, like every other you have hunted. It wants to fly. To be free. Like any other bird of prey.

The thunder tiger roared, as if it knew his heart.

How do you train a wild bird? Reel in that desire and make it see you as the master?

Masaru swallowed.

"Akihito, did Kasumi bring the nagamaki blades that Shōgun Kaneda gave us?"

The big man blinked away the storm. "Of course."

Masaru's face was a mask, hard as stone, rain washing over him as if he were granite. He clenched his fists, eyes never leaving the arashitora, drawing the back of his knuckles across his lips.

"Fetch me the sharpest."

12

TEARS IN RAIN

Yukiko crouched in the bow, the pale boy beside her, watching the beast rail against its prison. She reached out with the Kenning again, feeling only an unassailable rage tinged with a faint ozone scent. She gave it her regret, her pity, flooding its mind with helpless overtures. She tried to make it feel safe, warm. Her every plea was rebuffed; the buzzing of a troublesome insect.

Kin crouched low whenever a cloudwalker approached the bow. Yukiko gradually became aware that he was terrified of the men, skulking low, fear plain in his eyes.

"What's the matter?"

"They can't see me like this," he hissed.

"Like what? What are you talking about?"

"Like this!" he cried.

Yukiko frowned.

"Who are you, Kin?"

A dizzying arc of lightning cracked the sky a handful of feet away from the *Thunder Child*, blazing a trail through the thousand-span darkness to the waiting earth below. Yukiko flinched, pressed herself against the chi barrels. She cast a fearful glance at the balloon swaying above their heads, straining against its moorings in the grip of the monsoon.

"What happens if lightning hits us?" she whispered.

"That depends. If it ignites the fuel, we'll burn up. If it strikes the inflatable . . ." The sentence trailed off into a brief pantomime, pale, slender hands indicating a wobbling descent into the deck and an explosion on impact.

Yukiko squinted through the rain. Her father approached the arashitora's cage, halting a few feet away and taking the needle-thrower from Kasumi's arms. The beast roared and cracked its wings again, sending several cloud-walkers sprawling across the deck. Her father took careful aim and emptied an entire magazine of blacksleep into the creature's flank.

She felt a stab of sympathetic pain, overshadowed by near-mindless outrage. She could feel the beast's hatred, burning a picture of her father into its brain and vowing to tear him limb from limb, to bathe in him as if he were a fresh mountain stream. But the poison rose up on wings of tar; a smothering, reeking blanket that dragged him back down into oblivion.

Akihito appeared from below deck, carrying the long haft of one of the Shōgun's nagamaki. He removed the leather sheath from the blade, steel glittering like a mirror as lightning flashed dangerously close to the starboard side. Fear clutched Yukiko's gut and she stood, Kin forgotten, running down the deck toward the cage as her father unbolted the door.

"You're going to kill it?" she cried. "You can't!"

Masaru glanced over his shoulder, eyebrow raised.

"Where did you come from? Get below deck!"

"It hasn't done anything!"

"We're not killing it." Kasumi shook her head. "But it's going to crash the ship if it keeps up with the Raijin song."

One of the lookouts shouted a warning, and Yamagata tore the wheel sharply to starboard. A towering spire of jagged mountainside loomed out of the darkness in front of them, the ship's keel barely clearing a spur of sharp rock. The crew hung on for dear life, the hunters ducking low as the captain flooded more chi into the struggling engine. The *Child* rose a few precarious feet above the stone fangs.

The hunters stood slowly, uncertain, the deck rolling beneath their feet. Yukiko looked deep into her father's eyes, unable to banish the dread despite Kasumi's assurances.

"So what are you going to do?" she asked, fearing the answer.

Masaru hefted the nagamaki.

"Clip its wings."

Yukiko's jaw dropped, eyes wide and bright with outrage.

"What? But why?"

"It's like any other bird, girl," Masaru snapped. "If we were breaking in a falcon, we'd do the same. Anything with wings asserts dominance through superior altitude. Take that away, it breaks their spirit. We need to break this beast, and quickly. We don't have enough blacksleep to knock it out until Kigen. It's torn the ship to shreds."

"You're just going to make it angrier!"

"Aiya, girl. You don't know what the hells you're talking about."

"It's not just a beast, it thinks like we do. I fel—"

She glanced around quickly and lowered her voice, taking her father by the arm.

"I *felt* it."

"You Kenned it?" Masaru hissed, eyes narrowed.

"Hai." She lowered her gaze to the deck. "I couldn't help it. It was so beautiful. Like nothing I'd ever seen before." Her eyes shone as she looked into Masaru's face. "Please, father, there must be some other way."

Masaru stared at his daughter, his stony facade softening for a brief moment. She reminded him suddenly of her mother. He could see Naomi in the curve of her cheek, the determination in her eyes, that gods-awful stubbornness he had so adored. But just as quickly as it had come, the softness inside him was gone, replaced with a hunter's pragmatism and the knowledge that the beast would send them all to their graves if it wasn't calmed. His daughter among them.

"I'm sorry, Ichigo. There is no other way."

"Please, father—"

"Enough!" he barked, and the thunder rolled in answer, making Yukiko flinch. He turned without another word and stalked into the cage, Akihito following with an apologetic glance. Kasumi placed one restraining hand on Yukiko's arm, but the girl shrugged her off. Hugging herself tight, she stared at her father's back, numb and silent, rain spattering across her skin.

Knowledge that the beast could wake at any second bid Masaru to work swift and sure. Akihito knelt among the ruined nets beside the thunder tiger's right shoulder. The arashitora's wing structure was similar to an eagle's: twenty-three primary feathers, each as long as Masaru's legs and just as broad, glinting with an odd metallic sheen. Twenty-three secondaries, white as new snow. The greater and primary coverts were speckled gray, darkening to charcoal among the lesser coverts. Even slack in the blacksleep repose, Masaru could sense the terrible strength in each wing, enough to propel this impossible beast through the storm-tossed skies like a koi fish beneath the surface of a smooth millpond.

Akihito spread the primaries out in a fan. Masaru drew in one steady, measured breath, brow furrowed, exhaling softly. He gripped the nagamaki tight, knuckles white on the scarlet cord binding the haft. His fingers drummed upon the hilt.

My hands must be as stone. My hands and heart.

The blade fell. A clean slice. Razor-sharp, folded steel, hard as diamond. A faint tearing sound, barely a whisper in the wind. Feathers parted as if they were made of smoke, sheared back to half their length. The severed ends drifted to the deck, looking pathetic and fragile beneath the falling rain.

Behind him, Masaru heard his daughter begin to weep.

He nodded to Akihito, and the men moved to the other wing, repeating the procedure, swift and clinical. Despite the turbulence, the motion of the deck beneath them, the nagamaki fell true, cleaving the feathers like a hot blade through snow. Masaru pushed aside the feeling that he was cutting away a part of himself. He watched the scene as if in a dream, rolling with the motion of the ship, the long blade an extension of his own hand. A hand bloodied by the life of a hundred beasts. The hand of a hunter. A destroyer.

The only living thing he had ever created stood behind him, her tears disappearing in the rain.

When it was done, he stood back and surveyed his work with a critical eye. Clean cuts, not too close to the blood vessels, but enough that the beast wouldn't be capable of much more than a feeble glide until its next moult. He nodded his head.

"Good work," agreed Akihito.

They removed the needle shafts from the beast's flanks and slapped a thick green poultice over the punctures. Crimson stained its fur, dripping onto the deck, covering their hands. The blood smelled of ozone and rusted iron.

They heard a low growl, a rumble that shook their insides. The beast began to stir, claws flexing, gouging foot-long scores into the hardened oak deck. The hunters stood and left the cage, Masaru slamming home the door's thick iron bolts. The arashitora growled again, the shifting of tectonic plates beneath ice-white fur.

Lightning flashed, bright as the dawn, dangerously close. Small fingers of it arced through the roiling cloud around them, cracks spreading out across its black mask, poised to crumble away into terrible violence. The wind was a pack of wolves, all lolling tongues and razor-sharp frozen teeth.

Without looking at his daughter, Masaru turned and walked away.

I ts fury was terrible.

Yukiko sat on the sodden deck and stared as the beast clawed its way back to waking. Its eyes were the color of honey, crystallized, pupils dilated in the blacksleep hangover. She was struck by the complexity of its thoughts; a fierce intelligence and sense of self she'd not encountered in a beast before. She could sense its confusion, the weight of its wings lessened, a strange sense of vertigo as it flapped them for balance and regained its feet.

It thrashed its wings again, staring at the blade's work, glancing down to the severed feathers beneath its feet. And then it roared, an ear splitting scream of rage and hatred, a fury that tore its throat and flecked its tongue with blood. It cracked its pinions but no Raijin song would come, electricity sputtering and dying on the butchered tips of its quills. It slammed its body against the bars, once, twice, the dull sound of flesh on iron drowned out by the raging storm.

I'm sorry.

Yukiko poured the thought into its mind to comfort, to console. The beast recoiled from her touch, a howl of psychic fury almost knocking her senseless. It smashed itself against the cage again, tearing at the iron impotently with claws and beak, giving voice to its rage, the violation it had suffered at the hands of these wretched men.

KILL YOU.

I did not want this. If I could undo it, I would.

RELEASE ME.

I can't.

LOOK AT WHAT THEY HAVE DONE.

I'm so sorry.

DESPOILERS. USURPERS. LOOK AT THE COLOR OF MY SKY. THE SCARS ON THE GREEN BELOW. PARASITES, ALL OF YOU.

The beast fixed her in its furious gaze, and she felt tiny and afraid reflected in that bottomless black. She knew how pathetic her overtures must sound. She had stood by and let her father mutilate this magnificent creature, hadn't lifted a finger to stop him. And for what? A spoiled princeling's command? A dream born of ego and blind hubris?

This, the last great yōkai beast on the whole of Shima. And what had they done to him?

The beast shut off its mind, forcing her out into empty blackness. Its hate was palpable, a dark radiance that burned like the summer sun. It stared in unblinking, wordless challenge, and though it said not a thing, she could read every thought as surely as if it had spoken them aloud.

Look at what they have done to me. At what you allowed them to do. Look me in the eye, be you not ashamed of yourself and your entire wretched race?

Thunder rolled cold fingers down her spine.

Shuddering, Yukiko lowered her eyes and looked away.

Her father was lying in his hammock when she returned, staring at the ceiling. His sodden clothes hung on the walls, an old hakama tied about his waist, tattoos crawling on his arms and chest. The ink was old, black running to blue, edges blurred under the press of time. His flesh was hard, but carved from sickly chalk, gleaming with fresh sweat and the stink of lotus.

He didn't look at her as she entered.

She closed the door and sat beside the hammocks on a small wooden stool, rocking it back on its hind legs. Her eyes glittered in the lamplight, hooded, almond-shaped; the one gift she'd been allowed to keep from the mother who had abandoned her all those years ago. The eyes that had welled with tears in the Shōgun's gardens, staring at her father with dumb disbelief as he told her that her mother was gone.

"I wish I had gone with her." She kept her voice low, calm; she refused to allow him to think that this all came from hysterics. But the words were intended to make him bleed. "I wish I were anywhere but here with you."

A long pause, pregnant with anger and the sound of falling rain.

"Wishing for the impossible," Masaru said softly. "You get that from her."

"I pray that's not all I get."

Another pause. Masaru took a deep breath. "If you're going to hate me, at least hate me for the mistakes I could have avoided."

"Like mutilating that poor thing?"

"Its feathers will grow back. Like any other bird. It will moult soon enough."

"You're going to give it to him, aren't you? The Shōgun."

Masaru sighed. "Of course I am, Yukiko. I swore I would."

"He's just a greedy boy. He doesn't deserve anything that beautiful."

"Sometimes we don't get what we deserve. We play the cards we are dealt instead of whining about what might've been. Therein lies the difference between an adult and a child."

But I am a child, she wanted to scream.

"I know about you and Kasumi," she said.

He nodded, eyes never leaving the ceiling. "Your mother told you?"

"No. I see the way you look at her."

"Kasumi and I are over. I ended it when your mother—"

"Is that why she left? Without even saying goodbye to me?"

He paused for a long moment, licking at dry lips.

"Your mother left for many reasons."

"You blamed her for Satoru." Yukiko blinked back the tears. "You drove her away."

Masaru's expression darkened, as if clouds had covered the sun. "No. Satoru was my fault. I should have been there. I should have been a father to you. I was never very good at that, I'm afraid."

"You *are* afraid," she growled. "All your life you've been running away. You left us alone to go on your mighty hunts. You left your wife's bed for another woman's. You leave me every time you suck down a lungful of that stinking weed. You're a coward."

Masaru sat up slowly, swung his legs over the edge of the hammock and dropped to the floor. His eyes betrayed his rage, flashing like polished jet, clear of smoke. He stepped closer.

"If I were a coward, I would have run as your mother bid me." His voice was soft, dangerous. "I would never have returned to Shōgun Yoritomo's side after Sensei Rikkimaru died. She bid me to become an oath-breaker. Dishonored. Shamed."

"And if you had, she would still be here."

"Yukiko, I am warning you . . ."

"Satoru would still be alive."

He slapped her then, an open hand across her face, the crack of flesh on flesh seeming louder than the song from the arashitora's wings. She lost her balance on the stool and toppled over backward, head slamming into the wall, hair splayed across her face.

"Godsdamn you, girl," her father hissed. "I was sworn to the Shōgun. I still am to this day. If I break my word, he will take everything from me. Everything, do you understand?"

What about me, she wanted to cry. *You'd still have me.*

He stared down at his hand, at the palm print on her cheek. He looked suddenly wretched, an old man, body slowly turning to poison, life ebbing away one fix at a time.

"One day you will understand, Yukiko," he said. "One day you will see that we must sometimes sacrifice for the sake of something greater."

"Honor." She spat the word, unwanted tears welling in her eyes.

"Among other things."

"You're a godsdamned liar. There's no honor in what you do. You're a servant. A rent boy who butchers helpless animals at the behest of a coward."

Masaru hung his head, teeth gritted, hands curled into fists. His breath was low and measured, trembling in his nostrils. His eyes flickered to hers, glazed with anger.

"I hate you," she hissed.

Masaru opened his mouth to speak, and the world turned sideways. A tremendous boom rang out above the ship, shattering the small glass porthole and making Yukiko wince. They were both tossed across the room, walls rushing forward with outstretched arms to embrace them, unforgiving, hard as stone. Her forehead split on the wood, stars in her eyes as she and her father tumbled to the ground.

The whole ship trembled, her timbers shaking beneath their feet as if in the grip of an earthquake. The sound of boiling vapor filled the sky.

Yukiko opened her eyes, blinking away the blood as the *Child* rocked beneath them. Through the tiny cracked porthole, she could see the clouds were painted with flickering orange.

The acrid tang of smoke stained the air.

They were on fire.

13
DESCENDING

Staggering. Blood and swelling gluing her eye closed. Her father's hands on her shoulder, firm. Deck bucking beneath their feet. A stumble, a fall. Hands dragging her up. Her father's voice, from far away.

"Keep moving!"

Onto the deck. Light blinding above them, bright as the sun. Too close, heat curling the ghost-pale hair on her arms, leaving behind tiny black cinders. A roar, terrifying, crackling across the rigging with ruinous, hungry hands. The nightmare sound that woke cloudwalkers in the dark, stomachs in knots, soaked in sweat. Fire.

Fire in the sky.

The balloon was ablaze. The canvas had spilled wide open, the hydrogen within clasping hands with the lightning strike and giving birth to a conflagration, sucking the very breath from their lungs. The heat of a funeral pyre beat upon their backs. Screaming men, feet running across the deck, panicked voices. The hiss of rain, great gouts of pitch-black smoke rising in a veil from the marriage between fire and water. Vertigo swelled, the clutch of gravity denied by the speed of their descent. Falling.

They were falling.

Dragged up the ladder to the pilot's deck, vice grip on her wrists, press of bodies all around her. Across the shifting wood, steering wheel spinning free, Captain Yamagata's voice rising above the din.

"Masaru-san! Quickly!"

She felt hands on her, dragging her through a metal hatchway, the volume of the world dropping to a dull, reverberating roar. The smell of sweat, tang of iron in her nostrils, copper on her lips. Yukiko blinked away the blood, looked around her, trying to focus. She was surrounded by heaving, sweating bodies, packed into the confines of the life raft fixed to the *Thunder Child*'s stern. It was filled to capacity, two frantic cloudwalkers working to uncouple the small beetle-shaped pod from its burning mother.

"Hurry up, we're going down!"

"Lord Izanagi, save us!"

Hissed curses. The sound of iron crashing against iron. And then she heard it. A vibrato scream of fear, of rage. Louder than the thunder, tipped with electricity, grating across the back of her skull.

"Oh no," she whispered.

She turned to her father, pawing the blood from her eyes.

"Father, the arashitora!"

Masaru's expression darkened. His eyes showed no trace of dread; simply dismay at the loss of his prize. She could see the hunter in him, pragmatic and cold as steel. He glanced up as the beast screamed again, wiped the soot off his face with the back of his hand. His skin was damp with sweat, and he left one long black smear across his cheek.

"We can't." He shook his head, looked back and forth between Yukiko and Kasumi. "There's no time."

"Gods, listen to it," breathed Akihito, crammed against the far wall.

The cry was piercing, dripping with outrage: a trembling note of fear and anger, of disbelief that it could end like this. They heard the scraping of claws on metal, flesh pitting itself against iron in a repeated frenzy of terror. Rage. Red and boiling.

One coupling came loose with the snap of iron jaws, and the life raft swung as if on a hinge, crashing hard against the polished hull. The rain poured through the open door, soaking the miserable knot of humans huddled in the boat, blinding, blistering white as the lightning flashed. Raijin rejoiced at the *Child*'s destruction, his howl of triumph and the beating of his drums echoing across the clouds.

Yukiko could feel the thunder tiger's thoughts, its terror. She imagined its final moments: plummeting from the sky like a falling star, feathers and fur charring, praying for the impact that would end its burning agony. She shook her head.

Not like that. He cannot die like that.

Masaru sensed his daughter's intent, reached out toward her.

"Yukiko, no! You stay here!"

Too late. She leaped from the raft as the final coupling sprang loose, the small ship spinning off into the darkness with a brittle, metallic sound. Her father's anguished cry drifted off into the throat of the storm as the belly of the life raft lit up in a halo of blue flame, propelling the small craft away into the tempest.

Yukiko stumbled across the pilot's deck and down the ladder, smoke burning her eyes, the wood beneath her an untamed, living thing. She felt numb, head still swimming from the kiss on the cabin wall. The wind tore at her skin, burning hot from the inferno raging overhead, embers entwined with the falling rain and smoldering on the sleeves and shoulders of her uwagi. The balloon had been reduced to a blackened skeleton, lit from within by the blaze; a corpse lantern on the feast day of the dead. The *Child* began to roll toward its wounded port side, starboard engine still at full burn, shadows of sharp rock swelling up out of the darkness before them.

Down the ladder, holding on for dear life as the ship clipped a spur of mountain stone, tearing half its belly out with the roar of splintering timber. On the main deck she slipped and stumbled, lunging across to the cage and using its bars to hold herself upright. The arashitora was lost in a frenzy of fear, near mindless as she reached out to it, almost overcome with primal terror of the fire above. It roared, a thundering, metallic screech, pupils glazed with panic.

Be calm. I will free you.

OUT. AWAY. FLY.

The bolts on the door were slippery in her hands, palms sweaty in the shocking heat. She thrust them away from their housings, fear turning her arms to jelly. Blood dripped into her eye, sticky and thick on her lashes. The *Child*'s roll grew more pronounced, and she struggled to keep her footing as the deck listed, floods of rain spilling over the brink in a doomed, lonely waterfall. The snaggle-toothed face of a mountain appeared out of the darkness directly in front of them, jaws of jagged stone open in welcome.

The final bolt slid free and the door swung wide. The arashitora burst from the cage, talons scrabbling across sodden boards, half-sparks flaring on its ruined wings. As it thundered across the shifting deck, Yukiko reached out, desperate, snagging her fingers into a clump of sodden feathers and swinging herself up onto its shoulders. Wood shredded like rice-paper beneath razored claws, sinew and muscle snapped taut like iron cable as it spread its wings and plunged over the side of the burning sky-ship.

Fly! Fly!

The blaze dropped away behind her in a rush of freezing wind, flaring bright as the *Child* plowed into the mountainside. The barrels of chi lashed in the bow split and ignited like fireworks at Lord Izanagi's feast: a damp, thunderous explosion that sent burning timbers spinning off into the darkness. They plummeted out of the smoke toward the ground, burning embers falling bright between the raindrops. One flared blue-white, spiraling down into the yawning black below them.

The arashitora shrieked, pounding the air with its ruined wings. Yukiko was almost thrown from its shoulders, entwining her fingers in its feather mane and gripping tight with her thighs. Exhilaration and terror fought for her attention. The beast's muscles seethed beneath her as its wings tore at the air, futile, furious. Sharp spires of rock rose out of the storm around them, rushing toward them as a blur, rain hissing across the stone in freezing squalls. The beast spread its wings to their full breadth and managed to bank away from the fangs of black granite, spiraling into a clumsy glide. It rolled from side to side, trying to maintain equilibrium without the use of its primaries. Yukiko could feel a grim determination rise up and engulf the fear inside it: a refusal to fail, to lie down or roll over. It screamed in the face of death, defiant and proud as a king upon a wind-tossed throne.

They wheeled away in their broken glide, green treetops rising out of the rain curtain ahead. The beast was unable to maintain altitude; every flap of its wings simply sent them falling faster. The green fingers of giant cedars and maidenhead trees clutched at the beast's belly, pulling them down toward ruin.

GET OFF ME.

The arashitora bucked, trying to throw Yukiko from its back.

What?

GET OFF, INSECT.

You can't throw me off. I'll break my neck!

OFF. NOW.

The beast rolled from side to side, twisting through the air. Yukiko shrieked, daring a glance down through the treetops to the ground rushing away fifty feet below them. She clung to the tiger's shoulders, teeth gritted, knowing a fall from this height and speed would mean her death.

I just saved your life!

WOULD NOT NEED SAVING IF NOT FOR YOU. GET OFF ME NOW.

I wasn't the one who maimed you. You'd be a smear on the mountainside right now if it weren't for me. You want to kill me?

MY WINGS CANNOT HOLD US BOTH ALOFT. YOUR PACK SAW TO THAT.

I'll die!

BETTER ONE THAN TWO.

They descended below the canopy in a flurry of severed leaves, branches whipping at her face and snapping beneath the impact of the arashitora's wings. It banked sharply between two tightly spaced maples. Her stomach lurched up into her throat, and a thick bough caught her full in the chest. Yukiko's breath spewed from her lungs. The branch whipped her backward, she lost her grip on the arashitora's neck and sailed off between the raindrops. She screamed, spinning down through the branches, skin torn, tumbling toward her death. The world spun over and over itself before her eyes.

She shrieked as a branch snagged in her obi, ripping a long gash up her back. The green wood split but held, arresting her fall and leaving her suspended twenty feet above the ground, dangling like fresh meat outside the abandoned slaughter mills of Kigen city.

She gasped, white pain rushing up and spilling wet from the gouge in her back. The branch swayed, making ominous noises as she looked down at the stone below. Reaching up, wincing, she tried to pull herself off the snag, and with a sound of splintering wood and a despairing shriek, the branch snapped and sent her plummeting down into the black.

Lightning arced across the skies, illuminating the smoldering ruin of the cloudwalkers' vessel, strewn upon the mountainside in a thousand flaming fragments. Long streaks of burning chi were scored across the mountain's face—a halo of blue-white illuminating the swirling mists of rain, running through to orange as the foliage around it caught and burned.

The girl hit the stone hard. The thunder echoed across the trees like booming laughter.

Raijin was pleased.

She pawed away the darkness some time later, hours slipping by like shadows between sleep and the slow opening of her eyes. One was sealed shut by a scum of blood and dirt; she had to prise her lids apart with trembling fingers. The pain in her back was a dull ache. Merciful numbness had spread through her body, spurred on by the falling rain and bitter, brittle cold of altitude. It urged her back to sleep, to simply close her eyes and drift away, to worry no more.

She shook her head, forcing the thought back into the gloom where it had been born. Time enough to sleep when she was dead.

Yukiko pushed herself up on her elbows, wincing at the bruises all over her body. The forest floor was covered in a thick blanket of dead leaves and lush green moss; even the stones were bearded with great growths of it. She ran her fingertips across the spongy surface and touched her fox tattoo in thanks: a fall onto bare rock would have broken her bones, possibly killed her outright.

Kitsune looks after his own.

She climbed to her feet, brushing the sodden hair away from her face. Her dark eyes surveyed the surroundings, glittering with the occasional faint burst of lightning across the hidden clouds above.

Trees with trunks as thick as houses stretched up to blot out the sky. Rain dripped through the knotted canopy, drumming upon leaves in a thousand discordant beats. The trees were ancient and gnarled: bent old men, their skin crawling with fingers of thick moss, mushrooms clustered about their feet in multicolored growths. Her stomach growled and she picked several of the safer-looking fungi, stuffing a few into her obi for later. Panic bloomed as she groped at the small of her back, and she breathed a sigh of relief when her fingers brushed the polished lacquer hilt of her tantō.

She blinked about the darkness, each direction looking no worse or better than the rest. So, with a shrug, she set off down the slope in the direction the arashitora had flown.

"Ungrateful shit," she muttered.

Her father would have scolded her for the unladylike language. She looked around the darkness, and realizing that there were no adults nearby to chastise her, she began shouting every bad word she could think of. A rainbow of profanity rolled between the trees, gutter-talk bouncing among walls of wood and fern, beneath a ceiling of shadowed green. Spirits slightly buoyed by her tiny rebellion, Yukiko tromped off into the gloom.

Her thin sandals were soon sodden and torn, and she slipped and stumbled across the forest floor. The storm raged above, its volume muted by the lush canopy over her head, the great trees reaching out to entwine their branches like the hands of old, dear friends. There was a strange scent on the air, a smell that lay so far back in her childhood that she took a while to recall what it was.

The absence of lotus.

Everything in Kigen was polluted by it, lending its acrid tang to the food she ate, the water she drank, the very sweat on her skin. But here in the deep Iishi Mountains, there was almost no trace. The fields encroached closer every year, but she sensed there was still a purity here; the last stretch of true wilderness in all of Shima. She wondered how long it would take before the shredder-men set their sights on these ancient trees, this fertile soil, and put their blades to work. The motto of the Guild rang unbidden in her head, and she whispered it once into the darkness, fingers to her lips.

"The lotus must bloom."

D awn had spread its gloomy pall across the forest before Yukiko stumbled across the arashitora's trail: fresh gouges in the earth marking the broken gait of a creature unused to spending much time on the ground. She found no blood, and took solace that the beast wasn't injured beyond the suffering it had already endured.

She followed the trail for hours down the crumbling mountainside, stopping occasionally to rest and eat, to lick rain off the broad green leaves. Sandals torn, feet bleeding, dripping with the humidity trapped beneath the ceiling of overhanging leaves. She lost the trail several times on stony ground; she wasn't half the tracker her father was. *If only he were here . . .*

The memory of her final words to him echoed in her head. She could still feel the sting of his slap on her cheek, hear the anger and hurt in his rebuke. But beneath it all lurked the fear that he might have died in the crash, that the life raft and everyone aboard had lost the way in the storm and plowed right into a mountainside. Hot tears welled in her eyes, and she pawed them away with the heels of her hands.

He's all right. You're worrying for nothing. Everyone will be all right.

Hours passed, the mushrooms in her belt disappearing one mouthful at a time. She lost the trail again as the forest grew darker, cursing herself and stumbling over the uneven ground. Stopping beneath a towering maple, she re-tied her braid, damp wisps of hair clinging to her forehead. The forest had grown noisy as the sun rose, alive with chattering birds, spattering rain, small scuttling feet. She had felt their tiny pulses with the Kenning, searching for the fear that might linger in the arashitora's wake. But now, as dusk fell, she reached out and felt no sparks, no clusters of warm, furry bodies or sleek feathered heartbeats. Silence had descended: a sweaty hush that fell heavy as a moldy blanket.

Something's wrong.

Creeping through the undergrowth, she crouched low, her footfalls barely a whisper. Eyes darting about the gloom, pulse quickening at every snapping twig or shifting shadow. Steam rose up from the rain-soaked earth, cloaking the forest in mist. She could sense the faint glow of the setting sun through the canopy above, the chill of night creeping with slow, measured tread through the wildwood. No bird calls. No wind. Just the heavy patter of fat raindrops and the faint scrape of her heels on dead leaves.

Predator?

Touching the fox tattoo on her arm for luck, she reached out again, searching for the arashitora, or perhaps some hungry carnivore stalking her through the green curtain.

Nothing. A vast emptiness, creaking with the echo of old wood, the breath of the slumbering earth. Even when the wolf came, even after the snake strike, she had never felt more frightened or alone in all her life.

She crept onward.

A shape loomed out of the mist. Ragged walls of raw granite, covered with creepers and a thick fur of moss. A temple. Twisted. Timeworn. Rising from the forest floor to squat glowering and grim on the mountain's flank, surrounded by thick scarlet tangles of wild blood lotus. Yukiko swallowed, averting her eyes from the blasphemous kanji gouged into the stone; dark words calling to darker hearts. There was a palpable sense of *wrongness* about the place, something decidedly unnatural that took root at the base of her spine. The carvings lingered in her mind, shadows lurking in the dusk, dripping malevolence. A name.

Lady Izanami.

A long piercing scream sounded off in the mist; some animal or bird in the distance giving voice to her terror. Yukiko's heart thumped in her chest, frigid sweat beading on her skin.

This is a temple to the Dark Mother.

She turned to leave, and a nightmare shape swung down from the trees behind. Twice as tall as a man, long arms like an ape, rippling with ropes of sinew. Its skin was as blue as cobalt. Its face mirrored the fearsome masks of Yoritomo's Iron Samurai, but instead of polished metal, this face was carved in flesh, twisted and evil. A wide grinning mouth was flanked by two iron-shod tusks, a long black tongue lolling from between serrated teeth. Twin embers burned in dark eye sockets, spilling a ruddy glow across its jagged grin. A studded iron war club was clutched in shovel-broad hands, a rope of spherical beads was strung about its neck, each as big as her head. The blasphemous kanji on the temple walls was repeated on polished onyx.

It dropped to the ground in a crouch, one vast palm flat on the earth, regarding her with those awful, glowing eyes. Then it bellowed; a choir of screaming children reverberating across a rusted sky.

Amaterasu, Lady of the Sun, protect me.

Monsters from legend, the stuff of nightmare, a threat to disobedient children from exasperated parents. Never in her blackest dreams did she think they might actually exist.

In the distance, Yukiko heard another bellow in answer.

Oni.

14
GRAVITY

Hungry.

Belly growling. Footsore.

Stinking snarl of heat and green. Storm singing above his head, primal and complete, making his chest ache with want. Its pull like gravity, like moon to tide, urging him upward. But his wings wouldn't work. Couldn't fly. Wretched monkey-things maimed him. Scarred him. Cut him to pieces.

KILL YOU ALL.

Game fleeing at his clumsy approach. Claws crunching on fallen leaves and brittle twigs, wings dragging through soaking underbrush, making more noise than Raijin himself. Small fleshlings could hear him coming from too far away. No hunt. No food.

SO HUNGRY.

So he walked. Many steps. Too many for counting. Water flowed downhill, so downhill he stumbled, hoping for a river and fat, slow fish. Ignoring his growling belly. Ignoring the lessened weight of his wings, the flat shapes of his maimed feathers. The fury at what they had done to him swelling for hours at a time, until at last it would boil up and over and he would lash out with hooked talon and razored beak. Tearing saplings from their roots and fallen logs from their rotting beds, roaring his frustration at the rumbling clouds above.

No answer.

He would stand there afterward, chest heaving, tail lashing from side to side, head bowed with the weight of it all. And deep inside him, a single thought would raise its serpent head and whisper with forked and darting tongue, a truth so far beyond denying that it might have been carved into the bones of the earth itself.

SHOULD NEVER HAVE COME HERE.

He walked on. Stumbling through the curtain of emerald green, clumsy as a newborn cub. The same cycle of rage and release, building and breaking, over and over again. And then, amidst the fading echoes of his roars and the crash of black clouds and the voice of the howling wind, he heard it among the boughs of the ancient trees.

A scream.

It took a second for him to recognize it for what it was: the wail of the monkey-child. The one who had spoken in his mind, freed him from the cage, saved him from burning death. She was calling out in terror, breathless, desperate. And in answer to her wavering song of fear, he heard an echoing bellow. Deep as the grave. Twisted and gurgling. Behind him. Back toward the ruined stone and stink of grave soil that he had known well enough to avoid.

He sniffed the air. Smelled death. Heard the sound of running feet in the distance; one set as light as the dreams of clouds, another, pounding heavy upon the earth. Falling trees, a roar of anger and pain. And he thought of the monkey-child in the rain, flooding his mind with her wretched, unwelcome pity as he awoke to find his wings mutilated. He thought of her trembling fingers on the lock to his prison, sliding the bolt free as the flames reached toward them with hungry hands. He thought of debts unpaid, heard her voice in his mind; a memory of old words that filled him now with a faint and nagging guilt.

"I wasn't the one who maimed you. You'd be a smear on the mountainside right now if it weren't for me."

Blinking up at the ceiling of leaves and the hidden sky beyond, he flexed his crippled wings. The rain and wind caressed his ruined feathers as the monkey-child's words played over and over inside his head. He heard faint, gurgling laughter over the storm, dripping and malevolent. A black voice speaking, the tongue of the Dark Ones, poisonous and vile. Lightning stabbed at the gloom, the predator's instinct quickening his pulse. And then he was running, loping through the scrub, bounding over fallen logs and clawing branches toward the fading sounds of battle, azalea petals falling like perfumed snowflakes in his wake.

Figures between the trees. Smell of black blood. A raised sword. A demon, Yomi-spawn looming twelve feet tall over the fallen monkey-child, skin of polished midnight blue, ready to spill her open on the acres of swaying green. Thunder rolled across cloud, Raijin hammering his drums in the skies above, hollow, booming echoes sounding in the depths of the temple ruins at his back. He leaped on the oni's shoulders, a flurry of razors, broken blue sparks and beating wings. Tearing. Biting. Pounding the air and gagging at the foul blood on his tongue.

The taste of charnel pits and ashes. The stink of burning hair and open graves.

A war club scythed toward him from the darkness. He sprang from the demon's back and took to the air for a few brief and wondrous seconds, almost forgetting, tiny whirlwinds of falling leaves dancing in time to the thrashing of his wings. Weightless. Flying.

He heard the crunch of breaking spine behind him, the spittle-thick death rattle of the pit demon as it crumpled to the ground. He landed hard, unsteady on maimed wings, digging bloodstained claws into the earth. Turning his eyes toward the remaining oni, he breathed deep, inhaling the stench of black gore amidst the steaming green rot. The oni glanced at its companion's corpse, shifting the war club from one hand to the other.

CAN SMELL THE FEAR IN YOU, LITTLE DEMON.

A bellow. A war club raised high. Lightning arced across the skies, bathing the whole scene in fleeting, brilliant white: the endless wilds, the stranded arashitora, and the pit demon poised to cave in his skull.

A charge across broken ground and the pair collided, crashing earthward and tumbling about in a flurry of feathers, petals and screams.

Dark splashes staining the white azalea blossoms.

A crunch, a choking gurgle, and then a vast, empty silence.

He emerged from the shadows, feathers stained black with blood. He saw the monkey-child laid out in the dark, face spattered with gore. A tiny splinter of sharpened metal lay near her outstretched hand. He stalked toward her and lowered his head, a growl of challenge building in his throat. She groped toward the steel, even as her world began fading to black.

She was weak. Frail. No real threat at all.

If this was victory, it was his alone.

Gravity returned as the rush of battle faded, the weight of his flesh and bones painfully real. The wind and rain sang a melody he had known since birth, too distant now to be of any comfort. He felt like a child torn early from its womb, bound to wretched earth, helpless in the grip of its hateful pull. Longing to fly, he spread his wings, sparks breaking on the edges of mutilated quills. Listening to the song he was no longer a part of, he felt it calling like iron to lodestone. As a victim calls to vengeance.

He roared at the skies, emptying his lungs, a hurricane scream of rage and longing.

At his feet, the girl surrendered to darkness.

PART 2
SHADOWS

Yet all flowers fade.
Lady Izanami's life, childbirth's labor stole.
To reclaim love lost, Lord Izanagi walked deep, to black
    Underworld,
Yet to slay cold death, and break Yomi's bleak embrace, no
    power had he.
And there she dwells still; the broodmare to all evils,
Her name, Endsinger.

The Book of Ten Thousand Days

15
NAMING THE THUNDER

Eight years old.

Playing in the bamboo every day, she and Satoru, their favorite game. He the brave hunter Masaru, she the Naga Queen, arrows of venom and snakes for hair. She would topple the imaginary forms of the squires Akihito and Kasumi, slay the Hunt Master Rikkimaru and stand poised over Shōgun Kaneda, ready to end him. And with a fearsome shout, Masaru, Rikkimaru's brave apprentice, would snatch up his sensei's spear and thrust it into her heart, and she would sink to the cool ground, cursing his prowess, vowing that her children would avenge her.

Serpent Empress. Mother to All Vipers.

Almost a year to the day after the Naga Queen's death, their father had come home to stay at last. And though they didn't really know him, they loved him fiercely.

It was their mother who raised them, who forced them to do their chores and eat their vegetables and punished them when they misbehaved. Masaru had always returned from his long treks with trinkets and stories and broad smiles. Sometimes Uncle Akihito or Aunt Kasumi would come too, bringing small mechanical marvels from Kigen: music prisms or glittering spring-loaded contraptions that mapped out the path of the hidden stars. Masaru would sit by the fire and tell hunting tales. Satoru's eyes would fill with pride and he'd say, "One day I will be like you, father."

Masaru would laugh and tell his son to work harder at his numbers. But when he had time, he would take the twins out into the bamboo to hunt the small game that grew more scarce every season, or to fish the stream that flowed like crystal down from the Iishi crags. He would love them for a day or two, then disappear for months on end.

They loved him back. It's easy to lose yourself in the idea of a person and be blinded to their reality. It's a simple thing, to love a stranger.

But now, for the first time in as long as they could remember, he was home for more than a handful of days. At night he would sometimes tell the story of the Renshi swamps, the hunt Shōgun Kaneda promised would be his last. Satoru asked why the village minstrels sang tales of Kaneda the nagaraja slayer, and barely mentioned the brave apprentice Masaru, who saved his Lord's life. Their father said that it did not matter what the minstrels sang, that pride was the province of men who did not understand what was truly important.

Playing and fishing and breathing, a blessed handful of months beneath the scorching summer sun. Sometimes the twins would dance together in the dappled shade between the bamboo stalks, and he would simply sit and stare, motionless, his smile reaching all the way to his eyes. He was home. He was happy.

And then the letter arrived.

After fourteen months of agony, Shōgun Kaneda had succumbed to the nagaraja's toxin and gone to his heavenly reward, succeeded by his thirteen-year-old son, Yoritomo. The new Shōgun commanded Masaru to move his family to Kigen and take up Sensei Rikkimaru's old role: Hunt Master of the Shōgunate court.

Their mother refused to go. Naomi loathed the thought of leaving Kitsune land for Kigen's polluted labyrinth and choking fumes.

"Besides," she argued, "what is there left to hunt? The last of the Black Yōkai is dead. What need does the Shōgun have of hunters now, aside from indulging foolish pride?"

Masaru had been torn between love and duty; his wife and his honor. And so they fought, shouting matches that went on for hours, driving their children into the comforting veil of long emerald leaves and swaying stalks and cool dark earth. There they would play hunters, or chase the few remaining butterflies flapping on feeble, near-translucent wings. Even this close to the mountains, the lotus was beginning to leave its stain; the fields were encroaching further north every year, choking exhaust rolling among the morning mist. Every so often they would catch the scent of smoke on the air, and Satoru would decide they were hunting Kagé today, crashing off through the undergrowth. Yukiko would follow, whooping like a wild thing.

They ran through forest that day, Satoru swinging his stick of bamboo like a double-handed daikatana, hacking at imaginary foes. She raced along with him, flitting among the swaying green, eyes alight.

"Let's play nagaraja," Satoru said.

"Not today."

"Why not?"

"Because I'm always the Naga Queen." She made a face. "I always get killed."

"Well, that's how it happened." He was busy hacking at a thick tangle of akebi vines. "You slay Sensei Rikkimaru, though. You give Uncle Akihito his scars."

"Why don't you be the Naga Queen, then?"

"Because I'm a boy," he laughed, stabbing at the vines again. "Boys can't be queens. And you do the voice better than me."

Yukiko smiled and crouched low, pawing at the air.

"My children will avenge meeeeeee," she hissed.

Satoru's laughter was bright. Short-lived.

The snake was green as grass, fast as lightning. It uncoiled from the akebi vines and struck like quicksilver, fangs buried to the gums in Satoru's hand. The boy cried out, stumbling away as the terrified serpent struck again, punching twin holes in his forearm. The bamboo sword dropped to the moist earth. The viper slithered away from the noise and motion, its scales gleaming like polished glass. Yukiko watched her brother fall, eyes wide, mouth open.

"Satoru!"

She ran to his side and he blinked up at her in confusion and shock, jaw slack.

"Jade adder," he mumbled.

Yukiko took off her obi, tying the fabric above the wounds as tight as her little hands could. She heard her father's voice in her head, careful, methodical:

"You must cut the wound, draw the poison out with your mouth and spit. And you must be swift. Swift as the snake that bit you, or you will find yourself standing before the Judge of the Nine Hells, fearsome Enma-ō."

"But I don't have a knife," she wailed, cradling her brother's head.

Satoru was staring at the sky, holding her hand, a thin sheen of sweat rising over his body. He began trembling, first his fingertips, then his lips, breath coming in shallow gasps.

"Tell me what to do!" she pleaded. "Tell me what to do, Satoru!"

His tongue was swollen, lips turning blue. She made to stand and run for help, but he held onto her hand, refusing to let go. And in that moment she felt the world drop away beneath her, fell down into the warm darkness of his thoughts; the first and only time she had touched another human mind. Awash with poison, metallic tang in the back of her throat, muscles palsied. But she could hear him, feel his voice, like the wind up the valley in the warmth of spring.

Don't go.

But I have to get help.

Please don't leave.

Tears streamed down her cheeks, spattering across his upturned face. He couldn't feel his feet, his fingers were a distant blur. She was inside him and staring down at him at the same time, a glittering myriad of pathways in his mind, slowly choking closed with the onset of the venom. He was terrified, but he reached out and found some solace in her warmth, her touch, squeezing her hand as best he could.

I don't want to die, sister.

She screamed for help, screamed until her throat seized closed, grabbing him by his collar and dragging him through the brush. But he was so heavy, and she was so little. The rush of his thoughts was overcome with lethargy, spilling over into her mind and turning her hands and feet to lead. She dragged him and screamed, snot spilling from her nose, cheeks wet with tears, unable at the end to even find words. Inarticulate, shapeless sounds; a howling, threadbare wail until her throat could take no more.

And nobody came.

I'm sorry, brother.

He died in her arms.

I'm so sorry.

And for the first time in her life, she was truly alone.

S he opened her eyes.

The night wind kissed the sweat on her skin. The air was rank with the smell of burned blood and shit, two oni crumpled like broken statues and bleeding out black onto the snow-white azaleas.

The beast glowered down at her, pupils dilated, a thin, brilliant band of amber glittering like a ring of fireflies around bottomless pits. Its flanks heaved, breath snorting from its nostrils, talons and fur painted with steaming demon blood. Splashed with thick gore and gobbets of flesh, its beak looked sharp enough to cut through bone as if it were butter. It growled, deep and grating, echoing the clash of dark clouds slung high overhead.

AWAKE. GOOD.

It turned to leave, long tail swishing across the leaves. The ground crunched beneath its feet, wings curled back on its sides, sleek and pale. The scales on its forelegs were the color of iron, each talon as long as her tantō, sharp as any blade of folded steel. Lightning dappled its fur, the shadows in the leaves creating shifting patterns among the stripes across its back.

Wait. Wait!

The beast paused, aiming a narrowed stare over its shoulder.

Why did you help me?

DEBT OWED. NOW REPAID.

The image of small hands struggling with the cage door flitted across their minds. The beast turned and stalked into the darkness, moving with an unsteady, feline grace.

GOODBYE.

Please don't leave me.

Yukiko struggled to her feet, wincing at the bruises, the gashes up her back and across her ribs. Her hair was a ragged tangle over her eyes. She fumbled in the gloom, finally grasping the bloody tantō and slipping it into the scabbard at her back.

It had been a gift from her father on her ninth birthday.

OWE YOU NOTHING, MONKEY-CHILD. GO BACK TO YOUR SCAB.

Scab?

ANTS' NEST. WOOD AND STONE. SPEWING POISON INTO MY SKY.

We call them cities.

SCABS. BOILS ON THE LAND. YOU ARE SEPTIC.

If you leave me here alone, I'll die.

DO NOT CARE. DEBT REPAID. MILLIONS OF YOU. ONE LESS IS NOTHING. A GOOD START.

We thought your kind extinct. Where do you come from?

RAIJIN.

The beast looked up at the sky, wings twitching across its back. She could feel the anger, the distrust clouding its mind. Instinctual aggression, the aftermath of the battle with the oni still singing in its veins. But behind that, she sensed a tiny sliver of something more primal, blooming in its gut and crawling across the inside of its ribs.

You're hungry.

The beast glared.

STAY OUT OF MY MIND, INSECT.

You can't fly, can't swoop on prey.

The arashitora growled, pawing the earth with its hind legs. Its anger flared bright and hot at the reminder of its mutilation, the faces of her father and Akihito flashing in its mind's eye, dipped in the color of murder.

I can help you. I am a hunter.

DO NOT NEED YOUR HELP.

You can't hunt here. Game will hear you coming. You're too slow on your feet to catch them. You'll starve.

SWIFT ENOUGH TO CATCH YOU, MONKEY-CHILD.

Its eyes glittered in the dark like the long-lost stars.

We can help each other. I'll hunt for us. You protect me. Together we can get out of this. Up to higher ground.

DO NOT NEED YOU.

But I need you. I'll pay for your protection with tribute. Flesh. Hot and bloody.

The beast purred, the vibration thrumming in her chest, mulling the word "tribute" over in its mind. It was unsure of the exact meaning, but liked the sound, the mien of subservience Yukiko had adopted. She kept her eyes down-turned, shoulders slumped, hands before her like a penitent at temple. She could feel its stare, the knowledge that it could smear her across the forest with a casual wave of its talons banishing the realization that she was right; that it would starve to death without her help.

She would be a pet, it decided. She could atone for the insults of her pack with servitude. And if not, she could serve at the last by lining its belly.

VERY WELL. COME.

It stalked into the undergrowth, long tail whipping from left to right. Yukiko fell into step alongside, stumbling over roots and scrub in the dark. Off in the black she heard an owl call, the soft patter of the rain on broad leaves. Small sparks of life fled before them, unsure who these interlopers were, but certain they had little wish to know more. The arashitora's head was level with her own, and it eyed her with disdain as she blundered about, tripping and cursing in the gloom.

HUNTER OF BEASTS WITH NO EARS, PERHAPS.

I'm sorry. It's so dark. I can't see.

WRETCHED MONKEY-THING. WEAK. BLIND.

May I use yours?

MY WHAT?

Your eyes. I can see through your eyes.

A long pause, heavy with the sound of its breathing, the girl stumbling in the dark, the whisper of small, fleeing feet. Its stomach growled.

YES.

Yukiko slipped inside its mind, felt its muscles flexing, the damp warmth of its fur. The ground was uneven beneath them, and she realized how difficult it was for the beast to walk with forelegs simply not designed for land travel. But it held itself proudly, unwilling to stumble, a stubbornness that immediately put her in mind of her father. Arrogant. Arrogant and proud.

We need to find somewhere to rest. Away from that temple. Then I can craft some snares. What do you eat?

WE FISH. FROM THE MOUNTAIN STREAMS. NOTHING ELSE IN THIS PLACE. LAND CHOKED WITH YOUR WEED.

There are others like you? More arashitora? We thought you had died out.

NOT YOUR BUSINESS, INSECT.

Yukiko fell silent, walking as if in sleep, eyes half-closed as she stared through the arashitora's. She put a hand out to steady herself, laying her palm flat on the thunder tiger's side. Broad quills flowed down its flanks and belly, growing thinner and finer until it was almost impossible to tell where they ended and the lustrous tiger fur began. She marveled at its softness beneath her fingertips, thick and wonderfully warm despite the rain, sticky with oni blood. The beast smelled strange, a heady mix of pungent feline musk, gore and ozone. Its mind was alien: the sharp, predatory instincts of a bird intertwined with the sensual, vibrant impulses of a cat.

Its curiosity finally got the better of it.

HOW CAN YOU HEAR MY MIND?

A gift from my mother's people. I am a fox child.

KITSUNE.

She felt a vague approval radiating from a distant corner of its psyche.

WE REMEMBER KITSUNE.

My name is Yukiko. Do you have a name?

A long pause, filled with the voice of the storm.

. . . NO.

Then what should I call you?

MATTERS NOT TO ME.

She ran her fingers along its flanks, touched the tips of its feathers. She remembered the wolf coming down from the mountain with a belly full of hunger, so many winters ago. She remembered the friend who rose to defend her, to save her life without having ever been asked. The sense of safety she felt when he was nearby. Her protector. Her brother.

Her friend.

Then I will call you Buruu.

16
SKIN

Oni are the demon spawn of the Yomi underworld. Servants of the dark beyond darkness, children of the great black mother, Lady Izanami, born and beholden to the shadow.

Perhaps that's why Yukiko and the arashitora didn't see them coming.

Wind scrabbled through the trees, tearing blossoms and leaves from the branches and whipping them into blinding flurries, thunder and rain drumming in their ears until the entire world seemed one endless drone. The pair stumbled on through the deep of night, looking for a cave, a hollowed tree, anything to shield them from the elements. The demons fell on them as they entered a copse of oak, downwind and silent as vapor. Like spiders dropping from the trees, all long limbs and wicked teeth, studded tetsubos and ten-span swords clutched in clawed hands. In the split second before the war club landed on the thunder tiger's skull, Yukiko glanced up and screamed a warning. The arashitora moved quick as lightning, knocking her sideways and into a tangle of battered pink hydrangeas.

The war club smashed the ground like an anvil, the ten-span sword whistling over the thunder tiger's head. And then there was only motion, a kind of brutal poetry, lashing out with beak and talon and spraying the leaves with hissing, black blood. The first demon fell with its throat torn out, the arashitora spitting chunks of dark flesh onto the leaves. He hurled himself skyward, furiously thrashing his wings, landing atop the second's shoulders and raking the creature's gut with the hooked sabers on his hind legs. Coils of thick black intestine unfurled with a stench of funeral pyres, and Yukiko clapped her hands over her mouth to hold back the vomit.

A third demon dropped from the shadows above them and landed behind the thunder tiger, raising its iron club high above its head. Yukiko moved without thinking, pushing a warning into the beast's mind and darting forth from the hydrangeas. She hacked at the demon's Achilles tendon with her tantō. She felt a moment's resistance, as if cleaving through old, salted rope. But the blade was of the finest crafting, folded one hundred and one times by the venerable Phoenix swordsage, Fushicho Otomo, and blue flesh soon gave way in a mist of hissing ichor.

The oni screeched, clutching its ankle and tumbling to the ground. The arashitora was on it in a second, cutting like a whirlwind, a jagged scythe of blades and feathers that left little more than a blue-black smear in its wake.

When he was done, the thunder tiger shook himself as a dog might, spraying black gore in all directions. His flanks heaved, great gusts of breath hissing from his open beak and scattering the dead leaves. Steam rose off his fur in warm drifts, eyes glittering with the joy of the kill. He stared at her, gaze flickering to the tiny blade in her hand.

SMALL KNIFE.

Yukiko pushed her sweat-slick hair out of her eyes, nodding at the demon's severed ankle. Her arm was painted to the elbow in rancid black.

Big enough.

She felt a grudging respect rising in him despite his efforts to push it away. Though he didn't acknowledge it, she could sense his gratitude, the knowledge that the oni would probably have staved in his skull had she failed to call out in time.

BRAVE.

He wiped his claws on the dead leaves, and with a swish of his tail, turned to leave. Pausing, he looked over his shoulder, eyes fixed on her.

COME.

He moved off into the darkness.

Trying to stifle her smile, Yukiko followed.

The night stretched on, dark and soaking, and dawn seemed a thousand miles away. A chill settled over the forest, altitude and the howling storm slowly leaching the heat from the earth and her own tired bones. Yukiko's clothes were drenched, wind cutting through her like a nagamaki's blade through snow-white feathers, and she wrapped her arms around herself and shuffled along in the dark, almost too exhausted to keep her eyes open. The rain was a constant, a deluge pressing her toward the sodden ground, her mood sinking into the mud along with her feet. She tried to keep the misery at bay, thinking of the bamboo valley, the warm stretches of green grass and crystal-clear water, shimmering with heat. But thoughts of the valley brought her back to her father, the bitter words they had shared before the *Thunder Child* fell from the skies.

The slap on her cheek.

The hiss through gritted teeth.

"*I hate you.*"

She had meant it. Every word. And yet the thought of him lying bleeding in the wreckage of the lifeboat, of never seeing him again . . . it was almost more than she could bear. Her muscles burned, lungs aching with each breath, and she stumbled and fell into the muck, too tired to plant one foot in front of the other. The arashitora watched her trying to stand, her fingers curled into claws, chest heaving.

YOU ARE WELL?

No, I'm not well. It's pouring with rain and I'm so tired I can barely walk.

He eyed her up and down with disdain.

WEAK.

We need to find shelter. Somewhere I can start a fire. We're far enough away from the dark temple now.

WOOD WET. WILL NOT BURN.

Somewhere out of the wind, at least.

The beast snorted, flexed his wings. He stared for a long moment, wide pupils reflecting the arcs of lightning stretching overhead. She could feel the heat inside him, the warmth of the blood in his veins, pulsing beneath a layer of thick, soggy fur.

He nodded up the rise, pawing at the ground.

THERE.

Yukiko looked up, saw the dark shadow of a cave mouth set in the mountainside.

They scrambled up the slope, loose stones and mud, clawing branches and thorns. The cave entrance was a black pit in the stone, perhaps eight feet across, opening out into a deep circular depression in the mountain's flank. The thunder tiger sniffed the air, sensed no predator save small furry things too feeble to bother them. And so he squeezed inside and stretched out along one wall, facing outward and watching the lightning dance among the treetops.

Yukiko curled up against the opposite wall, damp clothes clinging to her skin like a rime of morning frost. Clawing the wet hair from her eyes, she hugged herself and sank down to embrace her misery. She felt the cold more keenly once she stopped moving, and the shakes soon grew so fierce that she was forced to lie on the floor, back pressed against the stone, every muscle a knot of pain. Dry twigs and leaves were scattered around the cave, but her hands were trembling so badly that she couldn't have started a fire even if she had the flint.

The arashitora stared out at the storm for almost an hour, motionless and unblinking. Occasionally, he would glance over at her and watch her curled in her miserable little knot, shivering uncontrollably. Then his wings would twitch, and he would scrape his talons across the stone and turn his gaze back to the clouds. Yukiko closed her eyes and gritted her teeth to stop them chattering.

At last, he drew one great, deep breath and sighed; a bellow that sent the dry leaves skittering across the cave floor. Yukiko watched as he wordlessly lifted his wing, inviting her closer. She blinked and stared for a long moment, meeting the even gaze of those bottomless eyes. Crawling across the stone, she snuggled down beside him, wrapped in the tremendous heat radiating from his body. He folded his wing about her, a blanket of down and sweet warmth tinged with the scent of lightning, the smell of blood. She could hear his heartbeat beneath inches of pale, velvet fur.

Thank you, Buruu.

QUIET NOW, MONKEY-CHILD. DREAM.

Sleep came at last, as deep and complete as any she had known. She lay motionless, a soft smile on her face, and dreamed of a little bamboo valley, sweating beneath a summer sun.

The rabbits were plump and juicy, Buruu's gorge swelling as he threw his head back and swallowed them whole: fur, bones and all. Yukiko poked at the fire and watched the small haunch sizzle, fat spitting among the embers. Her stomach growled; the mushrooms she'd lived on for the past few days were nourishing, but hardly enough.

Buruu was stretched out beside the flames along the rock wall, firelight gleaming in his eyes. Woodsmoke drifted out into the evening chill, up into the pouring rain. The rabbits had been hard won; a day's patience in the downpour, hovering above the snares until her muscles ached. But the smell of the roasting meat made it all worthwhile.

Buruu had slept while she caught their dinner, the beast stretched out above one of the snares in a maidenhead tree. He had woken twice during the day, once to tell her to hurry up, the second to pounce unsuccessfully on a small hare nosing about the trap below him. After his failure, he'd mustered a little more patience, and when she returned with half a dozen fat rabbits slung over her shoulder, he'd discovered his civility.

Now, she looked at Buruu across the roasting meat, flames sparkling in her pupils. During the drama on the *Thunder Child*, the shock of the last few days, she'd not really had the opportunity to study him as well as she would have liked. But at last, here in the flickering warmth, with dry skin and the promise of a full belly, she found herself transfixed. Simply amazed to be in the presence of a creature so beautiful.

The flames lent the pale, sleek feathers on his head and chest a strange sheen; a luminosity that was almost metallic. His shoulders were broad, thick with muscle, and the feathers there rose like hackles on a hound when he grew angry. The patterns of black in the snow-white fur on his hindquarters were like words, written in some savage tongue she couldn't quite comprehend. Strangely enough, it was his tail, not his face, that was the most expressive part of his body. It moved in long, lazy arcs when he was content, lashed from side to side like a bullwhip when he was enraged, hung poised and slightly curled when he was stalking through the dark. Though he was half eagle, she'd noticed he moved mostly like a big cat: lithe and sinuous, an undercurrent of cunning in every fluid motion.

"We have enough food to start moving." Her voice skipped across rough stone walls. "We can strike out for the cliff tomorrow. If we're lucky, we'll be able to see where we are once we get to the top."

He blinked at her, saying nothing. She realized that he couldn't understand her when she spoke aloud; her voice was a series of squeals and barks in his ears. She repeated the sentence into his mind, the liquidity of thought overcoming the barrier of flesh and bone between them.

When we climb the cliff tomorrow, we should be able to see where we are.

WE ARE HERE. WHAT ELSE MATTERS?

Yukiko took a few moments to answer.

I need to get home.

He snorted, preening his crippled wings with the elegant hook of his beak. Its tip was white like his fur, running through gray into a deep black encircling his eyes. The cool breeze rustled the feathers of his brow.

DO NOT UNDERSTAND YOU MONKEYS.

Meaning what?

THIS IS GOOD PLACE. FOOD HERE. WARM. DRY. SAFE. WHY DO YOU RUSH BACK TO YOUR SCAB?

My father. My friends. They could be dead for all I know. If they got away, they'd head back to Kigen. I need to find out if they're all right.

YOUR PACK.

The beast nodded, the gesture all too human.

PACK I UNDERSTAND.

Where is yours?

. . . NORTH. AMONG THE STORMS.

His eyes gleamed, honey shot through with shards of molten silver.

Why did you come here?

TO SEE WHAT YOU HAD DONE. THE OLD ONES WARNED ME. SAID THERE WAS NO LIFE LEFT IN SHIMA. DID NOT LISTEN. FOOLISH.

I don't listen to my father either.

Yukiko smiled.

THE ONE WHO MAIMED ME.

Her smile died, and she was surprised to find herself leaping to Masaru's defense.

He's a good man. He was only doing what he was commanded.

COMMANDED BY WHO?

The Shōgun. The leader of Shima.

DESPOILER LORD COMMANDED YOU HUNT ME. WHY?

He wanted you for himself. To ride you, like the Stormdancers in the old tales.

NO MAN WILL RIDE ME. THAT GIFT IS EARNED. YOUR RACE IS NO LONGER WORTHY. ARASHITORA DESPISE YOU.

Not all of us are evil.

LOOK AROUND. GAME DEAD, RIVERS BLACK, LAND CHOKED WITH WEED. SKIES BLEEDING, RED AS BLOOD. FOR WHAT?

I don't—

YOUR KIND ARE BLIND. YOU SEE ONLY THE NOW, NEVER THE WILL BE.

Buruu glared, the embers setting his eyes aglow.

BUT SOON YOU WILL. WHEN ALL IS GONE, WHEN THERE ARE SO MANY MONKEY-CHILDREN THAT YOU MURDER FOR A SCRAP OF LAND, A DROP OF CLEAN WATER, THEN YOU WILL SEE.

Yukiko pictured the recruitment posters slapped over the walls of Kigen city, the factories churning out weapons for the war machine, the constant updates about the gaijin conflict streaming across the wireless.

It's already happening, she realized.

AFTER THE LAST FISH IS CAUGHT. AFTER THE LAST RIVER POISONED. THEN YOU WILL KNOW WHAT YOU HAVE DONE. AND BY THEN IT WILL BE TOO LATE.

The arashitora shook his head, began sharpening his claws against the stone floor; iron-hard curves against sparkling granite. Yukiko found it hard to argue with him. Her mind had swum with uneasy questions for years, born in the gaudy opulence of the Shōgun's court, festering in the crowded streets beneath Kigen's poisoned sky. But even if Buruu was right, what could one person do about it? The world was so big. How could one girl make a difference? She could spend her whole life shouting from the rooftops, and nobody would listen. A common man doesn't care about dying birds or changing weather. He cares only for the food on his family's table, the clothes on his children's backs.

Are we any different? These rabbits died to feed our hunger. We killed them because we think our lives are more important than theirs.

She thought of her father, the blood of a hundred beasts on his hands. For all his faults, she knew if Masaru had to pollute a thousand rivers, exterminate a thousand species to keep her safe, he would. Realization struck, a grubby bulb turning on in her head and shining light in a dusty corner she'd always ignored.

She was all he had left.

Everything he had done, he'd done for her. The months away from home. The move to Kigen. The hunt. Clipping Buruu's wings.

"One day you will understand, Yukiko. One day you will see that we must sometimes sacrifice for the sake of something greater."

She frowned, pushing the tears down into the tips of her toes.

He hadn't been talking about the Empire, or his honor.

He was talking about me.

Buruu stared, saying nothing. He stretched out along the floor, lifted his wing to offer shelter, but she remained motionless. With something approaching a shrug, he nestled his head beneath his shoulder, closed his eyes and sighed.

She stayed awake and watched the fire burn.

Humid days followed chilled nights, rain dripping from the howling skies, heat trapped beneath the ceiling of green. Sweat ran off her body, soaking through sodden clothing, turning cotton to damp, stinking weight. The slope was ragged and steep beneath them. Buruu struggled worse than she did in some places, shale and mud sliding away beneath his weight. He would slip and stumble, flapping his near-useless wings to regain balance, and curse the children of men, calling down the wrath of his father on those who had mutilated him.

Yukiko would hang her head and say nothing.

It was near midday when they reached the crest. The granite crags looked as if they'd been beheaded by Hachiman himself; cleft flat by the War God's blade. Yukiko climbed a thick copse of ancient cherry trees to get a better view. Her goggles had been lost somewhere during the crash and, even hidden behind the clouds, the sun's glare made her wince as she poked her head through the canopy. Behind them, she could see the black scar across the mountain where the *Thunder Child* had met its end, and she wondered for a brief moment if it would be worth trying to salvage anything from the wreckage. The thought of having to trek back past the Dark Mother's temple quickly put her musings to rest.

The plateau stretched for miles ahead, clad in rich summer green, spotted with crimson wild azaleas and muted slashes of dandelion gold. The storm clouds threw a shadow over everything. The forest grew thick again further south, and it seemed a long, harsh trek back toward civilization. She hoped the lifeboat and her friends had cleared the mountains intact.

Touching her brow, her lips, she whispered to the skies above.

"Susano-ō, deliver them safely. Lord Izanagi, Great Maker, hold them close."

They shared the last of the smoked rabbit, Yukiko having only a mouthful of meat and a stray mushroom, washed down with wonderfully clear water from a small stream. She suggested they should follow the flow, perhaps stumble across a river where they could fish. Buruu's stomach growled at the mention of the word, and he purred assent.

It was near dark when they found the snare. Buruu caught blood-scent on the air and fell still as stone. She touched her fox tattoo for luck and crept forward in the deepening twilight, rain masking her footfalls on the leaves. There was a fresh hock of raw flesh dangling above a concealed net: an unwary carnivore pulling at the meat would set off the snare and find itself dangling high above the ground. She disarmed the device by cutting the counterweight free and brought the meat back to Buruu. The arashitora crunched it down in three mouthfuls, barely pausing to breathe between each bite.

Maybe the oni set the traps?

SNARES ARE THE WORK OF MEN.

I didn't think anyone dwelt in the Iishi Mountains. Not even the Kitsune clan.

WRONG, OBVIOUSLY.

They might have more traps about. Watch your step.

The arashitora eyed the contraption with contempt as they moved past. The net was made of old vines, twisted and knotted tight; he could shred it as easily as a child tearing a piece of damp rice-paper.

He snorted in derision.
THEY SHOULD WATCH THEIRS.

T hey slept in the trees that night, thirty feet above ground, splayed among
an intertwining cradle of maple branches. Buruu had proved an adept
climber, much to Yukiko's surprise, and the trunk was scarred with deep gouges
from his ascent. The wind moved like a wave across storm-tossed water, long
blades of liriope and forest grass swaying with its song. The rain was a constant
murmur, a heartbeat, and she curled up inside the nook of Buruu's wing and
dreamed of the safety of the womb, amniotic and warm.

A metallic, insectoid rasping startled her from her sleep sometime after
midnight. She sat upright. Buruu closed his wing around her, eyes shining in
the gloom.

QUIET. MONKEY-CHILD APPROACHES.

She squinted through a fan of downy feathers and into the dark. She could
hear unsteady, heavy footsteps, the sound of metal against metal. A rectangular slab of red light was moving toward them, a sawing rasp carrying above the
music of the storm. Yukiko's eyes widened as she made out a humanoid, mantis shape.

An Artificer.

WHAT?

Amaterasu protect us. It's a Guildsman. What is it doing here?

WHAT IS GUILDSMAN?

*They administrate the Lotus Guild. They grow the blood lotus flower all over
Kigen. Collect it for the Shōgun, process it into chi to fuel their machinery. And
they burn people like me.*

DESPOILER PRIEST.

She could feel the anger swell in Buruu's heart; a cold, black hatred.

It must be from the Thunder Child. *It must have missed the lifeboat. Gods
help us . . .*

DO NOT PRAY FOR US. PRAY FOR IT.

Buruu moved, razor-swift, whisper-quiet, stretching out his wings and leaping into the dark. Yukiko shouted at him to wait. The Artificer looked toward
her voice, sharp intake of breath hissing through its bellows as the shadow
swooped down. It turned to run, far too late. Buruu was on top of it, swiping a
fistful of bristling talons across its chest and sending it spinning into a nearby
tree. A flash of bright sparks accompanied the hollow crack of bursting pipes.

The Guildsman tumbled down into a tangle of wild roses, crying out in fright and pain amidst the groan of metal and hiss of acetylene.

Yukiko swung down from the maple branches, running toward the pair, hand outstretched.

"Buruu, stop!" she screamed. "Stop!"

"Yukiko?" The Artificer wheezed, one hand clasped to its ruptured breast-plate.

Buruu's talons hung in the air, poised for the deathblow.

IT KNOWS YOUR NAME.

Yukiko frowned.

It might have overheard it on the ship . . .

"Yukiko-chan, it's me." The Guildsman fumbled with the clasps on its helmet. There was a hiss of suction, compressed air bursting from the cuff around its neck as the throat unfurled like a mechanical flower. It peeled the helmet away from its face and she saw pale skin, close-cropped hair, eyes bright as a knife-edge.

"Kin-san?" she gasped.

YOU KNOW THIS ONE?

Yukiko was aghast, staring at the boy as if he were a ghost.

I met him on the sky-ship. But I never saw him in his suit.

"You're a Guildsman?" Her eyes were narrowed with surprise and be-trayal.

"Hai."

"But Yamagata-san said the *Child*'s Guildsman was called Kioshi . . ."

Kin had his hands up in surrender, back pressed against the tree behind him. Rose petals fell about him like snow. Thick red oozed from his ruptured breastplate, leaking down the brass in a sluggish flow. His eyes never left the arashitora's claws.

"Kioshi was my father. He died two summers ago."

"So?"

"So, it's Guild custom to take the name of an honored parent after they pass." He winced, moving slowly so as not to startle the thunder tiger looming above him. "Can you call off your friend, please? He seems to listen to you."

"You're with them." Yukiko took a step back, drew her knife. "You're one of them."

"I was born one. I never chose it." He looked up into her eyes. "You don't get to choose your family."

"But you burn people, Kin. You burn children . . ."

"No, that's not me," he shook his head. "I'm an Artificer, Yukiko. I fix engines. I build machines. That's all."

"You could have said something. You lied to me."

"I never lied. I just didn't tell you the whole truth."

"You said you were alone."

"I am alone."

"There's hundreds of you. Maybe thousands. You and your 'family' are everywhere."

"Just because you're standing in a crowd doesn't mean you belong there."

Buruu glowered at the boy, eyes alight with bloodlust. One flick of his talons and the monkey-child's life would be spilled over the forest.

WE SHOULD KILL HIM.

Yukiko chewed her lip, stared down at the Artificer.

I'm not so sure . . .

WHY NOT? DESPOILER. USURPER. HIS KIND OVERSEE THE RAPE OF SHIMA.

. . . I'm not sure he's like the others. He's gentle. Kind.

She pushed a picture into his mind, the image of Kin without his suit, standing on the *Child*'s prow and laughing in the clean rain. It was almost impossible to imagine that pale, fragile boy as one of the faceless monsters she so despised. Looking into Kin's eyes, she couldn't imagine him hurting a lotusfly, let alone lighting a fire under some poor child at the Burning Stones.

Give me a minute to talk to him.

YOU DO NOT TELL ME WHAT TO DO.

I'm not telling. I'm asking.

She ran one hand down the sleek feathers at his throat.

Please, Buruu?

The thunder tiger growled, a bass rumble that made the leaves above and the boy below tremble. But he lowered his claws and stepped back, eyes like arrowslits. His tail whipped from side to side, head cocked, shoulders tense.

"You're hurt," Yukiko said, kneeling beside Kin. Concern welled in her eyes as she looked down at the thick red spilling over his clockwork breastplate. The ruptured mechabacus whirred and clicked in a broken beat, spitting counting beads into Kin's lap.

"It's not blood, it's only chi." He reached out as if to touch her, make sure she was real.

"Why didn't you tell me, Kin?"

There was no anger in her voice now, only disappointment. She sheathed the tantō at her back.

Kin's hand dropped to his side.

"I thought you would hate me." He hung his head. "That you wouldn't trust me. Besides, being seen in public without our suits is forbidden. It's a great sin for your kind to see our flesh, for us to risk contamination from the outside world. If anyone found out . . ."

"Then why take it off at all?"

"To feel the wind on my face. To know what it is to be normal. To live like you, if only for a second."

Yukiko frowned, ran one hand across her eyes.

Normal . . .

"So you were on the *Child*'s deck before the crash. What happened?"

"I couldn't risk my flesh being seen. I stayed hidden, hoping the deck would clear, but when the lightning hit, the crew were everywhere. I had to wait until they abandoned ship."

"Did you see what happened to the lifeboat? My father?"

He shook his head.

"By the time I heard the pod detach, I was already below deck getting back into my skin. It was a close thing. I barely made it off before the impact."

"So you risked your life rather than be seen by the crew?" Yukiko raised an eyebrow.

"My chi burners can fly for twenty minutes before they run dry."

"But what if you didn't get into the suit in time? You'd have been incinerated."

He shrugged.

"Being killed in a sky-ship crash would be a mercy compared to my punishment if the Guild found out I'd taken off my skin in public. There are worse things than dying."

"Taken off your skin? What do you mean?"

"That's what we call it." He rapped his knuckles on the atmos-suit. "Our skin. The Purifiers say the flesh underneath is only an illusion. Flawed and powerless."

"That's ridiculous."

"That's Guild doctrine," he shrugged again. "Skin is strong. Flesh is weak." He touched his forehead with two fingers. "The lotus must bloom."

ENOUGH NOISE. STAND ASIDE. I WILL GUT HIM.

Buruu stepped forward, a low growl building in the back of his throat. Yukiko glared at him over her shoulder, refusing to move.

We can't kill him like this.

AH. YOU WISH TO LET HIM STARVE, THEN. SLOW DEATH. FITTING.

No, I think we should bring him with us.

Buruu blinked, cocked his head to one side.

TO EAT?

What? No! I mean we should help him.

. . . NO.

Why not?

DESPOILER. PARASITE. HIS KIND HAVE TORTURED THE SKIES. COUNTLESS BEASTS. COUNTLESS LIVES. ALL FOR GREED.

If you kill him, you're no better than them. You're just another murderer. And if we leave him out here, he's as good as dead.

Kin looked back and forth between them, a frown on his face.

Please, Buruu. Just for a while at least?

Buruu's frustration bubbled over in a snarl, but he backed away, finally turning and bounding up a nearby cedar. He nestled among the shadows and glowered down at the Guildsman, claws twitching on the branches. Waiting. Patient as a cat.

"It's magnificent." Kin shook his head, staring at the arashitora.

"I don't think he likes you." Yukiko smiled, apologetic.

"We didn't believe they existed. We thought that Yoritomo had finally gone mad, that this quest would end in dismal failure and his public humiliation." He shook his head. "Imagine his joy when you bring him such a prize." He looked at her, eyes sparkling. "You will be a goddess. You could ask for anything you wanted, and the Shōgun would grant it."

She stood, arms folded, uncomfortable beneath his stare.

"Can you climb a tree in that suit? It's probably not safe to sleep on the ground."

"I can get into the trees, hai."

"We'll set out at dawn. We're heading south, toward Yama."

"As you wish."

"Well . . . goodnight."

"Goodnight, Yukiko-chan."

She turned and flitted across the undergrowth, climbed up Buruu's tree and nestled beside him. He closed a protective wing around her. They watched as Kin placed his insectoid helmet back on, twisting buttons and levers at his wrist. The coiled pipes at his back roared to life, spitting bright blue lotus flame, propelling him upward into the branches of an ancient maple. He lay down among the boughs, securing himself with steel cable from a capsule on his thigh. Roses smoldered in his wake, blackened by lotus exhaust.

Buruu growled, staring at the ring of wilted, ruined blossoms.

DESPOILER. EVERYTHING THEY TOUCH, THEY DESTROY.

Yukiko stared at the clockwork silhouette. Intermittent blue sparks spat from ruptured metal. The blood-red rectangle glowed, the eye of some hungry ghost, a winter wolf come down starving from the mountain. She shook her head at the fancy, banishing it from her mind.

Still, it was a long while before she slept.

17

TO BE THE WIND

The storm raged all night.

Yukiko only managed a few hours of fitful half-sleep before the groggy morning light pawed its way through the canopy, pushing the sleep from her eyes. She had dreamed again of the green-eyed samurai, adrift on a crimson sea of lotus blossom. He had reached out to touch her lips, sending delighted shivers down her spine. She scowled now at the memory, cursing the stupidity of it all. Stranded in the deep wilderness with an impossible beast and a gods-damned Guildsman, and she was wasting sleep dreaming about boys.

As she peeled her eyes open, Buruu's gut was growling, and her own stomach murmured in sympathy. Kin was already awake, standing beneath the sprawling boughs of his maple tree, keeping a safe distance from the thunder tiger. He was trying to bend the torn plates of his skin closed with a hand-wrench, pounding the ruptured pipes with the hilt, sealing them as best he could. The dull clank of metal hitting metal drowned out the sound of the rain. Yukiko foraged around the damp roots below her tree, finding a few small mushrooms. She scoffed down half before wandering over and offering the rest to Kin.

"No need," he buzzed, gesturing to the cluster of pipes and compartments on his back. "It will be several weeks before I run low on nutrients."

Yukiko blinked.

"The suit feeds me intravenously. A complex string of protein and mineral supplements. It is forbidden for us to eat the food of the hadanashi."

Yukiko narrowed her eyes at the word.

"What do you mean 'hadanashi'?"

"People without skins." He shrugged. "People like you."

"What's wrong with people like me?" Yukiko put her hands on her hips.

"You're polluted by the lotus. The food you eat, the water you drink. We're forbidden to come into direct contact with the bloom or anything touched by it."

"Look around you," Yukiko laughed. "There's no lotus for miles. You can't even smell it up here. Go on, try some mushrooms."

Kin shook his head.

"It is forbidden."

"Well, it's forbidden to take off your suit and let your face be seen by a *hadanashi girl* too." She covered her mouth, feigning shock at the scandal. "But that didn't stop you on the *Thunder Child*."

WHAT ARE YOU TALKING ABOUT?

Shhh.

YOU ARE TALKING TOO MUCH TO HIM. TALK TO ME.

Buruu nudged her with his beak, almost knocking her over.

In a minute!

Yukiko held out the mushrooms to Kin, nodding encouragement. His sigh was soft and distorted. Peering around out of a ridiculous notion that someone might be watching, he worked the clasps on his helmet. The throat unfolded again, interlocking plates unfurling, a pretty, metallic ballet. The metal made a crisp, grinding sound, as if two blades were rubbing against each other. She heard a dry sucking noise as Kin pulled the helmet off and stowed it under his arm, the lengths of segmented cable spilling from its mouth rasping against each other. He took a mushroom from her outstretched palm and popped it between his teeth, chewing tentatively. He made a face, uncertain, but ate another nonetheless.

"They taste . . . odd." He shook his head.

"The Iishi's own recipe," Yukiko smiled. "Pure as can be."

"That's something at least."

"Why is the Guild so afraid of coming into contact with lotus anyway?"

"It clouds thought. Pollutes consciousness. We must remain untainted. Impartial. So we can govern its use correctly." He touched his brow again and shrugged. "Skin is strong, flesh is weak."

"But you're fine with the rest of us sucking it down? Becoming tainted by it?"

"Me?" He blinked at her. "This isn't me we're talking about. I don't make these rules."

"But you follow them."

"When I have to. We all bow to somebody, Yukiko-chan. Or did you travel up here hunting thunder tigers of your own volition?"

WHAT ARE YOU TALKING TO HIM ABOUT?

Shhh. I'll tell you soon.

"So you've never smoked it? Never touched it?"

He was silent for a long moment. When he spoke, his voice was hesitant, soft.

". . . Only once."

He placed the helmet back on, scanning the swaying green, the curtain of rain. His eye was aglow, her reflection crawling on the lens, a distorted scarlet portrait.

"We'd best be off. Your friend looks hungry."

He started clomping through the brush. Yukiko and Buruu followed.

I DO NOT LIKE HIM.

Yukiko smiled to herself.

Are you jealous?

HE TALKS TOO MUCH. SCREECHING HURTS MY EARS. HIS VOICE SOUNDS LIKE RUTTING MONKEYS. AND HE IS THIN. PASTY.

You are jealous!

FOOLISHNESS. I AM ARASHITORA. HE IS HUMAN. WEAK. PUNY.

Well, good, there's nothing to be jealous of. He's just a strange boy. He's harmless.

TELL THAT TO THE SPARROWS WHO FALL CHOKING FROM THE SKIES. THE FISH DROWNING IN BLACK RIVERS. TELL IT TO THE BONES OF MY FOREFATHERS.

Buruu growled, so low and deep that she could feel the vibration in her chest.

HE AND ALL HIS KIND ARE POISON.

Yukiko said nothing, and Buruu fell into a sullen and uneasy silence. The trio stumbled on through the downpour, each lost in their own thoughts. Lightning arced overhead, turning the world to brilliant white for split seconds at a time, clear and pure. But the gloom in its wake seemed all the more black for that moment's clarity, darker than if the light had never been.

The thunder sounded like laughter.

He couldn't take his eyes off her.

Even glazed in red behind the glass of his visor, her flesh illuminated by the occasional sparks bursting from his ruptured skin, she was beautiful. He slowed his pace and fell into step behind her, watched the way she moved through the trees. She was almost soundless, fluid, as if she danced to a tune only she could hear. Untouched by the snags and clawing undergrowth, dodging around the falling leaves; he fancied even the storm was afraid to touch her as she walked between the rain. Just the gentle kiss of the wind on her skin, running its fingers through her hair.

To be the wind . . .

He thought of her beside him on the prow of the *Thunder Child*, her face alight with joy and wonder. The way she had taken his hand, her flesh on his, the first time he could really remember touching another human being. The way she had spoken to him without fear, even after she knew what he was; the way he imagined regular people spoke to each other every day.

He found it hard to watch the girl and his footing at the same time, and so he stumbled, clumsy, crashing through the greenery like a drunken shredder-man. His boot finally twisted among some roots and he fell, crunching face-first onto the ground. The dead leaves beneath him smoked and smoldered in the shower of sparks from his skin. He looked up and she was standing over him, one hand extended, a small smile on her face. He wrapped his fingers in hers, feeling nothing but the press of his gauntlets against his flesh. His hands were shaking. As she struggled to pull him to his feet, she spoke, and her voice sounded like it came from underwater.

He didn't hear a word she said.

The beast would glare at him occasionally over its shoulder, radiating disdain. When they stopped to rest he would catch it watching him, tail extended and curling upward, and he would feel like something small and furry, making a desperate dash across a wide empty field, the shadow of wings blotting out the sun above.

So he kept his distance, ten or so feet behind them, and simply watched her move.

And so he began to notice it.

Small things at first. The way they changed direction simultaneously, the way the rhythms of their pace were mirrored, one step for another. Around noon, they both came to an abrupt halt for no apparent reason and stood, still as statues for two full minutes. Not a sound passed between them. Not a glance. He hovered, uncertain, as heavy seconds ticked by to the beat of the pouring rain, almost ready to open his mouth and speak when the spell was shattered and they began to walk again as if nothing had happened.

Once, she looked at the beast and laughed as if it had said something amusing. But it hadn't breathed a whisper. Not a growl or a purr, let alone something approaching words. Yet she smiled and touched it briefly on the shoulder, and beneath a vague sense of jealousy, an impossible thought took seed in his brain.

Could it be?

By late afternoon, Kin's ruptured breastplate was spitting out fingers of blue current with alarming regularity. Yukiko noticed he was having trouble keeping pace, shuffling and stumbling in the undergrowth. Even the eye in his mantis mask seemed to be dimming.

"What's wrong?" she asked.

He started, as if she'd woken him from a daydream.

"The rain is getting into my skin." The voice of an angry wasp. "Your friend ruptured the internal seals. The moisture is frying my relays."

"Can you fix it?"

Gears sang as he shook his head.

"My acetylene tank is ruptured. My cutter and welder won't work." A metallic sigh. "An Artificer who can't even fix his own skin. Although I suppose I should be thankful. He would have killed me if I were naked." He touched his brow, a now familiar gesture. "Skin is strong, flesh is weak."

An arc of raw current spilled from the rend above his heart, cascading in a waterfall down his breastplate. It skirted the pipes across his ribs in fingers of bright blue-white.

WHAT IS HE SAYING?

His suit is damaged. I think you broke it.

Buruu flexed his wings, fingers of stuttering voltage spilling off the mutilated feathers.

HE SHOULD LOOK ELSEWHERE FOR SYMPATHY.

The mountain stream was a constant babble on their eastward flank, growing gradually wider, white breaks flowing over submerged teeth of smooth river rock. Though drinking did little to ease their gnawing hunger, the water was wonderfully cool compared to the forest's cloying humidity.

The plateau began sloping downward, and as they trekked lower, the air grew thicker, the heat more pronounced despite the constant rain. The stream spilled over a short waterfall, forming a large pool in a natural depression of rock. Yukiko waded out up to her waist, sinking below the surface and washing the sweat and grime from her body. Her skin prickled in the delightful chill, and she ran her fingers along her scalp, hair flowing in the water behind her; black silk on sparkling glass.

Buruu took up watch on an outcropping of rock over the water, tail swishing, muscles coiled tight. Kin wandered the banks, chest occasionally spitting out a plume of bright sparks like a broken strobe light.

Yukiko sank below the water, felt the current wash over her. Beneath the rippling crystal, she thought of her father, of Akihito and Kasumi, hoping they might have reached safety by now. Resurfacing, she blinked up into the rain, the roiling wall of clouds overhead, clashing like great warships on a black sea. Monsoon thunder rolled down the mountain, echoed across ragged cliff faces, small stones tumbling into the depths.

She looked at Buruu, watching from the spur of black granite. Kin had wandered off somewhere into the woods.

The water is good. Come in. Wash off what's left of that oni blood.

She saw him tense, a subtle shift of involuntary muscle, tail stretched like a whip.

DO NOT MOVE.

What's wrong?

BE STILL. STILL AS STONE.

His tension became hers. She licked her lips, eyes roaming the water, bright with new fear. Without a sound, Buruu spread his wings and plunged into the pool beside her, talons outstretched. There was a tremendous splash, a wave that lifted her up and dunked her as she shrieked. She surfaced, spluttering, wiping the blanket of sodden hair from her face. Buruu lunged in the water, pupils dilated, gray silt seething in his wake. She scrambled for the bank, hauling herself out and drawing her tantō.

What is it?

Buruu pranced out of the pool, head high, gallons of chill water spilling off his fur. He shook himself, spreading out the impossible breadth of his wings to keep balance.

PREY.

Yukiko saw two fat trout in his claws, one still struggling feebly, mouth agape as it suffocated in the damp mountain air. The fear melted into relief and she sighed, trying to hold back her smile.

You scared me!

I AM NEAR. NOTHING TO FEAR.

He blinked at her, head cocked to one side, then tossed one of the trout into the air and caught it in his beak, swallowing it whole.

COME. EAT.

He bit the second fish in half, laid out the twitching remainder on the bank's smooth stones. Yukiko crouched beside it, started filleting it with her knife. She heard a faint cry off in the distance, the sound of breaking branches, a metallic bang. Twisting to her feet, she peered into the forest.

"Kin-san?"

A long pause, filled with drumming rain upon broad leaves.

"Help!" A faint reply, drifting from the depths.

She darted into the undergrowth, clutching her knife, Buruu bounding along beside her. Lightning flashed above, gloom deepening as they struggled deeper into the green. Kin called her name and she followed his voice. The wind shrieked through the trees, singing the song of the storm.

"Where are you?"

A faint cry in response, somewhere to the west.

"Keep talking!" she called, desperate.

They crashed on through the scrub, into the tropical heat and spitting rain. It was Buruu who finally found him, coming to a halt at the edge of a deep hole and peering at the boy trapped below. A woven layer of scrub and leaves had been draped over the pit. The Guildsman had blundered right into it, plummeting through the cover and down into darkness.

CLUMSY FOOL.

Kin had fallen among a series of long bamboo spikes, aimed upward like a fistful of knives. His atmos-suit had deflected the worst, but one shoulder plate had been wrenched away, and a shaft had impaled the instruments on his back. His hydraulic crane twitched about as if in a fit. Thick streams of chi flowed from ruptured fuel tanks, down the backs of his legs, pooling bloody in the mud at his feet. Blossoms of blue-white popped and spat from the torn spaulder, and the lens over his eyes was cracked and dark.

"Are you all right?" Yukiko called.

"Fuel line severed, main control down." He shook his head. "Can't fly out. Can't see."

"But are you hurt?"

He was struggling with his helmet, cursing under his breath. It finally folded away from his head like brass origami and he pulled it off, blinking up into the rain. He stabbed at a small button among the rends in his chest, twisting and pawing with thick metal gloves, hissing in frustration.

"Emergency skin release isn't working. These sparks might ignite the chi . . ."

He looked around in desperation, clawing the spike of bamboo that held him transfixed. The circular saw on his wrist was spinning intermittently, spitting sparks. He tried cutting the bamboo, but wasn't flexible enough in the suit to reach it.

"The cable," Yukiko called. "The one in your thigh. Throw it up to us."

Kin fumbled at the compartment on his leg, flipping it open and spooling out lengths of fine metal wire. There was a hook at one end, and Kin swung it in a circular motion at his side before flinging it up toward them. Yukiko lunged but the wire fell short, tumbling back down into the pit. There was another burst of blue sparks from Kin's shoulder, reflections dancing across grubby, bloodstained bronze.

"Try again," she cried over the thunder.

The wire sailed from his hand and plunked into the earthen wall two feet below Yukiko's outstretched fingers. Another arc of orphaned current tumbled down the armored shell, and with a dull *whumph*, the leaking chi ignited in a burst of blue heat. The boy screamed in terror.

"Throw it," Yukiko yelled. "Throw it!"

Sailing skyward, the length of cable fell short of Yukiko's grasp again. She wailed in frustration. Gray, scaled talons stretched out and seized hold of the hook; a clumsy fist, still smeared with trout blood. Buruu growled and snapped the wire up into his beak, heaving with all his strength. Kin was screaming and slapping the flames spreading across his body as two tons of muscle hauled him out of the trap. The thunder roared disapproval. Buruu spread his wings for balance and backed away, cable and claws cutting into moist earth as the boy emerged flaming at the lip of the pit. Yukiko beat the fire with soaking branches, and between the rain and bursts of strange white foam from valves at the suit's collar, the flames soon died.

Kin gasped, his throat and face charred. Yukiko clubbed at the jammed emergency release with the hilt of her tantō until she heard a dull, metallic snap. Clockwork seals grudgingly unwound, the atmos-suit peeled open, heated metal steaming in the rain. Beneath the shell, Kin's body was clad in pale skintight webbing from feet to throat. The strange covering was melted around his shoulder and chest, the skin beneath red and blistered. To Yukiko's horror, she saw black lengths of rubber piping inside the suit, plugged directly into Kin's flesh. Bayonet fixtures made of dark metal were studded along his ribs, the inside of his arms, one embedded just below his collarbone.

"Lord Izanagi save us," she breathed.

Buruu snorted, shook his head.

THEY DESPOIL EVERYTHING. EVEN THEIR OWN BODIES. MADNESS.

Kin blinked up at her, wincing with pain, licking blistered lips.

"It is bad?"

"You're burned." She swallowed. "It's not good. You need medicine."

"Aid kit," he rasped. "Left thigh. Opiates. Antibiotics."

"I have to get you out of this suit. These pipes in you . . . how do I release them?"

"Push in . . . counter-clockwise turn." His face twisted, teeth stark white against charred lips. "Gods, it hurts."

Yukiko fumbled with the compartment on Kin's left thigh, wrenching it open and spilling the contents onto the leaves. The boy began muttering, a repeated mantra, over and over, whispered under his breath: "Skin is strong, flesh is weak. Skin is strong, flesh is weak." Sorting through the jumble of instruments, Yukiko found several hypodermics marked with the kanji for "painless." She stabbed one into Kin's neck, auto-plunger depressing with a faint hiss. The boy sighed and swallowed, closing his eyes, head drifting back into her lap.

LEAVE HIM. HE IS DOOMED.

We can't just abandon him, Buruu.

Yukiko took hold of the cable above Kin's heart, felt it squirm under his skin. The rubber was warm beneath her fingertips, corrugated and vaguely oily. She grimaced, fighting back a wave of sudden nausea. Taking a deep breath, she closed her eyes and pushed, twisting the fixture in until she felt a faint click. With a small popping sound, the cable came loose from the metal stud in Kin's flesh. Broken motors whirred, the cable retracting partway back into the suit's lining. Gulping down great lungfuls of air, she repeated the process until Kin was unplugged, flesh pocked with a dozen of the round bayonet collars, sealed tight against the rain.

She drew her tantō, started to cut away Kin's undersuit. The flames had fused the pale webbing onto his flesh, and she was forced to tear it away, peeling off layers of skin with it. Her lips felt dry despite the rain, her mouth tasting of bile.

Emptying a hypo of antibiotics into his arm, she wrapped his burns in pressure bandages from the aid kit, tiny rolls unwinding into improbably long strips. She poked around the suit's compartments, salvaging medicine and a tube of gray slush that stank like boiled cabbage. Hoping the muck was Kin's "nutrients," she stuffed the items into a netting bag spooled in his belt. An impatient growl rumbled in Buruu's throat.

POINTLESS. BLOOD SICKNESS WILL KILL HIM. LET US GO.

I told you, I'm not leaving him.

THEN WHAT DO YOU PROPOSE? YOU CANNOT CARRY HIM.

We could put him on your back?

NO MAN RIDES ME. NO SHŌGUN. CERTAINLY NO DESPOILER.

Yukiko felt tears of frustration welling in her eyes but refused to let them flow. Blinking hard, she scanned the forest around them, gaze finally coming to rest on the pit trap beside her. It was the work of many men, cut deep into the earth and cleverly concealed. From the look of the walls, the age of the bamboo spikes and bloodstains, she'd guess it had been here for a long time, reset with regularity.

This is the second trap we've found in as many days. There are people living up here.

SO?

So, people who set snares have to come back and check them. And we need people to help us with Kin. I can't take care of him by myself.

Buruu paused, and she felt faint admiration swell inside him. He shook himself, rain spraying from his flanks, anticipation coursing through his veins.

HUNT THE HUNTERS.

Yukiko smiled, lightning reflected in her eyes.

Exactly.

18

TREETOP SHADOWS

The day drowned slowly beneath the constant deluge. Night fell like a hammer, echoes of thunder rolling across the crags as the tempest raged overhead. Yukiko was huddled under an outcropping of mossy stone, eyes on the pit trap, wondering how much longer the storm could last. As if in answer, the downpour increased in intensity, droplets as fat as her thumb soaking the world through to the bone. Cold and drenched and thoroughly miserable, she cupped her palms together and watched the rain pool in her hands. The water was like glass; clean and crystalline. No toxins, no corrosives, no black stain. It was perfect.

Still, it would be nice if it was a little less wet.

Buruu prowled from the darkness, quiet as a mouse under the monsoon's roar.

At least nobody can hear you in all this.

MIGHTY STORM.

He turned his eyes to the clouds, wings twitching at the sound of thunder.

Do you miss it? Being up there?

. . . MORE THAN ANYTHING.

Regret and guilt swelled inside her as she looked at his severed feathers, rain dripping from the ugly squared edges. She could still recall the sound of the blade shearing them away, the sight of their remnants scattered across polished wood. His tail swept from side to side as he watched the clouds above, chest heaving in a long, deep sigh.

I'm sorry, Buruu.

His growl ended almost before it had begun.

NOT YOUR HAND. NOT YOUR FAULT.

Father said you would moult your feathers. Like a bird. Is that true?

TWICE YEARLY. SUMMER AND WINTER.

You'll be back up there soon.

THERE IS NO SOON. ONLY NOW.

Well, I suppose for now you're stuck down here with me.

He blinked at her. She smiled, pushed clumsy affection into his mind. A feeling of warmth and gratitude, the sensation of her putting her arms around his neck and holding tight. She felt something inside him shift. Soften.

I'm glad you're here, Buruu. I'm really glad you're with me.

THERE ARE WORSE FATES.

Faint amusement glittered in his eyes.

MONKEY-CHILD.

She laughed out loud, chuckles trailing off into a yawn that she had to smother with both hands. She stretched and blinked, shaking herself to stay awake.

YOU ARE TIRED.

Yukiko shrugged, turned her eyes back to the pit trap.

I'm all right. They're bound to come back and check it soon.

GO REST. I WILL WATCH.

No, I'll stay with you.

IF THEY COME, I WILL CALL. REST. TEND THE BOY'S WOUNDS. UNLESS YOU WISH HIM DEAD NOW ALSO.

Yukiko made a face but assented, crawling from her foxhole. She ran one hand across his flank in gratitude and thought she heard the beginnings of a purr, deep in his chest. He stalked into the forest, lightning casting stark shadows across the undulating patterns of snow and jet on his fur.

She stole back to the small cave they'd discovered above the fishing pool. The floor was covered in a blanket of dry leaves and branches driven inside by the wind. She'd piled some dead scrub in a corner, hoping it would be dry enough to start a fire later. Kin leaned against the far wall, twitching and murmuring in his sleep, bandages soaking through with fluid. She felt his brow for fever and emptied another hypo of antibiotics into his arm, worried the supply would soon run out.

After nearly an hour of painstaking work and the rasp of flint across the blade of her tantō, she'd managed to cultivate a small spark into a blaze. Buruu had caught two more mountain trout and laid them out for her at the cave mouth. Once cooked, they were delicious; like nothing she'd ever tasted in Kigen. No bitter lotus tang, no hint of corruption. Pure and sweet, juice glistening on her fingers and lips. She sighed, looking out to the dark, wondering where her father was.

Kin woke with a start behind her, sucking in a lungful of air over clenched teeth. He glanced around wildly for a few seconds, fear in his eyes. She turned to look at him, pale and drawn in the fire's feeble light.

"How do you feel, Kin-san?"

His eyes fell on her as she spoke. He blinked, finding focus, breath coming a little slower.

"Thirsty." He winced, sat up straighter. "Sore."

She had salvaged a metal cylinder from the ruined atmos-suit and filled it with river water, now offering it to the boy. Kin licked at his burned lips and gulped it down without stopping, sighing after the last mouthful.

"Where is the rest of my skin?" His gaze was unsteady.

"I hid it. Behind some boulders upstream."

"There's a beacon inside." He winced again, hands hovering but not daring to touch the burns around his face. "Activated when the s-skin suffers catastrophic damage. Guild will b-be looking for me."

"We'll worry about them later. Right now we need to get you stable. Do you want more opiates for the burn? There's a little left."

"No," he shook his head. "I d-don't want to sleep any more."

He touched the bandages at his chest and throat, hissed in pain. His forehead gleamed with a sheen of sweat, but he was shivering. Yukiko could see the distress in his eyes.

"Why don't you want to sleep?" she asked.

"B-bad dreams."

"About what?"

He shook his head again, said nothing.

"You're in pain, Kin-san. You need to rest."

He swallowed, still licking at his blistered lips. The fire gleamed in his eyes. "Will you wake me up? If it l-looks like I'm dreaming?"

"I don't understand."

"You don't n-need to."

"What are you so afraid of?"

". . . It's forbidden to speak of it."

"Oh, gods!" Her voice rose, exasperation getting the better of her. "You know, you should take a look around, Kin-san. A hundred miles from nowhere, burned half to death, and you can't even bring yourself to trust the person who's keeping you alive."

He stared at her for a long, silent moment. The fire spat and crackled, and the wind outside was the howl of a hungry wolf. His sigh came from the depths of his chest.

"On the eve of our thirteenth year, all Guildsmen are forced to smoke l-lotus. Smoke so much of it that we have visions. Nightmares. They c-call it 'the Awakening'." He ran his hand over his eyes. "And every night after that, we dream about what we saw. The What Will Be."

"The What Will Be?"

"Hai."

"You mean the future?" A raised eyebrow.

"H-hai."

". . . What did you see?"

A haunted look came over the boy's face, and he stared at the crackling flames. His voice was a whisper.

"I c-cannot speak of it."

"Let me guess." She rolled her eyes. "It's forbidden."

"No." He looked back up at her, shook his head. "It's horrible."

Yukiko stared at him in the flickering light, looking for a lie in those knife-bright eyes and finding only pain and fear. Finally, she nodded, lifted the syringe. "If I see you dreaming, I'll wake you up."

". . . All right then. Thank you, Yukiko-chan."

She plunged the needle into his flesh, and he stared as if fascinated. Numbness crept over his face like a shadow at sunset, slowly dulling his eyes. He leaned his head back against the cave wall, watching her from beneath drooping eyelids.

"I know what you are," he breathed, lips numb.

She blinked, pushed the damp hair from her face.

"What?"

"I see you with him." Kin nodded to the cave entrance, lashes fluttering. "The arashitora. The way you look at each other. The way you speak without speaking."

Yukiko felt a slippery knot of dread in her stomach, and her heart began pounding against her ribs. Her mouth was dry as the ashes at the feet of the Burning Stones. Her tantō was a cold weight pressed into the small of her back.

"I know what you are." Kin frowned up at her, struggling to see through the velvet-soft chemical haze. "But it's all right. I won't tell them. N-never tell anyone. I won't let them hurt you. I promise, Yukiko."

She met his stare, watched the fire dance across his dilating pupils. Long moments passed, seconds slipping by like hours as her heartbeat calmed, the fear in her stomach slowly dissolved. Shadows flickered on the wall behind him, in the hollows under his eyes.

He smiled at her. She believed him.

"You're so beautiful," he said.

She felt a blush in her cheeks, turning to busy herself among the crackling flames with the last trout fillet.

It's the drugs talking, she told herself. *He doesn't know what he's saying.*

"A Guildsman could never marry a hadanashi girl." He frowned, trying to focus as the opiate swell rose up past his eyelids. "When you return the arashi-tora and the Shōgun asks your desire . . . perhaps you could ask him to set me free?"

Yukiko turned back to him, a dark crease between her brows.

"It would be good." His eyes fluttered closed as he whispered. "To be free . . ."

She watched him for a long moment, pity in her stare.

"Good"? It would be impossible.

Nobody ever left the Guild, everyone knew that. Its members were born into the chapterhouses and died there. Nobody escaped except into the judgment of Enma-ō, the endless cycle of atonement and rebirth. And even if he did get out, how could Kin possibly hope to get by in the real world? He'd lived all his days in that metal suit, never known anything but a Guildsman's life. What on earth would he do with himself?

Leave the Guild? The only way to do that was to leave this world.

"Now I know it's the drugs talking," she muttered.

Buruu's voice shook her from dreams of the green-eyed boy, reverberating like the sound of distant thunder. Unsure whether she'd imagined it, she sat up slowly beside the dying embers, brow creased with concentration.

Buruu?

THEY ARE HERE. MEN. TWO.

I'm on my way.

She checked her tantō and dashed from the cave, leaping lightly down the slope and into the seething tangle of green. The wind was a cutting chill after the cave's warmth, rain dashing into her eyes and pattering upon her skin. She touched the fox tattoo on her arm and crouched low, flitting from shadow to shadow without a sound, feeling for Buruu in the gloom. She could sense him off to the left, curled high in a vast cedar close to the pit, watching the two figures gathered beside it.

Yukiko could see them through his eyes: one around her age, long hair and sharp, angular features, the other older, broader, topknot peppered with gray. They were both dressed in dark gray cloth, swathed with stripes of deep green, like the patterns on the thunder tiger's haunches. Each was armed with a ku-sarigama—a sickle with a length of long, weighted chain attached to the handle. The older one also carried a katana in a battered scabbard on his back.

Possession of a blade that length would be enough to see you executed in any metropolis in Shima. These men care nothing for the Shōgun's rule. They are outlaws.

MY FONDNESS INCREASES. PERHAPS I WILL NOT GUT THEM.

We need to talk to them. Let me speak.

AND IF THEY DO NOT LISTEN?

Well, then you just swoop in and save me.

Yukiko could sense his amusement echoing in the Kenning, and smiled into his mind in return. The link between them was growing more complex; transference of subtle emotional content, interpretation of tone and pitch as easy now as simple colors or shapes. But more than that, the arashitora seemed to be growing in intellect—grasping concepts such as humor, even sarcasm, that just a few days ago would have been foreign to him. She realized that she'd never felt the voice of a beast in her dreams before, even the ones she'd known for years. She wondered if it was because he was yōkai, and where their growing bond might lead. But for now, she pushed the thought from her mind, focusing instead on the men. They were armed like bandits, and had covered the mountainside with traps. Obviously, they weren't fond of strangers.

She crept up behind them, silent as a ghost, fingers wrapped around her knife hilt. Close enough to hear their voices, crouching beneath the fronds of an elderly frangipani, a shadow against deeper black. A long wooden pole lay beside the pit, two animal corpses tied to it, their flanks pierced with bloody holes. Yukiko thought they might be deer.

"It was big," the younger one was saying. "But look at these tracks. Not oni."

"Is that blood?" The older one crouched beside the pit, pointing to the bamboo spikes.

"Too dark to tell. Want me to climb down?"

"Who are you?" Yukiko stepped out from cover. She was tense as a drawn bowstring, ready to bolt at the first sign of hostility.

The men raised their weapons and turned toward her voice, peering into the darkness.

"Who goes there?" the older one demanded.

"I asked you first, old man." Yukiko kept her voice steady, ignored the pounding of her heart. "Your pit trap nearly killed me. You might at least give me the courtesy of your name."

The pair squinted into the gloom, then stared at each other, incredulous.

"A girl?" the younger one laughed.

"What in the name of the Nine Hells are you doing out here?" The older man stepped forward, kusarigama raised, chain looped in his other hand.

"That's close enough." Yukiko's fist tightened about her tantō. "I'm warning you."

"A lone girl in the wilderness isn't exactly in a position to be warning anyone, young miss."

"But I am not alone." She flashed them a dangerous sort of smile.

The arashitora rose from his nook in the cedar and swooped down into the clearing, wings spread wide, infant lightning crawling over sheared feathertips. He landed among the undergrowth with a bellow; a screeching roar that split the air and sent a flurry of petals shivering from their blossoms.

"Izanagi's balls," hissed the young man, cowering low.

"Arashitora," whispered the elder, slack-jawed, wide-eyed.

"This is my friend, Buruu." Yukiko crossed her arms, stood a little taller. "I will have the honor of your names now, please."

"Isao," muttered the young man.

"Kaiji," said the other, eyes still glued to the beast. He pinched himself on the arm and shook his head, as if to reassure himself that he was still awake.

"What are you doing up here?" Yukiko looked back and forth between them. "Why have you set these snares?"

"We hunt game, young mistress," said Kaiji, blinking rapidly. "To feed the village."

"What village?"

"We live nearby," said Isao. "We are simple folk."

LIARS. BE WARY.

Yukiko glanced at the katana on the old man's back.

I know, but . . .

She stopped, frowned at the arashitora.

Wait—you can understand what they're saying?

. . . NOT WORDS. IMAGES. PATTERNS.

How can that be?

DO NOT KNOW. BUT I BEGIN TO SEE THE SOUNDS.

Buruu blinked in the darkness, pupils as wide and deep as the night sky.

THROUGH YOU.

Kaiji watched the pair stare at each other, cleared his throat to break what seemed an uncomfortable silence.

"The village is not far, young mistress. There is shelter there. Food also."

The mention of shelter hushed all questions about Buruu's revelation, pulled her back into the gloom and forest's chill. She shivered in the rain, remembering Kin lying alone and burned on the floor of the cave.

"Do you have healers in your village? Medicine?"

"Are you injured?" The old man looked her up and down.

"No, but my friend is." Yukiko nodded toward the rock pool. "We were in the sky-ship that crashed not far from here. He was burned."

"We saw the ship go down." Isao nodded.

"Did you see the life raft?" Yukiko took a step forward, anxiety etched plainly on her face. "What happened to it?"

"It got away safely." The boy pointed. "Over the southern range."

Yukiko felt dizzy with relief. "Thank the gods."

"We can help you." Kaiji was watching Buruu warily. "You and your friends."

"Please don't lie to me, old man." Yukiko shook her head in warning. Buruu growled and moved forward, feathered hackles rising down his spine. She could feel the menace vibrating in her chest.

"I swear on the souls of my ancestors." Kaiji thumped his kusarigama across his heart. "If you are friend to the yōkai, young mistress, you are friend to us."

THEIR FEET ARE SURE ON UNEVEN GROUND. THE GRIP ON THEIR WEAPONS IS STRONG. THESE ARE WARRIORS, NOT PEASANTS.

I know. But what choice do we have?

KILL THEM. LEAVE THEM IN THEIR PIT.

A mental shrug, as if he were stating the obvious.

Without medicine, Kin will die in that cave.

GOOD.

I can't let that happen, Buruu. I couldn't forgive myself. Will you come with me?

The voice of the wind was mournful, lonely as a lost child. The arashitora stared for a long moment, the girl reflected in the liquid amber of his eyes.

Please?

A slow, heavy nod.

. . . I WILL COME WITH YOU.

She smiled into his mind again, gratitude and affection in equal measure.

"All right, Kaiji-san," Yukiko nodded to the older man. "Follow me."

She moved off into the darkness. The men followed her silently, glancing over their shoulders at the arashitora. With a faint growl bubbling in his throat, Buruu scowled and stalked after them into the black.

There it is," said Kaiji, pointing down into the valley.

Yukiko squinted, seeing only the green of the forest canopy, rippling in the wind.

"Where?" she asked.

They had built a makeshift stretcher for Kin, Isao lashing it to his waist and dragging it behind him. The young man had struggled with Kin's weight and the deer carcasses, but didn't whisper a word of protest. Yukiko walked behind them, Buruu beside her, watching Kin with concern. His fever was getting worse, and he seemed to be delirious, muttering nonsense in his sleep. She had tried to wake him several times, but he had barely opened his eyes before sinking back down into unconsciousness.

There were no paths to follow, and burdened as they were, the trek seemed to take hours. The mud was slippery beneath her feet, caked on her ruined sandals. They finally stopped on a small ridge overlooking a crescent-shaped valley, nestled between two spines of jagged, black stone. The rain had sputtered and finally stopped, a blessed, merciful silence descending to kiss each of her numb ears and echo inside her head. Heavy black cloud still covered the sky, but a stubborn shaft of feeble moonlight was stabbing through the thick curtain, illuminating the valley below. Yukiko scanned the greenery but could find no trace of a village.

"I don't see it," she whispered.

The men laughed and proceeded down a rocky slope along a rough, almost invisible track. Buruu found the going so difficult that he was forced to glide down to the valley floor on his maimed wings. He waited below, eyes upturned, fretting as he paced back and forth.

"I have never seen the like of him," Kaiji shook his head. "We thought them extinct."

Yukiko shrugged.

"I could have said the same thing about oni until a few days ago."

"You have seen oni? Where?"

"North. Above this ridge. There was a temple, I think. Dedicated to Lady Izanami, the Dark Mother. We killed five of them altogether."

"Aiya," breathed Kaiji. "So many . . ."

"What happened to its wings?" Isao interrupted. "Why can't it fly?"

Yukiko noted the sudden change in topic. Wary of revealing too much to the strangers, she feigned indifference to the boy's question.

"Our ship was commissioned by the Shōgun. The court Hunt Master was aboard with us, commanded to catch the beast. When it became enraged, he clipped its wings to break its spirit."

"Masaru, the Black Fox?" asked Kaiji.

Yukiko nodded slowly.

"Desecration." The man shook his head. "No wonder Raijin tore you from the skies. To treat his offspring so . . ."

Isao muttered under his breath, hands curled into fists. Buruu rejoined them at the bottom of the rocky slope. The arashitora stared at the men with open suspicion, purring as Yukiko ran a reassuring hand over the back of his neck. They made their way further into the forest, Yukiko stumbling in her weariness, eyelids heavy as the world became a dark, whispering haze.

Buruu's thoughts snapped her from her reverie.

MORE MEN. MANY. I SMELL STEEL.

Be ready for anything.

Shapes dropped from the trees in front and behind, clad in gray and green that tricked the eyes, melting into the forest around them. They were masked, faces hidden by thick sashes and hoods, only their eyes exposed. Split-toed tabi socks made barely a whisper across the dead leaves. Each was armed; bo staves, short tonfa clubs, kusarigama sickles, all tense and ready. Buruu dug his claws into the earth, growl building and bubbling out of his throat.

"Hold, Kaori." Kaiji held up his hand. "These ones have spilled oni blood."

A short figure swathed head-to-foot in gray-green stepped from the shadows, an exquisitely crafted wakizashi held poised to strike. The sword's blade was perhaps two feet long, curved and single-edged, dark ripples flowing in the steel. The scabbard at the figure's waist was black lacquer, golden cranes taking flight down its length. Yukiko couldn't see the maker's mark, but had no doubt it was the work of a master artisan.

"Do I walk sleeping, Kaiji-san?" The figure's voice was female, low and smoky. "Or do you walk with an arashitora beside you?"

"No dream," Kaiji shook his head. "A miracle, perhaps. The arashitora is called Buruu. The girl is Yukiko. They are comrades in arms, slayers of five oni."

Yukiko felt a multitude of eyes on her, instinctively stepping closer to Buruu's side. He unfurled a wing, curled it about her. The handle of her tantō was cool in her grip, slippery with sweat. She could sense him in her mind, reaching out across the Kenning and absorbing the conversation. It was true that he couldn't really understand their words. He was discovering meaning through her; a filter processing the tumbling jabber of monkey noises into colors and impressions and images he could comprehend. His muscles were tense, and that tension flowed back into her; hands curled into fists, the sharp tang of adrenaline on the back of her tongue.

The woman stepped closer, and Yukiko tried to stifle a gasp as she took off her mask. She was in her early twenties, possessed of the kind of beauty that inspired poets; the kind that a man might happily murder his own brother to taste for a single heartbeat. Porcelain skin, high cheekbones, full lips, waves of blue-black velvet falling past her chin, glinting with a moonlight sheen. Her eyes were the color of water reflected across polished steel. But the scar ruined it all. Angry red, bone deep, it ran in a diagonal line from her forehead, cutting down across her nose to a jagged conclusion at her chin.

Knife work.

"Yukiko-chan." The woman covered her fist with her palm and bowed slightly. She tossed her head, her long diagonal fringe spilling down to cover the worst of the scar.

"Kaori-chan." Yukiko repeated the bow and covered fist.

"You may be a strange sight, but any oni-slayer is welcome here." Kaori's eyes flickered to the arashitora, back to Yukiko. "My father will want to meet you. Have no fear. There is no evil here but what you bring with you."

Yukiko bowed again, and she and Buruu allowed themselves to be led further into the forest gloom. She could feel the men and women around her: all fluid motion, drifting soundless through the clawing green while she stumbled along on exhausted, clumsy feet, making a small ruckus in comparison. Though the rain had stopped, the drip and patter of water upon the leaves was a constant off-tempo beat all around them. She could smell moist earth beneath her, and above that, the faint, sugar-sweet perfume of wisteria blooms. Breathing deep, she kept one hand on Buruu, running her fingers through the feathers at the join between shoulder and neck. She could sense him trying not to purr, to stay on edge amidst these strangers and their dark, hooded eyes.

After what seemed like an age, Kaori signaled a stop with a closed fist.

"We are here."

Glancing about, Yukiko caught sight of a cleverly concealed ladder cut into the bark of one of the ancient maples beside her. Buruu looked up, and even staring through eyes as keen as his, she could barely make out a series of nets, woven through with greenery and strips of cloth; camouflage for the rope walkways linking the canopy high above. She could see the vague silhouettes of houses squatting in the branches of the timeworn trees. Carefully obfuscated by more netting and leaves and great tangles of wisteria, but houses nonetheless; a large village stretching out through the boughs, peopled with countless folk, all staring down with curious, bright eyes. She blinked, scanning the canopy, mouth open in wonder.

SIMPLE PEASANTS, EH?

They are far from that.

WHY DO THEY DWELL HERE IN THE DEEP WILDS? YOUR KIND FEAR SUCH PLACES.

These are not my kind, Buruu.

She placed her hand on the hilt of her knife, trying to keep her face impassive.

These are not my kind at all.

19

AVALANCHES AND BUTTERFLIES

His skin was the leather of old boots, brown and weathered, cracking at the edges. Cropped hair, shaved so close to his skull that it seemed a shadow on his skin, old scars crossing his scalp and puckering the flesh above one narrowed eye. An ancient pair of goggles hung about his throat; custom Shigisens that in their day would have cost a small fortune. His irises were the same color as his daughter's; steel-gray, shot through with a thousand splinters of cobalt. He knelt in front of a low table set with a saké bottle and simple cups, salt-and-pepper mustache reaching almost to the ground.

"This is my father," Kaori had said softly. "Daichi."

Yukiko blinked, a flickering of remembrance in her mind.

I think . . .

She stared hard, a small frown darkening her brow.

I think I know this man.

They sat in a rectangular room, walls of raw wood, caulked with tar. Daichi's house crouched atop one of the larger trees, a shadow among the swaying foliage, nestled between a fork in the branches. One bough reached up through the floorboards and disappeared into the roof, letting in a faint draft and sweet wisteria perfume. Yukiko was reminded of her family's old hut in the bamboo forest.

She had waited until the others ascended before climbing the ladder. Buruu had climbed beside her, bleeding gouges left in his wake, talons and claws sticky with sap. Unable to fit through the door to Daichi's dwelling, the arashi-tora crouched on a branch outside, motionless save for the rhythmic sweep of his tail. His tension was palpable, radiant, eyes glittering like blades. Yukiko

152

could feel his pulse, the rhythm of his breathing. Without even being conscious of it, her own heart and lungs fell into pace with his.

She knelt across from the old man, pressed her forehead to the floorboards. "Daichi-sama."

"Yukiko-chan." The old man nodded, covered his fist with his palm. "Friend to arashitora. You honor this humble house with your presence."

Kaori and the rest of her group knelt in a semi-circle around Daichi, respectfully silent. Yukiko glanced around her: rough furniture, fire pit in the center of the room, crude metal chimney stabbing up through the ceiling. Three closed doors, leading off into different rooms. An old-fashioned katana lay sheathed in a groove on the wall at Daichi's back, its scabbard exquisitely crafted: black lacquer, golden cranes on the wing. There was another groove beneath it, and Yukiko had no doubt that Kaori's wakizashi had once sat there, part of the same daishō pair. Only the noble-born were permitted to carry the daishō, the proud symbol of their status among the samurai caste.

He must be ronin.

WHAT IS RONIN?

An ex-samurai. A noble-born warrior without a Lord.

WHY DOES LORD MATTER?

All samurai follow the Code of Bushido. It's like a religion and a philosophy and a set of laws all mixed together. Loyalty and sacrifice and humility—they live their entire lives by it. But above all, the code demands servitude. Allegiance to a master. If your master dies, or you break your oath, you become ronin. It is a source of shame. A great loss of face.

HE IS OATH-BREAKER, THEN? LIAR?

Yukiko lifted her head from the floor to look for the man's irezumi, the symbol of his clan inked on his flesh. But his arms were covered with the sleeves of his uwagi, gray cloth running down to his wrists, frayed at the cuffs. He followed her eyeline, something like amusement twinkling in that steel-gray.

"Where are you from, Yukiko-chan?"

"Kigen, Daichi-sama."

"And you served on the sky-ship that crashed into Kuromeru Peak?"

"Hai," she nodded, keeping her eyes low.

"Mrmn," he grunted, running one hand through his mustache. There was something reptilian about the man; something ancient and slow, all muscles and teeth and endless, cold-blooded patience. "You were not aboard the life boat. How did you survive the crash?"

"I set Buruu free from his cage. When he leaped over the railing, I jumped on his back."

"You flew on an arashitora?"

A faint murmur rippled among the assembled figures. Kaori narrowed her eyes.

"Hai," Yukiko nodded.

"Aiya." Daichi shook his head. "One hundred summers could come and go, and we would never hear another tale like that."

"It was either that or die," Yukiko shrugged.

"And you killed four oni?"

"Five, Daichi-sama," said Kaiji. "The northern slopes. Near Black Temple."

"Mrmn," he nodded. "Have you heard of the Stormdancers, Yukiko-chan?"

She looked up from the floorboards and met Daichi's stare. He was older than her father but unmarked by lotus smoke, gaze still sharp, skin clean. His body was hard, lean, calloused fingers and old scars. The katana on the wall behind him was within easy reach of his hand.

"Stories." Yukiko shook her head. "From childhood. Kitsune no Akira and the Dragon of Forgetting. Kazuhiko the Red and the hundred ronin. Widow's Bridge, and the doomed charge of Tora Takehiko into Devil Gate."

"One of my favorites," Daichi smiled.

"They're just stories."

"Some might say," he nodded. "Tales of halcyon days can serve to promote nationalist pride. The Communications Ministry invokes past glories to inspire new ones among the working class, to wring more sweat from the karōshimen's backs. To convince more young men to take up arms and spill their heart's blood beneath the Shōgun's flag in a war they know nothing about. The Stormdancers have become pulp heroes, serialized on the Guild wireless, their stories drained of all meaning and truth. It is easy to see why you'd think them nothing more than propaganda. Such is the shape of the world in which we live."

Daichi nodded toward the doorway, in the direction of Buruu.

"Your . . . friend, you call him? If there were any justice, our kind would have never seen his kind again. But here he is, a miracle in flesh, proof that there is truth even in their lies. And what do they do when they learn one of these creatures still exists?" The old man sighed. "Hunt him down and cripple him like some wretched sparrow in the palace gardens."

"The Shōgun commanded it."

"The Shōgun." Daichi chuckled, amusement spreading like an infection among his cohort. "The Shōgun commands only that which we allow him to."

"Everyone on these islands owes Yoritomo-no-miya their allegiance."

Steel-gray eyes glittered.

"Nobody in this room owes Yoritomo a thing, Yukiko-chan."

"So you are ronin, then?"

"Hai, I am ronin." Daichi's smile faded. "Once I served the Shōgun's house. I wore the ō-yoroi and the golden jin-haori of the Kazumitsu Elite guard. I know Masaru, the Black Fox, who mutilated your friend's wings. I know Yoritomo, who sits as Shōgun of the Four Thrones and would be my Lord."

Daichi's hand moved slowly, rolling up the sleeves of his uwagi. Where there should have been irezumi, there was only a blanket of patchwork scars, stretching from his elbows to his shoulders. The skin was rough and uneven, pale in comparison to the rich tan on his face.

"You burned off your tattoos?" Yukiko frowned.

"I have no zaibatsu. I will suffer no Lord such as Yoritomo. None of us here carries the symbols of slavery any longer. No clan save our own. No masters save ourselves."

Conscious of the irezumi running down her left arm, Yukiko thanked Kitsune that her uwagi's sleeves were long enough to cover it. Daichi smiled, as if he knew her thoughts.

"Symbols of slavery?" Yukiko tilted her head.

"When a man's fate is not his own, when he may die at the behest of a man born luckier or wealthier, when he sweats all his life for scraps from another's table, then he is in peril." Daichi's eyes glittered in the half light. "But when he accepts it in his heart, when he ceases to struggle against that fundamental injustice, then he is a slave."

Yukiko's face burned. She was no slave. Her friends, her family, they were all freemen. Who did this man think he was?

"Most men would rather be a slave than an oath-breaker."

"An oath to a liar is no oath at all," Daichi growled. "Yoritomo broke his oath to me."

"How?"

"He demanded what was not his to take." Daichi's eyes flickered to his daughter, back to Yukiko. "And when it was denied him, he decided that no other man should possess it either. Nor should they ever want to."

Yukiko looked at the scar running down Kaori's face, beauty forever spoiled, feeling sick to her stomach. She nodded. Not in understanding, because nobody who claimed to be human could possibly understand something like that. But she nodded. She *knew*.

MADNESS.

"So it has always been with the line of Kazumitsu." Kaori's voice shook with remembered anger. "What they see they want, and what they cannot possess, they destroy. Look at your friend outside. If not for your Shōgun, he would be free, soaring over the desolation that Yoritomo names 'Empire'." She shook her head. "I wonder why he ever came here."

"Perhaps he was brought here," Daichi answered, his eyes never leaving Yukiko's. "Perhaps you were too."

Yukiko stood on a broad footbridge, watching maple leaves spiral toward the ground. She held a wisteria bloom in her hand, fragile as spun sugar, petals shaped like an upturned bowl, white as pure snow. A hush had fallen over the world, a pre-dawn silence that held the night in a fragile embrace, waiting to break in the sunrise with the first birdsong. The horizon was aglow with the promise of impending daylight.

Though she'd suppressed her yawns as long as she was able, Daichi had realized Yukiko was tired. He told her that Kin was being cared for, that she should rest, but she knew it was only a matter of time before someone discovered the bayonet fixtures in his flesh. Yukiko had no idea how she was going to explain them.

She and Buruu were taken to an empty dwelling high in the branches of an old oak. The tree was overgrown with wisteria vines, twisting up from the forest floor in thick, fragrant growths. Buruu had stretched out on a branch shaped like a cupped palm as she began pacing across the footbridge, too restless to sleep.

She let go of the flower, watched it spiral into the drop below her feet. Staring down through the camouflage nets, she blinked in wonder at it all: the squat houses covered in creepers and wrapped in twisted branches, the bridges, dwellings and storerooms blending in seamlessly with the greenery around them, mere shadows in the canopy to anyone looking up from below. A hundred men would have to slave for a decade to build a place like this. The will it must have taken to craft it out of nothing made her marvel.

These people are fanatics.

Buruu opened one eye, blinked sleepily.

YOU SHOULD REST.

I don't trust them. What are they doing here?

LIVING FREE. AWAY FROM YOUR SCABS AND DESPOILER LORD. ADMIRABLE.

There is hatred in their eyes. Darkness. I can feel it. They are not just men who seek freedom from the Shōgun's rule. There is more to it than that.

SLEEP. I WILL WATCH IF YOU FEAR.

Yukiko heard soft footsteps. She turned and saw Kaori approaching across the bridge, surefooted, hair rippling in dark, velvet waves. The diagonal fringe hung over her face, obscuring much of the scar, one eye visible between twin curtains of black. She stopped beside Yukiko, leaned against the railing and stared out into the whispering gloom.

"You should sleep." Kaori's voice was as soft as smoke. "You look exhausted."

"Soon."

"Rumors are already spreading among the people here." Kaori glanced at her sidelong. "The girl who rides the thunder tiger. Slayer of half a dozen oni. I fear you will be inundated with attention tomorrow. You should rest while you can."

"It wasn't half a dozen. It was only five."

MUST HAVE BEEN DIFFICULT. LITTLE THING LIKE YOU ENDING FIVE PIT DEMONS ALL ALONE.

Yukiko made a face.

"Buruu did most of the work, anyway."

SHOULD THINK SO . . .

"The oni will be angered," Kaori sighed. "The loss of so many of their number . . ."

Yukiko stayed silent, staring off into the dark. There was something wrong with all of this; the simple folk with warriors' weapons, the burned tattoos. Suspicion gnawed at her insides, the feeling of being constantly watched prickling the back of her neck.

"Your friend is running a fever." Kaori stood on tiptoe and peered over the railing, waves of raven hair falling about her face. "We have given him antibiotics, something to help ease the pain."

"And where did you get the medicine?"

Ever so slightly, Kaori narrowed her eyes. "What do you mean?"

"Well, do you trade for it? You seem intent on keeping this place secret. But unless you're growing the antibiotics yourselves, I'm guessing someone knows you're out here."

Kaori turned toward her, shoulders square. Her face had hardened; a sudden shift to smooth stone. She glared behind her fringe.

"You ask a lot of questions, Yukiko-chan. They can be dangerous things so far from home."

Buruu growled; a low rumble full of menace. Yukiko met the older woman's stare coolly.

"There are all sorts of dangerous things around here."

Kaori's eyes flickered to Buruu, now rising to his feet. The thunder tiger stared at her the way an avalanche stares at a butterfly.

"As you say." The woman gave a small bow, palm covering her fist. "Get some sleep. We will talk more in the morning."

Kaori turned away, her feet making barely a sound, the bridge unmoving beneath her. Yukiko watched until she disappeared among the shadows, eyes narrowed.

I do not like this, Buruu.

20
MYTHOLOGY

Yukiko was awoken late the next day by the arashitora's voice in her head, warning her of approaching footsteps. She had dreamed of flying above the mountains, high and free, thermals cupping her wings and bidding her higher until the whole world lay on display beneath her claws. She knew it was Buruu's dream. She wondered if he sometimes dreamed of the boy with the sea-green eyes.

The footsteps belonged to Isao and a girl around Yukiko's age, who peeked in the door and introduced herself as Eiko in a small, shy voice. Isao had brought Buruu a brace of fresh trout, and the arashitora began tearing the flesh with relish. The boy bid Yukiko good evening and handed her a pair of old polarized goggles, explaining that the sun was still bright enough to burn her eyes if she ventured beyond the forest shade. The glass was scratched, the leather strap so timeworn that it felt like sandpaper under her fingertips.

Eiko offered a bowl of nigirizushi and fresh, fat plums; Yukiko had missed both breakfast and lunch, but it was not yet time for dinner. Giving genuine thanks, she began wolfing down the food, asking Eiko's background between mouthfuls.

"I have lived here six years," replied the girl, watching Buruu with unashamed wonder. "My family moved here when we could no longer afford inochi, and our fields began to turn to deadlands without the fertilizer."

"Why would the Guild let your fields run to ruin?" Yukiko mumbled around a mouthful of plum. "Why charge so much that your family couldn't afford inochi? That just means less lotus next year."

"It's not the Guild, it's the clan Daimyo," Isao explained. "Their soldiers run the farmers off the land before the deadening gets too bad. They drain money from the farmers' pockets by charging land taxes, ensuring the little man hasn't got enough coin left over to afford fertilizer. Then they kick him off his land under the guise of environmental protectionism: 'If you can't afford to preserve the soil, then we will.' It's all about consolidation of power. Taking the land away from the common people."

"But who works the fields once the farmers have been kicked off?"

"Slaves," Eiko shrugged. "Why do you think the zaibatsu support the war? Most nobles run their fields almost entirely under slave power now. Every shipload of gaijin from the war zone is more cheap labor. Labor you can starve, sweating the skin off their bones until they drop. Then you just buy another shipload with spoils you make from the war. Gaijin aren't people. What do the Daimyo or noble-born care?"

WHAT IS DAIMYO?

The leaders of the clans. Powerful military Lords.

LIKE SHŌGUN.

Well, the Tiger Daimyo also claims the title of Shōgun. The other three Daimyo—Fox, Dragon and Phoenix—all swear allegiance to him.

"They've got bigger problems, anyway," Isao was saying. "Inochi can only delay soil-death for so long. Covering the earth with that sludge will buy you a handful of years. A decade or two at most. And now land is running out. They've razed all the scrubland, 'reclaimed' the swamps, clear-felled every forest. We're standing in the last wilderness left in all Shima. The only reason the shredder-men haven't leveled it is because of superstition and the fact that some genius discovered it's more profitable to enslave gaijin instead." The boy counted off on his fingers. "You get more land to seed overseas, cheap slave labor back home, the market on a war-footing, and an enemy for the common people to hate." Isao made a face. "The nameless, round-eye barbarian, rather than the barbarian sitting on the country's throne."

Yukiko shook her head, thoughts tumbling inside her skull.

They're speaking sedition. The Iron Samurai would execute their whole family for talking this way back in Kigen.

THIS IS NOT A SCAB.

No. But these are not simple displaced farmer folk either.

When the feast was done, Eiko offered to take Yukiko to the bathhouse, and Isao suggested he should come along. Eiko punched him in the stomach, threatening to cut his privates off, and the boy soon took his leave. With a small smile, the girl produced a bar of soap from within her obi. It smelled of honeysuckle and fresh daisies, and Yukiko closed her eyes, inhaling the fragrance and trying to calculate how long it had been since she'd had a warm bath. Her skin tingled at the thought of it.

"Hai," she breathed. "Please."

The girls walked together across creaking boards and swaying rope bridges, listening to the voice of the wind in the leaves. The thunder tiger padded a safe distance behind them, ropes creaking dangerously under his weight, wings slightly spread in case the bridge beneath him decided to give way. The sun was beginning to set in the west, fingers of burning red piercing the forest canopy, deepening the shadows amidst the treetops. Yukiko found herself astounded at the scale of it all; teahouses and storerooms among the winding branches, sprawling family homes, even a crude village center, fashioned from a broad platform of unfinished cedar wood.

As they drew closer, Yukiko realized some kind of gathering was taking place in the square, and she stopped, uncertain, reaching out with nervous fingers toward Buruu. With a smile, Eiko took hold of her hand and led her toward the group.

Two dozen children were sitting in a wide semi-circle, scattered across the landing in the long, muted light of the afternoon sun. Daichi was perched on a rough wooden stool at their center, loose, worn cotton draped about his body, a ceramic cup full of clear water clutched in one hand. His sword was tucked into his obi, his other hand on the hilt, all calluses and scarred knuckles. He leaned closer, one elbow on his knee, and looked each child in the eye.

". . . but the Maker God, great Lord Izanagi, refused to accept his wife's death after the birth of Shima. His love for her was as deep as the ocean, as wide as the great blue sky, for indeed, the sky was blue in days long past. And, ignoring the warnings of the kami spirits, the Maker God traveled by long and hidden roads, to bring his beloved Izanami back into the land of the living."

Yukiko and Eiko took up position quietly at the back of the crowd, leaning against the railing, towels and soap in their hands. Buruu stood beside them, tail sweeping from side to side, tense and irritable. The platform groaned as he shifted his footing. One of the children looked back and caught sight of the arashitora, breath catching in his lungs. He tugged on the sleeve of a friend's uwagi, eyes like saucers, mouth opening and closing without making a sound. The friend looked up to see what the fuss was about, several others followed his gaze, and all of a sudden there came a great shout from the children; a jumbled clamor of overjoyed shrieks, a tumult of little hands and feet across the floorboards, running toward the arashitora as if he were some new puppy dog with which to play.

A single deafening roar rang out among the treetops, windows rattling across the village, wisteria petals drifting down to the forest floor in gentle, tumbling showers. The stampede halted as suddenly as it had begun, and the children scampered back to Daichi's circle, pale and petrified.

The old man nodded a greeting to Yukiko, a small smile on his lips.

"Forgiveness, sama." Yukiko covered her fist, bowed. "Buruu means no harm."

"Do not apologize, Yukiko-chan." Daichi glanced around at the children, a mock frown on his face. "Respect is a lesson well learned in the presence of thunder tigers."

"We did not wish to interrupt."

"It is no imposition. Please, stay. Listen."

Eiko shuffled a little closer to Yukiko, whispering as the children resumed their seats.

"This is a kind of ritual up here. The children gather in the square at weeksend, and Daichi tells them stories of yesteryear. Gods. Heroes. Myths."

"Is it weeksend already?" Yukiko blinked.

"Hai."

Yukiko was astonished to learn that so much time had passed since she left Kigen. The days in the mountains had become a blur, one melting into another. It must have been almost three weeks since they first set out on the *Thunder Child*.

The truth was, it seemed like a lifetime ago.

The children watched her out of the corners of their eyes as Daichi resumed speaking, whispering to each other and pointing when they thought she wasn't looking. Rumor about her battle with the oni had obviously spread, just as Kaori promised, and the youngsters peered at her with a mixture of open fascination and slack-jawed awe. Buruu growled whenever he felt little eyes on him, and most of the children had the common sense to avoid his gaze.

"And so it was, after many dark trials, great Lord Izanagi found the entrance to Yomi." Daichi leaned back and took a sip of water, his voice rough as sandpaper. "The Devil Gate, here in these very mountains. And there in the underworld's pitch black and endless cold, deep enough to freeze a man's flesh from his very bones, he found his beloved. He could not see her face, but he could hear her voice, felt the touch of her lips on his own. His heart swelled, and he knew her for his wife, and her voice drifted in the dark like the sweetest perfume.

"'You must not look on me, my love,' she said. 'For the light will draw the hungry dead near, and they are cold as morning frost and fierce as tigers. But lie with me now, like we did when we were young, and the islands of Shima were but a dream in my womb, yet to be born.'

"And so Lord Izanagi lay with his wife, and held her in his arms, and they remembered what it was to be young again—"

"Did they have sex?" A young boy piped up from the front row, eliciting a few sniggers from the older children. Daichi reached out with one quick, calloused hand and tweaked the boy's nose. Yukiko laughed along with the crowd as the boy yelped in pain.

"Now, you mind your tongue, young Kuon." Daichi wagged one mahogany-hard finger in the boy's face. "I have the telling of this tale. When you are my age, you might know better than to interrupt your elders when they are speaking. Until then, my hand will have to serve in place of wisdom. Hai?"

"Hai." The boy covered his fist and gave a little bow. "Apologies, sama."

"Tsk, tsk," Daichi shook his head. "A boy your age should not even know the name of such things, let alone speak of them in public." The old man took another sip of water. "Now, where was I?"

"In Yomi," offered a young girl.

"Ah, hai. Yomi." He leaned forward to heighten the drama, his eyes wide. "The deepest and blackest of the hells, where the hungry dead dwell in cold and silence for all eternity. Why was Lady Izanami there, you might ask, and you would be wise to. For she was not wicked, nor cruel in her life. But these were the earliest days of this land, before the one hell became nine, and before Enma-ō was charged to judge the departed souls of the living. Before that, all of the dead dwelt in the dark and despair of Yomi.

"Lord Izanagi awoke in the blackness, his beloved Izanami still in his arms. And though he knew he was in peril if the hungry dead were to see his light, he longed to look on the face of his wife again. And so, taking the comb from his hair, he lit a flame upon it, and gazed down at his bride. But what he saw was not the face of his love.

"Lady Izanami had become rotten, as the bodies of the dead. Her flesh crawled with worms, and her eyes were empty holes and her tongue as black as pitch. For she had eaten at the hearth of the underworld, and was forever to be touched by death's hand."

Several of the younger children gasped. One little girl hid her face in her hands.

"Lord Izanagi was horrified, and cried aloud. And at the sound of his voice, Lady Izanami awoke and saw the burning comb in his hand. Her rage was terrible. She leaped at him, intending to keep him in Yomi, where they would be together always. Lord Izanagi ran, as fast as any god might, pursued by the hungry dead. But the Maker God was swift, and he sealed shut the entrance to the underworld with a mighty boulder, trapping his wife inside. From the other side of the stone, Izanami screamed that she was now with child, and that the demons birthed from her womb would destroy one thousand of Shima's children every day to punish Lord Izanagi for abandoning her. And her husband replied thus:

"'Then I will give life to fifteen hundred.'"

The old man straightened on his stool and cleared his throat, gave a small cough. He swirled a mouthful of water and spat on the decking, wiping his mouth with the back of his hand.

"And there the boulder stayed for a thousand years, trapping all of Yomi's evil inside it. Until a young and foolish boy . . ." he frowned at Kuon, ". . . moved the boulder aside and let Hell loose on the world again."

Daichi looked up, fixing Yukiko in those steel-gray eyes. He stared at her for a brief moment, then turned his gaze back to his audience.

"All right, that is enough for one day."

A universal wail of disappointment went up from the children.

"Aiya, I will tell you more next week. The tale of a great battle, and a greater sacrifice." He looked around at the upturned faces. "The charge of the Storm-dancer Tora Takehiko into Devil Gate, and how Yomi was sealed shut once more. Now go on, off with you. Mind your parents and see to your chores!"

The children stood and began to shuffle off, many of them stopping to cover their fists and bow to Yukiko, whispering behind their hands. A deep growl from Buruu sent the stragglers scampering to catch up with their fellows.

Daichi stood and walked over to the railing. Eiko covered her fist and bowed low as he approached. Yukiko watched him carefully, trying to recall where she knew him from. All around, the forest was alive with the sound of birdsong, the perfume of fresh flowers. The old man stared out into the ocean of leaves, wrapped in the smell of wisteria.

"The children have heard of your battles," he smiled. "They are quite impressed."

"Impressed that I'm still alive?" Yukiko watched him carefully. "Or that oni exist?"

"You forget where you are, Yukiko-chan." Daichi waved his hand across the vista. "The haunted valleys of the Iishi Mountains. Demons are as real as the trees or the sky to the children who grow up here."

"Then why do you stay?"

"Long shadows. Dark nights. As far from the Shōgun's throne as a man can be, and a thousand and one myths to keep superstitious eyes away."

"I thought oni were just that." Yukiko looked down at her hand, curling and uncurling her fingers. "Stories to frighten the simple and the young."

"I am afraid not."

"Where do they come from?"

Daichi blinked, as if he didn't quite understand the question.

"From Yomi, of course."

"Yomi?" Her voice fairly dripped skepticism. "The deepest hell?"

"Hai." His reply was flat. Iron. "The deepest hell."

"But the old tales . . ." Yukiko shook her head. "Even if they're true, the gate to Yomi was sealed shut. And the Stormdancer Tora Takehiko gave his life to see that it would remain forever closed. My father used to tell us that story all the time."

"It was a great sacrifice," Daichi nodded. "But the cracks are big enough for the little ones to slip through."

"Cracks?"

"The great boulder that the Maker God pushed into place over the Devil Gate is only stone. Stone breaks under enough force. Enough hate."

"So it's all true? The old stories? The myths my father told us at bedtime?"

Daichi tilted his head and frowned, motioned toward Buruu.

"You walked into this village with a thunder tiger beside you. You have slain demons with your own hands. Are the old myths really that hard to believe?"

"They wouldn't be myths otherwise, would they?"

"Then have a care, Yukiko-chan," Daichi smiled. "Keeping the company of the last arashitora in Shima sounds like an excellent way to become a myth yourself."

The old man covered his fist and bowed. Clasping his hands behind his back, he walked off across the rope bridge, eyes still on the forest. Yukiko stared at his back until Eiko waved the soap in front of her face, a gentle smile on her lips. With a mumbled apology, Yukiko allowed herself to be led to the bathhouse, conscious of the many eyes on her.

Her tantō was a comforting weight in the small of her back.

Their nook was on a branch behind the bathhouse, obscured by thick tangles of wisteria blanketing the walls and the deepening light of dusk. Isao crouched low, eye to the peephole. His friend Atsushi, a wiry, quick-fingered lad one year his junior, sat beside him. The younger boy had drilled the hole several months ago, and the experiment had proved so successful that he'd since expanded the venture across the bedrooms of at least half a dozen girls in the village. His name meant "industrious," after all.

"Is she in there yet?" Atsushi whispered.

"Hai, shhhh," Isao hissed.

"Let me see."

"You go to the Nine Hells. I found her in the forest. Besides, you hogged it yesterday."

"Well, Hachiro's wife was in there."

"Gods above." Isao pulled away from the peephole and scowled at his friend. "She's old enough to be your mother."

"What can I say? I fancy older women."

"Well, if you fancy being torn to shreds by the arashitora, keep talking."

"Aiya, it's days like this I wish we had a picture box."

"Shhhh!"

Isao pressed his eye to the hole again. He could see Yukiko sitting to one side, running Eiko's brush through her long, black hair. Steam uncoiled in a pale haze from the water's surface, several sputtering candles the only illumination. As Isao watched, the girl stood and untied her hakama, letting it slip to the floor in a dirty heap. He could see the long, smooth line of her legs, leading up to the delightful curve of her buttocks just peeking out from the edge of her uwagi. His eyes widened and he broke into an idiot grin. Atsushi tried pushing him aside and he hissed, punching his friend in the arm. The boys struggled briefly, slapping one another and pressing fingers to their lips, each urging the other to shut it. Emerging the victor, Isao put his eye back to the hole.

"Oh gods, she's taking her top off . . ."

Another brief flurry of slaps and hisses for silence. Yukiko untied her uwagi and slipped it off her shoulders. Isao caught his breath, drinking in the sight of the naked girl. Pale skin, bruised and gashed, the elaborate fox running down her right arm, one of its nine tails curled under the swell of her small, high breasts. Her skin was the color of honey in the candlelight. She turned toward him and stretched her arms above her head, sighing, slender, hourglass-shaped.

"You're right," Isao breathed. "We need to get a picture box."

The girl padded toward the bath, a silhouette now against the flames. She dipped her toe into the water, hands of steam caressing her body. Sinking up to the waist, she turned her back toward him. Candlelight flowed over her skin, falling into shadows along the valley of her spine. She turned and Isao saw a small mole on her collarbone, hair flowing down over her left shoulder, a black curtain parting to reveal the tattoo underneath.

"Oh, shit," Isao whispered.

"What? What?" Atsushi pushed his friend aside, pressing his eye to the hole, hands cupped about his face to cut off the light.

The tattoo was stark red against creamy flesh, spilling across her shoulder and bicep, striated rays reaching out toward her elbow. It was the hated symbol of a corrupt regime, an engine of greed bleeding the land and its people dry. The flag of the enemy.

"Oh, *shit*," Atsushi agreed.

21
DYING LIGHT

Imperial suns drifted in a choking breeze, embroidered on long shreds of golden cloth, deep scarlet against a rippling, sunset sky. Despite the dying light of the day, the heat was a blanket; a living, breathing thing, smothering the stunted palace gardens with a leaden, sticky weight and soaking the flesh beneath in glistening perspiration. Servants stood poised beside spring-driven fans, waiting to turn crank-handles at the slowing of the blades, broad-brimmed hats and brass-trimmed goggles shielding them from the sulfur glare on the western horizon. A chosen few of the Tora court stood in the long shade of the broad palace eaves, cups of water growing milk-warm in their palms, doing their best to appear fascinated as Yoritomo-no-miya, Ninth Shōgun of the Kazumitsu Dynasty, hefted his iron-thrower and slaughtered another defenseless cantaloupe.

The melons sat in a neat row, impaled on the tips of nagamaki spears, juice trickling down the wooden hafts buried in the ground. As the shot from the iron-thrower rang out across the garden, the centermost melon exploded into a haze of pulp and shattered rind. The wilted sugi trees behind were painted in its innards, orange, slick.

Polite applause rippled among the spectators, compliments murmured behind the brass and rubber of their breathers, silken armpits stained with sweat. Why the Shōgun insisted on taking target practice in this awful heat seemed beyond them, but if any harbored resentment at being dragged outside to slap their hands together like trained monkeys, they swallowed it without a word.

The Shōgun raised his iron-thrower and drew a bead on the melon at the far left of the row, elbow slightly bent, chin lowered, feet spread. He struck a formidable pose; the ugly lump of pipes and barrels and nozzles in his hand was the only thing about him that lacked symmetry. His robe was woven of deep scarlet and pale cream, embroidered in golden thread with tall grass and prowling tigers. Long black hair fixed in a topknot, pierced with gleaming pins, his face and eyes obscured by his elaborate tiger-maw breather and its golden jagged smile. Fading sunlight glittered on the glass over his eyes. A thin patina of lotus ash dulled the bronze of his skin to cloudy amber. The servant beside him adjusted his grip on the broad rice-paper umbrella, doing his utmost to keep his Lord in the shade.

The Lady Aisha watched her brother from beneath the swaying arms of a maple tree, surrounded by a dozen serving girls, wilting like flowers in the heat. Pale, porcelain skin, motionless as stone until the moment Yoritomo pulled the trigger. She flinched then, despite herself, jaw clenched, hand at her throat. The hollow boom of the iron-thrower was frighteningly loud, as if someone had chained Raijin inside the hollow tubes in Yoritomo's hand, leaving the Thunder God only a tiny, black opening through which to bellow his rage.

Another cantaloupe shattered, a spray of bright orange against bloody sky. Another round of feather-light applause floated among the gray leaves.

The hiss and clank of ō-yoroi armor broke the stillness in the shot's wake, the hollow report still echoing across high, glass-topped walls. The heavy tread of metal boots thudded against the veranda. Yoritomo was bringing the iron-thrower to bear on another melon when a thin, hoarse voice rang out across the garden.

"Great Lord, your humble servant begs forgiveness for this intrusion."

Yoritomo did not bother to look over his shoulder, instead glaring down the barrel at the mottled rind of his next victim.

"What is it, Hideo-san?"

The old man paused, drew a crackling breath on his pipe.

"News from the Iishi, great Lord."

Yoritomo's arm dropped to his side and he turned toward his minister, hidden in the shade of the palace's eaves. He squinted into the shadows, making out the looming forms of several Iron Samurai surrounding the major-domo, wreathed in chi exhaust, two more figures lurking in the gloom behind. The Shōgun beckoned. The samurai trod down the stairs onto the river-smooth stones of the garden path, pushing the figures before them. As the pair stepped out into the fading light, a hiss of surprise escaped from between Yoritomo's teeth.

"Masaru-san." Confusion in the Shōgun's voice, tinged by faint suspicion. "And Captain Yamagata."

"Your humble servant, Seii Taishōgun."

Yamagata's clothing was worn and travel-stained, his skin filthy, his hair a bedraggled mess shoved back into a rough tail. He still wore his custom Shigisen goggles, but appeared to have lost his breather, mouth covered instead with a torn strip of gray rag. Masaru was in a similar state, hair and clothing disheveled, his skin smeared with chi smoke and grime. The right lens of his goggles was smashed, cracks spreading out across the glass like a spider web, the kerchief around his mouth drenched in sweat. Both men knelt on the ground, pressed their foreheads into the dying grass at the edge of the path.

Yoritomo pulled off his breather with a wet, sucking sound.

"I was not informed that you had set sail back to Kigen."

The statement was aimed at the huntsman and cloudwalker, but the Shōgun's glare was fixed firmly on his chief minister.

"They informed no one, great Lord." Hideo's long, narrowed eyes roamed the backs of the two kneeling men, blue-black smoke drifting from his lips. "They arrived late this afternoon by heavy rail direct from Yama, presented themselves at the palace gates and begged for audience. I brought them here immediately."

"By rail?" Yoritomo glanced down at Yamagata, cold and iron-hard. "Where is your ship, Captain-san?"

"Destroyed, great Lord." Yamagata's voice was muffled against the ground. "Lightning struck us in the Iishi. Our inflatable was set ablaze. The *Thunder Child* fell to her death in the accursed mountains."

Yoritomo's face darkened, muscles at his jaw clenched. He licked once at his lips. A servant materialized at his side as if conjured from the spirit realms, offering a mug of tepid water on cupped palms. The man faded into the background just as quickly when he caught the gleam in his Lord's eye.

"You failed to find the beast." A statement, not a question. "Undone by misadventure before the hunt even began. And now you wish to beg for mercy."

"All respect, great Lord," Masaru kept his tone steady, his fingers pressed into fists. "We did not fail. The beast was found, exactly as you commanded."

"You saw it?" Yoritomo's eyes widened. "It exists?"

"Hai, great Lord." Masaru dared a glance up from the ground, pulled the grubby kerchief down around his throat. "I swear it on the souls of my ancestors. The beast exists. And moreover, great Lord, we captured it."

A strangled snatch of laughter spilled from the Shōgun's mouth, spittle flecked on his lips. He stared at Hideo, a bright, brittle joy shining in his eyes, the corners of his mouth drawing upward as if pulled by hooks in his cheeks.

He took a step forward, cast his gaze among the courtiers, to his sister, dragging shaking fingers across his lips.

"It exists." Another gasp of strangled laughter, longer than before. "Hachiman be praised, it *exists*!"

Yoritomo roared, veins standing taut on the flesh of his throat, a triumphant, wordless challenge to the sun sinking toward the horizon. He stomped about in a small circle, grabbed a nearby servant by the cloth at his throat, shaking the little man back and forth until the umbrella dropped from his hands.

"It exists, you beautiful little whoreson!"

The Shōgun shoved the servant away, the man tumbling across dead grass and smooth stones, one sandal flying from his foot. Yoritomo seized hold of Masaru's uwagi, dragged him to his feet, pulling his face close enough that the Hunt Master could see the veins scrawled across his Lord's eyes. The Shōgun tore the broken goggles from Masaru's face, chest heaving, laughter caught in his teeth.

"Where?" Yoritomo's grin stretched his lips to splitting. "Where is my arashitora, Masaru-san?"

Masaru took a deep breath, swallowed hard. A bead of perspiration trickled down pale skin. There was pain in his eyes, distant and clouded by lotus smoke.

"It is dead, great Lord." His voice was tiny, choked. "The beast is dead. And my daughter with it."

The garden was as still as the portraits hanging in the palace halls, as the ancient statues standing among the trees, gray leaves frozen, not a breath of wind. Only Lady Aisha moved, rising up from her seat into a half-crouch, one hand stretching ever so slowly in the direction of her brother. The fire in Yoritomo's eyes flared and died, breath dragged over a fading smile into strangled lungs. The grip on Masaru's collar slackened as the Shōgun exhaled, long and ragged, moving his lips at the terminus of breath to frame one trembling word.

"Dead?"

A blink, wiping the confusion from his eyes, rage in its wake. Yoritomo hissed through clenched teeth, "How?"

"The crash, great Lord." Masaru hung his head, lotus ash caked on dry cheeks, tears swimming in his voice. "They both died in the crash."

"We were laid low by the might of the heavens themselves, great Lord." Yamagata rose to stand beside Masaru, keeping his gaze on the floor, hands clasped behind his back. "The Black Fox brought the arashitora to its knees, chained in a cage of iron on the deck. But Raijin . . ." The captain shook his head. "The Thunder God grew angry at the conquest of his offspring. Hurled lightning from the clouds to strike the *Child*'s inflatable. It was an inferno, spreading like we were made of tinder. I ordered the crew to abandon ship. There was no time to save the arashitora."

Yoritomo's glare slipped sideways, over Masaru's downturned face, coming to rest on the captain. His voice was a whisper.

"Say that again."

A tiny frown creased Yamagata's brow. "Great Lord?"

"Say it again." Yoritomo took one step closer to the cloudwalker. "You ordered the crew . . ."

"I ordered the crew to abandon ship." Yamagata swallowed, pawed beneath his goggles at the sweat burning his eyes. "There was no time to—"

A hollow boom, thunderous, too close. A rush of air, the brittle crackling of tiny sparks. A sound Masaru would never forget. Yamagata's head rocked back on his shoulders, the back of his skull popping like an overfull balloon, full of bright red sweets. Masaru flinched away, spattered in something warm and wet. The captain's body seized tight, rose up on the balls of his feet and tumbled backward like a marionette as the music died. Somewhere in the distance there was a shriek, painted lips muffled by pale, grasping hands. The cloudwalker's body hit the path, stones washed smooth by the hands of ancient rivers, now washed again in a flood of sticky gray and scarlet. Heels beat a staccato rhythm against the rock, a thin, broken-finger wisp of smoke rising from the shattered lens and bloody mess where Yamagata's right eye used to be, another drifting from the barrel of the iron-thrower in Yoritomo's outstretched hand.

Soft sobbing from the direction of the maple trees. Aisha's hissed command for silence.

Masaru swallowed thickly, eyes still downturned, refusing to look at the shattered lump of carrion bleeding on the stones beside him. In the distance, he could hear the sounds of the bay, the Market Square. The churn and growl of sky-ship motors, the reverb of a thousand voices, the song of life swelling beyond these walls. He looked up at the sky, eyes narrowed against Lady Amaterasu's light burning on the horizon. He thought of his wife.

His son.

His daughter.

The years that had flown by so quickly, the span of days and nights that now seemed only a heartbeat long, just one more heartbeat remaining until it was all over.

He almost welcomed the thought.

Yoritomo raised the iron-thrower, leveled it at Masaru's head.

"Failure," he hissed.

And Masaru closed his eyes.

22

DAIYAKAWA

"Come out here, you lying whore!"

Yukiko sat upright, blinked in the steam. The candles had burned low, dim shadows playing on the bathhouse walls, pale wax pooled at their feet. The shout had come from outside, Kaori's voice, shattering the evening hush. Had it been aimed at her?

Buruu?

MONKEYS ANGRY. CARRYING STEEL.

She closed her eyes and looked through Buruu's, feeling their muscles tense, their claws digging into the branch below, aggression flaring out along their veins. Kaori stood before them, a cadre of twenty men behind, Isao holding a struggling Kin. The boy looked sickly pale and terrified: eyes bruised, flesh blistered, unsure of where he was, or who these people were. Only certain of the blade at his throat.

Yukiko leaped from the bath and threw on her clothes, hair clinging to her skin like seaweed. She drew her tantō and dashed barefoot into the muted evening light. Buruu was on his feet, wings spread in a show of threat, broken sparks of electricity skirting his feathers and making the shadows dance. Yukiko took position beside him, his wings at her back. Arms spread, knife in hand, wisteria perfume strung across the twilight. She could feel the anger in him, the rumbling deep inside his chest. When she spoke, the word almost emerged as a growl.

"Kaori?"

"You must think us idiots, eh? Troublesome little firebugs without a brain between us?"

"Kaori, what are you talking about?"

"Just deckhands on a sky-ship, hai?" Kaori's lips were peeled back from her teeth. "You and your little friend here?"

"I never said he was a deckhand." Yukiko frowned, narrowed her eyes.

"You never said you served the Shōgun, either," Kaori hissed, spittle on her lips. "And yet you wear the imperial sun on your shoulder. Is Yoritomo so arrogant that he brands his infiltrators before sending them up here to spin their little webs?"

Yukiko swallowed, instinct bringing her hand up to her tattoo.

Oh, no.

WE SHOULD KILL THEM.

They'd cut Kin's throat.

ACCEPTABLE.

"Yukiko, who are these people?" Kin asked, voice feeble, face twisted in pain.

"Let him go, Kaori." Yukiko took a step forward, white knuckles around the grip of her tantō, bloodless cheeks and flashing eyes.

"You really think me an idiot, don't you?" Kaori laughed. "I let this boy go, your beast tears us to pieces. How did you pressgang it into Yoritomo's service? Its kind is almost extinct because of your Shōgun. Is it blind, or merely stupid?"

"He doesn't serve the Shōgun."

"It serves you," spat Isao. "And you serve Yoritomo."

"I've had this tattoo since I was nine years old. That doesn't make me a spy." She raised the knife, Buruu's growl filling the air. "Now, let my friend go."

"Your friend, eh? Then perhaps you can explain this?"

Kaori tore away the fluid-soaked bandages around Kin's chest and throat, exposing the black bayonet fixtures studding his skin. The boy moaned in agony, his face pale as death.

"What the hells are these? They reek of the Guild's hand."

Yukiko sighed inwardly, licking her lips.

Be ready for anything, Buruu.

"He's an Artificer."

There was a murmur of outrage among the assembled men. Kaori drew her wakizashi, the sharp sound of polished steel ringing out across the treetops. Isao grabbed Kin by the neck and delivered a savage kick to the back of his legs, forcing him to his knees. The long, razored knife sat poised above the boy's throat.

"Say the word, Kaori. I'll gut this pig right here."

"No, don't!"

Yukiko took another step forward, and several of the men turned on her, weapons ready. The arashitora stood up on his hind legs and bellowed, wings cracking at the air. The atmosphere became tinged with a faint static electricity, the hairs on everyone's flesh standing rigid. A flock of groggy sparrows spilled from the leaves and tumbled off into the night, squawking an angry protest. The men backed off a few steps, palms sweating on the hafts of their weapons. Nestled inside Buruu's mind, Yukiko could feel the power radiating across their shoulders, the electricity crackling down their spine and reaching out along their feathers.

They growled with her voice.

"Hurt him and we will kill you all."

"What goes on here?"

The question rang out high and clear across the throng, snow-white wisteria petals falling loose and tumbling into the empty spaces between the cedars. Daichi walked slowly across the footbridge, hands clasped behind his back, Eiko several paces behind. His katana was tucked into his obi, still sheathed, gilt cranes taking wing across gleaming black lacquer. The crowd parted before him, respectful, heads bowed. He drifted between the men and placed a restraining hand on Isao's shoulder. The boy loosened his grip, but still pressed his blade to Kin's throat.

"Daughter, why are there blades drawn among our guests?"

"Father, this girl is a spy." Kaori never took her eyes off Yukiko, sword still clutched in her hand. "She wears the Shōgun's irezumi on her shoulder."

Daichi raised his eyebrow and looked at Yukiko, stroking his mustache.

"A deceiver . . ."

Buruu growled again, the report rolling down their spines and landing in each man's gut.

"Daichi-sama, Kaori is mistaken." Yukiko's words tumbled over each other in their haste to escape. "My father serves the Shōgun, and I wear the imperial mark. But I'm not here to spy on any of you. We crashed in a sky-ship, just like I said. This boy was the Guildsman on board. We had no idea anyone lived up here. Please believe me."

"A Guildsman?" Daichi looked down at the boy with hatred. Ice cold. Crystalline.

"We are not spies!" Yukiko insisted.

"As for you, I cannot say," the old man growled. "But this boy is our enemy. His Guild is a rotten sore on the face of this land."

"Who are you people?" Kin moaned, voice taut with pain.

Daichi knelt in front of Kin, glaring into the boy's eyes. "We are the flame to cauterize your disease. Plant by plant, throat by throat, until you drown in ten times the blood you have spilled for your precious chi." He hawked a mouthful of phlegm, spat into the boy's face. "You say the lotus must bloom. We say it must burn."

"Burn." The word was echoed by a dozen other voices. Not raised in anger, but soft with menace, rolling among the gathering like a prayer.

"I knew it," Yukiko breathed. "You're the Kagé."

Daichi looked at her, eyes narrowed, as if weighing her on a scale inside his head. He glanced at Buruu, running finger and thumb down through the length of his mustache, his mouth a thin, hard line.

"We are the Kagé," he nodded. "We are the clenched fist. The raised voice. The fire to burn away the Lotus Guild, and free Shima from the grip of their wretched weed."

"You burn the fields," Yukiko scowled.

"We burn more than that."

"The refinery fire." Yukiko searched their faces.

"The first of many. The Guild's propaganda machine calls it an accident. But their lies will not shield them much longer. We have infiltrated the airwaves. We have fists in every metropolis in Shima now. Shadows in the Kazumitsu court itself. Closer to the Shōgun than he could ever dream."

"People died in that fire." Yukiko looked around at the crowd in disbelief. "Not just Guildsmen. Innocent people."

"Lotus is killing this country." Daichi stood, hands still clasped behind him. "Choking land and sky, enslaving all it does not outright destroy. Absolute power over the state rests with a single man who rules by fiat, not merit, empowered by an elite that the common man can never join, nor understand. A regime of deception and murder, blood in the gutters, decades of war on foreign shores, all for the sake of more chi."

The evening air grew more oppressive, a cloying blanket of sticky tropical heat, slicking Yukiko with sweat. She began to feel very alone, and a long way from home.

NOT ALONE. I AM HERE.

"Innocent people," she repeated.

"Sacrifices must be made," said Kaori. "The people of Shima are addicted to chi. The system will not die willingly, it must be killed. Those enslaved will adapt or perish, like any addict denied his fix. But better to die on your feet than live on your knees."

"That's not your decision to make!" Raised voice, Yukiko's hands clenched into fists, eyes flashing. "People can decide for themselves!"

"Can they?" Daichi's tone was a counterpoint to her own, measured and soft.

177

"Every word they read or hear is Guild controlled. There is no truth, only the reality that the Communications Ministry weaves. When was the last time you heard the wireless tell you about a farmer who went under? A daughter raped by a nobleman whom the law will not touch? A species that ceased to exist?"

"Well, what about all of you?" she demanded. "You made up your own minds."

"Have you heard of the Daiyakawa riots?"

". . . No."

"Nor would you if this scum had his way." Daichi kicked Kin in the stomach, the boy grunting and curling into a ball. "Ten years ago, the Prefect of Daiyakawa province allowed his farmers to stop growing foodstuffs and switch their crops to lotus. It was worth five times its weight in any other harvest, after all. The problem was, the government had designated Daiyakawa a breadbasket province—they had been commanded to grow nothing but rice, according to the administration's grand design." Daichi stroked his mustache, scowling. "Such is the state of affairs in the countryside of this nation. A man cannot even choose what he plants in the ground any more.

"It did not matter to the Shōgun if Daiyakawa's farmers were forced to tithe so much of their harvest that they could barely feed their families. No matter that their children starved to death surrounded by fields of food. And so, when the farmers saw that there was more money to be made in growing lotus, they decided to claim a slice of that profit for themselves. The Shōgun ordered them to desist, to sow their fields with food again. They rioted, burned the local guardhouse, killed the magistrate. So Shōgun Kaneda and Minister Hideo ordered in the army.

"I was the captain sent to quell them."

Daichi's voice was shaking, he took a deep breath before continuing.

"Have you ever seen Iron Samurai in action against men of flesh and blood, Yukiko-chan? Farmers, with empty bellies and pitchforks for spears?"

Yukiko said nothing, a look of horror on her face.

"Kaneda sent his herald when we were done, decreeing that any farmer who sowed lotus would suffer the same fate as the prefect. Then we dragged the man into the street and executed his family in front of him. Wife. Two sons. A baby girl." Daichi swallowed, looked down at his trembling hands. "Then we forced him to commit seppuku."

"Gods," whispered Yukiko.

"Daiyakawa province grows rice to this day." Daichi curled his hands into fists. "But they don't teach you why. Shima's people never heard of the riot on the wireless, never heard the sound of that baby screaming."

"It was Shōgun Kaneda who commanded you. Perhaps Yoritomo—"

"Yoritomo is his father's child," Daichi growled. "I have seen oceans of blood spilled by his command. Children. Pregnant mothers. Beggars hold out their hands to him and draw back stumps. He rules side by side with a cabal of zealots, turns a blind eye to Purifiers burning people alive for the sake of their ridiculous dogma." He glared down at Kin, shaking his head. "And all the while, these monsters meld their flesh with machines and fill our lungs with cancer."

Daichi looked up at Yukiko, steel-gray irises growing dark with anger.

"We've burned dozens of fields since I arrived in this village, gods know how many more before that, and not one blaze has ever been reported to the people. We burn the refinery, the Communications Ministry says it was a fuel leak. We could cut off the Shōgun's head and parade it down Palace Way on a spike, and the Guild would say he died of natural causes. And the people would believe them."

"The Guild print the history books," Kaori said. "The Guild control the airwaves. Every report, every word they speak to the common man is like a kick to his head. Cowing him. Making him stupid."

"His kind," growled Daichi, kicking Kin again, "are poison."

Buruu purred, eyes fixed on the gathered men and their steel. Yukiko could feel his approval. The arashitora agreed with the philosophy of the Kagé. She was shocked to realize that a part of her did too.

"Daichi-sama, please, let him go."

"Wake up. The lotus must burn. The Guild must burn."

"Burn," murmured the Kagé.

THEY SPEAK TRUTH. THEY SEE CLEARLY.

They kill innocent people.

CHANGE IS SELDOM BLOODLESS. SOME EYES WISH TO REMAIN CLOSED. SOMETIMES THEY MUST BE CUT OPEN.

I can't believe that. I won't.

"Just let us go, please. We won't breathe a word about you, I swear it."

"Let you go?" Kaori laughed. "So you can take Yoritomo his prize? Hand over this beast to that rapist so his bastard Hunt Master can mutilate it some more?"

Yukiko felt a flash of anger, tilting her head and glaring at the woman through her lashes.

"Don't you call my father a bastard. He is a man of honor."

Daichi turned pale, slack-jawed and breathless as if she'd punched him in the stomach. Kaori's eyes widened, and she glanced back and forth between her father and Yukiko.

"You are Kitsune Masaru's daughter?" Daichi's voice was a whisper. "Then your m—"

"Oni! Oni!"

A boy of eight or nine was running across the rope bridge toward them, hissing the word over and over, as loud as he dared. The assembled Kagé turned toward his voice, hands on their weapons. The boy broke through the crowd and knelt before Daichi.

"Daichi-sama, Kaiji-san reports oni on the western rise. A raiding party from Black Temple. Dozens."

"Aiya, so many," murmured Isao.

"Angered at their brethren's deaths." Kaori stared directly at Yukiko. "They seek vengeance. Skulls for their mother, Lady Izanami."

DEMONS. MAGGOTS FROM THE YOMI PITS.

Do they come for us?

Buruu blinked at her, pawing at the ground.

DOES IT MATTER?

Daichi pulled the boy to his feet, one hand on his katana. His calm had returned as swiftly as it vanished, voice low, hard as steel.

"Isao, take this filth to the holding cells and lock him down." He pointed at Kin. "Kaori, fetch the other captains. Make sure they are armed and ready to move. The rest of you, come with me." He turned to leave, his cadre with him.

"Daichi-sama," Yukiko called.

The man turned to look at her, eyebrow raised.

"We will help you," she said. "If Kaori-chan is right and they seek revenge for the blood Buruu and I spilled, honor demands that we help send these things back to the deepest hell."

She tossed her head. Defiant. Proud.

"I am also my father's child."

A long pause. A knowing glance shared with Kaori. A sigh. But finally Daichi licked his lips and nodded to Yukiko, running one hand across his scalp.

"If the Black Fox's daughter asks it, then it will be so." His stare unsettled her. "But when we return, we will speak more. There is something I must ask of you. Something important."

He turned to his men and nodded.

"We move."

23

SURFACING

They are many.

Birthed from the stinking cracks of the Iishi hell gate, heeding the call of the Red Bone Warlord. Dragging themselves from beds of flint and pits of rancid blood, thunderous drums echoing across dark places, bidding them up into the light of the night.

Servants of a deeper darkness. Crouched on her bone mountain in the sunless depths of the Yomi underworld, empty eyes and blackened womb, a tarnished wedding band clutched in the palm of one bloodless hand. She Who Feasts in the Dark, Broodmare of Demons, Queen of the Hungry Dead, whom the Book of Ten Thousand Days calls Endsinger. They, her servants, her faithful, her children. Leaking through rifts of stone into a world she has promised to destroy, a dark and rising tide, swelling drop by drop until it becomes the flood that heralds the Last Day.

Their feet are as an earthquake upon the ground. Their swords are sharp as razors. Their war clubs thick as tree trunks. Black words crawl along their spines, thrumming in their veins, filling them with blackest rage at the loss of their brethren.

The bay and howl, the cry for blood.

The hymn of the Endsinger.

Yukiko crouched in the tree beside Buruu, knife clutched in her hand, nestled inside the arashitora's mind. Eagle eyes, needle-sharp, piercing the darkest shadow. There was no movement in the forest but the flutter of tiny beasts and birds, mirrored in the flutter of the pulse in her veins. But she knew they were close.

She reached out with the Kenning, straining to her limits, feeling the terror of small warm things at the oni's approach: a multitude of giants, belts of skulls, eyes aglow, feet thundering upon the earth and sending tiny, frightened shapes scampering into the dark.

The Kagé crouched in the trees beside her, mere shadows against the pattern of green and black, swelling and shifting in the chill night wind. Yukiko could see Kaori, wakizashi naked in her hand, folded steel painted with lampblack to avoid the glint of lightning or stray moonlight. The approaching monsoon growled in the dark skies overhead. The crack of thunder shook her insides and Buruu purred like a kitten in the aftershocks, the boom resonating in his chest as he stared with longing up at the gathering clouds.

The Kagé were grouped in a tight knot, three, sometimes four to a tree. Isao was wrapped around the branch above Yukiko's head. She looked up and found him glaring at her, eyes narrowed to knife-cuts. Her voice was a whisper, "How do you know the demons will come this way?"

The boy lifted his mask to spit down onto the leaves below. He stared at her for a long, pregnant moment before he answered.

"The mountain gives them only one approach." He nodded west. "The pit traps funnel them in this direction. We have been preparing for this night for years. Though, in truth, we thought it would be men of flesh who came for us, not oni. Iron Samurai and bushimen. Servants of your Shōgun."

Yukiko felt a grudging admiration in Buruu's chest.

You like these Kagé.

THEY SEE. THEY KNOW.

What do you mean?

THEY TURN WEAKNESS TO STRENGTH. THEY USE THE EARTH. NO BARRICADES OF DEAD TREES. NO BULWARKS OF STONE. THEY ARE FEW, FACING MANY. AND THEY ARE NOT AFRAID TO DIE.

No fanatic ever is.

THEY WILL WIN. THOUGH IT TAKE A HUNDRED YEARS, THEY WILL TOPPLE YOUR SHŌGUN. BURN HIS FIELDS AND CITIES. FADE AWAY INTO SHADOW. INTO PLACES HIS ARMIES CANNOT REACH. MORE THAN FLESH. THEY ARE AN IDEA.

She watched the thunder tiger in the darkness, acutely aware of how much he had changed since the crash. His animal instinct, the primal aggression inside him, was being gradually tempered with elegant thought, complex concepts, all too human impulses growing through their bond. She realized that the link between them was changing him, her humanity leaking into him like irezumi ink spilled on cotton weave. He was becoming *more*.

But what might she become?

He is not my Shōgun, Buruu.

He blinked, tossed his head.

SO. ARE YOU RONIN TOO, THEN?

I cannot be ronin. I was never samurai.

YOU SEE. THE RED SKY. THE BLACK RIVERS. YOU KNOW.

She sighed, running her hand across her eyes.

I don't know anything.

She looked up again, found Isao was still watching her, open hostility in his stare.

"What are you looking at?"

"The servant of my enemy," he growled, averting his gaze. "Do not expect many here to weep if the oni kill you, girl."

Buruu's growl was low and soft. Yukiko reached out a comforting hand to quiet him. The thunder tiger stiffened, rising up into a half-crouch, hackles raised. Yukiko closed her eyes and looked into his distance, saw tall silhouettes moving in the dark, tiny pinpricks of glowing blood-red. She ignored the cold dread seeping into her gut.

"They're coming," she hissed to Isao.

The boy nodded and cupped his palm to his mouth, making a sound like cricket-song. The signal echoed among the trees, a chorus of insects armed with sharpened steel. A subtle shift among the shadows; weapons being drawn, grips tightened. The world held its breath for a moment, as if preparing for a deep plunge. And then, with a blinding flash of lightning and a deafening crack of thunder, it began to rain.

It was a chattering hiss on the leaves, a gray veil drawn across the eyes of the oni as they lumbered forward. No order or form to their line, just a tangled mass of tetsubos and ten-span swords hacking the undergrowth, glowing eyes and guttural, croaking voices, a language too black for human ears to comprehend. The rain glistened on their skin, myriad shades from azure to midnight blue, fangs of ivory and rusted iron, eyes like fresh blood. The scrub behind them was flattened, swathes of green cut low, bleeding sap into trampled earth.

Gods, there are so many.

The thunder crashed again.

SOON THERE WILL BE LESS.

The demons drew closer, slashing their path across the emerald green, wading through the curtain of rain. The Kagé remained motionless as the horde passed below, not a single red eye upturned, black speech coursing under the sound of thunder. As the last oni drew level with their positions, the cricket-song rang out in the dark, drifting among the shadows and giving birth to sudden, savage motion.

Silhouettes dropped from the trees, sword and spear buried glittering to the hilts in the backs of the oni rearguard. Bubbling screams. Black blood hissing in the rain. Steam rising from awful, mortal wounds. Heads lopped from shoulders, throats opened to the bone, guts spilling and steaming in the dark. The first to fall had no chance at all.

The horde turned at the wails of their brothers, blinking in the darkness. They saw corpses crumpled on dead leaves, shadows of men in the black. The one who walked in their vanguard, bone armor on his chest and the ancient skull of a sea dragon covering his face, raised a bloody femur into the air and roared; a guttural, reverberating command in a language that none of the Kagé spoke, but every one of them understood.

And so it began.

Buruu dug his claws into the branch as Isao dropped past them, black shuriken stars spinning from his outstretched hands. Yukiko felt the bloodlust build inside the arashitora, the hair on her flesh standing up as raw electricity cascaded along his wings. She bared her teeth and growled alongside him, fingernails biting into her palms.

CLIMB ON MY BACK.

. . . What?

YOU HEARD. FLY WITH ME.

Yukiko blinked away the amazement and scrabbled up the arashitora's shoulder, thighs clamping his ribs, one hand wrapped in his feather mane. Buruu unfolded his wings, stretching out in the darkness, and Yukiko had a brief moment to catch her breath before the world was rushing up toward them, leaving her stomach on the branches above.

They plummeted from the gloom, screaming with one voice, crippled lightning flashing at the edges of their feathers. They were clutching an oni a moment later, shoulders caught in their fists as their claws tore its insides out, spitting a mouthful of throat onto the ground as blood scalded their tongue. The flesh that was Yukiko rolled off into the grass and crouched among the lightning strobe, hacking at the ankles of another oni as the flesh that was Buruu rose up and tore off its arm in one razored talon.

Two sets of eyes watched the enemy, moving in symbiosis between the scything arcs of sword and war club. Fluid as water, flowing beneath iron and steel, crashing with sudden ferocity, liquid between the spittle and death screams.

Flesh parted before their fingers, steel and talon slicing midnight blue and giving birth to great floods of steaming black.

There was no time. There was no gravity. There was no Yukiko. There was no Buruu. There was only motion, bloody, brutal motion as their father screamed his joy overhead, thunder rumbling across the clouds, lightning painting the butchery as bright as the day. The shapes of men fell about them, red blood washing away in the rain, screams of pain lost beneath the roaring sky. But they were unstoppable, untouchable, eyes in the backs of their heads, transcending thought and laying all before them to rest.

Their flesh was together again, one astride the other without knowing who was which, feathers wrapped in fingers and pounding at the air, longing to fly again. The need swelled inside them, denial of an impulse so primal that it filled them with rage, spreading across their severed quills and screaming at the sky, spattered in warm black blood.

The red warlord answered, holding the bleeding bone into the air and bellowing, a cruel iron sword twisted in the other fist. It charged toward them, lips curled back from jagged tusks, knocking aside its fellows in its haste to taste them. They turned to face it, roaring again. Two mouths, one voice, echoed by the raging storm.

The curved sword fell in a ten-ton arc, slicing raindrops in two. They bounded into the air, wings tearing at the space where flight was born, finding only momentary lift and the awful clutch of gravity. But it was enough to carry them over the blade and onto the oni's torso, claws tearing its chest, piercing bone armor, knuckle-deep in steaming black. With a bellow, it brought the bleeding bone across their brow. A blinding white light arrived with it and knocked them senseless. They rolled apart, shaking their heads, blinking the blood away from their eyes. The flesh that had been Buruu staggered, eye swelling closed, sharing the pain with the flesh that had been Yukiko and feeling it fall away by half. She loaned him her eyes and slipped into the shadows beneath a cedar, his fingers running across the fox tattoo on their shoulder. They began to climb.

The warlord lunged, Buruu's flesh lashing out at the thing's face with one razored fist, bringing it back, sticky with blood. The oni roared and they answered, laughter rolling across the clouds. Rain turned the blood-soaked earth to mud, the sounds of battle around them dropping away to whispers. There was only this. There was only them.

Me.

Lightning cracked the sky, burning away the black.

WE.

The flesh that was Buruu danced backward, bringing the oni with it, eyes aglow with hatred. The flesh that was Yukiko sprang from the tree, twelve feet high, tantō clutched in both hands. The knife plunged to the hilt in the oni's back, gravity and momentum pulling them earthward, flesh parting down to the spine and peeling away like the rind of swollen fruit. The blood was blinding, the scream of deafening white pain filling their ears, drowning the storm. They leaped toward the wounded oni, claws outstretched, smashing the sea dragon skull to splinters and tearing away the demon's face in their hands. Beak to throat, savaging until there was nothing left but broken bones and empty, twitching meat.

The storm howled in triumph.

They screamed, faces to the sky, knife clutched in their bloody claws. What was left of the oni band turned and fled into the night, pounding back through the broken green, spears and shuriken whistling about their ears. Broken and defeated.

And then there was only the sound of the falling rain. The Kagé didn't cheer, didn't goad or gloat. They simply watched the giants disappear into the shadows, nodding to each other, heads bowed in silent prayer for their dead.

Kaori was looking at Yukiko and Buruu with awe, swallowing great gobs of hot, wet air, drenched to the elbows in steaming black gore. Daichi wiped a sluice of oni blood off on his sleeve and slid his katana back into its scabbard. He watched them as their blood calmed, the Kenning receding as the heat of the battle died in their veins, leaving them sundered in its wake. Yukiko felt lessened somehow, reaching out toward Buruu as if to reassure herself he was still there. He purred, satisfaction rumbling across the ground, tectonic and primal.

GOOD. IT IS GOOD.

"You are one," Daichi said, wiping the sweat from his eyes. "You and the arashitora are one in the same. You are yōkai-kin."

"Stormdancer," whispered Isao.

Yukiko glanced at the boy as he covered his fist and bowed, eyes turned to the ground in reverence. She looked around at the other Kagé as they repeated the gesture, bowing one after the other in the pouring rain. She felt the hair on her arms and the back of her neck rise, a thrill of fear surging in her gut, tightening her throat, the word rippling among them like the forest wind through the liriope grass.

"Stormdancer."

She knew what she must look like. Spattered with demon blood, knife clutched in one white-knuckle fist, the arashitora beside her spreading the saw-toothed fan of his wings and roaring at the storm above. She felt Buruu's triumph rising in her chest, and it was all she could do to stop herself from screaming with him again, to hold onto some small part of what she'd been, and see in Daichi's eyes a stark reflection of what she was becoming.

"You are yōkai-kin," he repeated.

"I am yōkai-kin," Yukiko nodded, breath still burning in her lungs. "I hear the voices of beasts in my head, can speak to them as easily as I speak to you now. Do you really think the Shōgun would send one of the Impure to spy on you, Daichi-sama? When Guildsmen burn others like me on pyres in the Market Square for sport? Do you think Yoritomo would be stupid enough to brand an infiltrator with his own irezumi before sending her up here?"

The old man stood silent for a handful of heartbeats, amidst the clawing wind and shapeless white noise. With agonizing slowness, he finally shook his head.

"No. I do not."

Yukiko ran her hand across Buruu's flank, smearing the blood through his fur. "So where does this leave us?"

Daichi looked around at his men. Some still stared at Yukiko, but a few were busy slinging the bodies of their fallen comrades over their shoulders. Two others had begun the grisly task of dismembering the oni corpses so they could be disposed of elsewhere. The rain washed the blood from their flesh, down into the earth, soaking into hungry roots and sodden mud. All so transient. Soon there would be little to show that they had ever been here at all. Nothing but the shadows they left behind.

"We must talk, Kitsune Yukiko." Daichi nodded in the direction of the village and turned to walk away.

Yukiko's voice pulled him up short, "Talk about what?"

The old man looked over his shoulder, a strange sadness in his eyes.

"Murder."

Yukiko tried to swallow the cold lump in her throat, ignore the dread in her belly.

"Murder and treason."

Fire seethed across the maple logs, greedy fingers lapping on dry bark, breaking the wood into glowing cinders. Yukiko cupped a warm bowl of broth in both hands and nestled closer to the blaze, hair hanging in a tangled curtain about her face. Buruu sat outside by the open door, preening his feathers, watching the blood run from his fur beneath the chattering rain.

The battle with the demons seemed like a distant memory now; the dim recollection of a dream in the cold light of morning. She could recall the blood-lust in her veins, the haze of red that clouded her eyes. The feeling of her wings at her shoulders, slicing through the air and failing to find purchase, the joy she felt at the roar of the storm above. Watching Buruu preen in the rain, she knew none of this was hers; that he was leaking into her as surely as she was into him.

What am I becoming?

Daichi and Kaori sat beside Yukiko around the fire pit, cross-legged on thin hessian cushions. Kaori was watching Yukiko with that same awed expression, her father was staring at the blaze, at the smoke writhing up the chimney. The smell of wisteria drifted in through the open windows, entwined with the song of the storm.

"Our scouts have reported a Guild-liner in the skies above the crash site of your ship," Daichi murmured. "They are looking for something."

"Kin-san," she said. "He told me they could find his suit. I hid it in the rocks upstream."

"So. Escape beckons. Do you wish to leave this place? Take Yoritomo his prize?"

Yukiko clawed the hair from her eyes, tucked it behind her ears. Her voice sounded like it came from a thousand miles away.

"I want to know my friends are all right. That they escaped the crash in one piece." She stared through the open door at Buruu, pained and weary. "But I don't want to hand Buruu over to that maniac. I don't care about what was promised to him. I don't care about honor. Honor is bullshit."

Daichi heaved a sigh that seemed to come from the tips of his toes.

"I envy you, Yukiko-chan." He stared at her across the pit, flame glittering in the steel-gray of his eyes. "It took me forty years to learn that lesson. For the longest time, from the day I first held a wooden sword in my hands, I thought honor was defined by servitude. By carrying out the will of my Shōgun, and living by the Way. I thought I was a man of courage, to do what others would not. But I know now that this kind of loyalty is cowardice. That the nobility of this country have abandoned the Code of Bushido, paying it lip service at best. To be a servant can be a noble thing, but only as noble as the master served."

He wrung his hands, staring hard at calloused flesh.

"These hands of mine drip with blood. It will never wash away. I have killed women. I have killed children. I have killed the innocent and the unborn. And though it was my Lord that commanded it, it was I who wielded the blade. I know this. I know I will answer for it one day to Enma-ō, and the great judge will find me wanting. A demon lives inside my mouth, and speaks to me in quiet moments with blackened tongue. Wresting me from peaceful slumber and waking me sweating in the night. Two words. Over and over."

He swallowed, shook his head.

"Hell-bound."

"Why are you telling me this?" Yukiko watched him through her lashes, uncertain, afraid without quite knowing why.

Kaori squeezed her father's hand, shook her head fiercely. He stared at the fire for what seemed like hours, watching the logs blacken and char. Finally he looked at Yukiko.

"I would have you do something for me. For all of us. I would have you free this land."

"And how do I do that?"

"Kill the Shōgun."

Yukiko dropped the bowl with a clatter, broth splashing across the boards. She could swear her lower jaw was sitting in her lap.

"Wh— you want me . . ."

"Hai," Daichi nodded. "I want you to assassinate Yoritomo."

"But I'm not . . . I'm just a . . ."

"Yoritomo is childless. For all his rape and geisha, he has not sired a single heir. The line of Kazumitsu dies with him. Without a figurehead, the Tora clan and its government will splinter. One of the Kazumitsu Elite might have the strength to take control of the Tiger army if Yoritomo dies, but none of them is strong enough to seize power over the entire country. The Daimyo have their own troops, and each will resist any attempts by other zaibatsu to place their own man on the throne. There is no love lost between the clan lords, nor their generals." He sighed again, seemed suddenly too old for his skin. "I know how their world works. I was part of it for forty years."

"You're talking about . . . you want to start a civil war?"

Daichi shook his head.

"I want chaos. Formlessness."

Kaori spoke, her voice soft, a snatch of verse from the Book of Ten Thousand Days.

"*Our prelude was Void. The vast possibility, before life drew breath.*"

Daichi nodded his head.

"And within this void, the people of Shima will find their voice. We will show them how. Show them that their addiction to lotus is killing them, killing everything around them. Show them that the only power governments wield is the power given to them by the people. And now, they must take that power back."

"I'm not a killer," Yukiko said.

YOU KILL ONI.

That's different, Buruu.

HOW?

Oni are demons. Hellspawn. We're talking about a man of flesh and blood here. A real person.

RAPIST. SLAVER. LORDING OVER A DYING LAND, AND HE ITS MURDERER . . .

I am not killing anybody, Buruu!

Daichi watched her carefully, hands steepled under his chin.

"There is a place, and a time, for all endings to begin—"

"The Shōgun might be the most evil man in the world," Yukiko glared across the fire, sudden anger flaring in her eyes, "but I'm no assassin. What the hells makes you think I'd kill someone for you?"

"Because I know what Yoritomo has done to you. You and the Black Fox."

"Yoritomo never touched me, wha—"

"He killed your mother."

A perfect, absolute silence. A stillness inside her, complete and untouchable, as her entire world fell away and tumbled down into the dark. Cold sickness in her belly, a lump of frozen lead in her throat, tongue cleaving to the roof of her mouth as lightning licked the sky, turning all to horrid, lurid white.

"What did you say?" A whisper, barely a breath.

"He killed your mother." Daichi's voice was flat. Dead. "Or rather, I killed your mother. Your pregnant mother. At Yoritomo's command."

"My mother isn't dead. She left us when—"

"No." Daichi shook his head. Palms upturned, calloused and scarred, stained to the bone. "She left this world. My hands. Yoritomo's word. A warning to your father."

Yukiko glanced from the old man to his daughter, saw awful truth gleaming between the tears in the woman's eyes. Buruu was on his feet, growling, hackles rippling down his spine. A splinter of his rage broke through the rime of disbelief and Yukiko found her hand wrapped around her tantō. She could feel the wood grain beneath the lacquer, fingertips running over the faint undulations; a Braille mantra repeating over and over inside her head. She was on her feet before she knew it, one hand wrapped in Daichi's collar, the other holding the knife to his throat.

"You're lying," she hissed. "You're a liar."

"I am many things." Daichi met her stare, calm, accepting. "Assassin. Fire-starter. Murderer of the innocent and the unborn." He shook his head. "But never a liar, Yukiko-chan."

She pressed her blade against Daichi's flesh. He tore his uwagi open, exposing chest and abdomen, the awful scars left in the wake of his tattoos.

"Here." He slapped his belly, the sound of flesh drumming against mahogany. "Strike here. I deserve no cut throat, no quick kill. A death by sepsis. A screaming, coward's end. But before you strike, promise me you will give the same to Yoritomo. That is all I ask. Give us both everything we deserve."

Kaori wore a look of horror, hands clenched at her sides, tears tracing the line of her scar. She dropped to her knees, pressed her forehead against the floor. Her voice was faint; tiny and pale and fragile.

"Please, Yukiko-chan, mercy. Mercy."

KILL HIM.

Yukiko clenched her teeth, lips peeling back in a snarl, bubbling in the depths of her throat. Tears blurred her vision. Daichi was still as stone, unafraid, listening to the simmering grief threatening to spill over into a scream. Yukiko pressed the knife against his throat, blood welling under the blade's edge and spilling down his chest.

Daichi stared into Yukiko's eyes, his voice as hard as the steel in her hand.

"There is a place, and a time, for all endings to begin. If not here, then where? If not now, then when?"

Yukiko gasped, short of breath, spit hissing from between her teeth. Blinking. Blinded. She clutched Daichi's collar as the world rolled beneath her feet, knuckles clenched white in the cloth and on the handle of her knife.

"Promise me."

HE HAS TAKEN FROM YOU.

She blinked the tears from her eyes.

I . . .

HE BEGS FOR IT, YET YOU FALTER.

Buruu glared from the darkness, eyes of polished glass. She felt his rage swelling inside her, a black cloud of frustrated bloodlust and hate. She struggled to push it away, to find some kind of clarity, a moment's silence to seize on the thought that held her back.

KILL HIM.

The tantō was as heavy as lead in her palm. She looked down at the blade, remembered the glint of steel falling between the raindrops. The sound of tearing paper. Severed feathers on the *Thunder Child*'s deck. Kaori's sobbing drowned out the rumble of the storm above her. Yukiko glanced at the woman, head pressed into the boards, shoulders heaving.

"Mercy," she whispered.

My father . . .

WHAT?

She could feel her pulse pounding behind her eyes. Cold sweat on her palms.

When he took your wings, did you hate him, or the nagamaki in his hands?

The arashitora fell still, a cold sliver of logic breaking through the animal rage.

THAT IS NOT . . .

Did you hate the weapon, Buruu? Or did you hate the hand that wielded it?

Yukiko tightened her grip on Daichi's collar, face twisting, a single tear spilling down her cheek. The world was too loud, the firelight too bright, reflected in cold folded steel and painted blood-red.

The old man grabbed her wrist and squeezed, stared hard into her eyes.

"Promise me!"

The words spilled from her lips. Reluctant. Metallic.

". . . I promise."

The knife fell from her grip, plunged point-first into the wood between Daichi's legs. Blood ran down the patterned blade, pooling around the razored edge and soaking into the grain. She loosened her grip on the old man's collar, shoved him backward, breath spilling over trembling lips. Her hands were shaking, mouth dry, chest heaving. She wiped the back of her hand across her mouth.

Daichi lay sprawled where she had pushed him, looking up at her with something close to bewilderment in his eyes. He touched the wound at his throat, the thin line of red that welled and spilled down his chest. Deep enough to remember her by. But not deep enough to end him.

"Why?"

YES. WHY?

"Yoritomo." Yukiko curled her hands into fists to stop them trembling. "He is the one. He ordered you to kill her. And if you had refused, you would be dead, and the Shōgun would have just commanded someone else to do his bidding. You're just a tool. A weapon. And a broken one at that."

Kaori crawled across the floor, threw her arms around her father's neck. Yukiko couldn't read the old man's expression through the tears in her eyes. Relief? Disappointment?

"You deserve it for all you've done." Yukiko looked from father to daughter. "But she doesn't deserve to see it. And in truth, Daichi-sama, your death won't avenge my mother." Her voice cracked, almost broke. "You're the one who took her life, but you're not the one who murdered her."

. . . YORITOMO.

Yes.

HE IS THE HAND.

Yes.

Yukiko stooped and retrieved her tantō from the small puddle of cooling blood. Thunder crashed in the skies above her head, a rumble that shifted the world beneath her feet and settled in her bones. She slid the blade into the scabbard at her back and wiped the tears from her eyes.

It's time someone cut it off.

PART 3
BLOOD

We who yet remain;
Clans born of water, fire, mountain and blue sky,
We with beating hearts, cursed by dread Izanami; hater of all
*   life,*
To the Maker God, to Bright Moon and Lady Sun, our voices
*   are raised,*
To the God of Storms, to any who hear, we pray;
Great Heavens, save us.

The Book of Ten Thousand Days

24

BRETHREN

The girl stood on the sky-ship's deck, holding her mother's hand. Eyes bright with wonder as they stared at the city beneath them, wet with the sting of chi smoke. It hung in a pall over the city streets; a blanket covering the dozens, hundreds, thousands of people that scurried back and forth, a flood of sights and sounds, underscored with that oily, rancid smell. Kigen city was a living, breathing thing, a beast with a constantly writhing hide, people clinging to its flanks like an army of ticks. She had never imagined anything like it in all her life.

From above, it was intricate, beautiful and terrible, a winding maze of squeeze-ways and alleys twisting between the cracking sores of bleached buildings. The broad square of brick at its heart, cobbled arteries worming off in labyrinthine patterns that mimicked a maniac's scrawl. A great cluster of broad, grand roofs on the hill, red flags crowing among its stunted gardens. A five-sided fist of yellow stone amidst a growth of hunchbacked, abandoned slaughterhouses, the great nest of pipes and tanks and vomiting chimneys that must be the refinery, a rusted length of intestine spilling from its bowels and leading off north toward First House. Winding serpents of filthy river water, spilling out into a bay of char and floating refuse, shoals of garbage drifting on a dirty sea breeze. The streets were choked with a black-tongued haze, a dirty stain smeared across the skies, hovering over the crust of concrete and brick on the harbor's skin.

The ship kissed the sky-spire as gentle as the summer rain. Cloudwalkers lashed them tight; thick rope knotted on corroded couplings. Yukiko climbed onto her father's back, breathless with excitement as he descended the rungs. Her new goggles slipped down her nose, and she tightened the strap behind her head. She looked up at her mother climbing down after them, swift and sure, the fox tattoo on her arm proudly displayed for all to see.

"Mother," Yukiko called. "Do you see all the people?"

"Hai, Yukiko," she smiled down at her daughter. "I see them."

"Father, why are there so many?"

"This is the capital of Shima." He smiled, ruffling her hair as his feet touched the ground. "People from all over the Empire come here. Brave warriors, traders, priests. Sooner or later, every man turns his feet to Kigen."

Masaru helped Yukiko scramble up onto his shoulders. She peered at the throng, face alight with wonder. Her mother stepped down beside them, wrinkled her nose.

"Before he turned his feet here, perhaps he should have washed them."

Yukiko giggled.

"Naomi, please . . ." Masaru said.

"Mother's right," Yukiko nodded. "It smells here."

"You'll get used to it, Ichigo." Masaru pinched her toes, eliciting a yelp.

The motor-rickshaw waited for them, strange men with growling swords ushering them inside. They rode through the crowded streets and Yukiko pressed her nose to the pockmarked glass, watching the people drift by, wave after wave of seething flesh. The giant samurai in their clanking armor, the grubby children fighting in the gutters, the sararīmen and neo-chōnin, peddlers and beggars. And such a noise! Noise like she'd never heard, near deafening compared to their little bamboo valley, breeze whispering through the stalks in breaths a lifetime wide.

She wished Satoru could see it all.

Further up the Palace Way, an impossible cluster of towers and buildings beckoned, tiger flags waving in the toxic wind, daubed in red and gold, bigger than any building she had ever seen.

"Who lives there, father?"

"That is the Shōgun's palace. We will visit it often, if we decide to stay. Would you like that?"

Yukiko looked uncertain.

"Can we fish there? Are there butterflies?"

"No," her mother said, staring at her father. "There are no butterflies here, Yukiko. No birds. No flowers either."

"What is that?" the girl cried, pressing against the window. Beyond the glass, a strange figure was clomping through the crowd, clad in chattering brass, all cogs and wheels and spinning teeth. Its head looked like the fighting mantis that used to clash across the bamboo forest in spring. Its eyes were red as blood, glittering in the muted sun.

Her mother had answered softly, for her ears only.

"That is your enemy."

I mpure."

Yukiko whispered the word, watching the Iishi crags grow smaller and smaller, tiny lightning flashing among the now-distant storms. It was such a simple thing; two syllables, the press of her lips together, one on another, tongue rolling upon her teeth. She breathed it again, as if savoring the shape. Tasting it.

"Impure."

It was a word their mother had taught them, her and Satoru, sitting by the fireside late one night and swimming in their hound's mind. She told the twins not all people had the Kenning; that there were some who could never know an animal's thoughts or feelings, who were locked in the prison of simple sight, sound and smell.

"And they are jealous," she'd warned. "So you must never tell another of the gift, not unless you trust them with your life. For if the Guild discover it, they will take it from you."

The twins had nodded then, pretended to understand. Yukiko could remember those words like they were yesterday.

"If she could see me now," she sighed.

She stood at the carven bow of the Guild ship *Resplendent Glory*, sun on her goggles, hair streaming in the wind. The whirr and clank of atmos-suits and mechabacii was a constant hum, an itch between her shoulders that she couldn't scratch. The sound of metal boots and engines. Insectoid clicking. Grease and transmission fluid.

Chi.

Buruu stood beside her, glaring at any Guildsman or cloudwalker who drifted too close. The ship bristled with cannon and shuriken-throwers; the crewmen who manned it were all armed. A full platoon of marines in Guild colors drifted about the deck; mercenary soldiers in the employ of the Lotusmen. They eyed the arashitora warily from behind face-length breathers and grubby panes of glass. The *Glory* was a warship of the "ironclad" class; slow-moving, bullet-shaped, plated with metal the color of rust. The soldiers aboard had trekked north in response to the distress call of Kin's sundered suit, spoiling for a fight. The marines had been surprised when they'd stumbled across the girl and her thunder tiger, dragging the unconscious, naked flesh of a Guildsman behind them, just two miles from where they'd found his ruined skin. In truth, they had expected to find nothing but a corpse.

Instead, they had found the impossible.

The storm had calmed as the ironclad lifted off from the rock pool, almost as if Susano-ō wanted to be rid of them, bidding them to hurry away from the Iishi and back to their filthy scab. The ship trekked south, retching black fumes onto the mountains silhouetted at its back, dark clouds drifting among snow-capped peaks. Buruu kept his gaze pressed forward, but Yukiko knew he wanted nothing more than to look behind them and stare at the storm. To close his eyes and remember the wind rushing beneath his wings, the lightning playing in his feathers.

Soon.

She ran her hands across his shoulders, fingers entwined in his fur.

Soon, Buruu.

Daichi had watched them leave the Kagé stronghold, Kaori by his side. Yukiko had looked back at the village as they climbed out of the valley, just shadows now among the treetops, hung thick with wisteria perfume. She wondered if she would ever return. It had felt as if she were leaving home all over again, nine years old, packing her bags to depart for Kigen. Her mother had refused to cry or bid their house farewell, her mind already made up that she would hate the city, that they would return once she had begged the Shōgun's pardon.

Yukiko blinked away the tears, tried to smother them with rage.

She was pregnant.

She gritted her teeth, clenched her fists tight. She must be stone. Unfeeling. Unblinking. They must not see. They must not guess. She must wear the mask, the triumphant daughter of the Black Fox returning from the wilds with a legend by her side, delivering unto the Shōgun his glittering prize. And when he leaned close, guard down, offering her the world as her reward, she would take it. His life. Cut from his chest, beating in the palm of her hand, blood on her face and on her tongue.

She knew what she had to do. But try as she might, again and again, she felt the sorrow swell up past the rage, drowning the spark of anger inside. She felt weak and frail: a tiny girl inside the gears of a great, crushing machine, oiled to murderous precision with the blood of innocent women and children.

Women. And children.

She was pregnant, Buruu. I might have had a baby sister. Or another brother.

She felt steel in him, folded and sharp, light rippling across the surface and glinting on his edge. He flooded her with it, tempered and hard, a resolve forged in lightning and thunder and cooled by the pounding rain. He was strong. So *they* were strong.

I AM YOUR BROTHER NOW.

On the evening of the third day, a Lotusman approached the bow with halting steps, the flat black barrel of a Sendoku shuriken-thrower clasped in its gauntlets. Buruu turned and stared, his subsonic growl making the plates of the Guildsman's suit chatter and squeal against each other. His claws dug into the deck as if it were butter. The Lotusman stopped a good ten feet away and cleared its throat.

"Kitsune Yukiko." The voice sounded like a dying lotusfly. "The Artificer you rescued is awake. He requests your presence."

Yukiko eyed the Lotusman's weapon, running her hand down Buruu's cheek.

I will call if I need you.

AS YOU WISH.

"Lead on, sama," she said.

The air below deck was rank with chi, the sweat of marines, the vague cabbage stink of the Guildsmen's "nutrients." She tied her kerchief around her mouth, fighting the familiar nausea. The Lotusman led her down a long hallway pocked with doors, into what she presumed was an infirmary.

The light was low, tungsten buzzing inside amber housings above her head, the faint rumble of the engines pitching a tent behind her eyes and helping to stoke her growing headache. A long cot stretched along her right-hand side, racks of strange lead-gray apparatus lining the walls. Gauges and dials and lengths of pipe snaking down the wood and into the flesh of the figure on the cot. There was a sheet of opaque gauze draped over the bed like a mosquito net; the figure behind it was only a silhouette swathed in what she presumed must be bandages. The stink of antiseptic hung in the air like smoke.

The figure shifted as she entered, making the pipes and cables plugged into his flesh quiver obscenely; the shadows of metal serpents writhing on the gauze.

"Kitsune Yukiko." Formal tone, his voice stronger than it had been since the accident. She couldn't see the face, but she recognized Kin nonetheless. "Thank you for coming."

"How do you feel?" Yukiko kept her voice neutral, conscious of the Lotusman and its Sendoku hovering by her side.

"They tell me the fever has broken. The infection is not bad. It is a good thing the antibiotics in my pack lasted as long as they did."

". . . Hai. It is."

"I wanted to thank you." She could almost feel his stare through the curtain between them. "For keeping me safe. Wandering alone in the wilderness all that time could not have been easy. I am indebted to you."

Kin had tilted his head slightly when he said the word "alone," a subtle underscoring for her eyes only. Yukiko's glance flickered to the Lotusman beside her.

She nodded, "Think nothing of it, Guildsman." Cold. Distant. A good ruse.

She covered her fist with her palm and gave a small bow. Turning to leave, she refused to spare another passing glance for Kin. Better for the Guild to think they were simple strangers. Less trouble for him. Less trouble for her.

"Kitsune Yukiko." The metallic rasp of the Lotusman's voice pulled her up short at the doorway.

"Hai?" She glanced at it over her shoulder.

"The Kyodai also wishes to speak to you."

"What is a Kyodai?"

"The rank and file of the Guild are called 'Shatei,'" Kin explained. "Little brothers. The ones who look after us are 'Kyodai.' Big brothers."

Yukiko looked at the Lotusman in its suit, those cold eyes of impassive glass.

"What does it want to speak to me for?"

"It was not my place to ask." The Lotusman turned, walked out into the corridor. It motioned to the door at the end of the hallway. "Come."

Kin's voice was a whisper, so low she could barely hear it.

"Be careful, Yukiko-chan."

Yukiko checked the tantō in her obi, then walked from the room.

The Kyodai's quarters were opulent, trimmed in brass and stained teak. A small crystal chandelier in the ceiling swayed with the ship's motion. Maps covered the walls: countries she had never seen, studded with small red pins and long arcs of black. A thick carpet woven with intricate designs lay on the floor, and Yukiko kept her eyes fixed on it as she entered the cabin. The weave pictured a multitude of arashitora silhouettes, solid black against a backdrop of pale blue. Shadows moved beneath the swinging bulbs, reaching out across the floor toward her.

"Kitsune Yukiko," said a voice, thick and buzzing.

Yukiko glanced up to the squat figure behind the low table. The Kyodai was fully suited, bloated belly sheathed in yards of glittering metal, fat fingers encased in elaborate gauntlets. If nothing else, the trim of the skin marked it as a senior Guild member. Extravagant gothic flourishes decorated its spaulders and cuirass, scrolled around the faceted, glowing eyes. Breath hissed through the filters on its back, punctuated by the occasional burst of chi exhaust. A stubby matt-black iron-thrower lurked in a holster on its belt.

"Guildsman," she answered, eyes returning to the floor. She did not kneel.

"Leave us," the Kyodai ordered.

The Guildsman at Yukiko's side touched two fingers to its forehead, rasped, "The lotus must bloom," and clanked out the door.

"Do you like it?"

Yukiko glanced up at the Kyodai. It nodded to the carpet beneath her feet.

"Very pretty, sama." She used the term of respect, hoping to impress.

"Morcheban," the Guildsman mused. "Taken from a gaijin castle last summer; spoils of the glorious war. It seems some of the barbarian aristocracy have a fondness for Shiman folklore."

Yukiko couldn't tell beneath the helmet, but she thought the Guildsman might be smiling. She found the smooth insectoid lines and empty, glowing eyes of its mask unsettling, so she turned her gaze earthward and remained mute.

"I am Kyodai of this vessel. You may call me Nao. You are Kitsune Yukiko, daughter of Kitsune Masaru, the Black Fox of Shima."

"Hai, sama."

"It would trouble you, then, to learn that your father is in prison."

Yukiko glanced up to the impassive mask.

"For what?"

"Failing Yoritomo-no-miya." A lazy shrug. "Be thankful he is not executed as Captain Yamagata was."

"My father didn't fail." She tried to keep the anger from her voice. She remembered Yamagata's kindness, his strong hands on the *Child*'s wheel as the storm drove them toward the jagged rocks. "Nobody on that trip failed. We captured the impossible."

"And then let it escape." The Guildsman drummed heavy fingers across the table, leaving shallow impressions in the wood. "But it would seem the daughter succeeded where the father did not. No mean feat for one so young, to tame a beast such as that. I am wondering how you managed it."

"Its spirit was broken after my father clipped its wings, sama." She shrugged, tried to keep her voice casual. "It is a beast, like any other. I tamed it with a little patience, and the offer of food."

"Remarkable."

"I have a way with animals, sama."

"So it would seem."

The Guildsman's faceted eyes glittered; a trick of the light that nevertheless sent butterflies tumbling across her stomach. She met his featureless stare with mute defiance, refusing to be afraid, to back down or beg. She would not think of the Market Square, of those charred stone pillars coated with ash. She could feel Buruu prowling behind her eyes, seized hold of his anger and held on tight. A long, silent moment passed, Nao's fingers beating a slow rhythm upon the tabletop. Yukiko kept her breathing steady, felt the comforting weight of the tantō at the small of her back.

"We have taken the liberty of radioing ahead to inform the Shōgun of your success. He is most anxious to meet his prize. You will tell it to behave, hai?"

"I cannot tell it to do anything. It's not a dog."

The Guildsman's disbelief hung almost palpable in the air. "It dotes on you like a loyal hound. Like the pup that bit Lady Aisha, hai?"

Yukiko swallowed, saying nothing.

"You have a measure of control over it," Nao rasped. "Do not deny it."

"Only the same that anybody does. The control it allows me to have."

"I hope that is enough." Nao shifted his immense bulk. "For the beast's sake and yours. It will not take much to convince Yoritomo-no-miya to put you both to the pyre."

Yukiko forced her eyes down again, studying the woven patterns beneath her feet. Black wings and claws and tails interwoven in a frozen dance across the long-lost color of the sky; the blessed spirit-beasts that had once been so much a part of this island that even foreign artisans knew their shapes by rote. All of them gone now. Gone because of men like this one, bloated with greed, a pig grown fat on the sweat from poor men's backs. Gone into the mists of memory, obscured behind a rolling blanket of choking blue-black smoke, like a curtain falling after the last notes of music died.

She put her hand to her brow, headache pounding inside her skull.

I am thinking like a Kagé.

"I will do my best to serve the Shōgun's wishes." She kept her voice low and even. "As I have always done. As my father has always done."

"Of course you will." The Guildsman sniffed, waved her away like a troublesome insect. "You may go. Enjoy the rest of the journey. You may visit Kioshi-san if you wish, but you will seek my permission first."

They call him by his father's name.

Yukiko frowned, feigning confusion.

"Who is Kioshi-san?"

"Ah." The Guildsman's laugh was a short, humorless bark. "You had no chance to learn his name while ripping the skin from his flesh. Kioshi-san is the Artificer you rescued from the crash. I misunderstood. I presumed you two had become . . . close."

"Oh." Yukiko blinked. "I did not think any of you had names."

"We do not." Nao pointed toward the door. "The lotus must bloom."

Yukiko covered her fist and bowed, backing away and slipping out quietly. The Guildsman hovering outside regarded her with those glowing, bloody eyes, clockwork and gears rippling down its chest. She nodded to it, and hurried up the stairs.

The noise of the mechabacus behind her sounded like a growl.

25

A DAUGHTER OF FOXES

Yukiko had never seen so many people in Docktown before. As the *Glory* pulled into its berth, she looked over the ship's railing at a sea of upturned faces, thousands upon thousands, respirators and kerchiefs and bare, filthy flesh, goggles bright, fingers pointing. Humble sararīmen and slick neo-chōnin, filthy karōshimen and filthier beggars, guards, gaijin and geisha. Rumor had obviously spread; half the city had turned out to clap eyes on the legend. The word was a whisper, riding a tide on a multitude of lips, lapping in waves of growing volume until it became a tsunami, an impossible thought given voice and crashing among the dust and cobbles.

"Arashitora."

Buruu poked his head over the railing to glower at the crowd and they burst into thunderous cheers. Startled, the thunder tiger ducked back out of sight, tail between his legs. He shook himself like a wet dog, as if to shake the trepidation away.

SO MANY. INSECTS, ALL.

I am with you. I am here.

I WOULD LEAVE THIS PLACE.

I know. But we have work to do.

WHEN IT IS DONE, WE WILL FLY FAR FROM HERE. FAR FROM THIS SCAB AND ITS POISONED SKY. WE WILL DANCE IN THE STORMS, YOU AND I.

Until then, we must be careful. He must think me a simple girl, you a dumb beast.

Buruu glanced over the side again, ignoring the crowd's rapture, glaring at the arriving convoy of low-slung motor-rickshaws. They glittered in the sun like beetle shells, crawling with men and their growling swords, surrounded by a choir of wailing monkey-children. Reeking of wealth, of stinking excess, of blind, mad hubris. He had yet to lay eyes on this Yoritomo-no-miya, and he already despised him.

I WILL PLAY MY PART. FEAR NOT.

Yukiko smiled, ran her hands along his flanks.

I fear nothing when you are near, Buruu.

The arashitora purred, nuzzled her with one broad, feathered cheek. He prowled about her, brushing gently with his wings, wrapping his tail about her legs. Yukiko watched him with a smile on her face, dragging her fingers through his fur. There was a subtle cough, and the Guildsman standing a respectful distance away spoke with a sandpaper tongue.

"We will descend and pay our respects to the Shōgun now."

Yukiko nodded and fell into step beside the Lotusman, Buruu staying on the *Glory*'s prow. She stepped across to the sky-spire and began climbing down, painful memories of the day she had first arrived in Kigen welling in her mind. She could see herself sitting on her father's back as he descended, the entire city at her feet. The applause of the crowd was a dirge in her ears now, the hum of her mother's funeral hymn.

She wondered where they had buried her.

Yukiko reached the ground, flanked on all sides by Guild mercenaries and Lotusmen, the air abuzz with the noise of their suits, the rasp of their breath. The greasy reek of lotus crawled over her tongue and the back of her throat, making her feel ill. The pristine air of the storm-wracked Iishi seemed a distant memory now, so far back in time, so far away she could only barely see the edges, a blurry haze on a distant horizon. She tried to remember the taste of clean rain, and failed.

The crowd looked at her with unabashed curiosity. This dirty, bedraggled girl who had tamed a thunder tiger and brought it from the heart of the wilds to lay at their Lord's feet.

"Arashi-no-ko," she heard them whisper.

She could feel Buruu frown in her mind, puzzled by the word's shape.

WHAT DOES IT MEAN?

She smiled, embarrassed, turning her eyes to the floor.

Storm Girl.

His pride warmed her insides.

I LIKE THAT.

The first rickshaw opened and Herald Tanaka stepped out, golden breastplate reflecting dirty scarlet sunlight. Yukiko pressed her forehead to the dirt as

Tanaka crowed the full list of Yoritomo's titles, the speakers at his throat amplifying his voice into a rasping shout. "Guardian of the Holy Empire," "Resplendent Sword of the Four Thrones," "Son of the Nagaraja Slayer." It was all a blur, an insectoid humming in her ears, empty slogans and hollow words until the final phrase, a sharp kick to her gut that sent a murmur of appreciation through the crowd.

"Next Stormdancer of Shima."

Yukiko kept her head low, swallowed the rage boiling up inside her. She imagined tearing the scroll from Tanaka's hands, shoving it down his throat and screaming the truth to all these docile sheep.

Rapist.

Murderer.

Butcher of unborn children.

CALM. BE CALM. SOON WE WILL RIGHT THESE WRONGS.

She smiled to herself, reached out and touched Buruu's mind. She kept her forehead to the floor, watching the scene through his eyes.

Soon.

Tanaka rolled up his scroll and the central rickshaw cracked open. Yoritomo-no-miya stepped out with a flourish, and the assembled mob dropped immediately to the dust. The Shōgun wore a brand-new respirator, solid gold, crafted so that his face resembled an eagle's, twin filtration cylinders sitting either side of a curved beak, eyes hidden behind amber glass. His embossed breastplate was fashioned with a small golden wing on each shoulder, the corners of a red silk cloak spilling out from each metal pinion and billowing in the contaminated breeze.

RIDICULOUS.

She could feel Buruu's snort of contempt rumbling in her own chest, pressed her lips together lest it spill out of her mouth. The Shōgun helped his sister from the rickshaw as the herald pronounced her name. Yukiko risked a glance up at the woman, the impeccable facade hidden behind mirrored lenses and the blades of her golden respirator fan. A full dozen serving girls flowed out of the rear carriage and flocked to their Lady's side, swathed in slippery red silk. There was the barest flicker of recognition in Aisha's face as she stared at Yukiko, glanced down to the puppy in her arms. And then it was gone.

Yoritomo approached Yukiko, one hand resting on his sheathed katana, stopping within arm's reach. He took off his respirator and handed it to Tanaka, slinging his long plait over his shoulder with a toss of his head.

"Rise, Kitsune Yukiko."

His voice had an edge to it. A fervor she'd never taken note of before.

Yukiko stood, kept her eyes to the floor under the pretense of respect. Her fingertips tingled, the tantō in her obi felt heavy as a brick. She could hear her mother singing by the fireside in their little house, her voice filling the night, weariness of the day giving way to gentle dreams.

"Great Lord," she said.

She felt his hands on her chin, and it was all she could do to hold back the scream; to not lash out with the knife and open his throat wide, bathe in his blood. He forced her gaze up from the ground, tilting her head back until they looked into each other's eyes. There was a faint tittering among the geisha, whispers drifting in the throng.

"You have served your Shōgun well, daughter of foxes."

"Thank you, great Lord."

"You bring honor to your father. I am glad I did not kill him."

"My great Lord is truly merciful."

"Indeed. I am." Yoritomo released his grip and glanced up and down her body, a lingering stare that made her stomach turn. "Now, where is my arashi-tora?"

Yukiko stepped backward out of his reach and gave a shrill whistle, fingers to her lips. The sound of claws on wood was heard overhead, a sudden rush of air, and a great silhouette blotted out the sun. The children shrieked and pointed, men and women gasped in wonder as Buruu stretched his crippled wings and dropped from the *Glory*'s deck. He could manage only a brief, wobbling glide, spiraling down far too quickly and sending the Guild marines and gathered bushimen running for cover. Landing clumsily, he skidded across the cobbles and gravel, talons tearing deep furrows in his wake.

He opened his beak and roared. A deafening sound, broken lightning flickering across his outstretched wings. The stupefied crowd crouched low in terror. Even Yoritomo was taken aback, stepping away and clutching the braided hilts of his daishō. The Iron Samurai drew their own blades, the chattering chainkatana growl lost in the reverberation of the thunder tiger's wings. The bushimen advanced as the arashitora prowled toward their Shōgun, weapons at the ready, uncertain glances. Yoritomo held his ground but his face was bloodless with fear, knuckles white on his sword hilts. And as the assembled crowd gasped in wonder, Buruu dipped his head and scratched at the ground before the Shōgun's feet.

The beast was bowing to their Lord.

Applause. Jubilant, euphoric, a giddy wave spilling over the throng and turning Yukiko's stomach. An awful sound; all slapping sallow skin and bare, stamping feet, row upon row of grubby kerchiefs hiding a streetful of empty, crooked smiles. But the mob was overjoyed, filling the air with whistles and shouts, ecstatic that this beast from the pages of legend had immediately abased itself on seeing their Shōgun. Truly, this was a man who deserved their obeisance. Truly this was a Lord worthy of the title. His father's son.

Yoritomo smiled and nodded, holding his hand up to the people. At a signal from Tanaka, a tarpaulin was pulled away from the back of the rearmost motor-rickshaw, revealing a large cage with bars of thick pig iron. Yoritomo strode to it and pulled aside the door, looking at the arashitora expectantly.

"Forgive this crude transportation." He gave a small, mocking bow. "But since he cannot fly himself . . ."

Yukiko put her hand on the beast's flank, running her fingers through his fur. She could feel his fear, saw the images painted across his mind's eye; the moment he had awoken in that cage on the deck of the *Thunder Child* and found his wings mutilated.

Buruu, you don't have to . . .

NO.

The arashitora shook his head defiantly, pushing the fear away.

I SAID I WILL PLAY MY PART.

"Up," she said, voice harsh with command. "Get in there."

The beast padded toward the cage, aiming a glittering amber stare directly at Yoritomo. And then as the crowd dropped into a breathless hush, he folded his wings and leaped inside.

Applause. Nauseating, deafening applause.

"Great Lord," said Yukiko, staring at Yoritomo's split-toed boots. "With your permission, I will ride with the arashitora to the palace. He may become unnerved by the noise of the city."

"Your family seems to enjoy the view from behind bars." Yoritomo laughed, still waving to the crowd. "But do as you wish. Just keep it calm until we get to the arena."

"Arena, my Lord?" She swallowed.

Surely he cannot intend to have Buruu fight for sport?

"You will see, Kitsune Yukiko." Yoritomo dropped his hand and strode toward his waiting rickshaw. "You will see."

B uruu prowled the arena floor, tail lashing. The chain tether rasped across stone and straw, clanking as he paced. The rock beneath his feet was dark with the blood of a thousand gaijin: victims in the spectacles that kept Kigen pacified on festival weekends and feast days. Countless pale throats dragged across the waves, opened up to the tune of the roaring crowd.

The arena pit was sunk ten feet into the ground, a hundred feet in diameter. The stone floor had been pierced at its center with a single bar of black iron, driven deep into the rock. Empty stone benches rose in concentric circles all around the pit, wind howling mournfully in the vast, hollow space. Above them sat the empty imperial box, tiger flags whipping in the breeze. Though there were no bars above his head, thick chain and crippled wings kept Buruu firmly tethered to the hateful earth. He looked up at the red sun and squinted, shook himself like a soggy tomcat. The iron collar at his throat clanked with the motion.

AT LEAST I CAN STILL SEE THE SKY.

I'm sorry, Buruu.

I WILL ENDURE.

The Guild Artificer affixed the other end of Buruu's tether to the iron spike in the middle of the arena, its arc torch flaring sun-bright, blobs of molten solder spattering thick on the floor. A rectangular eye of black glass reflected the white-hot flare. As Yukiko watched, the Artificer turned off its welding iron and stabbed a switch on its chest. The black pane over its eyes slid aside to reveal a slab of malevolent red. She stared at the brass mask, wondering who was really inside that suit, whether they were truly as evil as the Kagé would have her believe.

She thought of Kin lying burned in the rain, murmuring the Guild mantra over and over to himself. The desire to ask whether the boy had been punished was tempered with the knowledge that a hadanashi girl showing any kind of concern for him might only make his punishment worse. And so she kept her questions to herself, picturing her friend standing in the rain on the bow of the *Thunder Child*, and prayed for Kitsune to watch over him.

Yoritomo stared at the Guildsman, nodded when the task was done. He was surrounded by half a dozen Iron Samurai in the golden jin-haori tabards of the Kazumitsu Elite. Each warrior stood nearly eight feet tall, clad in great, hissing suits of ō-yoroi armor, gleaming black, chi exhaust spitting from the power units at their backs. Their masks were iron, crafted to resemble the faces of oni, twisted and grinning. Chainsaw katana and wakizashi were worn at their waists, heavy iron gauntlets never straying far from the hilts. Beside the Shōgun stood Herald Tanaka and the bent figure of Chief Minister Hideo. The old man clutched a walking stick in one hand, a lotus pipe in the other, occasionally lifting his breather to suck down a lungful of smoke. The scent reminded Yukiko of her father.

I hope he is all right.

Buruu pawed at his collar, glanced at his ruined wings and said nothing.

"So." Yoritomo addressed the Guildsman. "You will begin constructing the saddle immediately. I have drawn the one I saw in my vision. It must be exactly as I have illustrated here."

Yoritomo snapped his fingers, and Minister Hideo dutifully handed a carven mahogany scroll case to the Artificer. The Guildsman accepted it, nodded slowly.

"I expect it to be ready in time for the bicentennial celebrations next month." Yoritomo's eyes were fixed on Buruu, glazed with hunger. "The Kazumitsu Dynasty has ruled these islands for the past two hundred years. I intend to usher in the next two hundred on the back of this arashitora. Am I understood?"

"As you command, great Lord." The clicking of cicada wings.

"The lotus must bloom."

"The lotus must bloom," the Guildsman repeated, touching its forehead with two fingers. With a hiss of chi smoke and the whirr of a dozen clockwork engines, the figure clanked off across the stone floor under the watchful eye of the Iron Samurai. Two other Guildsmen waited as patiently as spiders beneath one of the outer arches. Yukiko watched the trio exchange brief words, casting glowing stares in her direction before departing. Dread clutched at her stomach. Heavy footsteps rebounded across sweating stone, their shadows sliding down the wall and out into the lotus-choked light.

"How long until its feathers grow back?"

Yukiko took a moment to realize the Shōgun was addressing her.

"Ah . . ." She stammered, staring at the floor, hands clasped before her. "Forgive me. I do not know, great Lord."

"Ask it."

Yukiko dared a glance at the Shōgun's face. He was studying her intently, dark eyes glinting like star metal, smile like a razor. His long jin-haori tabard writhed in the warm, cancer wind, golden tigers prowling across scarlet silk.

"Great Lord?"

"The Lady Aisha changed her perfume after our meeting at the sky-docks. Her dog has seemed quite content ever since. Strange that you guessed the root of its misbehavior in a handful of seconds. Almost as if you knew its mind . . ."

Yukiko glanced between Yoritomo and his bodyguards, hands on their chainkatana hilts. A tiny, childish part of her realized that the samurai to Yoritomo's left had green eyes.

"I . . . I have a way with beasts, my Lord." She swallowed, turned her eyes back to the ground, squeezing her hands into fists to stop the shakes.

"You are yōkai-kin."

"No, Lord, I—"

Yoritomo's raised hand was as good as a slap, cutting her sentence in half. Buruu edged closer, eyes on the Iron Samurai, hackles rippling.

"You have nothing to fear, Kitsune Yukiko." The Shōgun's smile never reached his eyes. "I have no interest in revealing your secret to the Guild. I do not care for their zealotry, their crusade for 'purity'. The Book of Ten Thousand Days has many interpretations, and theirs is only one." He motioned to Buruu. "This beast will accept me as his master quicker with you telling me his thoughts, and conveying mine to him. That is all that matters to me."

The Shōgun ran one hand across the thunder tiger's flank, fingers spread into claws, buried deep in the thick fur. He inhaled the arashitora's scent, the heady mix of musk and ozone, tracing the line of one thick black stripe over Buruu's spine.

"Magnificent. My vision was true. Do you see, Hideo-san?"

He turned to glare at the minister.

"I see, great Lord." Hideo bowed deep, voice distorted by his pulsing breather-helm. "Truly, the God of War has spoken to you. None can now doubt that you are Hachiman's chosen. Astride this creature's back, you will become the greatest general in the history of Shima. The gaijin will quail before you. After twenty years of war, your hand will bring an ending, and the barbarian hordes will hail you rightly as conqueror, and sovereign Lord."

Yukiko scowled at the minister, despising him for his sycophantic little liturgy. Yoritomo seemed too intent on Buruu to notice, running his fingers along the arashitora's wing. Buruu rankled at the touch but kept himself calm, still as the stone beneath their feet. The Shōgun grinned, bloodless lips across perfect teeth.

"So." A glance at Yukiko. "How long?"

Yukiko remained mute, terrified beneath that iron stare. For her to admit her gift here in front of the Shōgun was to place herself in mortal danger. She recalled her mother's words, urging her and Satoru never to risk death by revealing the secret. To admit it now would be to invite the executioner's blade, or worse, a screaming death chained to the Burning Stones in the Market Square.

And then, glancing at the Iron Samurai, she realized her life was in danger anyway. Regardless of what he knew or what he didn't, Yoritomo had the power of life and death over every man, woman and child in Shima. If he wanted her dead, she'd be dead; he didn't need a reason. He certainly didn't need a confession. One snap of his fingers would be all it took.

So to the hells with being afraid.

Be clever instead.

"The beast has a simple mind, great Lord," she said. "It thinks in scent and sight, not words. I would measure it no smarter than a dog. It understands concepts that any hound might; only day and night, not months or years. But I believe it will moult at the end of autumn, when it grows its winter coat."

"That is nearly four months away," the Shōgun hissed.

"It may be sooner, Lord." She kept her eyes on the ground. "But it is looking forward to winter. I do not think it will fly before then."

NO SMARTER THAN A DOG . . .

Shhh.

The Shōgun snarled, cheeks flushed with blood. He took a few deep, calming breaths, clenching and unclenching his fists. Yukiko could see the tension in Hideo's stance, the nervous glances between the samurai at their Lord's growing rage. Yoritomo closed his eyes and breathed deep, blotches of color fading on his cheeks. Finally, he gritted his teeth and nodded.

"So be it." He opened his eyes and glared. "You will break this beast, get it accustomed to the notion of a rider, of being steered with bit and bridle. When the Artificers have completed my saddle, we will begin training. You will stay in the palace, one of my Elite will accompany you at all times." His tone became darker, edged with steel. "I remind you that your father is still imprisoned in the dungeons. Should you fail in this task, you will not be the only one to suffer for it."

COWARD.

"May I see him, great Lord?"

Yoritomo seemed surprised by the request. He stared at her for a long, pregnant moment, drumming his fingertips on the hilt of his katana.

"Very well," he finally nodded, turning to the green-eyed samurai. "Hiro-san, you will be the Lady Yukiko's escort while she is our guest. Should any trouble come to her, or *because* of her, you will pay the forfeit. Is this clear?"

"Hai!" The samurai strode to Yukiko's side and bowed to his Lord, palm over fist.

Yukiko realized the Shōgun was watching her, something unpleasant coiled in his eyes. As she met his stare, he let it linger a minute longer, drifting down to her throat, over her breasts. She felt naked and exposed in her tattered clothing, folding her arms and turning her eyes back to the floor.

"It is settled," he nodded. "Visit your father, then Hiro-san will show you to your quarters. Your desire is his command. I will check in occasionally to monitor your . . . progress."

"As you say, great Lord."

Yukiko covered her fist and gave a deep bow. The Shōgun replaced his respirator, collar folding over his throat with a small, metallic hymn. Spinning on his heel, he stalked from the pit, red silk billowing behind him. His retinue fell into step after him, heavy metal tread cracking on the stone. Faint trails of chi fumes twisted through the air in their wake, weaving among each other and drifting up into the red sky overhead.

How long until you begin to moult?

WEEKS. PERHAPS THREE. WHEN THE SUMMER BEGINS TO DIE.

We must keep your wings hidden while your new feathers grow in. Yoritomo must think you crippled. He must underestimate us both.

HE WILL.

Yukiko finally turned to the Iron Samurai looming over her, breath hissing through his tusks. Embossed black steel covered his body, spaulders broad and flat and studded with rivets, expression entirely hidden behind the twisted oni mask. Yukiko looked into his eyes, at those irises colored like creamy jade. Though he was the right height, she couldn't see enough of his face to confirm her hopes. Butterflies floated through her stomach on lead-lined wings.

Is it really him?

YOU MONKEYS ARE SO STRANGE. SO MUCH FUSS OVER COUPLING.

Buruu!

WHAT? YOU WISH TO MATE WITH THIS ONE. YOU ARE OF AN AGE. THERE IS—

Gods, stop it! You're worse than my father.

"We meet again, daughter of foxes," the samurai said.

"It *is* you."

Her pulse pounded in her veins, the memory of her dreams rising with the flush in her cheeks. She shoved them away in a dark corner of her head, barred and locked the door.

"You remember me?" A hint of a smile in his voice.

"You remember me." She shrugged.

"How could I forget?" He covered his fist and bowed. "I am Lord Tora Hiro, sworn of the Kazumitsu Elite."

"Kitsune Yukiko."

"I know who you are, Lady." The smile in his voice was unmistakable now. "It is my honor to serve you."

BE WARY. HE SERVES THE SHŌGUN FIRST AND FOREMOST. HE IS A WEAPON IN THE MACHINE.

. . . Maybe he's not like that.

DO NOT BE BLINDED BY YOUR DESIRE TO—

Gods, if you say "couple" again I'm going to scream.

CALL IT WHAT YOU WISH, THEN.

I know what he is and who he serves. Not everyone who swears to the Shōgun is evil, Buruu. I wear Yoritomo's irezumi on my flesh too, remember?

Buruu snorted and prowled away, lying down near the spike that kept him tethered. He heaved a great sigh through his nostrils, straw dancing off the ground, slipping and spinning through the air. The Iron Samurai watched with unashamed wonder.

"It is beautiful," Hiro said. "Can you really hear its thoughts?"

"Hai," she nodded, watching the Iron Samurai carefully. "I suppose that repels you."

Hiro checked over his shoulder, ensuring they were alone.

"I am no advocate of the Guild, or their views." A small, clanking shrug. "The Guildsmen give us many amazing gifts. Sky-ships, chainkatana, ō-yoroi. Yet I do not understand how this gives them the right to dictate morality to my Lord or his people. They are not sworn to the Code of Bushido. They are mechanics, artisans. Not priests. Not to me."

The quiet conviction in his voice sent a tingle down Yukiko's spine, and she stared deep into his eyes, resisting the urge to just plunge in and drown. The revelation that he resented the Guild was a welcome relief, but Buruu's warning was an insistent echo in her head. Even by a fool's estimation, this samurai was now her keeper. Her jailer.

A jailer with the most beautiful eyes she had ever seen . . .

"There is nothing you could do that would repel me, Lady."

Yukiko could barely hear his voice over the sound of her heart pounding in her chest.

RAIJIN, TAKE ME NOW.

She shot Buruu a withering glance as he rolled over on his back and pawed at the sky.

HAVE MERCY ON ME, FATHER. TAKE MY WINGS. CHAIN ME TO STINKING EARTH. BUT THIS TORTURE I CANNOT ENDURE.

Oh, shut it.

"Come on." She glanced at the Samurai, nodded toward the exit. "I have to see my father. If you're to be my babysitter now, I suppose you'd better come along."

She turned to leave, sparing one last glance for the arashitora on his chain. He looked thoroughly miserable, a beast of thunder and open sky caged in a filthy pit built for murder and mindless bloodshed. Her heart swelled with pity, the knowledge that if not for her, he would never have come here.

I'll be back, Buruu. Very soon.

He blinked at her, eyes of molten honey. To a stranger, his face would have seemed utterly impassive. No lips to smile, no brows to frown. Just a mask of sleek lines and white feathers, smooth and motionless. But she could see it in the tilt of his head, the way his tail switched from side to side, the rise and fall of his flanks as he breathed.

She could feel it inside him, the rock he had set his back against, the core of his being. A compass that would steer him through this darkness, this torture at the hands of insects, safely out the other side into blinding lightning and howling wind. It would lead him home.

It was love.

He nodded, curled his head beneath one crippled wing.

I WILL BE HERE.

26

PORTENTS

It was waiting for him every time he closed his eyes. A shadow in a darkened room, breath held in anticipation of the candle's flame that would give it life. Yet he could feel it lingering even when he was awake, seen or unseen, just a nightfall away. A part of him as integral as the heart that pumped his blood, the metal skin encasing his flesh.

The vision.

It had been with him since his Awakening, the night they took him from his bed and pushed the smoke into his lungs and opened his eyes to the future that awaited him. And in that awful moment he had seen what he would become. Witnessed the horror and majesty of it all, listening to the grim march of inevitability inside his skull. And from that day to this, the dream had been lurking in the warm dark space behind his eyelids. And he had been dreaming of a way to escape it.

He heard their voices now. Hundreds of bloody eyes upturned, hundreds of faces watching him with as much fervor as could be found in smooth lifeless brass. Hands held high. Metallic voices echoing on blank stone. They were calling him as they always did.

"Kin-san."

And he answered as he always did.

"That is not my name."

"Kioshi-san."

The voice was harsh and metallic, the drone of a fat and hungry lotusfly, pulling him into the harsh light of waking. He blinked away the blur of sleep, pawed at his eyelids in the dirty halogen glow, searching for the source of the sound. He was lying in a metal cot, gray sheets, walls of sweating yellow stone at his back. He recognized the hum of the air filtration system and the groan and clank of great engines throbbing in the background. It was a tune he had lived with since the day of his birth; the lullaby of the Kigen chapterhouse. The air was moist, and a sheen of sweat on his flesh made the gauze at his throat and shoulder itch, crinkling like dry paper as he ran his hand across it. He realized that he was still skinless, but they had already plugged him back into a mechabacus, bayonet fixtures speared at his collarbone, under his ribs, relays worming toward his spinal column. Out of instinct, he flicked several beads across the device to test the transmission conduits, and received a brief acknowledgment in return.

"Kioshi-san."

Kin turned to the source of the sound, the buzzsaw rasp of heavy breathing, a shadow falling across the light above. He took in the broad silhouette of a Guildsman looming over him in the grubby warmth, dull light gleaming on the sculpted, muscular lines of the atmos-suit, eyes burning like a smog-choked sunset.

Dread stabbed at Kin's stomach, and he licked at suddenly dry lips. He recognized the suit, the tiger-stripe pattern of iron-gray filigree across burnished brass. The authority dripping from every word the figure spoke. But most of all, he recognized the face. Unlike the hard insectoid helms of most Lotusmen, the elaborate mask staring down at him was almost human. The sculpted brow and rounded cheeks of a boy in the prime of his youth, rendered in smooth, polished brass; a perfect symmetry that should by all rights have been beautiful. Perhaps it was the cluster of segmented cables spilling from the mouth, as if the child were in the middle of vomiting up a stomachful of iron squid. Perhaps it was the burning red eyes that cast a bloody glow on those full, flawless cheeks. Whatever the reason, there was something wrong about that face; something in it that Kin had always feared.

The man towering above him had been the closest thing to a friend Kin's father had ever known. If they were normal people, he might have taken Kin into his own house when Old Kioshi passed away. If Kin were a normal child, it would not have seemed strange to any if he called the man "uncle."

But being who and what he was, Kin used the title that everyone else did.

"Shateigashira." He tried to make his voice sound strong, covered his fist, bowed as best he could. "The Voice of Chapterhouse Kigen honors me with his presence."

"You wake. Good."

The huge figure flicked several beads across the mechabacus on his chest, transmitting to the grand library hub at First House. A thousand receivers gathering and transcribing a thousand chits of data every minute, relaying information to the Ministries of Communication, Ordinance, Procurement, Division. Adding to the constant machine hum inside the heads of anyone plugged into the system. The pulse of the machine he had lived with his entire life.

"How do you feel?"

"Sore." Kin touched the bandages again. "Thirsty."

"To be expected, after so grand an adventure."

There was no trace of amusement in the Shateigashira's voice. Kin blinked, saying nothing, watching the mechabacus click back and forth on the broad clockwork chest.

"When your skin transmitted its distress beacon, there were fears you had met your end in the Iishi. But I knew better. We both know you are intended for grander things, Kioshi-san." The Shateigashira ran one gauntleted hand along the metal railing of the cot; a grinding rasp that set Kin's teeth on edge. "And yet the Kyodai of the *Resplendent Glory* tells me that you were naked when his troops found you. Outside your skin. In the company of a hadanashi girl."

"The fire." Kin swallowed. "The damage to my skin. It was unavoidable, Shateigashira."

"It was unfortunate, Kioshi-san." A shake of his head, red light casting frightful shadows across those perfect, frozen features. "A great loss of face. Your father would be ashamed to witness a blessed child fall so low. I am glad he is not alive to see this day. An example must be made to the other Shatei. Even for one such as yourself. There must be punishment."

Kin took a deep breath, tried to still the pounding of his heart.

"I understand."

"And yet, the example may be tempered with mercy. The retribution meted out for your transgression may be lessened through your cooperation."

Kin already knew what they would ask. As if the act of asking made it any less of a command. As if he had any choice in the matter whatsoever. He breathed deep, tried to remember the taste of clean rain, the feel of the cool mountain breeze on his face, the way her hair rippled like black silk in the wind. He spoke the words as if they didn't quite fit properly in his mouth.

"What would you have of me, Shateigashira?"

"The girl they found you with. The one who tamed the arashitora."

"Hai?"

The towering figure leaned in closer.

"Tell me everything you know."

27

WISTERIA PERFUME

The prison was a stinking cesspit of oily stone and rancid air. A forgotten hole into which Kigen justice poured criminals spared from death in the arena or outright execution; a pitiful, lucky few. Debtors and thugs, petty thieves and one-percenters crammed into tiny cells with bars of pitted iron and rotten straw on the floor. No sunlight. No air. Stale bread and black water and bare rock for a pillow.

The gate guard had taken one look at Hiro in his golden tabard and hissing, clanking suit of ō-yoroi before fumbling for his keys and opening the gate to the cell block. He bobbed and shuffled along a dank corridor, looking back over his shoulder every few feet as if to make sure they were still with him. Beckoning them down twisting stairs into the reeking dark. Small rats scurried away from the torchlight in the guard's hand, larger ones with tails thick as Yukiko's thumb standing their ground and screeching in defiance. Buzzing lotusflies swam in corpse-stench as they passed one cell. She covered her mouth and averted her eyes.

The guard halted deep in the prison bowels, indicating a cell door at the end of the corridor. Handing the torch over, he bobbed his head again at Hiro and retreated a respectful distance. Yukiko turned to the Iron Samurai, nodding toward the cell.

"I would speak to my father alone, Lord Hiro."

He bowed, whirring gears and hissing chi smoke.

"As you wish, Lady."

She approached the cell with slow, heavy tread, torch held high, heart breaking when she saw the pale, filthy figure hunched in the cage. Naked but for a vomit-stained rag, gray skin glistening with a sheen of sallow sweat, palsied with the agony of lotus de-tox. Teeth chattering, head bowed, arms clasped about his knees. Locked in a private hell and not stirring an inch at the light's approach.

"Father?" The sob caught in her throat, voice breaking.

She knelt in front of the cell door, jamming the torch between the bars. Flickering light crept across Masaru's tattoos, the nine-tailed fox seeming to dance among the shadows. She reached toward him, fingers spread. The reek of the bucket in the corner made her want to retch.

"Father," she repeated louder.

He lifted his head slowly and squinted at the light, knotted tangles of graying hair hanging in dirty strings over his face. Recognition broke through the crust of withdrawal and he blinked, eyes widening, uncurling from his crouch.

"Yukiko?" he whispered, crawling toward her across the filthy stone. "Lord Izanagi, take me. Are you real, or another smoke vision?"

"It's me, father." She tried to smile, tears rolling down her cheeks, clasping his hand between the bars. "It's your Ichigo."

His face was alight with joy, creeping past the pain and shining in his eyes. "I thought you were dead!"

"No." She squeezed his hand. "I saved him, father. The arashitora. He's here with me."

"Gods above . . ."

"Where is Kasumi? Akihito?"

"Gone." He shook his head, dropped his gaze to the floor. "I commanded them to flee before we reached the city gates. I knew Yoritomo's wrath would be black. Yamagata . . ."

"I know. I know what Yoritomo did. To Yamagata. To us. I know everything, father."

He glanced up, confusion and fear dilating his pupils. The creases at the corners of his mouth and eyes were cut deep; dark furrows in gray stone, scars of a torturous secret held for years. Drowning the pain in lotus smoke, seeking oblivion in drinking dens and gambling pits, hoping for some kind of end to it all. Hollow respite from the secret twisting inside, whispering in the dark. The secret they now shared.

"You . . ." There were tears in his eyes. The first time she had ever seen them. "You know?"

"I know."

His sigh seemed to come from the depths of him, someplace dark and poisonous, an exhalation of the toxin he'd breathed since that crushing day. Some part of her had known, had always known. Ever since he'd crouched down beside her in the Shōgun's garden and told her that her mother was gone, that she had left and would never be coming back. That Yukiko couldn't say goodbye. And she had blamed him. She had hated him for it.

"Naomi . . ." His voice cracked at the name. "Your mother, she begged Yoritomo to release me from his service. Beseeched him on behalf of our family. The babe in her belly. You had grown up without me. She did not want that life for our new child. The Shōgun smiled and nodded, told us he would think on it. That he would give us his answer on the morrow."

Masaru blinked hard, screwing his face up tight and willing away the tears. Yukiko held his hand as hard as she could, reached out and brushed his cheeks.

"They killed her the next morning. I returned from the bathhouse and found her still in bed. Eyes closed. Throat cut." His voice broke. "The blood . . ."

He stared down at his open, empty palm, silent for a long, terrible moment, eyes filled with hatred.

"I snatched up the nagamaki his father had given me, and went in search of Yoritomo, intending to take his head. I found him on a terrace overlooking the garden, watching you play with the sparrows. He was only a boy, barely thirteen, but he looked at me with the eyes of a madman. And do you know what he said?"

Masaru hung his head, swallowing thickly, "'If you defy me again, I will take everything you have left. Everything.'" A low growl. "'And I will *hurt* it first.'"

He punched the floor beneath him, splitting his knuckles, bone grating across stone.

"Then he smiled down at you and walked away, without a backward glance." Masaru ran a hand across his eyes, smearing his face with blood. "I couldn't tell you. If you knew what he had done, he might have seen you as a threat. And so I told you she had left. I told everyone that she had left. It was easy to believe. I was never home. I had been unfaithful. But I loved her, Ichigo. Despite everything, I did not stop loving her for a moment. And you were all I had left of her."

He looked up at her, face streaked with blood and grief. "I could not lose you too."

The tears rolled unheeded down her cheeks, pattering on the floor with the sound of rain. Washing it all away, the hate, the anger, leaving her with the knowledge that she had wronged this man. That he had shackled himself to a madman's throne so her life would be spared.

"Forgive me," he whispered, squeezing her fingers.

"Forgive me," she begged.

He reached through the bars and pulled her close, the metal between them pressing into their flesh as they embraced. She could feel the hard muscle coiled beneath gray skin, the strength in his arms beneath the lotus tremors. But it was nothing compared to the will it must have taken to kneel every day, to give up all he was for the sake of his daughter. A strength beyond strength.

She could hear the words he had spoken to her on the *Thunder Child*, ringing in her mind as clearly as if he had said them aloud. And at last, she understood what he had meant.

"One day you will see that we must sometimes sacrifice for the sake of something greater."

"I'm going to get you out of here," she whispered, holding him tight. "I promise."

S hateigashira Kensai, exalted Second Bloom of Chapterhouse Kigen."
   Hideo's pale voice traveled the length of the reception hall and into the throne room, up the woven red carpet and among the high tapestries swaying in the afternoon breeze. The minister clapped his staff against the floor three times, and the Iron Samurai manning the doorway stepped aside as one, perfectly timed; a silicone-slick machine precision to match that of the Lotusman.

The courtiers gathered in the hall outside parted respectfully, fluttering fans in front of painted faces and elaborate breathers, eyes staring behind goggles of tinted glass or slitted against the long afternoon light shearing through the windows. Representatives from every zaibatsu in Shima were present at Yoritomo's court. Emissaries from the Daimyo of the Ryu clan stood in their rippling blue silks, obi fashioned like dragon scales. A cluster of Kitsune nobles, skin pale as snow, thick as thieves, shrouded in kimono of whispering black, glaring across the court at their Dragon neighbors and muttering darkly behind their fans. Beautiful men and women from the Fushicho lands, flesh around their eyes shaded with the color of flame, blond streaks bleached in their hair, breathtaking finery the hue of newborn sunflowers bleeding through to vibrant orange. As always, the Phoenix did their best to ignore the obvious enmity between Dragon and Fox, concentrating instead on outshining both. Of course, the vast majority of the assembly was clad in red: brilliant, bloody red, the symbol of the Tiger clan embroidered on their robes in precious golden thread. Each of them fell silent now, the innuendo and gossip fading to nothing as Shateigashira Kensai, Second Bloom, the voice of the Guild in Kigen city himself stepped through the double doors and approached the throne room.

The hiss of gears, the song of the mechabacus on his chest. Heavy tread sounded upon the carpet, the dying day glittering in those blood-red, faceted eyes. Kensai was a monster of a man: six feet tall and almost as broad, impressive bulk stuffed inside an indulgently decorated atmos-suit. The metal was crafted to emulate hard lines of muscle, embossed with gothic flourishes and filigree in the pattern of a tiger's stripes. But his face was an anomaly; the features of a beautiful gilded youth, retching up a lungful of chattering iron cable.

Hands in fists, breath hissing through his bellows, the Second Bloom stopped before the throne with barely a bow. His backpack spat a mouthful of chi smoke into the air as the Iron Samurai closed the doors behind him. Spring-driven ceiling fans clicked and swayed in the exposed beams high overhead. Somewhere in the distance a servant roamed the halls, ringing in the Hour of the Wasp on his iron bell.

Yoritomo had watched the Guildsman approach, languid in the heat, face impassive behind a small indoor respirator. Rumor had it that Kensai was a bloated pig beneath his suit; the sheets of metallic muscle were a facade hiding slabs of soft, spotted blubber, the beautiful childlike face covering a mongrel visage that not even a mother could love. Hideo also had it on good authority that Kigen's Second Bloom had a predilection for gaijin women. Imagining the sweaty, faceless hog soiling himself with some poor, abducted barbarian girl, Yoritomo found it easy to ignore Kensai's intimidating stature. The Shōgun actually found himself stifling a smile at the scandal.

"Shateigashira," he nodded. "Voice of Chapterhouse Kigen. You honor us with your presence."

"The honor is mine, Seii Taishōgun, Conqueror of Eastern Barbarians, equal of heaven." Kensai's voice was a deep, metallic rumble, completely at odds with the youthful lines of his mask. "Amaterasu shine on your fields, and bring bounty to your people."

"You are here to discuss the bicentennial, I presume? I trust my saddle will be ready on schedule?"

Hideo materialized beside Yoritomo's throne, the long stem of his pipe resting on bloodless lips. The throne itself was twice as tall as the little minister, a twisting amalgam of golden tigers, sweeping lines and silken cushions. Tapestries swayed in the dirty breeze, slapping against the columns behind. The pillars were black granite shot through with cobalt, sleek and polished as the Guildsman's eyes.

"The venerable Second Bloom wishes to discuss the Kitsune girl, great Lord." Hideo bowed, exhaling a puff of sweet blue-black, narrowing his bloodshot stare.

"Ah," Yoritomo nodded. "My arashitora wrangler. What of her?"

"Forgive me, great Lord." The Guildsman gave an almost imperceptible bow, barely worth the charade. "I wish to give no cause for insult, nor weaken the ties of friendship and honor that bind First House and your court together. I know you have offered shelter to this girl in your own—"

"Spit it out, Kensai." Yoritomo's eyes flashed, pretense sliced to ribbons and slumped bleeding on the floor. "We both know why you are here."

"The girl is Impure, great Lord." His voice was a storm of bumblebees, plump and chitinous. "Tainted by the blood of yōkai. As is commanded in the Book of Ten Thousand Days, her filth must be cleansed. Purity's Way must be walked."

"Mrnm." Yoritomo did his best to look troubled. "Yōkai-kin, you say?"

"It is our deepest-held suspicion, Seii Taishōgun. The incident with the Lady Aisha's dog. The way she handles the arashitora . . ."

"Suspicion?" A raised eyebrow. "You mean to say you have no proof?"

A long pause, filled by the sound of the mechabacus spooling on Kensai's chest. As Yoritomo and Hideo watched, the Guildsman reached up and flicked several of the beads across to the other side. His tone was that of a man choosing his words with utmost care.

"With all due respect, great Lord . . . since when has proof ever been required?"

The guest suite sprawled along the western wing of the palace, thin rice-paper walls, polished teak and no real privacy at all. Every inch dripped with excess. The furniture was hand-carved, masterpieces by Ryu Kamakura and Fushicho Ashikaga hung on the walls, long aquariums of clouded beach glass were set into the floor and populated with thin, miserable koi fish in all colors of the rainbow. But it all felt pompous. Fake. Coin spent not for the comfort of the guest, but for the sake of the Shōgun's majesty.

Yukiko turned to Hiro, hovering by the door.

"You can come in if you like."

"That would be unseemly." His armor sang as he shook his head. "Lady Aisha would have me branded if she discovered I had entered a Lady's bedchamber unaccompanied."

"So, are you just going to sit outside?"

"Hai."

Yukiko thought she could hear a smile hidden behind his fearsome iron mask.

"Can you take that thing off?" She pointed to the mempō. "I've seen enough oni to last a lifetime."

"You have seen oni?" To his credit, there was only a small trace of skepticism in the samurai's voice. "Where?"

"It's a long story." She shook her head. "It doesn't matter. Can you just take it off, please? I can't tell if you're making fun of me under that thing."

Hiro worked the clasp at his throat, the faceplate swung away with a wet sucking sound and he peeled the helm from his head. His hair was plastered to his scalp, face damp with sweat. Strong jaw, small pointed goatee, smooth cheeks beneath those glittering, wonderful eyes.

"I am not making fun of you, Lady."

She stared for a long moment, remembering her dreams and feeling that ridiculous flush rising in her cheeks again. She chided herself; a quick, seething anger that banished the nocturnal fantasies, reminding her that her father and best friend were imprisoned by her mother's murderer. If she could have slapped herself, she would have.

You have more important things to think about than boys.

"I need a bath and a change of clothes." She tried to keep her voice even; it wasn't his fault she was being an idiot. "So find yourself a comfortable chair in the hallway."

Hiro smiled, covered his fist with a small bow. Stuffing his oni helm beneath one arm, he backed out of the room, sliding the door shut behind him. She could see his silhouette painted on the rice-paper by the scarlet sun, like a shadow puppet from the festival pantomimes. Stalking into the dressing room, she sat down in front of the looking glass and began attacking her tangles, refusing to think any more about dreams or childish fantasies or the boy waiting outside her bedroom door.

The girl reflected in the mirror was filthy: chi-stained skin, dirt and oni blood spattered across her clothes, bare feet, knuckles scabbed.

She felt ugly. Ugly like this city and the people who ruled it.

The suite had a private bathhouse, and she soaked in the deliciously warm water for what seemed like hours, watching dried blood and sweat reconstitute and form a dirty scum across the surface. The shampoo smelled like wisteria. She drifted, eyes closed, remembering the village in the trees. The knife in her hand. The blood on the floor.

The promise.

In the solitude and rippling hush, she gradually became aware of an emptiness inside her. It was as if someone had taken a piece of her and pulled it away, so slowly and gently that she didn't notice until there was only a hollow left behind. But now it ached. There was an absence in her head, the feeling that she'd forgotten something as vital as her own name or the shape of her face.

She tried to grasp the feeling, to find a source. Her father? Her mother? And then she blinked, running her hand over her eyes.

Buruu.

She missed him. Not like a lotus-fiend missed his fix, or a drunkard his bottle. It was a softer longing, gentle and sad and deep; the lonely ache of a morning without birdsong, or a flower without sunlight. She reached out with the Kenning and felt him on the periphery, a smudge of heat on the edges of her senses. And though she was too far away to hear his reply, she pushed out toward him; a mute, clumsy affection, the ache of his absence.

I miss you, brother.

She closed her eyes, felt warm tears in her lashes.

I need you.

Drying herself off, she heard the outer door to the bathhouse slide open. She reached down into her dirty clothes, wrapped her hand around the handle of her tantō.

"Hiro-san?" she called.

A small figure appeared in the doorway; a girl about her age with perfect skin and big, beautiful eyes, dark as ebony and smeared with kohl. Her lips were plump, pouting, glistening with a long vertical stripe of deep red paint. White cherry blossoms drifted across the silk of her beautiful scarlet furisode robe. Her hair was tied up in an exquisite coil, pierced with ivory needles and blood-red tassels. She held an enormous bundle of clothing in her arms, straining under the weight, her long sleeves dragging on the ground.

"Forgive me, Lady." She bowed at the knees, eyes on the floor. "The Mistress of the house bid me to bring you these."

"Lady Aisha?"

"Hai." The girl bowed again, placed the bundle at her feet. "I am Tora Michi. My honorable Mistress asks that when you are bathed and rested, you visit her for tea. She wishes to convey her heartfelt gratitude to you for Tomo."

"Tomo?"

"Her dog, Lady." The girl politely covered her mouth to hide the smile. "She wished you to have this jûnihitoe to wear for the occasion. She commands that I help you dress."

"Um, that's all right." Yukiko eyed the pile of fabric with vague suspicion. "You can leave it there."

"Have you ever worn jûnihitoe before, Lady?"

". . . No."

The smile grew wide enough that the girl's hand couldn't cover it.

"Then you will need my help."

It took an hour to get into the dress, and by the end of the procedure, Yukiko had sworn a dozen times that she would never wear one of the damned things again. Layer upon layer was wrapped about her: undergarments of white silk first, eleven more layers to follow, each more complicated than the last. The outfit must have weighed a good forty pounds.

When the dressing was done, Michi applied make-up to Yukiko's face: bone-white powder for her skin, thick kohl around her eyes, that same vertical stripe of red paint for her lips. Her hair was twisted up into a broad coil, held in place by golden combs. The girl peered over Yukiko's shoulder into the looking glass when she was done and smiled.

"You are very beautiful, Kitsune Yukiko."

"All this just for tea?"

Michi covered her grin.

"Lady Aisha is the sister to the Shōgun. Most ladies of the court would spend an entire day preparing for an audience with her."

"Gods, what a waste. There are people out in the street begging for bread right now."

Michi tilted her head to one side, narrowed eyes, bee-stung lips pressed tight together.

"We should depart. The Lady will be waiting."

Walking in the jûnihitoe proved just as cumbersome as putting the thing on. The hem of the dress was tight around her ankles, and Yukiko found she could only manage short, shuffling steps across the polished boards. When Michi opened the bedroom door, Hiro was still kneeling on the other side. He caught sight of Yukiko and snapped to his feet with a whine of gears and a spitting hiss of exhaust, leaving his jaw behind on the floor.

"You . . ." Hiro stammered. "You look . . ."

"Ridiculous," Yukiko said. "So the less said about it, the better."

Hiro marched behind as the girls shuffled into the palace proper. Polished pinewood boards stretched in every direction, rice-paper walls adorned with beautiful artwork and long blood-red amulets of curling paper, scribed with protective kanji. Ceiling fans creaked overhead in the stifling heat, and Yukiko felt a bead of sweat running down her spine to the small of her back where her tantō was hidden. Servants stopped and bowed at the knees as they passed, eyes on the floor. By the time the trio reached the gardens, Yukiko's feet were throbbing, calf muscles protesting at the bizarre, shuffling gait she'd been forced to adopt.

They walked along a broad veranda, sweeping gardens to their left, the hoarse chirping of miserable sparrows piercing the reek. The trees were bent, twisted, leaves a sickly shade of gray. A large stone statue of Hachiman spilled cloudy water from its hands into a little creek, but Yukiko could see no koi fish swimming below the surface; just dead leaves and smooth, round stones. She remembered playing in these gardens as a child, chasing the birds, searching in vain for butterflies. She remembered her father kneeling down in front of her, telling her that her mother was gone. That she wasn't coming back.

She blinked back the threat of tears and coughed, lotus pall creeping across her tongue. Squinting up at the darkening afternoon sky, she saw that it was the color of old blood.

The bushimen guards murmured as they passed, more and more of the scarlet tabards appearing as they proceeded deeper into the palace. When they reached the royal wing, the scarlet was replaced with golden tabards of the Kazumitsu Elite, simple iron breastplates traded for great hissing suits of ō-yoroi. The Iron Samurai would bow to Hiro, fists covered with one palm, and he would stop and return the gesture, the pistons and gears of his armor singing. Once the formalities were done, the Elite would look at her, silent as ghosts, curious eyes behind their oni masks.

The hallway floorboards creaked and chirped beneath their feet: the song of the so-called "nightingale floors," meant to dissuade assassins and the unwelcome eavesdropping of nosy servants. Yukiko felt eyes upon her even when nobody was around, her skin prickling with unease. The robes were heavy, stifling, and she wished for all the world to be back in her simple uwagi and simple life.

The creaking stairs up to the tearoom were torture. Hiro knelt on the ground just outside as Michi slid open a set of double doors and announced her name. Yukiko stumbled inside, nearly tripping, blinking in the gathering dusk amidst the tittering of a dozen young girls.

"Shhh," hissed the Lady Aisha, snapping her fingers. The giggling died immediately.

Yukiko stepped out of her sandals and peered around the room. Walls painted with tiger motifs, prowling in a stylized jungle. Balcony overlooking the garden, piteous sparrow song drifting through the open doors, entwined with a blessedly cool breeze. Mats of lotus wicker across the floor, a low table in the middle of the room surrounded by silken cushions. A dozen serving girls in scarlet furisode lurked on the periphery, staring at her with unmasked curiosity. But it was the woman in the center who caught Yukiko's attention and held it tight.

The Lady Aisha was a few years older than she, a woman in the prime of her beauty. She seemed carved out of alabaster, a statue come down from its pedestal to swim among the flesh. Make-up, hair, dress, everything about her was immaculate. High cheekbones, rivers of coiled, raven locks, full, painted lips. Yukiko wondered how many serving girls had slaved for how many hours, all for the sake of her appearance. Though the Lady was stunning—breathtaking in fact—all Yukiko felt was disgust; a disdain at the wealth on display, the effort behind the facade. She could feel it roiling behind her teeth as she pressed her forehead to the floor.

"Lady Tora Aisha."

"Kitsune Yukiko," Aisha replied, husky, smoke-scarred. "We thank you for visiting us."

"It is my honor, Lady."

The terrier in Aisha's lap bounded down to the floor, bounced up to Yukiko and started licking her ear. She sat upright, squirming, and a chorus of bright laughter rang out again from the legion of serving girls. Aisha drew her fan-shaped respirator from within her sleeve to cover her smile. Yukiko ruffled the puppy's ears, feeling the world fall away beneath her feet, the vertigo of the Kenning turning the earth upside-down.

Hello! Happy! Play?

Yukiko felt Buruu's absence like a fresh wound as she stared into the puppy's eyes.

Not now, little one.

The puppy barked and danced in a small circle.

"Come, sit with me, Kitsune Yukiko," said Aisha.

Yukiko dragged herself forward on her knees until she knelt before the table. The puppy gnawed at the geta sandals she had left by the door. She watched Aisha prepare the tea; a stylized, elegant dance of pot and saucer and sweet-smelling steam. Three of the girls began plucking at shamisen, filling the air with soft, hypnotic music. The instruments were almost six feet long, crafted of exquisitely carved kiri wood, inlaid with mother-of-pearl. They were played laid flat on the floor, the girls kneeling beside them, striking the thirteen strings with fingers and thumbs. The wavering notes were long and sweet, almost melancholy in parts, as if the instruments were searching in vain for a voice beautiful enough to match their own.

"They tell me that you captured the thunder tiger." Aisha's eyes were fixed on the tea service, scooping a bowlful into Yukiko's cup. "And saved a Guildsman's life. All alone in the Iishi for days."

"Hai." Yukiko turned her cup three times before accepting it, bowing to Aisha.

"That must be an extraordinary tale." Aisha bowed back, filled her own cup. "You must tell it to me sometime."

"If you wish, Lady."

Aisha glanced down at Yukiko's cup, waiting for her guest to drink first.

"How old are you, Kitsune Yukiko?"

The jûnihitoe pressed down on Yukiko like the air in a tomb. Sweat burned her eyes. She longed to rub them, but was afraid of smudging the wretched make-up. She tried to blink the sting away instead, lifting her cup and taking a small sip of the steaming liquid.

"I am sixteen, Lady."

"So young. And yet here you are, the toast of our city."

". . . I would not know, Lady."

"And so modest!"

The serving girls giggled. Aisha took a sip of her tea, watching Yukiko over the rim of the cup.

"You are very beautiful, Yukiko-chan."

"You honor me, Lady."

"Your accommodations are suitable?"

"Hai, Lady."

"I trust that Michi-chan was of assistance?"

"Hai, Lady. Very much so."

"The jûnihitoe suits you."

"My thanks for your gift, Lady."

"My brother, the Seii Taishōgun, is overjoyed."

"As you say, Lady."

"I have not seen him this happy in many years. You have brought him a great prize."

Yukiko found herself growing angry, impatient at this silly ritual and this pointless one-sided conversation. She felt as if this painted doll was talking *at* her, not to her. That she didn't care what Yukiko said or felt, that this was just a momentary distraction in Aisha's life of banality, of pretty dresses and hours in front of looking glasses.

She knew she should keep her mouth shut, that she should nod her head and sweat in this ridiculous dress and sip her bloody tea with a smile. But she couldn't.

"And yet your brother has my father locked in his dungeon," she said. "Starving. Almost naked, with bare rock to sleep on and a bucket to shit in."

A collective gasp, music stopping dead, corpse-pale painted faces turning paler still. Aisha was motionless as stone, cup poised before her lips, blinking once at Yukiko with dark, liquid eyes. She heard Michi behind her, whispering something under her breath. A prayer, maybe.

"Leave us," said Aisha, an iron note of command in her voice. As one, the serving girls stood and fled the room, tiny steps scurrying across the wicker matting.

Yukiko bowed her head, uncertainty getting the best of her anger. This aggression, this impatience; it wasn't like her. She was normally level-headed, grown pragmatic beyond her years in the shadow of her father's addictions. It was almost as if . . .

Of course.

Buruu. Once so primal. Impulsive and feral. But now he showed capacity for restraint, patience, complex thought, reason overcoming his bestial nature. Their shared dreams. Shared feelings. The bond between them growing by the day.

He's becoming more like me.

"I am sorry, Lady," she murmured. "I beg your forgiveness."

And I'm becoming more like him.

Aisha put her cup down on the table carefully, her hand steady.

"What do you want, Kitsune Yukiko?"

Yukiko's gaze flickered up to the Lady's face. She didn't seem angry, or offended. Aisha glanced up and down Yukiko's body, as if taking her measure inside her head. Her eyes glittered with a fierce intelligence, a calculating precise cunning that matched the unveiled authority in her voice. The shamisen music began playing again from the room next door, a smoke-screen over their conversation behind the paper-thin walls. Yukiko began to suspect that there was more to this woman than pretty dresses and tea ceremonies.

"What do I want?"

"Hai," said Aisha. "What is it that you wish to achieve here in Kigen?"

Yukiko blinked, said nothing.

"You may speak freely."

"Well." Yukiko licked carefully at her bottom lip. "First of all, I want my father out of prison."

"And you believe that insulting me is the best way to achieve this?"

"N-no," she murmured. "I am sorry, La—"

"Do not apologize for your mistakes," Aisha interrupted. "Learn from them."

"I don't—"

"Women in this city, on this island, we do not seem like we are important. We do not lead armies. We do not own lands, nor fight in wars. Men consider us nothing more than pretty distractions. Do not for a second believe that this means we are powerless. Never underestimate a woman's power over men, Kitsune Yukiko."

"No, Lady."

"You are young, have not been educated in courtly ways, instead growing up wild with that drug-addled father of yours. This is a disadvantage you must learn to overcome quickly. For believe me when I say that, second only to myself, you are currently the most powerful woman in all of Shima."

"What?"

"Yoritomo needs you, Yukiko." Aisha held her pinned in that dark, glittering stare. "I know what you are, yōkai-kin. The whole court knows. The entire city has heard your story by now. Street minstrels sit on the corners, watch their offering cups fill with kouka as they play songs about the brave 'Arashi-no-ko,' who slew a dozen oni and tamed the mighty thunder tiger. Did you know that the Guild has already sent an emissary demanding you be put to the pyre?"

Yukiko felt her gut lurch with fear as she mumbled a negative.

"Yoritomo laughed in his face. Can you imagine? The Shateigashira himself, the Guild made flesh in this city. And Yoritomo *laughed* at him." Aisha shook her head. "My brother thinks of nothing but his dream. Of riding that arashitora to a final victory over the gaijin that a dozen different generals under the command of our father failed to bring. A triumph the historians will tell of for generations. And you can give that to him, Yukiko-chan. Only you."

Aisha picked up her cup and sipped the tea.

"Why do you think I brought you here today? Made you wear that dress?"

". . . I do not know, Lady."

"You are not just young, you are beautiful. And now half the men in this palace know it, and have told the remaining half what a prize you are. Men are idiots. They think with their loins, not their heads. Beauty is a weapon, sharp as any chainkatana. Men will do almost anything to possess it, if only for a second. In the face of that desire, a girl blushes and turns her gaze to the floor. A woman plays it like a shamisen." Aisha gestured to the musicians next door. "And she gets her way."

"Why are you telling me all this?"

Aisha smiled. "Because you have a good heart. A kind spirit and a brave soul. Most people in this palace have none of these things. I know what has been done to you. You and your family. I want to see you get what you want, Yukiko-chan. And I want to see others here get what they deserve."

Aisha drained the last of her tea, placed the cup down, a faint stripe of blood-red paint left behind on the glaze.

"I received a message from a dear friend today. One I have not seen in many years. She told me her father is well. She wanted me to pass on her regards to you."

"To me?"

"Hai."

Aisha reached into the sleeve of her robe, placed something on the table between them. Unfurling her fan respirator, she fluttered it in front of her face. The eyes floating above it were diamond hard.

Yukiko looked down to the white shape, stark against stained teak. Fragile as spun sugar, petals shaped like an upturned bowl. Her heart thundered as she inhaled the scent, the sweet perfume of the Iishi.

It was a wisteria bloom.

28

FRAGILE AS GLASS

Sweat burned her eyes.

The arashitora tossed his head and steered himself away from the obstacle course again, jerking the reins from Yukiko's hand. The circuit ran endlessly around the iron spike in the center of the arena; a ring of packing crates, bales of dirty yellow straw, and crumbling statues of bent, wizened men. Losing her grip with her thighs, Yukiko slid off the thunder tiger's neck and tumbled to the ground, landing in a painful heap on her rump.

"You stupid idiot!" she yelled. "Can't you tell left from right?"

The beast growled at her and tossed his head again, clawing at the steel-shod bridle around his beak. His talons rasped across the metal weave, giving birth to tiny sparks.

"If you break another one, you get no dinner tonight," she warned him.

A roar of defiance.

"Maybe he's had enough for one day," Hiro ventured.

The lone Iron Samurai sat in the benches above their heads; a spectator to the ongoing farce that was the arashitora's "training." Several bushimen were scattered among the seats and along the arena walls, laughing in appreciation whenever Buruu misbehaved. To say that the beast's education was going badly was an understatement.

"Maybe he's just too stupid," called one. "No wonder the damn things died out."

FIVE MINUTES ALONE. WE WILL SEE WHO IS STUPID, INSECT.

Peace, brother. You're doing so well.

Yukiko stood up slowly, wincing, and made a show of rubbing her behind where she'd fallen on it. She stretched to touch her toes, feigning a cramp in her lower back, sensing the eyes of the bushimen on her body. Hungry stares and dry mouths.

Aisha was right. These men are fools, suspecting nothing.

THIS CHARADE GROWS TIRESOME.

We'll have time for pride when we're far away from here. Until then, we both have to swallow it. For my father's sake as well as our own.

THIS HARNESS ITCHES.

It had been on the second day, after Buruu bucked her off with his wings for the fifth time that afternoon, that Yukiko suggested some kind of device to strap them down. She drew a rough sketch and had Hiro take it to the Shōgun.

The Guild Artificers had complied sluggishly with Yoritomo's request, delivering the harness five days later. Thick straps of padded rubber and flexible iron mesh now bound Buruu's pinions to his flanks. Ostensibly, the harness prevented him from trying to take flight and giving Yukiko a fresh set of bruises. In reality, it also did a fine job of concealing the new feathers sprouting along Buruu's wings, and catching the old feathers as they moulted away.

Yukiko had found a small box tucked inside the harness on the day it was delivered, her name written on top in precise, beautiful kanji. Inside she found a small mechanical arashitora, sculpted out of paper and brass, no bigger than the palm of her hand. She wound the tiny spring and set it on the floor, watching the wings become a blur, lifting the toy off the ground in short, whirring bounds.

At the bottom of the box, she found a note.

"Grounded in Kigen until my burns heal. Was sorry to hear about your father and Yamagata. I miss you.—Kin."

She had scanned the note, hidden it inside her obi. Later that night, she tore the message into tiny pieces and scattered it to the wind. She hadn't the heart to throw away the tiny arashitora. In all the noise and motion of the past few days, she had almost forgotten about Kin, and she was surprised at how relieved the knowledge that he was still living and breathing made her feel. A week spent under the watchful eyes of the bushimen and Lord Hiro was starting to fray her nerves.

I AM LOSING ANOTHER FEATHER. FOURTH PRIMARY. LEFT WING. FIRST PRIMARIES ARE GROWING IN.

How long until you can fly?

DAYS. PERHAPS A WEEK.

Then we'd best start work on freeing my father.

HOW DO YOU PROPOSE WE DO THAT?

We don't.

THEN HOW . . .

We get the Kagé to do it.

YOU WERE WISE NOT TO KILL DAICHI. DID YOU SUSPECT KAORI KNEW AISHA?

Gods, no. They said that they had people closer to Yoritomo than he could ever dream, but I had no idea it would be his own sister.

PERHAPS YOU HOPED IT WOULD BE SOMEONE DIFFERENT?

I don't know what you mean.

INDEED.

Anyway, it makes no difference. I didn't spare Daichi because I thought it would be to our advantage. I spared him because it was the right thing to do. If it were right of me to blame him for obeying Yoritomo's command, then it would be right of you to hate my father for what he did to your wings. And it's not.

FEATHERS GROW BACK. MOTHERS DO NOT. AND I DO HATE HIM.

Daichi wasn't the one who took my mother away. And my father isn't the reason you're chained here. You and I both know that. You're going to have to forgive him one day, Buruu.

. . .

Buruu made no reply.

"I think we should take a break," Yukiko sighed, rubbing her rear again. She walked across the arena floor, stepped through the gate leading out of the pit. Securing the exit behind her with two iron bolts, she started trudging up the stone stairs toward ground level.

"I am sure Lord Hiro is very sorry to hear there will be no more stretching today." Michi handed her a pitcher of water and a towel. The girl shot a stern glance up at the Iron Samurai in the seats. Hiro was looking intently at his gauntlets, pretending not to have heard. Wiping the sweat from her eyes, Yukiko gave the girl a broad smile.

Aisha had commanded Michi to wait on Yukiko after the tea ceremony. The girl was to ensure Yukiko conducted herself as a lady of the court should, but in secret she also carried messages back and forth between the conspirators. Michi had a black sense of humor and an infectious laugh, and her insight into courtly affairs was as sharp as razors. Against her better judgment, Yukiko found herself liking the girl.

"Can you ask Lady Aisha if she will have tea tonight?"

"Hai." Michi bowed at the knees. "I will prepare a cushion for your shadow to kneel on in the hallway."

Casting a mock frown in the samurai's direction, she tiptoed off to the motor-rickshaw waiting outside. Yukiko waited until she had gone, then climbed the stairs and sat down on the same bench as Hiro, keeping a respectable distance away. She pulled off her goggles and kerchief, wiped the sweat from the back of her neck and drank deeply from the water pitcher.

"Training is taking longer than I thought," she sighed.

"You have many months until he is ready to fly." Hiro glanced at her, careful not to stare. "And you are making progress. Yoritomo-no-miya is pleased at our reports so far."

"You report on me?"

"The Shōgun commands it." Pistons hissed as Hiro shrugged.

"But you're saying nice things?" She looked at him sidelong, risked a teasing smile.

"I could never say otherwise."

"Even about a commoner like me?"

"There is nothing at all common about you, daughter of foxes." He looked at her then, as if offended by the suggestion. He didn't look away. "Or should I start calling you Arashi-no-ko?"

She turned to face him, and they stared at each other for what seemed like an age, poisoned wind wailing around the arena in words she could almost understand. Even at a distance, Yukiko could see her reflection in his irises, curved and splintered on that field of sea-green. His skin was statue-smooth, turned to copper in the light of a strangled sun, lips parted slightly to breathe. Time stumbled, sand slipping through the hourglass one tiny grain at a time, falling earthward with that same gravity that dragged her forward, inching closer, pulse pounding in her ears.

She found herself wishing they were somewhere else. Somewhere private. Anywhere but this.

"Come on," she finally sighed. "We should be getting back."

D id he try to kiss you?"

"No."

"Did you try to kiss him?"

"Of course not, Michi!"

Yukiko scowled at the maidservant in the looking glass, trying to keep the flush from her cheeks. The girl was up to her elbows in Yukiko's hair, drawing the thick coils back into an elaborate golden headpiece studded with tassels and pins and tiny prowling tigers. Michi raised an eyebrow and shrugged.

"A matter of time. That boy is so heartsick he's practically green."

"Stop it."

"He's probably out there in the hallway right now, composing bad poetry in his head."

Michi cleared her throat, her voice taking on a breathless lilt:

"Pale Fox's Daughter,
Her cherry lips haunt my dreams.
Something, something, breasts . . ."

"Don't you think I've got more important things to worry about than Lord Hiro?" Yukiko's hiss cut Michi's laughter in half. "Don't you think I should be avoiding undue attention?"

"You already have undue attention." Michi wiped the grin from her face, shrugged again. "It can hardly be avoided, so use it to your advantage. A man will turn a blind eye to the misbehavior of his lover more readily than that of his prisoner."

"You'd do that?" Yukiko blinked. "Sleep with a man just to get your way?"

Michi stared at Yukiko as if she had asked the color of the sky. "There is nothing I would not do to free this land from the yoke of the Shōgunate."

"Why?" Yukiko watched her in the mirror. "What did they do to you?"

"What makes you think they did anything to me?" She returned to arranging Yukiko's hair, deft fingers wrapped in ribbons of gleaming black.

"Because people don't just wake up one day and decide to . . ." Yukiko caught herself, lowered her voice again, ". . . to do what we're going to do."

"And what is that?"

"I'm not in the mood for games. What did they do to you, Michi?"

The girl paused, meeting Yukiko's stare in the mirror. All trace of amusement was gone now, and it seemed that a shadow passed over her eyes. When she spoke, the facade of the impetuous, lively young girl Yukiko had spent the last few days with fell away, and for just a fraction of a second she caught a glimpse of the rage that lurked beneath that pretty mask.

"Daiyakawa," Michi said.

"What about it?"

"I was born there. I was six years old when the riot happened. The prefect. The one they forced to commit seppuku . . ."

"You knew him?"

A nod.

"My uncle."

"Then the children they killed . . ."

"My cousins." She swallowed. "Right in front of me."

"Gods . . ."

"My family gave their lives in resistance against the Kazumitsu Shōgunate." A black light burned in her eyes, her skin deathly pale. "So, yes, I would give my body. My final drop of blood. The last breath in my lungs to see this country freed."

"What about Aisha?" Yukiko tilted her head, eyes a fraction narrower.

"What about her?"

"What does she have to gain from any of this? Why does she care? It can't just be because of Kaori's face."

"You dishonor her, Yukiko-chan." There was steel in Michi's voice. "She is stronger than you or I could ever dream."

"Is she? If Yoritomo dies, she inherits the throne, right?"

"You do not know what you are talking about."

"Then teach me. What is she risking, exactly?"

A long moment of silence passed, each of them staring at the other's reflection. The only sound was the creak of the ceiling fans, the distant murmur of the city beyond high, glass-topped walls. Yukiko was beginning to think she'd pushed Michi too far when, at last, the girl began to speak.

"Think on this." Michi began to arrange Yukiko's hair again, her hands a touch less gentle than before. "Your mother. My uncle. The Shōgun and the Guild have *bled* us. Our resolve is built on scar tissue. It is easy to rail against injustice when the authorities have given you a reason to hate them. What have they given Aisha?"

Yukiko shrugged, said nothing.

"Everything she could ever ask for," Michi continued. "Anything she could dream. If she wished, she could live her entire life inside these walls, never touched by the growing rot beyond. She *chose* to open her eyes. She *chose* to refuse all of this, to risk everything they have given her, everything she could ever be. The Dynasty, the Guild, they've never taken anything from her. And still she wants to tear them down. Why?"

"I don't know why."

Yukiko stared long and hard at the girl's reflection, as if seeing her for the first time. She realized that the Michi she knew was simply a costume, a role adopted for the sake of ruthless expediency. She began to feel distinctly out of her depth, sinking to the eyes in black, cloudy water, reaching out instinctively for Buruu's warmth in the distance. She began to understand the scale of it all, the machine she was pitting herself against, the fact that she really knew nothing about the allies she had thrown in with.

Buruu. Her father. Her own life.

A lot to risk in the hands of strangers.

Michi watched her carefully, speaking as if reading her thoughts.

"I asked Aisha the same thing once. Why she risked all, and where she found the will to do it. She said that from the outside it seems an enormous thing, for anyone unscarred to choose to resist. To look around at the smiling faces of their peers, and step willingly outside the warmth of that contented little circle. She said that every part of her being rebelled against the notion at first. Because there is something in us that loves the momentum of the mob, Yukiko-chan. The comfort of swimming in the current with our fellows. Something in all of us wants to belong."

She was staring at Yukiko's reflection, but her eyes seemed focused at some distant point inside the glass.

"Yet as sunset approaches, all anyone needs do is look ahead and see where this current will lead us. To realize that if we do not stop and swim against the stream, eventually we will find the precipice over which it flows. We all of us know it. As surely as we know the sound of our own voices. We see it when we look in the mirror. We hear it when we wake in the long, still hours of the night. A voice that tells us something is deeply, horribly wrong with this world that we have made." Michi's voice became a whisper. "Aisha said it became a simple thing after that. As simple as speaking. As mustering the will to say one tiny little word."

"What word?" Yukiko whispered too, without quite knowing why.

Michi breathed, a tiny syllable as fragile as glass.

"No."

"Training is going well, I hear," Aisha said, sipping her tea.

The sun had slipped below the horizon, bringing a cool dusk. The whispering sea breeze was a mixed blessing; banishing the scorching heat, but blowing in the suffocating stink of Kigen Bay. The summer's worst was over, and autumn would soon be approaching on dry, yellow feet. Yukiko wondered if she would be back in the Iishi by then, to watch the trees shed their green dresses. She hadn't seen the shades of the world turn to rust since she was a little girl.

"Hai, Lady," Yukiko replied. She was kneeling on a flat silk cushion before the low, polished table. Three of Aisha's maidens were playing music again, deft, pale fingers flitting across taut strings, loud enough that curious ears passing by the rice-paper doors would only hear the haunting melody of the shamisen.

"And you are enjoying the attentions of Lord Hiro, among others."

Yukiko gulped a mouthful of tea and said nothing.

"He is a handsome man. Loyal to a fault."

"My Lady, forgive me. I did not come here to talk about Lord Hiro."

"Does talking of your lover embarrass you?"

"Wha—" Yukiko nearly choked on her tea, cast an accusing stare at Michi. "He's not . . . I would never . . ."

Aisha laughed, bright and musical, perfect teeth and ruby lips. Yukiko felt a blush rise in her cheeks. She stared hard at her lap, fingers twitching on embroidered silk.

"You are too easy, Yukiko-chan. You wear your heart on your sleeve. Guard it more carefully, lest others see it and pluck it out. People in this palace have a fondness for taking away what others desire most."

"I don't love Lord Hiro."

"Well, perhaps you should." Aisha raised an eyebrow. "Treasure your joys while you may. Gods know there are few enough in this world."

"Michi said you had word of my friends?" Yukiko lunged away from the subject. "Akihito and Kasumi?"

Aisha stared for a long moment, still smiling, then finally nodded.

"Akihito-san is safe. With friends of mine, in a house in Docktown."

"Thank Amaterasu," Yukiko sighed. "And Kasumi?"

"She is here."

"In Kigen?"

"In the palace. I had her smuggled in this morning. She is waiting to speak to you."

Yukiko was incredulous.

"Why didn't you tell me?"

"I just did, Yukiko-chan."

Yukiko fought down the anger, tried to hide it behind the mask as Aisha had bid her. Just when she thought she had some understanding of who and what Aisha was, the woman showed her how little she truly understood. Yoritomo's sister was an impossible enigma, a puzzle box with missing pieces. No matter what Michi said, Yukiko realized she had no idea what was going on behind those smooth puff-adder eyes, what secrets twisted in the dark beneath the plastic, death-pale facade. All she knew about Aisha was what she'd been sold. Who was to say she really was Kaori's friend? Did she actually want to see the country freed from the yoke of the Guild and the Shōgunate, or was she just making a play for the throne herself? Despite Michi's assurances, all her talk of resistance, how much could Yukiko really afford to trust this woman?

How easy would it be for Aisha to just cut her loose if things went badly?

And even if all went to plan, how easy would it be for her to sell Yukiko as her scapegoat after the fact?

She kept the trepidation from her voice, the questions from her eyes.

"May I see her, please?"

Aisha clapped her hands, and a rice-paper panel in the northern wall slid aside. Kasumi stood on the other side in a servant's kimono, knotted muscle, nervous eyes. But when she saw Yukiko, her face lit up with joy. She dashed into the room and they were in each other's arms, hugging fiercely, afraid to let go. Yukiko closed her eyes, felt the tears pour down her cheeks despite herself.

"I thought you were dead," Kasumi breathed into her hair. "Gods, I thought we had lost you."

They laughed and held each other tight, swaying with the shamisen song until the tears stopped. Eventually, they knelt together before the table, and Lady Aisha wordlessly offered Kasumi a cup of tea. The older woman accepted, drinking the steaming brew with shaking hands and tight, pale lips. She asked Yukiko to tell her all that had happened since the tempest on the *Thunder Child*. Aisha's eyes glittered in the flickering amber light as Yukiko spoke, beginning with the crash, ending with the arena and Masaru's filthy cell in the Shōgun's dungeons.

"So he is imprisoned," Kasumi said. "That is a small mercy at least."

"No mercy for Captain Yamagata, though," Yukiko murmured.

"I did not want to leave Masaru, Yukiko." Kasumi's eyes flashed. "I told him I wouldn't. That if he were going to die, I would die with him. Akihito refused too, threatened to knock Masaru out if he ordered us away. So three days before we arrived in Kigen, he poisoned us with blacksleep. When we woke the next morning, he and Yamagata were gone. The captain, to beg for the lives of his crew. And Masaru, to beg for ours."

"Akihito threatened to knock him out?" Yukiko couldn't help but smile.

"Akihito loves Masaru." Kasumi reached out to touch Yukiko's hand. "I love him too. Most dearly."

Yukiko stared at Kasumi for a long, silent moment. This was the woman who had betrayed her mother, who had shared her father's bed. And though she'd truly blamed Masaru for the infidelity, Yukiko had long ago written Kasumi off as a predator, venomous and sly. Treated with thin civility maybe, but never respect. Never love.

Yukiko looked at her now and saw differently. The truth was, Kasumi probably knew Masaru better than her mother had. She had always been there, the long nights in the wilderness, the treks through swamp and jungle, spilling blood, sleeping under the stars together.

Did Yukiko have a right to be angry? Yes. But could she understand what a person would do for love? Could she sympathize?

"I know you do," she whispered.

"We have to get him out of there."

"We will." Yukiko nodded, squeezed her hands into fists.

"Indeed?" Aisha said. "You have a plan?"

"No." She turned to the Lady, cold stare, white knuckles. "But I'm sure you can come up with one. You're the most powerful woman in Shima, after all."

"Masaru-san can be freed when Yoritomo is dealt with." Aisha waved with one pale, lacquered hand. "I mean no offense, but there are larger stakes in play here than your father's life. The Dynasty's bicentennial celebrations begin in two weeks' time. All of Yoritomo's court will be caught up in the noise and motion—a perfect distraction for the shadow games we must play. Why would I break the Black Fox out now and risk all, when the fate of the entire country rests on this one throw of the dice?"

"Because that's my price," Yukiko scowled. "I want a show of faith."

"Faith?" Aisha tilted her head. "You do not trust me, Yukiko-chan?"

"You just got through telling me not to wear my heart on my sleeve. I'm the one risking my own life, and the life of my friends. And yet the way I see it, everyone is getting something out of this bargain but me. The Kage get their revolution, you get a scapegoat for Yoritomo's murder, maybe even a throne. What do I get, aside from a death-mark on my head?"

"Vengeance. For your mother."

"If I wanted vengeance, I would have killed Daichi. I don't care about revenge. I want my family back. I want my father free by the end of this week. I want him and Akihito and Kasumi on a sky-ship to Yama. And when they're far from this stinking city, then I'll stick my neck out for you. After they're safe, you get what you want. Until then, you don't get a godsdamned thing."

Aisha smiled, a broad grin right to the eyeteeth that left Yukiko's stomach cold. The world seemed breathless. A darkened hush descended as night deepened, the pale moon limping through a poisoned sky toward the hour of treason. Somewhere in the dark, a sparrow flapped its crippled wings and began to sing.

"Now, that's the spirit, Yukiko-chan." Aisha clapped her palms together, delighted. "We'll make a woman of you yet."

H is name was Tora Seiji no Takeo.

A careful and proud man, thin limbs, clever hands, greatly learned in the keeping of tora—the great tigers of the Shima isles. He had inherited the craft from his father, Takeo no Neru, dead of blacklung some ten years past.

Seiji was Yoritomo's Keeper of Tigers; an expert on an island where only three of the beasts remained alive. It was a profession that, naturally, left him with plenty of free time on his hands. This he spent chasing servant girls, or writing thoroughly ordinary poetry, or listening to pirate radio while smoking with his friend Masaaki the Stable Master (the last horse on Shima had died eighteen years before, and Masaaki had devoted his overabundance of leisure time to cultivating a truly impressive lotus addiction).

The three sickly cats that prowled Yoritomo's gardens were kittens really, born and bred in captivity. Any idiot could feed them. Any fool with a pair of hands could pick up the dung when Naoki, the most mischievous of the trio, decided to do his business outside the kitchen door again. But Shōgun Yoritomo had insisted on keeping Seiji despite his obsolescence. Paying his wage, just like the Hunt Master and the Hawk Master and the Keeper of Cranes. It wasn't a bad life, really. Just a dull one.

That is, until last week.

And now here he was, with a kerchief mask and a shovel as wide as his arm, picking up thunder-tiger shit.

The beast was snoring in the center of the arena, great flanks pulsing, straw dancing with each heave of those mighty lungs. It had opened its eye briefly as Seiji entered the pit (the iron gate squeaked—he must remember to get some lubricant from one of the Lotusmen) but had immediately dropped back to sleep after a brief, disdainful stare.

Seiji crept on tiptoe among the lotusfly hum, wincing at the scrape of metal across stone as he scooped up another shovelful. He knew that the beast's chain was too short to reach the pit's periphery were he to run there. But still, he couldn't help the tremors in his hands, the cold fear crawling in his gut. This was a beast of legend, one of the great gray yōkai, child of the Thunder God, Raijin. It had about as much in common with a tora as a tiger had with a housecat.

But Seiji was a loyal man, sworn to his oath of service, grateful to Yoritomo-no-miya for sparing him from the breadlines and the overflowing gutters of Downside. And so, when he'd been commanded to care for the arashitora, he had bowed and murmured thanks to his great Lord, Ninth Shōgun of the Kazumitsu Dynasty, next Stormdancer of Shima, and set about finding a bigger shovel.

As he wiped his brow, Seiji stole a glance at the arashitora again. It was magnificent, possessed of a majesty that demanded attention; a beast from children's stories and dusty histories sprung inexplicably to life. Rumor was already rife about the strange (and, Seiji had to admit, pretty) girl who had arrived with it. "Arashi-no-ko," they called her. "Storm Girl." The bushimen whispered that she was training the beast for the day it would begin its moult, growing new feathers to—

Wait.

Seiji squinted in the gloom, shovel poised in his hands.

What is that?

The Keeper of Tigers crept forward in the dark, soft slippers muffling his footsteps on the stone. Head tilted, eyes narrowed at the white shape under the straw a few feet from the arashitora's hind paw. The beast snorted and rumbled in its sleep, and Seiji froze as still as kabuki dancers when the music stops. Flies tickled his skin for several agonized minutes before he felt safe to move again.

He knelt down and snatched it up, hurriedly tiptoeing back to his barrow and holding the object out in the grubby light of his chi lamp. His breath caught in his throat as he turned it over in his hands. As broad as his thigh, snow white, cut cleanly in half by what must have been a razor-sharp blade.

It was a feather.

A moulted feather.

29

MAYFLIES

Yukiko sat atop Buruu's shoulders, off-balance, face gleaming, reins wrapped twice around her fists. The arashitora weaved through the obstacle course, a continuous circuit around the iron pillar he was chained to, like a dog endlessly chasing its own tail. Their pulses pounded in time with each other, a single heartbeat holding hands with itself. She could feel the muscles at play beneath his feathers, smell the faint mix of ozone and sweat, like the promise of rain hanging in the air before a storm.

She had taken a fall once already for the benefit of the bushimen, relaxed her muscles, ready to take another.

Now.

She tugged hard on the reins and Buruu tossed his head, veering left and crashing into the straw. With a curse and a convincing shriek, Yukiko flew from his shoulders, bounced across the bale and crashed onto the stone in a tangle of limbs. Buruu stood on his hind legs, making a grating noise in his throat that sounded suspiciously like chuckling. Several of the bushimen watching the show burst into laughter. Yukiko tore off her goggles, glowering up at the beast as she pushed the hair out of her face.

"Clumsy oaf!" Her shout drowned out the laughter from the benches above. "How hard can it be? Are you blind or just stupid?"

Buruu's defiant roar was a comforting vibration in her chest. She smiled into his mind even as she cursed aloud, overjoyed simply to be close to him again. Amidst all the whispered conversations and shadowed intrigues of the past weeks, he was a constant, a true north by which to find her way. She felt his absence as a dull ache when they were separated, but in the few hours they spent together every day, she felt more complete than she had since Satoru died.

She realized his words on the deck of the Guild liner had been true.

He *was* her brother now.

AISHA AGREED TO YOUR DEMAND?

Yes. They're going to smuggle my father from his cell in the next few days. She'd rather wait until the bicentennial celebrations, but she didn't see him locked in that hole. What it was doing to him. I don't care if she says it will be difficult. As long as it's not impossible.

NOTHING IS IMPOSSIBLE.

A sigh as she tossed her hair over her shoulder, hauling herself up from the stone where she'd fallen. She winced and rubbed at her hip, massaging her thigh as she stood.

Only a few more days of this charade. And then we are gone.

A FEW MORE DAYS OF THIS AND YOU WILL BE NOTHING BUT BRUISES.

Somber applause cut through the sound of Buruu's laughter in her head; a single pair of hands clapping, reverberating along the arena floor and up into the empty grandstand. All eyes turned toward the noise, surprised gasps and the sound of men slapping their palms over their fists soon followed. All deep bows and stern faces, the bushimen threw off their smiles and studied the floor.

"Shōgun," one whispered.

Hiro was on his feet amidst the lubricated swish of gears and whine of tiny motors. He bowed deeply and hurried to his Shōgun's side, sparing a quick nod for the four Iron Samurai that Yoritomo had brought with him. Like Hiro, the men wore the gold-trimmed jin-haori of the Kazumitsu Elite, oni masks, the daishō blades of chainsaw katana and wakizashi paired at their waists.

"Seii Taishōgun," Hiro said. "Your arrival was unannounced. Forgive me, I would have ensured a suitable . . ."

Yoritomo held up his hand, words dying on Hiro's lips. The Shōgun's eyes were still fixed on Yukiko. He strolled down the stone stairs between the seats to the arena floor, unblinking, holding the girl pinned in that glittering, reptilian stare.

"A fine performance," he smiled. "My compliments."

Yukiko bowed deeply.

"You honor me, great Lord."

A nearby bushimen unlocked the iron gate leading into the pit. Yoritomo handed the man his breather mask and stepped inside. Golden breastplate, small wings on his back, broad swathes of red silk dragging a trail through the straw. He walked toward Yukiko, one casual hand on the hilt of the old-fashioned daishō swords at his waist. The Elite retinue filed in behind him, the whirr and hiss of ō-yoroi amplified in the vast, circular space. The last Iron Samurai through the door held up his hand to stop Hiro entering, slammed the bolt home with a clang, locking the gate behind him.

"I think perhaps you missed your calling, Yukiko-chan," Yoritomo said, stepping closer. "Instead of a hunter, perhaps you should have been a playwright?"

"My Lord?"

BEWARE.

"Oh, indeed," he nodded. "Such pleasant fictions you might have woven."

Yoritomo moved, viper-fast, seizing Yukiko by her wrist and hyper-extending her elbow into an agonizing armbar lock. Buruu roared, a terrible, booming report cracking across the stone, lunging toward the Shōgun. Two Iron Samurai stepped forward, drawing their weapons and shouting a challenge. Buruu's talons opened one up across his stomach; soft, feeble meat inside a thin tin can. The body tumbled away, spooling a writhing mess of entrails. Yoritomo twisted Yukiko's arm behind her back, drew his wakizashi and held it to the girl's neck. The second samurai swung his growling blade with a fierce cry, only to see his arm bitten off at the elbow, Buruu's beak shearing through the iron like hot steel through snow. The man's scream was high-pitched; a long quavering note of disbelief.

"Hold, or she dies!" Yoritomo shouted. "She dies, I swear it!"

YUKIKO.

Buruu!

Buruu stopped short, eyes ablaze with fury, talons sending a shower of sparks across the arena floor. Yoritomo's face was pale, pupils dilated, dragging air through clenched teeth as he pulled Yukiko backward toward the gate. The arashitora took a few hesitant steps toward them, growl building in his throat, vibrating across the pools of blood beneath his feet. Ripples in the scarlet.

"No closer," Yoritomo warned. "I'll cut this whore's throat."

The growl spilled over into another roar.

"He *does* understand me." Yoritomo twisted Yukiko's arm, eliciting a gasp of pain. "No smarter than a dog, eh?"

"My Lord, what goes on here?" Hiro cried, fists wrapped around the bars of the gate.

"Betrayal," Yoritomo spat, eyes never leaving the arashitora. "The vile reek of treason."

"My Lord?"

Yoritomo nodded to the other samurai and they seized Yukiko's arms, one apiece, dragging her backward in a grip of smoke and iron. Her hair was a tangled curtain over her face, pitch-black on pale skin. She stared up at Yoritomo with unbridled hatred in her eyes, struggling in those implacable, chi-powered grips. He smiled, placed the tip of his wakizashi beneath her jaw and forced her chin up, parting the hair away from her face with the razored point.

"You think yourself a clever fox, eh? Clever enough to outwit the Lord of all Shima?" An empty chuckle. "Pathetic little girl."

He slapped her, striking downward, the weight of his body behind the blow. Her head snapped to the right, the crack of skin on skin louder than a bull-whip. A grunt, cheek splitting, bright red spraying through the air. Buruu lost his mind, charged forward with a terrible, blood-flecked roar, claws tearing chunks out of the rock. Yoritomo drew the iron-thrower from his belt, pressed the snub-nosed barrel against Yukiko's temple and forced the girl to her knees.

Buruu reached the edge of his tether, chain snapping taut, links groaning dangerously as two tons of momentum was pulled up short. The iron spike in the floor bent forty-five degrees, making a high-pitched squeal, flakes of metal shedding like old skin. Buruu roared, spittle and tongue and rolling eyes, tal-ons swiping the air five feet from Yoritomo's face.

"Enough!" Yoritomo pulled the hammer back on the iron-thrower.

Buruu fell still, breath heaving in his lungs, shaking with adrenaline and rage. He whined, feral and grating, trembling haunches and wild eyes. His tail whipped from side to side, claws digging into the stone beneath his paws.

"Swords," Yoritomo barked.

With their free hands, the surviving Iron Samurai drew their katana and kicked them to life. The serrated growling of the blades drowned out the moans of their dying comrade. The man rolled about in a widening pool of blood, clutching the stump where his arm used to be.

"If the beast even coughs in my direction, take this bitch's head off."

"Hai!"

Yoritomo holstered his iron-thrower, slid the wakizashi back into his scab-bard. Eyes fixed on Buruu's, he stepped closer, slinging his plait over his shoul-der with a toss of his head. The smile on his face was arctic, the clenched grin of a corpse mask.

"You have spirit, great one. I will give you that."

YUKIKO. CAN YOU HEAR ME?

. . . Buruu?

A blurred consciousness, skull still ringing from Yoritomo's blow. Blood in their mouths.

"Move, and she dies," Yoritomo whispered.

The Shōgun drew his katana, steel sliding across the scabbard's lip with a bright silver tone. He sliced away the harness that pinned Buruu's wings with one stroke, rubber and steel mesh crumpling on the floor. Three feathers spilled from the remnants, broad and pale, severed neatly across their spines. Buruu flinched as Yoritomo ran his fingers across the new feathers growing at his wingtips, gleaming with a faint metallic sheen, whole and perfect. A sharp intake of breath rasped across the Shōgun's teeth; a hiss of incredulity and imperious, narrow rage.

"So it is true." Jaw twitching, gnawing his lip.

"Great Lord," called Hiro. "I am certain Yukiko knew nothing of this."

"She can hear the beast's thoughts." Yoritomo didn't even look in the Iron Samurai's direction. "Yet you tell me she knew nothing?"

"I am certain there is an explanation . . ."

"Then explain!"

"Perhaps she was unaware—"

"No, it was *you* who was unaware!" He turned on Hiro with a roar, pointing with his katana. "This treachery happening under your very nose and you were blind to it! You have failed me, Lord Hiro, and shamed yourself."

Hiro aimed a desperate, helpless glance at Yukiko. Then he dropped to his knees, pressed his head against the stone.

"Forgive me, great Lord."

The Shōgun turned back to Buruu, hissing through clenched teeth. The Iron Samurai lowered their swords, spinning blades of the chainkatana hovering bare inches from Yukiko's neck. Strands of her hair were caught in the turbulence, wafting up to be severed on the furious razors and then drift slowly back down to earth.

Yukiko blinked, ears ringing, trying to clear her head. Blood flowed from her swollen cheek, pooling sluggishly under the curve of her chin and spattering at her feet.

"Where is your respect?" Yoritomo growled at the arashitora. "You think this insolent child could outwit me?" He pointed his katana at Yukiko, shaking his head. "You will learn what I am. What it means to defy Hachiman's chosen. I will teach you. Hold out your wings."

YUKIKO.

Buruu, don't . . .

THEY WILL KILL YOU.

They'll kill me anyway. Don't do it.

"I know you understand me!" Yoritomo roared. "Hold them out or she dies!"

No, don't. Please, Buruu. Don't let him touch you.

The future stretched out before him, days without end, life in a rusty cage beneath this choking sky. Slave of this princeling and his madness, gawped at by insects and denied the freedom of his skies. The loss of his feathers was one thing. But the fear of this madman hacking off his wings whole was almost overpowering.

Yet it was nothing. Nothing compared to the thought of losing her. Of watching her spilled open in front of him, bleeding out on the floor as he ended them all, giving in to rage and pride and being left at the finale with their blood on his tongue and her blood on his soul.

What would it mean to fly again, knowing that she was rotting in the cold ground?

"Kill her," Yoritomo spat, stepping back. The Iron Samurai raised their blades. Hiro gritted his teeth, shaking his head and refusing to look away. The bushimen on the benches held their breath, wincing in anticipation. And with a sound like unfurling canvas, Buruu spread his wings.

Twenty-five feet of gleaming silver-white, new feathers glinting with a strange, electric opalescence. The hair on Yoritomo's flesh stood up, static electricity coursing over his skin and setting his eyes ablaze. The arashitora spread his feathers. His coverts were tickled by the warm breeze, rippling like snow-white waves across a broad expanse of muscle and voltage.

Yoritomo breathed deep, sweat turning the hilt of his sword damp and greasy. He pointed his blade toward the sky.

"There it is. Just above you. The desire you would risk everything to attain. And had you but the courage to serve, it would be yours for the taking. But now it falls to me to take instead." He sighed. "Such a waste."

He lashed out with his katana, scarlet light swelling along patterned steel. A faint ripping sound, no more than a whisper; a flurry of severed white. The perfect fan of the beast's outstretched feathertips was reduced to a flat, ugly shape, an amateur mutilation cutting the anticipated promise of flight to pieces. The tips of the new quills split asunder, ruined all over again, falling to earth with the sound of tearing paper.

Yukiko gasped as if she'd been stabbed, a rasping intake through a throat squeezed closed by grief, exhaled in an agonized, choking sob.

Kill him. Forget me, brother. Fight. FIGHT.

FEATHERS GROW BACK.

"No, please," she moaned under the growling steel. "No."

SISTERS DO NOT.

"This is the way the immortals feel," Yoritomo breathed. "To take anything and everything away with a simple wave of the hand. A wing. A face. A civilization."

He stared at the blade of his katana, transfixed by the light dancing along its edge.

"I am god-sized."

Buruu closed his eyes and hung his head as Yoritomo strode around to his other wing, katana falling with the weight of an anvil. Not a single drop of blood, not even a vague sensation of pain as the blow sliced away his quills. And yet, he felt as though the sword were cutting the heart out of his chest. His feathers sprayed through the air, sleet and whispering snow, falling earthward in slow motion. He felt the storm wind on his face, felt the rain dashing against him as he wheeled among the clouds, echoing the thunder with the song of his wings. So close. So close he could taste it.

And now so far away.

"Now you see," hissed Yoritomo. "All you possess, I allow you to have. All you are, I allow you to be. And that which you desire most is mine to give and take as I will. Think on this now, and in all the dark hours between this moment and the day these feathers grow back again, and know each one of them is an hour I *allow* you to have. I am Yoritomo, Chosen of Hachiman, Emperor of the world. Defy me again, and I will take everything you have left. Do you understand me? Everything." A feline sneer. "And I will *hurt* it first."

He drew close to the arashitora's face, put his blade beneath its chin and forced it to look up into his eyes. Amber swam with cold fury, coiled like a spring, held in check by a will as fierce as the storms themselves.

"Now show Yoritomo the respect that he is due," he hissed. "Kneel before him."

The Shōgun stepped back, sheathed his katana and held out his hands. Defenseless. Unarmed. It would take a single twitch to end him. Everyone in the room held their breath, the growl of the chainkatana poised above Yukiko's neck the only sound. And as she looked on, near blind with tears, Buruu bowed his head, curled up his talons and pressed his forehead into the stone at Yoritomo's feet.

"No."

She cried into his mind, a bitter, broken-glass grief, cutting her insides and flooding over her limits. He reached out and touched her thoughts, held her tight, safe and warm.

OUR TROUBLES ARE BUT MAYFLIES, RISING AND FALLING BETWEEN THE TURN OF DAWN AND DUSK. AND WHEN THEY ARE GONE TO THE HOUSES OF MEMORY, YOU AND I WILL REMAIN, YUKIKO.

He closed his eyes and folded his wings, lighter now than they had been a lifetime ago. Her sobs the only sound, echoing across the stone, cold and empty. His feathers lying severed on the floor, her heart beside them, torn and bleeding.

WE WILL ENDURE.

30

IDLE HANDS

They left her lying on the bloodstained stone.

A boot to the ribs, a gob of fresh spittle, and they were gone. Metal footsteps rang through the floor and into her skull, echoing behind her closed eyes. She couldn't bear to look at him, at what they'd done to him. All because of her. A bargaining chip, a pawn threatened, forcing the king to its defense. Used. Just like she'd been used against her father all those years ago. A stone around the necks of those she loved.

She could hear his voice in her mind, far away, telling her it would be all right. But she closed herself off, slamming the door and curling up in a dark room inside her head. She didn't deserve his understanding. She didn't deserve his friendship. She'd failed him, failed herself, thinking some simple sleight of hand and luck would be enough to see them through to the end.

Kitsune looks after his own.

Not any more.

She pressed her cheek into the floor, gravel denting her flesh. After the longest time, she felt strong hands pulling her up, into someone's arms. Cold, metallic skin, the whirr and hiss of ō-yoroi, the smell of fresh sweat and chi. She kept her eyes shut, hair draped over her face, a curtain of tangled black to hide behind. Childish fantasy; hoping that if she couldn't see the world, then it wouldn't see her either. Fingertips numb, cold sickness in the pit of her stomach, Buruu's voice outside the closed door fading away into the black.

Hatred, poisonous and seething. For Yoritomo. For herself. Veins running thick with it, throat painted with bile, teeth grinding so hard she felt the enamel might crack, spitting splinters of jagged white and blood along with her curses. Floating impotent in the empty black behind her eyelids, sickness her only company. She could feel it filling her lungs with every breath, seeping into her skin. So complete and terrifying that it made her want to scream.

Sick of being used as a weapon to hurt the ones she loved. Sick of being the weak one, the frightened one. Sick of being a pawn, being a prisoner, being one tiny girl in a world so cold and brutal. Just fucking sick of it all.

Hiro pulled the bedroom door aside, carried her to the futon and tried to put her down. She held on as if her life depended on it, cold, unforgiving iron under her grip. Beneath the metal she could feel his warmth, threw her arms around it, pressed her cheek against his, wet with tears.

"Don't let me go," she whispered.

"I have dishonored myself." He shook his head. "I have failed my Lord. I must beg forgiveness, or seek atonement in seppuku."

"Don't let me go."

She drew away and stared into his eyes, down to his mouth. She felt the hate inside, the desire for blood swelling and roiling. She shied away from that darkness, put her hand to his cheek, thumb running across the smooth expanse of skin, lips trembling. She lunged at his mouth with her own, a desperate, hungry kiss that tasted of chi and old tears. He held her tight as she pressed against the iron encasing him, wishing it were her skin, her flesh inside, sealed in cold, hard lines, safe and untouchable.

He kissed her back, just like he had in her dreams. And if she closed her eyes for long enough, maybe she would wake up and none of this would be real. Not the failure. Not the hatred. Not the severed feathers lying on the floor.

"Make it go away," she breathed around their tongues. "Make me feel something. Anything but this."

She sat up in the bed afterward, watching him sleep, sweat drying on her skin. She traced the line of his irezumi with her fingertips, the beautiful tiger stalking down his right arm, the imperial sun on his left. She looked down at her own arm, to the mirror image of that hateful icon on her flesh. She knew what Daichi had meant now, when he called it a mark of slavery. She considered scorching it off with a red-hot knife, blood cauterized and burning black, peeling the mark of that maniac from her skin once and for all.

But would that make her free?

She could sympathize with the Kagé all she wanted, but that didn't make her righteous. She knew that her spiraling hatred of Yoritomo came from her own pain, not some sense of injustice at the land's rape, the mass extinctions, the bleeding sky. From her own hurt. Her own suffering, just like Michi had said. And as she recalled her words to Aisha, they rang false inside her head. The truth was she didn't want justice any more. She wanted revenge.

Was Daichi any different? Were any of the Kagé? They talked of liberation and revolution, but she wondered how many of them would be singing that refrain if they'd been born a Lotusman, or the fat child of some zaibatsu noble. A conscience is easier to swallow on an empty belly, simpler to swing with a broken wrist. The people who hate money are the ones who don't have any. The people who hate power are the ones who are powerless.

Were these even her feelings? Or were they Buruu's?

In the end did it matter?

Gods, I don't know what's real any more.

She pushed her knuckles into her eyes. Warm breeze caressed her naked skin, flesh crawling with remembered goosebumps. Looking down at Hiro, recalling the taste of him. Expecting the palace guard to burst into the room at any moment and drag her off to prison with her father. At least she'd known his touch; at least she'd had this.

This was real. Right here. Aisha spoke truth: treasure your joys while you may.

She looked around the room, at the pieces of ō-yoroi scattered across the floor. She picked up a gauntlet, heavy as stone in her small hands. It was black, lifeless, power cable snaking out from its cuff, ending in an open, empty mouth. She smiled with the memory of clumsy fumbling, of switches and clasps and buckles, metal clattering to the wooden floor piece by piece. Slipping her hand inside the glove, she watched her tendons stand taut with the weight. She ran her fingers across the surface, metal embossed with unreadable Guild kanji and prowling tigers. The beasts stared at her, lifeless, etched stripes across flanks and faces.

She thought of Buruu alone in his prison and closed her eyes.

How he must hate me.

She wriggled her fingers inside the gauntlet, fingertips pressed against cool iron. A dozen pseudo-tendons flexed, the hand drawing partway closed. Even without power, the raw movement of the machinery was a beautiful dance. She wondered what it would feel like to wear a suit like this, to feel its strength at her command. To be impenetrable. Untouchable.

And then she thought of poor Kin, trapped in that half-body and half-life, plugged into his suit like an infant to its mother. Cables and wires and nutrients, never knowing the sun on his face or the breeze on his flesh, save through a few stolen moments in the dark and the quiet. What a price to pay, to be impervious. Never to be touched, all the days of your life.

She realized that she missed him. It had been nearly a month since their time in the Iishi. She wondered how he was, if his burns were better. She wondered how she might get a message to him. She knew now that he felt more for her that she did for him, that those long nights in the forest had made him see something in her that simply wasn't real. But if she could speak to him, tell him the way she felt . . .

She looked down at Hiro again.

How do I feel?

Sick. Guilty. Nothing close to righteous.

Buruu was the victim here. The only real innocent. He hadn't asked for any of this. He'd trusted her, trusted that she would lead them through the storm and out the other side, wind beneath their wings as they left this stinking city behind. And now they were nowhere. Her father imprisoned. Buruu grounded until his winter moult. How would he make it through six more months trapped in that reeking pit? How would her father?

They won't. They're going to die in those holes.

She narrowed her eyes, clenched her fist inside the gauntlet, feeling the sickness swell inside her again. And then she saw it, glinting in the light of the setting sun on the bedside table: the tiny mechanical arashitora Kin had made for her. She placed it in the palm of the ō-yoroi gauntlet, held it up to her face.

It was beautiful, intricate, spools of wire and pistons and interlocking teeth. Deft fingers and a mind of machines had sculpted it out of thin brass and clockwork. An Artificer's idle hands and idle mind, slumped on a sickbed while his flesh limped back to a half-remembered shape.

A small face had been etched in the metal; proud eyes and a razor-sharp beak. Yukiko smiled. Kin had always liked Buruu, even if the arashitora hadn't liked him back. It was a good likeness, a tiny portrait of better days painted in metal and solder.

The wings were strong, light, lengths of rice-paper reinforced with a skeleton of brass. She ran her fingers along the paper feathers and caught her breath, lips parted, eyes growing wide. She wound the spring, and the tiger leaped from her hands, wings blurring, floating down onto the bedspread with a sound like cricket-song.

An Artificer's hands . . .

"The answer," she whispered. "Gods above, that's it."

31

SURPRISES

People didn't have expressions there. Just faces.

A hive. Pentagonal, honeycombed walls, illuminated by quartz halogen flickering in oily housings. The air was abuzz with the hymn of a thousand machines: a choir of gears, falsetto of pistons and hydraulics, baritone of iron on hollow brass and crackling voices. Slow interlaced choreography unfolded inside it, lubricated ball-joints and transmission fluid, glinting in the glow of blood-red eyes and swimming with the ever-present stench of chi.

His skin was supposed to filter it out. His purity screens were always green, blood untouched by the poison they'd filled their world with. But he swore he could taste it, clinging to the back of his throat and creeping across his gums. Ever since his thirteenth birthday, and the agony of the Awakening. Their gift to him, along with the metal shell for his flesh, the tubes plugged into his meat parts; the constant fear that what he'd seen, what they'd shown him that night, might one day come true.

"Skin is strong. Flesh is weak."

The words were a whisper in his head, a conditioned response to the presence of self-doubt, destructive thought, drilled into him since before he even knew their meaning. He remembered the days when they used to bring him comfort, silence the questions that had no answers. The days he used to believe.

Kin touched his fingers to his brow as he passed three Shatei—Guild brethren—in the hallway. He stepped back against the wall to make way for the squat servitor that trundled along after them. The thing paused to query him with a single glowing red eye, two of its fine motor claws fluttering like antennae. It resembled a faceless fat man with spider-legs for arms, cast in metal and set trundling on two broad rubber tank tracks. He sometimes had nightmares about them, hatching moist in some vast sweltering nursery deep in the bowels of the chapterhouse. Not made, but grown.

The thing chattered at him and rolled after his fellows.

Smoke in the air, burning coal and chi, solder and sparks. The chapterhouse workshops were a vast series of cocoons, connected by stone umbilicals and irises of radiating steel, contracting and dilating as figures passed through. The broad test spaces of the Munitions Sect, the warrens of the False-Lifers, the endless corridors of the Skin-Weavers. A dozen different kinds of Artificer, thousands of machines, always in motion. No daylight lived here, no windows to let in the outside world. Just the constant hum of halogen bulbs, pressing bright fingers against sticky, smoke-stained yellow.

He walked out into the main hub, into the press and swell of skin on skin. A new shipload of gaijin were being pored over by the Inochi Techs; the only real livestock left in all of Shima now that the great slaughterhouses stood empty. The techs singled out a few large, fierce-looking men for future arena games; a short, brutal life spent killing their fellows to the deafening approval of the crowd. The strong and hale were pushed into motor-wagons bound for market, and from there, some endless pollen-choked field. The rest were hustled away in chains toward the inochi pits, more fuel for the machine.

He looked at their faces. Old and young. Women and children. Bewildered expressions, thousand-yard stares roaming this hellish pit peopled with metal insectoids and burned-flower stink. He wondered what the people outside these walls would do if they knew that their glorious war against the barbarian hordes was not fought for honor, nor renown, but because almost every warm-blooded creature in Shima had already been rounded up and slaughtered. Processed in the inochi vats and liquefied for orderly dispersal among the growing fields of swaying scarlet blooms that pumped the heart of the Shōgunate. How casually would Shima's people sip their tea or smoke their pipes if they knew the flower that birthed their empire was called blood lotus for a reason?

He stared at a skinny gaijin girl, maybe five or six, her grubby hand entwined with a tall, wretchedly thin woman. Rags for shoes. Backs of her thighs smeared with filth. Face wet with tears.

It will all be over soon, little one. The lotus must bloom.

One of the bigger gaijin yelled in his guttural tongue as the Inochi Techs pulled a woman from his arms. He lashed out with his foot, tackled one of the techs to the ground. Shatei descended from all over, a swarm of clicking brass and hissing exhaust. Fists rose and fell; a metal percussion beneath the song of the woman's screams. Kin closed his eyes, trying to block out the sound. It was easier to take if you didn't think of them as people. If you imagined they were just one more commodity. That they didn't think or feel. That they hadn't once loved and laughed and dreamed of bright and wonderful things. It was easier to take if you could manage that. Somehow.

A familiar nausea swelled in Kin's stomach as the sound of brass pounding on weak flesh faded. He could swear he tasted chi again in the back of his throat. He opened his eyes, pity-sick, watching them drag the bleeding body of the big gaijin toward the pits, silence the weeping woman with a popping spray from the barrel of a handheld shuriken-thrower. A Kyodai barked orders to gather up her body, pointing at the gleaming pools of blood and berating the murderer for "inefficiency." The taste got so bad Kin thought he might vomit.

He turned and walked on, quick as he could without raising attention, through the heart of the chapterhouse and onto the elevator spire at its gut. He stepped inside the chamber of burnished steel and glowing numbers, floating skyward to the fourth floor. The habitat level was austere, dimly lit, row upon row of faceless black irises radiating out from a central hub.

He pulled a lever, stepped inside his habitat. His mechabacus was relaying the latest crop report from the Fushicho quartermasters into his skull: pounds of lotus (yield), numbers of dead slaves (collateral shrinkage), deadlands still growing at an exponential rate (corruption percentile). Figures and kanji flowed in his head and in his veins. The air filtration system spat its rattle and hum into the little room. He cranked the door shut behind him with a sigh of relief, the iris contracting with the sound of metal grating on metal, pressure seals sucking closed with an intake of hot breath.

He waited a few minutes to allow the vents to cycle. The diode on the purity monitor smudged slowly from red to green, a bright silver sound indicating it was safe to take off his skin. He touched the release, neck unfolding like lotus in bloom, pulling the helmet away from his head. The rubber seal clung to his flesh as if terrified to let go.

He sloughed off his gauntlets, ran a hand over close-cropped hair, trying to forget about that little girl, the sound of the woman's screams. He was dripping with sweat, and the thought of a cool shower was a tiny promise of momentary escape, easing the frown on his face. He inspected his flesh in the small mirror above his cot. His burns were healing slowly, gauze coming away easily from the dimpled flesh of his throat.

Not too bad. Not so ugly that no one could want him.

Would she?

He closed his eyes, banished thoughts of Yukiko. The memories of their time together in the Iishi were locked in some small and hidden corner of his mind, a secret, brilliant joy he kept for himself, visiting only when the stench got too bad, the days grew too dark. But this was his life. Here in this chittering, steaming ants' nest, bent over a tool station and working on the Shōgun's pet projects until he was well enough to ship out again, away from the slaughter and the inescapable stink. Presuming they ever let him fly again, of course.

His father had been a great man. Third Bloom; a Fleet Master. He had made engines sing like the legendary nightingales, knew the troubles of an injection system or combustion chamber with a touch of his hands. Kin had inherited his father's gift for machines, and Old Kioshi had passed on the bounty of his knowledge, raising his son high in the esteem of Second Bloom Kensai before he died and was processed in the vats. A great family. An honorable legacy. Kensai's patronage had been enough to see Kin posted to a flagship like the *Thunder Child*, enough for them to allow him to carry his father's name.

Problem was, he liked his own.

And now he'd lost face. Been seen skinless by a hadanashi. An *Impure* one at that. A source of quiet disdain from his fellows, stinging rebukes from his Kyodai. Even with Kensai speaking on his behalf, an example needed to be made. And so they'd locked him in some far-flung workstation, given him a scribble marked with Yoritomo's seal and commanded that he turn the lunatic's vision into reality. They'd promised Yoritomo that the best Artificers in the entire Kigen chapterhouse would be working on his ridiculous saddle. That a dozen brethren would not rest until the Shōgun had his desire. In reality, there was only Kin and old Tatsuo pottering away on alternate shifts.

Truth was, antipathy for Yoritomo had been spreading among the Kigen Chapter for years. His excesses, his arrogance, his inability to provide final victory against the gaijin. But ever since Shateigashira Kensai's recent meeting, the contempt from the Upper Blooms had become almost palpable. An indignant hush had descended when news of Yoritomo's defiance spread among the Shatei. Who did this princeling think he was, to deny the Way of Purity?

We supply the weapons. We supply the armor. We supply the fuel for the war machine, and only we know the secret of its creation. We are Shima. Defy us at your peril, for what is given can be taken away.

The Shōgun had already been informed that "regrettable delays" meant his saddle would not be ready in time for the bicentennial. That Shateigashira Kensai would not be attending the gala due to "pressing Guild business."

Secretly, Kin was overjoyed to hear of Yoritomo's rebuke to Kigen's Second Bloom. The thought of Yukiko kept him up at night: dark eyes reflecting emerald green, those brief, wonderful moments in the Iishi swimming so vibrant in his memory that sometimes he swore he could still feel the wind, taste the water.

He could see the line of her face, closed his eyes now to reach out and touch it, aching with de-tox. She was in his veins. In his head.

"Skin is strong. Flesh is weak."

He opened his eyes, seeing it for the first time. A flat sheet of paper, folded beneath his temperfoam futon, corner peeking out into the dim light. A smooth high-pitched whine came from his skin as he crouched down, picked it up, noting the fine misting of dust on the floor under the ventilation duct.

Someone had been in his room. Crawling through the vents, dropping down and depositing this paper beneath his mattress. Why? Who?

He opened the quartered sheet, sharp folds, a little over a foot wide. It was a square of opaque parchment, marked with simple drawings of an arashitora. An overlay of translucent rice-paper sat on top. A contraption was drawn on it, sitting neatly over the thunder tiger's frame.

There was a note in the corner. A five-word fist in his gut, his heart threatening to burst through his ribs and fly from his chest.

"We need to talk—Yukiko."

Masaru woke from the dream with a moan, images glowing in his memory like the afterburn of a sun stared at too long. A rolling field of animal bones, ribs and skulls and empty eye sockets, overgrown with mile after mile of blood-red lotus. He'd stood in the dark, a flickering light in his hand, and then dropped the torch and watched it burn. Sucking in lungfuls of smoke, listening to the screams piercing the night and realizing, finally, that they were his own.

He sat up on raw stone, hands shaking, smudging the dream from his eyes. The cell stank of old sweat, shit, vomit. His skin felt greasy, smudged with gray. But, for the first time in as long as he could remember, he felt clean. No lotus in his veins, no ashen fingers snaking through his skull. Unshackled, weight falling from his shoulders and drifting away in rolling clouds.

"Masaru-sama."

A voice in the dark outside his cell. Was he still asleep?

"Masaru-sama." Urgent. Muffled. A girl's voice.

"Yukiko?"

"A friend."

He could make out eyes in the dark, a thin strip of flesh between folds of a dark cowl, skin painted black. Silhouette of a kusarigama's hooked, sickle blade at her belt, a sword on her back—a tsurugi by the look—straight blade and square hilt-guard. A weapon that long in the hands of a commoner was a death sentence.

"You're no samurai. Who are you?"

"I told you. A friend."

"My friends don't carry swords."

"Perhaps that is something they ought to think about."

"What do you want?" He rubbed his eyes, blinked in the dark.

"For you to be ready."

She slipped a package between the bars, wrapped in hessian, tied with twine.

"Ready for what?"

"Freedom."

The headache had been sent by Lady Izanami herself.

Yoritomo-no-miya closed his eyes and tried to relax, let the hands just drift over his skin. Deft fingers pressed at the anxiety knotting his shoulders, crouched among the muscles of his neck. Gentle hands cupped his cheeks, forced his head sharply to the right. A loud crack in his ears, as of last winter's firewood burning in the hearth, and the fist of tension at the base of his skull dissolved. The constriction of his veins mercifully eased, flooding his head with endorphins.

The Shōgun breathed deep, letting the gentle notes of the shamisen pick him up on a wave and carry him far from his cares. The geisha kneeling by his shoulders stepped lithely up onto his back, walking up and down his spine with small, surefooted steps. Little pops among his vertebrae accompanied her on her journey across his irezumi, her weight pushing the breath from his lungs as her toes wriggled into his aching flesh.

He heard the sound of the nightingale floor, wooden boards squeaking across a nail fretboard, the whisper of the rice-paper door sliding aside. He frowned.

"I told you I did not wish to be disturbed, Hideo-san."

"I beg your forgiveness, great Lord, equal of Heaven," the minister replied. Without looking up, Yoritomo could tell he was bowing as low as his old back could afford. "The Lady Aisha wishes to speak with you."

A sigh.

"Send her in."

Shuffling footsteps, muffled voices, geta across the floorboards and the smell of jasmine perfume. Yoritomo could feel his sister staring at him. He did not look up.

"Seii Taishōgun." Her voice hung in the air alongside the incense.

"Lady Aisha." He winced as the geisha ground her heel into a knot beneath his shoulder-blade. "All right, get off, get off," he waved.

The girl flinched and stepped off his back immediately, shrinking a few steps away, hands drawn up to her face. Fear in her eyes. Bruise on her wrist.

"Leave us," said Aisha, and the music stopped as if someone had choked it, the sound of instruments being set aside and scurrying feet filling the silence. Aisha slipped off her geta and walked to her brother's side, her split-toed socks only a whisper across the floor. She knelt beside him on the matting, began slapping his back with the heels of her hands, up and down his spine, air filled with the wet sound of flesh on flesh. Yoritomo twisted his head, felt his neck pop again.

"You are upset," said Aisha.

"You are perceptive."

"The arashitora?"

"I should have killed it. And that insolent Kitsune bitch."

"But your dream, brother," Aisha said, kneading his flesh. "Hachiman has sent you this gift. You were right not to squander it."

"Gift or no, that little whore belongs in prison with her bastard father. We will see how much of her spirit remains after a few months in the hole."

"And what do you think the arashitora will do without her to speak to it? How will you manage the beast without the girl keeping it in check?"

"It knows me well enough by now. I hold the key to both their fates. It would not dare raise a talon to me, not when I can have her killed with a snap of my fingers. I want that Kitsune trash under lock and key. Breathing the stink of her failure, and slowly going blind in the dark."

"She will die in that prison, brother. She would be food for corpse-rats, you and I both know it." She shook her head, kneaded the tension in his flesh. "No, your punishment was just. Harsh enough to leave no ambiguity about who rules their fate. Yet merciful enough to leave no permanent scars. You were wise, Shōgun. The beast knows the hand of its master now."

"One would hope. I have never had to teach that lesson twice."

A long silence, broken by the rasp of a crippled swallow. Her hands fell still on his skin.

"No," she finally said. "No, you have not."

"Yet now I am forced to wait." Yoritomo pushed himself off the floor; sudden, startling motion. He began pacing, candlelight rolling across inked muscle. "How long until it moults again? How long until I can lead my armies astride its back? The arashitora is worth nothing to me chained in a gods-damned pit."

"Then why did you cut its feathers, brother?"

"They lied to me. They *deceived* me."

"But there were any number of punishments you could have inflicted for the transgression. Starvation. Beatings. Torture. Why cripple its wings?"

He spoke like a parent to a simple, mewling child.

"Because it *wanted to fly*, Aisha."

She fell silent, face like stone, watching him pace the room.

"Yet until the beast moults again, my armies languish with weaklings in command. Not one of my generals is worthy of the title. Not one!" He wiped his knuckles across his lips. "The gaijin must be broken. We need more slaves, more inochi. Twenty years and a dozen different commanders, and we are no closer to victory than when father ruled. And what do we fight? Men of honor? Samurai? No! Skinthieves and blood-drinkers."

"They will fall before you, brother. It is only a matter of time."

"Time?" The word was a snarl. "If you listen to the Guild we have precious little left. They wave their productivity charts and deadlands maps in my face, spitting rhetoric about the 'fundamentals of the exponential equation.' And every day they demand I expand the fronts. Demand! Of me! Seii Taishōgun!" He slapped at his naked chest. "I decide! I say when we will move and when we will stay. I decide where and when the deathblow falls."

"Of course, brother," Aisha rose smoothly, voice soothing, folding her hands inside her sleeves. "The Guild does not understand. They have minds of metal. They are not men of flesh like you. They hide in their shells and their yellow towers, quivering with fear over children who speak to animals."

"Cowards," Yoritomo spat. "If only . . ."

The sentence hung in the air, dripping impotence.

"I have a gift for you," Aisha said finally.

"I have no need of your ladies tonight."

"No." She licked carefully at the wet stripe of red on her lips. "Something else. A way in which you might realize your dream and silence the Guild's demands. And best of all, it will be them who pays the cost."

"What is it?"

"Ah," she smiled, lowering her eyes. "It is a surprise, my brother."

"A surprise." A smile began creeping toward the corners of his mouth. His eyes roamed his sister's body, all of a sudden enjoying the game. "What kind of surprise?"

"The secret kind." She laughed, mischievous, slipping her geta back on her feet. "I will deal with the Guild, take care of it all, and in the end you will have your dream. But I will need the Kitsune girl. Not imprisoned. Not chained."

"Why?" Yoritomo's eyes narrowed.

"The little whore can make herself useful to atone for her treachery. And if she defies me, the thought of prison will seem like a mercy to her, and she will wish you had not stayed your hand. I do not possess your capacity for restraint, Shōgun."

"You are possessed of other qualities, sister. Far more tangible."

She turned aside, avoided his lingering stare.

"No snooping, do you hear? You tell Hideo-san to hold his little spy network at bay. I want this to be special."

"Aisha . . ." he warned.

"I mean it!" She turned back to him, took a step closer. "We will speak no more of it. There will be comings and goings and much noise about the arashitora's prison and you will ignore all of it. And when I bring you your gift, you must act surprised and remark what a clever sister I am. And everything you deserve will be yours. Agreed?"

She was a vision of beauty in the low, sooty light. Her face was so pale it seemed faintly luminous, punctured by two pools of kohl-stained, bottomless black. The paint on her lips was the color of their clan, the color of blood, seeming to drip down and stain her golden jūnihitoe with a scarlet pattern of lotus blooms. Twelve layers to paradise.

He finally smiled, bowed his assent.

"Agreed."

He leaned down to kiss her mouth, and she turned her head so that his lips brushed her pale, perfect cheek. She bowed at the knees and turned away, leaving him with the sweet scent of her perfume. He watched her sashay out the door, a river of black hair, bloody silk, soft curves. He smiled to himself.

Yoritomo loved his sister. Like no other man ever would.

K in held one of the severed feathers, running his fingers along the path of the sword blow. He could sense a faint discharge of electricity from it. The broken plume was reflected in his rectangular eye, heavy as stone in his gauntlets.

"I am sorry, Buruu."

The arashitora glared, motionless, curled around the twisted metal stanchion he was chained to. The arena floor was littered with cut feathers, shifting in the noxious wind. The skies overhead rolled with dark, threatening clouds.

The black rain would begin falling soon, skies spitting toxin back onto the people who had poisoned them, turning all to pitted, hissing scar tissue. Kin found it strangely reassuring; nature's ability to cleanse itself of the filth they pumped into it. He was sure that, if the planet were somehow rid of its bipedal infection, it would right itself eventually. He wondered how long it would take for the world to muster anger enough to shake them from its skin. Quake and flood, disease and storm. Open the fault lines, let it rain, flush all of it away.

Farewell and good-bye and goodnight, everyone. Remember to shut off the light when you're done.

Buruu stood abruptly, claws clicking across the stone, staring into the dark with his head cocked to one side. Kin turned, and she was standing there in the black, pale and perfect and beautiful.

"Yukiko," he breathed, his voice a choir of flies.

"I'm glad you came, Kin-san." Quiet. Lips barely moving.

"I didn't see you there."

"Kitsune looks after his own," she shrugged. "But do you see what they did to him?"

"A blind man could see that."

She moved past him in the gloom, across the arena floor. Padding softly along the straw, hands clenched, hair hanging over her face. He could see she had been crying. She reached out with trembling fingers. The arashitora stood, pushed his head into her arms, enfolded her in his crippled wings. He purred; deep thunder rumbling beneath a cloak of warm, white fur. She hugged him fiercely, face crumpling like it were made of paper, sodden with tears.

Kin watched them mutely, wondering what passed between them. He couldn't help but feel jealous of the beast, to know the inner workings of her mind and heart, to speak volumes without ever saying a word. What a strange thing for the Guild to want to exterminate. What a wonderful gift. To never be alone. To know the truth of another's soul. Maybe that was why they were afraid. Truth in the Guild was a dangerous thing.

Yukiko sniffed, swallowed thickly. She turned to Kin, scraped the hair from her eyes, one arm still resting on Buruu's neck.

Gods, she's beautiful.

"I can't stay long. They will be looking for me." Her voice was so small and fragile it made his chest hurt. "Can it be done?"

His boots rang on the stone, skin spitting chi smoke into the warm, sticky air. Walking across the arena floor, he had an almost overpowering urge to tear off his helmet, to see her again with his own eyes.

"I think so."

"And will you help us?"

"There is nothing in this world I would not do for you, Yukiko."

She smiled at him then, so sad and flawed and perfect that he almost cried.

She flung herself around his neck and he wanted nothing more than to hold her in his own arms, to smell her sweat, feel her hair on his face. If he could have given up every day of his life at that moment, for just one minute with his flesh pressed against hers, he would have done it with a smile on his face.

She drew away, and it was all he could do to let go, to hold back from squeezing her as tightly as he could, fusing them into a single, breathing—

"How long will it take?"

He blinked, shook his head. The mechabacus on his chest spat and chattered, a voice in his head, wheels and numbers and probabilities. He could see the apparatus in his mind's eye, felt metal being shaped beneath his hands in the stuttering light of the cutting torch amidst the smell of smoking solder. A creation for the sake of something more than destruction. Not a war machine. Not an engine to drive a slave ship or chainkatana. A gift. A gift for the one he loved, for the one she loved.

He would not sleep until it was done.

"A week," he finally replied. "They have me working on Yoritomo's saddle. Perfect subterfuge. I can come and go here as I please. I told them I was taking measurements tonight."

She couldn't see him smiling behind his mask. His heart ached.

"A week." She smiled, tears in her eyes.

"Will you be able to get away? Won't they be watching you?"

"I have friends in the palace. Even guards have to sleep sometime." She shrugged. "And Kitsune looks after his own."

"Well, let's hope he looks after me too."

"I know what you're risking to do this. Thank you, Kin-san."

"Thank me later. When we are far from here."

"We?"

"We," he nodded, dropping the severed feather to the stone. "I am coming with you."

32

A KNIFE IN THE CHEST

The days of waiting were almost unbearable. A few of the nights were not so bad.

Hiro had been taken off her guard detail, and the two new Iron Samurai stationed outside Yukiko's door had barely spoken a word to her. They would step aside to allow servants to bring in her meals, to change the linen, fill the bath. Her attempts at conversation were met with metallic silence. Michi was her only real company when the sun was up, and the two girls whiled away their time over decks of cards or listening to the sound box, speaking in tiny, hushed voices about the wheels that had been set in motion around the city.

Michi had brought her small folded maps of the palace, outlining the entrances that the servants used to move from wing to wing, or exit into the grounds. She had showed Yukiko how she could stand on her dresser and shove aside the panels in the roof, squeeze through the space between beam and shingle and circumvent the nightingale floors entirely. Told her about the bent maple tree in the southeastern corner of the garden, and how the serving girls used it to slip over the wall and tryst with their lovers in the city proper. How the palace of the Shōgun was not the impregnable fortress he believed, and that it was compromised by people he considered beneath his notice every single day.

The bicentennial of the Kazumitsu Dynasty was fast approaching, and the court was abuzz with excitement. A grand gala had been planned, and Yoritomo was set to make one of his rare appearances before his people. Since the arena was already occupied, the sky-docks had been chosen as the venue for the celebration. Free food and drink for every citizen of Kigen, followed by a magnificent parade of the Shōgun and his court down the Palace Way into

Docktown. A few hours before the Hour of the Fox fell, and the third century of Kazumitsu rule over Shima began, the gala would culminate in a twilight fireworks display the likes of which the city had never seen.

"As the sun sets over Kigen Bay," Michi said, "it sets for the final time over Yoritomo's dominion."

"What about my father?" The bruise on Yukiko's cheek was turning an ugly yellow at the edges. "Kasumi and Akihito?"

"The sky-ship they escape on will be in dock tomorrow. Papers are already drawn up for the return trip to Yama. The authorities will suspect nothing, nor will they have time for scrutiny with all the traffic around the gala. The ship flies Phoenix colors, but her captain is a friend of ours. We have friends ready at the docks too."

"Where do these 'friends' come from? Can you trust them?"

Michi tilted her head at the questions.

"You are not the only one who has been wronged by the Shōgunate of Shima, Yukiko-chan. Aisha and Daichi-sama have been gathering contacts for years, waiting for the opportunity to strike. In a system as brutal as this, there are always people who slip through the cracks. Countless lives ground between the gears of the machine." She shrugged. "This is how the rain becomes a flood. One drop at a time."

"There will be bushimen everywhere around the sky-docks during the celebrations. Iron Samurai too, if Yoritomo is making an appearance. Isn't there a safer way to smuggle them out? By train, maybe?"

"There will be so much noise and saké at the gala, three more shadows in the mob will not be noticed. Besides, the bushimen and samurai will have more pressing concerns, assuming you have done your part."

"Have no fear of that."

"Are you certain you are ready for this?"

Yukiko glared, iron in her eyes, not saying a word. Her fists were balled on her knees, jaw clenched, her whole body as still and quiet as midnight. Michi met her stare for a silent moment, a faint, grim smile curling the edges of her mouth. She nodded.

"You are ready for this."

On the third night, as she was preparing to slip into the crawlspace in the roof, Yukiko heard urgent, hushed conversation outside her bedroom door. Creeping closer, she could make out three male voices under the clank and hiss of ō-yoroi. The first two were her new guards, their tone stiff with challenge. When she recognized the third, her heart skipped a beat.

The door slid open and there he stood, wrapped in a kimono of dark red silk, embroidered with gold. Chainsaw daishō tucked into his obi, long hair drawn back into a simple tail, the light of flickering globes reflected in irises of beautiful sea-green.

"Hiro," she breathed.

He looked over his shoulder, covered his fist and bowed at his fellow Elite. And with the only hint of compassion they had shown in three days, the men turned away without a word and closed the door behind him.

She was across the room and in his embrace before he could speak, pressing hard against his chest, arms wrapped around him so tight she feared his ribs might break. And as his lips met hers, as he put his hands on her body, for a brief, intoxicating moment, any thought of crawlspaces and nightingale floors and maple trees fled from her mind, and all she was left with was the smell of his fresh sweat, the faint taste of saké on his lips, the ache his touch left between her thighs. The silk around her body fell away beneath his hands, and as her skin pressed against his, she closed her eyes and sighed his name and forgot the sound of her own.

Afterward in the sweat-stained dark, she laid her head against his chest and remembered. Guilt raised its head; subtle poison seeping into a cool mountain stream and turning it black as the rivers that flowed through Kigen's heart. She thought of her father and Buruu in their prisons. Kin slaving over his workbench. Even Hiro lying here beside her, oblivious to the plan unfolding under his nose. And there, wrapped in the warmth of his arms, she felt completely and utterly alone.

"I can't wait to get out of this place," she whispered.

"Am I that awful?" Hiro raised an eyebrow.

"No." She smiled and kissed his skin. "But everything else around me feels . . . polluted. There are so many wheels and lies within lies here." She shook her head. "I feel like it's rubbing off on me. Turning me into something I'm not. This place is poisonous."

"You will be here for some time. Try to make the best of it. When the Shōgun has calmed down, I will petition him for permission to court you. I have sent a letter to my father—"

"Court me? What the hells for?"

"So I can be with you." He frowned, leaning up on one elbow.

"Hiro, you're here with me right now," she laughed, kissing him again.

"In public." He searched her eyes. "I risked my life coming here without permission, Yukiko. And if it were only me, I would gladly risk more to feel you in my arms. But my comrades who guard your door? The servants who turned a blind eye to my passing? We risk their lives also, meeting this way." He took her hand, ran his thumb across her knuckles. "But more than that, I want people to know you are mine. This hiding, this skulking about like a thief, it dishonors us both."

"Gods, who cares what anyone else thinks? All that matters is the two of us."

"That is not true. We must think of our families. Of our names. I am sworn to Yoritomo-no-miya."

"I know that, Hiro."

"Then you know that, first and foremost, I am his servant. I live and die by the Code of Bushido. I must honor my oath."

"An oath to a liar is no oath at all," she muttered.

"What did you say?"

A sigh. She sat up and threw a thin kimono over her shoulders, slipped out of the bed. Padding barefoot across the polished boards, she stopped at the tiny window, staring out into the dark Kigen night. Summer's edge was growing dull; autumn would soon be here, and from there the world would slip into the cold depths of winter. Would he understand when he stood by this window alone? Should she tell him she'd be long gone before the first snows began to fall?

She looked at him, folded her arms about herself.

"You're a good man," she said. "But there are things about your master you don't know. Things that might make you rethink your obedience."

"Without his oath, without his Lord, a samurai is nothing. Honesty. Respect. Loyalty. Honor. This is the code of the warrior. I am samurai before all, Yukiko. To wield the long and the short sword and to die. This is my purpose."

"Someone once told me 'To be a servant can be a noble thing, but only as noble as the master served.'"

"Your father?"

"A friend." A quiet sigh. "I wish you could meet him."

She stared out into the dark, heard the wind whispering through the stunted gardens below.

The tantō was in her hand, the thin river of blood spilling down Daichi's chest. She could hear the knife as it clattered to the floorboards, hear Daichi asking her why.

She had been reborn that night. Become something more. Something better.

"Why are you speaking this way?" There was anger in Hiro's voice, bewilderment in his eyes. "You talk as if you wish me to question my Lord. But without my oath, I am nothing. Bushido is my purpose, my heart. It is the Way. Yoritomo-no-miya is Lord of this Empire. All his people owe him fealty. Including you, Yukiko."

She could see his eyes in the dark; the beautiful sea-green that had haunted the dreams of a girl lost in the Iishi. It all seemed so terribly long ago—the oni and the Kagé, the endless swaying ocean of rain-washed gloom. The girl who had crashed in those woods and dreamed of those eyes was a stranger now.

Yukiko sighed again and turned from the window, toxic, muted moonlight at her back. She shrugged the robe from her shoulders, slipped naked into the bed beside him and wrapped herself in his arms again. Closing her eyes, she pretended the next few days would be enough. Pretended she wasn't lying to him with every breath she mustered.

"Loyal to a fault." Aisha said.

She lay in the dark, eyes wide open, listening to his heart beating.

I can't tell him.

H ideo watched the grubby dawn light filter through the beach glass, shadows of the windowpane creeping across the floor to his master's bed. The pipe in his hands was long-stemmed, bowl carved like a tiger's head, smoke drifting from its open mouth. His morning fix was almost done; after two more puffs he would be dry, and soon the scratching, sour-tongued need would begin building again. The monkey on his back, chattering and digging its fingers into his spine. The demon who knew all his secrets.

What an old fool you are. Master of the Imperial Court. Eyes in every tavern, ears on every street corner. Not a man nor mouse who could hide from you in all of this land, and you cannot find a way to rid yourself of this wretched weed.

Poring over another document, he dipped his calligraphy brush into the cuttlefish ink. He made three short, precise strokes, giving permission for the Dockers Union to stop work and attend the bicentennial gala at weeksend. It could just as easily have been a purchase order for a hundred new slaves to toil and die on the Shōgun's lands. An arrest order for a dissenter who would disappear one night and never speak again. A death warrant.

Inhale. Close your eyes. Feel the dragon slide down your throat, spreading heavy coils throughout your veins. Hold your breath. Listen. Hear the emptiness inside your head. Embrace it. Be nothing. Know nothing. That you are nothing. That the need to breathe inside your lungs, building, burning, like all things, is only an illusion. Exhale. Open your eyes and watch the smoke dance in the muted light.

He blinked at the calligraphy brush and fancied it a blade in his hands. A weapon that had killed more men than a bushiman or Iron Samurai could ever dream.

I am consort to Lady Izanami, Mother of Death. This ink is the blood of my victims.

Yoritomo yawned and sat up in bed, blinking around the bedchamber as if confused. He ran his hand across his irezumi, palm rasping on his skin, eyes finally falling on his minister kneeling in the sitting room outside.

"I commanded that the lady wait in her own chambers, great Lord, equal of heaven." Hideo's tongue felt too thick for his mouth. "She can return when we are done if that is your wish."

Yoritomo sipped at the water by his bedside, grimacing at the chemical tang.

"No." He shook his head. "Send her back to her father with some iron for her dowry. I have no more need of her. Ryu women leave an aftertaste if savored for too long."

"As you say, great Lord. The lady will be returned to her family once the marks of your . . . affection fade."

"Is there anything important this morning?" Yoritomo waved at the stack of documents on Hideo's table. Smoke curled up from the tiger's mouth, drifting across the pages. The minister put the pipe to his lips.

"Lord Hiro asks again to beg your forgiveness personally, Seii Taishōgun. He seems genuinely contrite, and seeks to make amends to his sovereign Lord and master."

"Hiro," Yoritomo growled. "I should have had him commit seppuku for his failure."

"My sister and her husband have asked that I convey their eternal gratitude for sparing their only son your wrath, great Lord. Hiro is most dear to them."

"He is too young to wear the ō-yoroi and the golden jin-haori. He is too young to stand among the Kazumitsu Elite. You spoil him, Hideo."

"My sons are dead, great Lord." An old man's sad smile, his eyes red with lotus smoke. "Fallen before their time in the glorious war, green saplings cut down beneath the Empire's flag. You will forgive an uncle his indulgences to his only nephew, and make time to hear Hiro's lament?"

Yoritomo sighed, nodded, "Very well."

"Your generosity is boundless, Seii Taishōgun. My heartfelt thanks."

"What else?" Yoritomo waved at the table.

"Preparations for the gala are well underway. The marching order that the courtiers will use during the parade has *at last* been finalized." Hideo waved his pipe as he spoke. "Tora first, naturally. The Ryu retinue will march in front

of the Fushicho, followed by the Kitsune. The ruffled feathers of the Phoenix emissaries have been smoothed over after some initial difficulties."

"What did you promise them?"

"That a Phoenix commander would receive your careful consideration when you replace General Tora Hojatsu as head of the gaijin invasion force."

Yoritomo snorted. "If they wish to lead the entire army, perhaps the Fushicho should bring me victories in the skirmishes I have already allotted them."

"I promised your consideration on the matter, great Lord. Nothing more." A tired smile. "With that quibble silenced, all is now on schedule for the celebrations at weeksend. The fireworks have arrived from Yama, Fushicho Kirugume has composed a special piece to be played in your honor. I hear tell that the orchestra accompanying him will be at least fifty strong. The court is quite abuzz with excitement."

"Very well." The Shōgun stalked to the coral basin, splashing tepid water in his face. "Are we done?"

"There is one other matter, great Lord." Hideo's brow was creased with a small frown. "There has been much activity around the arashitora these last few days. Artificers coming and going at odd hours, taking measurements, poking and prodding. It seems a great deal of trouble for a simple saddle."

Yoritomo smiled.

"Do not concern yourself, Hideo. My sister is arranging a gift for me."

"Lady Aisha is—"

"Indeed. And she wishes to keep it a surprise. So be not alarmed."

Hideo's eyes narrowed slightly and he finally drew the last puff from his pipe. The smoke was cloying and warm, flowing down his throat, lungs open wide. Larynx to bronchi, alveoli to bloodstream and from there to bliss. The dragon uncoiled inside him, giving voice to his suspicion, serpentine form to his paranoia. Glittering scales. A cold, quiet hiss inside.

"A surprise, great Lord?" The old man smiled, smoke drifting from between his lips. "Well, you know how much we all enjoy those."

T wo days from now."

Yukiko kept her voice low, her eyes scanning the arena, listening for the sounds of the bushimen patrols. She had slipped from her bedroom as soon as the sun set, crawled through the roof and stolen out over the garden wall. From the cover of a nearby squeezeway, she'd watched the soldiers as they circled the periphery of the arena; two pairs marching clockwise and counterclockwise, walking through the archways and patrolling the inner walls every

second circuit. Each trip around the circumference took the men almost ten minutes. She had a little under seven left before she'd have to slip back into the shadows. She felt nervous and exposed on the broad expanse of the arena floor, crouching low beside Buruu's forelegs, one hand on his chest. She needed to get back to the palace before anyone missed her.

The Artificer was bent over Buruu's wing, testing a series of metal cuffs around the alula and marginal coverts, assessing length and breadth with a small, clicking measure-reel. The mechabacus on his chest was a constant, clattering hum, singing an equation of sedition.

"Two days," Kin replied, swapping one cuff for another. "It will be ready."

"It needs to be, Kin-san. The whole city will be at the bicentennial. Almost every bushiman in the palace will be part of the parade. Iron Samurai too. The prison will be almost empty, and all eyes will be on the sky. We get one chance at this."

"I will play my part."

DO YOU TRUST HIM?

Do I have a choice?

FROM THE FIRST TIME YOU MET, HE BEGAN LYING TO YOU. FACE HIDDEN BEHIND HIS MASK, THINKING THE WORLD DOES NOT SEE THE POISON.

He's not like the rest of them.

THEY ARE ALL THE SAME.

She reached up to Buruu's neck, dragged her fingernails between the sleek feathers under his chin. His purr was a tiny earthquake, rumbling deep inside her chest.

"I want to thank you, Kin-san," Yukiko said, searching the featureless, brass mask. "You are risking so much for us. I'm not sure I know why."

"Do you not?" A rasping buzz from within his helmet. "Can you not guess?"

She licked her lips and stared at the floor.

HE WANTS YOU. THAT IS WHY HE HELPS US. NO OTHER REASON.

"Kin, I—"

He held up his hand, thick leather and heavy brass, clockwork and spinning gears. Yukiko could see herself reflected in that single bloody eye, saw herself for the liar she'd become. She knew Kin was in love with her. But she was afraid that if she told him how she felt, he'd abandon her, leave Buruu to die in here. And she needed his help.

Was that something she could forgive herself for? Lying for the sake of a greater good? Deceiving this boy so her best friend would be spared his tor-

ment, her father could be free of his prison? Was tearing one heart out a fair price for the lives of two others?

"You don't need to say it," Kin shook his head. "When we are far from here, when we look to the horizon and see nothing but emerald and jet, then we can talk. Say everything we have wanted to say." He stuffed the metal cuffs back into his belt, took one last appraising look at Buruu's wing. "It will be ready, Yukiko-chan. Two days. I give you my word."

He touched two fingers to his brow, nodded to Buruu, then clomped from the pit and off into the darkness, leaving behind the faint stench of chi smoke. Yukiko stood and wrapped both arms around Buruu's neck, pressed her face into his feathers, breathing him in. He was warm and soft, like the blankets she would curl up in near the fireside when she was a little girl. She wanted nothing more than to be far from here, cool wind in her hair, clean rain on her face. Alive and breathing.

This is not me. I hate this.

IT WILL BE OVER SOON. AT LEAST OUR PART. THE KAGÉ WILL HAVE THEIR REVOLUTION. THE LOTUS WILL BURN.

I don't care. I don't care about any of that. None of it matters.

OF COURSE IT MATTERS. YOU ARE PART OF THIS WORLD. YOU HAVE THE POWER TO MAKE A CHANGE FOR THE BETTER.

How many people will die in this revolution?

HOW MANY WILL DIE WITHOUT IT?

I don't want to be the one who starts it all. I just want my family back. My father safe. You free. That's all I want.

YOU CANNOT HAVE THAT WITHOUT THE KAGÉ.

I know, I know. Yoritomo deserves to die. He killed my mother. Tortured my father. I hate him so much it's turning me black inside. But doesn't murdering him make me no better than he is? And what if killing him only makes things worse?

IN THE END, ALL QUESTIONS CAN BE DISTILLED INTO ONE. WHAT ARE YOU WILLING TO GIVE UP TO GET THE THINGS YOU WANT?

I'd give up my life for any one of you.

DYING IS EASY. ANYONE CAN THROW THEMSELVES ONTO THE PYRE AND REST A HAPPY MARTYR. ENDURING THE SUFFERING THAT COMES WITH SACRIFICE IS THE REAL TEST.

She was back on the *Thunder Child*, her father's voice ringing in her head.

"One day you will understand, Yukiko. One day you will see that we must sometimes sacrifice for the sake of something greater."

She nodded, wiped the tears from her eyes, locked them in a room inside her mind and threw away the key. No more fear. No more regrets. Not for vague ideology or someone else's notion of what was "right." For the ones she loved. For her family.

All right then. Let's start a war.

"What are you doing here?"

Yukiko flinched. Buruu's growl rumbled through the floor, up through the soles of her feet. His hackles rose in ragged peaks across his back, eyes flashing. She frowned into the dark, recognizing the voice.

"Hiro?"

He stepped from the shadows, bare chest beneath his red silk kimono, embroidered tigers prowling down his arms. He was wearing a black obi, neo-daishō crossed at the small of his back, crouched in their lacquered scabbards. His hair flowed loose, a frown darkening that beautiful, sea-green stare she'd dreamed of a lifetime ago.

"I came to see you, and you were not in your room. What are you doing out here without an escort, Yukiko?"

"Visiting with Buruu."

"How did you get out of the palace? The guards did not see you leave."

"Kitsune looks after his own." She tried a shy smile, hoping to win him over.

"And the Guildsman?" His eyes narrowed, looking down the corridor Kin had left by. "Why was he here?"

"I didn't ask." She shrugged, hands clasped behind her back to hide the shakes. "I have nothing to say to their kind. I think he might be working on Yoritomo's saddle."

"Yukiko," Hiro frowned. "If the Guild is plotting something . . ."

"Nobody is plotting anything."

"You are lying." He shook his head. "I can see it in your eyes."

TELL HIM NOTHING.

"Nothing is going on," Yukiko insisted. She stepped forward and pressed against him, arms around his waist. "You worry too much. Buruu is my friend. He gets lonely in the dark and I wanted to be alone with him. I miss him, Hiro. That's all there is to it."

"Swear to me."

"I swear." She looked directly into his eyes as she spoke, and the lie tasted like ashes in her mouth. "Nothing is going on."

Hiro looked down into her face, expression softening, voice a soft murmur.

"I am sorry." He touched her cheek, brushed stray hair away from her eyes. "I know you miss your friend. I know that he is dear to you in a way I cannot understand. But you should not be sneaking out of the palace without permission. You deceived the Shōgun before under my guard. I am . . ." He shook his head. "I am just afraid his faith in me will prove misplaced. If I fail him again . . ."

And there in the evening gloom, Yukiko saw him as if for the first time, as if the dark was somehow brighter than the day. Hiro wasn't like her father. He didn't serve Yoritomo because he'd been coerced or threatened. Hiro served because he believed it was right. Honor, loyalty, the Bushido Code, it was everything to him. He'd die before he betrayed it, one of Buruu's happy martyrs. His life was meaningless without his Lord. He was a spinning, razor-sharp cog in the engine, born to privilege and never once questioning the rightness of it all.

This was a mistake.

In her heart she had known it all along. And, truth be told, he had never pretended otherwise. But she had wanted so badly for them both to be wrong, hoped against hope that he might be different from the others. If someone like Aisha could grow to see the truth of things, then anyone could.

Anyone who allowed themselves to, that is.

She felt Buruu in the back of her mind, no judgment or rebuke. He'd tried to warn her, told her Hiro was just another part of the control machine. She wished she'd listened.

Hiro pressed her tightly to him, hands clasped at the base of her spine, staring with those beautiful eyes that had once haunted her sleep. He began to speak, time slowing to a crawl as his lips parted to tell her the one thing she didn't want to hear.

"I lo—"

She kissed him, stood on tiptoes and threw her arms around his neck and crushed her lips into his before he could finish the sentence. She didn't want to listen to those three awful words, feel them open her up to the bone and see what the lies had done to her insides. She pressed her body against his and kissed him until they died on his lips, the impulse to speak slowly strangled in soft, blessed silence.

She kissed him like it was the last time.

Somewhere deep inside, she knew it would be.

A knife in his chest.

A jagged splinter of rusted metal, shoved between his ribs and twisted until the bones popped. He couldn't breathe. Couldn't see. Nausea and vertigo, world swaying in some invisible wind as the ground split under his feet and yawned wide.

Kin leaned against the wall, fingers splayed on concrete as his universe dissolved. The measure-reel fell from numb, trembling hands, the figures he'd wanted to recheck drifting off into some dark, forgotten corner of his mind. He stared at Yukiko and the samurai in each other's arms and felt vomit bubbling up in the back of his throat. The taste of rage in his mouth, hard and metallic, a razor's edge.

What a fool you've been.

He turned and staggered away, clutching his heart as if to hold back the blood.

What a stupid, blind fool.

33

THE BREAKING STORM

A lifetime. The blinking of an eye. Two days long.

Whispers to Michi, shrouded in bathhouse steam or the silken rustle of the dressing room, those small pale hands with the sword-grip calluses she'd never noticed before running a comb through her long, dark hair. Whispers beneath a blanket of shamisen music, the whisking and steeping of tea, Aisha's diamond-hard eyes betraying no hint of treachery. A fast Fushicho sky-ship with fake permits waiting at the docks. A note from Akihito, written in broad, clumsy kanji, a promise that he and Kasumi would be with the Kagé as they freed Masaru from his cell. A rendezvous in Yama city, one week from today. Sleepless nights and excuses for Hiro and long hours alone, staring at the ceiling in the dark.

And no word from Kin.

She stared at the mechanical arashitora on her dresser, warm moonlight flickering on the brass, waves of leaden butterflies in her stomach. There was no chance she would sleep tonight. She wished the moon would be on its way across the sky and the dawn arrive, bringing with it Yoritomo's grand gala and distracted guards and empty arena. To be out. To be free.

Lightning kissed distant skies. The first autumn storm was rolling down from the Iishi, stretching dark fingers toward Kigen Bay. She prayed it would be dry tomorrow, that Susano-ō would hold back the black rain long enough to let Yoritomo's soldiers avert their eyes and drop their guard.

She held her tantō tight in her hand. She saw the picture clearly in her mind: Yoritomo standing tall on his podium, arms spread wide as the sun sank below the horizon and he called for the fireworks to begin. The people's faces upturned and soft with wonder as the dragon cannons and kindling wheels lit up the sky, spitting colored fire and blue-black fumes to choke all the good little boys and girls. And like a stone they would drop from the skies, thunder and blinding light behind them. And in their wake there would be blood, and screams, and the last male of Kazumitsu's line lying dead on the ground.

An empty throne.

A new beginning.

War.

"Godsdamn this accursed heat," Hajime swore.

"Aiya," Rokorou muttered. "Moaning about it will help?"

The two guards were slumped in the thin shade of the prison gate, sweat beading on their skin. The air was moist with storm-threat, clouds gathering to the north for a final push on the city. Hajime wiped his brow with his jin-haori and cast a mournful glance in the direction of the docks, listening to the sounds of music and bustling crowds drifting from the bay. The gala was well underway; the crackle of smoke sticks and spark poppers could be heard among the multitude of voices floating on the wind. He imagined his son's eyes lit with delight as he watched the real fireworks tonight.

Lightning flashed on the horizon.

"At least we get off at dusk," he sighed. "The real party will start then, assuming this storm doesn't piss all over everything."

"You're also assuming they'll relieve us. Daisuke was too drunk to show up last festival."

"If we're stuck here all night, I'm going to . . ."

His sentence trailed off as the girl appeared, sashaying around the corner in a sleeveless, split-leg black kimono. She held a wicker basket in her arms. A beautiful tiger curled around one bicep, the imperial sun radiating across the other. Flawless make-up, polished lenses, gleaming, candy-red lips.

"Michi-chan," Rokorou nodded, straightening slightly and sucking in his gut.

"Good day, brave bushimen," she smiled.

"Why aren't you at the gala? The parade will be starting soon."

"My Lady commands me to bring refreshment to those stalwart souls who do honor to her brother, Yoritomo-no-miya, and forsake the gala's joys for duty."

The girl gave a mock salute, then reached into the basket and produced two bottles of rice wine and two ripe nectarines, fresh and plump. The guards' eyes widened; the fruit was easily worth more than a week's pay. They bowed thanks and took the offerings, shooting each other broad grins.

"Not so bad a duty after all, eh?" Rokorou took a long swig of wine.

"Your Lady does us much honor, Michi-chan." Hajime bowed again. Shrugging off his gauntlets, he cut the fruit and popped a slice between his teeth.

"Aiya, it's good," he groaned.

Rokorou plowed into his own fruit as Hajime remembered his manners, offering a slice to the serving girl. She blushed and bowed from the knee, looking to the floor.

"My thanks, sama, but the gift was for you alone."

"At least have a drink with us?" Rokorou took another pull from the bottle, glaring up at the suns. The sky began to blur around the edges.

"Hai, drink and be joyful, give thanks to Yoritomo-no-miya, next Stormdancer of Shima." Hajime laughed, stumbling back against the wall. He frowned and stared at the fruits in his seven hands, feeling the stone beneath his feet turn to jelly.

A gasp. The sound of metal and bone hitting stone. The stink of urine.

Shapes emerged from the shadows, moving swiftly. Two men grabbed the slumbering guards and dragged them down an alleyway. A young boy dashed a pail of brackish water onto the floor to wash away the piss and blood. Akihito rounded the corner, broad-brimmed straw hat, long scars showing on his chest between the folds of his uwagi. Kasumi walked beside him, surefooted, feline grace, bo-staff in her hands.

"Are we ready?" the big man asked.

Michi glanced to the alley mouth as her fellows returned in the uniforms of the poisoned guards. One of them tossed a ring of keys, glittering in the scarlet glare. Michi snatched them from the air without looking. She glanced up to the big man, nodded to Kasumi and drew her tsurugi from the basket. The blade was two feet long, straight and double-edged, keen as razors.

"Now we are."

Thunder rolled in the distance.

"No mercy."

Yukiko padded into the arena, split-toed socks on bare stone, hands folded inside the sleeves of her uwagi. She nodded to the bushiman guarding the archway, her shy smile returned with lecherous enthusiasm. He held up his hand as she approached, fingers spread, wrapped in banded iron.

"And what are you doing here without an escort, little one?"

A roar from the arena, deafening, bellowing, reverberating off the warm stone. The bushiman turned toward Buruu, eyes narrowing, tightening his grip on the war club at his waist. The hypo was heavy in her hands, slipping from her sleeve, black liquid sloshing viscous in the syringe. She slid it through a gap in his breastplate, just below his armpit. He gasped, clutched the pinprick and collapsed on the ground in a blacksleep stupor.

The echoes of the roar had died by the time his comrade returned from the privy, still tying up the waist of his hakama.

"What the hells is it making noise about now . . ."

The bushiman glanced up from his obi and saw his fellow passed out cold on the deck. He ran to his comrade's body and knelt beside it, sloughing off his gauntlet and checking at the throat for a pulse. Yukiko stepped out of the shadows behind, footfalls soft as baby's breath, needle gleaming between her fingers. The bushiman collapsed onto his friend's body with a bleeding puncture in his neck.

The third and fourth bushimen were standing on the upper walls at the other side of the arena, staring out toward Kigen Bay. Music drifted on the sweltering wind as they spoke in hushed tones, cursing their misfortune at landing guard duty on today of all days. Her feet were quiet as ghosts behind them, a murmur of soft cloth on cool, hard gray. Dull sunlight flashed on surgical steel, a needle in each hand, thumbs poised on the plungers. Spots of blood welled from the needle-pricks, staining the fabric beneath their arms a deeper red. Each man collapsed without a whimper, and the sound of iron crashing hard onto stone echoed among the empty benches.

Looking down at the slumbering soldiers, Yukiko was reminded of a poem her mother had taught her when she was a little girl:

> *Tiger proudly roars.*
> *Dragon dives and Phoenix soars.*
> *Fox gets the chicken.*

"Kitsune looks after his own," she whispered. She tossed the empty blacksleep hypos onto the unconscious bodies and touched the tattoo on her arm for luck. Buruu growled on the arena floor below.

THE STORM GROWS CLOSE.

I know.

Looking up at the fingers of dark cloud drifting over the noonday sun, she prayed Kin would arrive soon.

A length of weighted chain flashed out of the darkness, wrapping around the bushiman's throat. He gasped and clutched at the metal links turning his larynx to pulp. Akihito loomed out of the black, fist descending to knock the man senseless. Black shuriken stars whizzed from the shadows, cutting the second guard down as he drew breath to shout for help. Blood sprayed across the walls, random patterns of deep scarlet on dull, sweating rock.

Michi stepped from the dark, more throwing stars poised between her fingers. Kasumi prowled close behind, casting anxious glances back the way they'd come. Akihito's eyes had adjusted to the gloom, and he could see the tension in Kasumi's stance, swimming in her eyes. Her knuckles were white on the haft of her iron-shod bo-staff.

"Are you all right?" he whispered.

"I'm worried about Yukiko."

"This way," Michi nodded.

The trio stole along the corridor, creeping down narrow spiral stairs. The chattering and screech of rats echoed off moist stone, air growing thicker as they descended. The stink of rotting meat and human waste clung to their skin, slick with sweat. Stone walls pressed in around them, all sweltering heat and noxious vapor.

Michi signaled a stop, crept forward in the darkness. Sounds of a scuffle, leather and metal on stone. A soft, wet exhalation. The girl returned and motioned for them to follow, a splash of someone else's blood across her forehead and running thick down one cheek. The tsurugi in her hands gleamed black in the gloom.

"You don't need to kill them," Kasumi murmured.

"You think they would spare you, Hunter?"

"Why do you do this?" Akihito whispered. "Why help us?"

"Yoritomo must die," Michi replied flatly, squinting into the black ahead. They arrived at a T-junction, stopped to listen, pressed against the damp stone.

"He hurt you?" Kasumi asked softly.

"Look at the world around you, Hunter," Michi growled. "He's hurting everyone."

*H*E APPROACHES.

Yukiko peered from the grandstand shadows as the sound of clockwork and pistons rolled off the arena walls. She could see an Artificer emerging from one of the entryways, peering around the benches, a squat mechanical contraption on tank treads rolling behind him. The mechanoid dragged a four-wheel trailer covered with a dirty gray oilskin.

"Kin-san!" Yukiko bounced down the stone stairs, feet so light she felt she could fly. She couldn't help throwing her arms around his neck, eyes alight with her smile. "You came."

The Artificer disentangled himself from the hug, voice crackling like beetle shells underfoot.

"I gave you my word that I would."

"I hadn't heard from you in days. I feared something had happened to you."

"We should start." He turned, motioning to the servitor. "We don't have much time."

Yukiko helped him unload the trailer and bring the gear into Buruu's pit. The thunder tiger eyed the Guildsman's contraption, tail tucked between his legs. Long lengths of hollow metal, enameled with the same strange iridescent coating as the Shōgun's motor-rickshaws. Sheets of treated canvas, the same lightweight skin as the balloon bladders of the sky-ships. Hydraulics and pistons and clockwork teeth.

THERE IS SOMETHING WRONG.

What do you mean?

THE WAY HE MOVES. THE WAY HE SPEAKS.

"Is everything all right, Kin-san?" Yukiko frowned.

"Ask Buruu to spread his wings, please." Kin pulled a leather harness from the trailer, ridged with a series of interlocking gears and pistons. "I need to install the spinal axis first."

The arashitora spread his wings, crippled voltage playing along his flat feathertips. The hairs on her arms prickled, the faint scent of ozone pierced the lotus reek. She stepped back and watched Kin work, unable to comprehend the machine he was strapping to Buruu's back. She could see tension in his movements, hear a catch as his breath billowed from the apparatus coiled on his back.

"Kin, what's wrong?"

"Nothing." He shook his head, eye aglow with the arc torch. "I need to concentrate."

Yukiko fell silent, watching the pretty rain of sparks, the motion of his hands as he assembled his creation. Long curved rods of iridescence were affixed across the arashitora's scapular quills and the line of his marginal coverts, extending beyond the severed primary flight feathers. Kin fixed the sheets of hard canvas over the skeletal frame, strapping them in place, tinkering at the series of gears and pistons that ran like a spine down Buruu's back. Yukiko watched as the minutes ticked by, one atop the other, holding her breath as the mechanism neared completion.

"It's beautiful," she whispered.

Kin paused for a second, sighed and shook his head.

"All right, try that," he finally said, stepping back from Buruu.

The arashitora looked uncertain but spread his wings regardless. Kin's machine whirred smoothly, unspooling into wide fans, a broad series of canvas quills sitting where the tips of Buruu's feathers should have been. Bones of shimmering metal, hydraulic muscles and reinforced joints. Buruu flapped again, bounding a few feet into the air, electricity crackling along the iridescent frame. The wings worked perfectly: a sleek song of lubricant and metal teeth, the rush of wind, straw dancing in the downdraft.

RAIJIN SAVE ME. THE BOY HAS DONE IT.

"Gods above, they work," Yukiko beamed. "It works!"

Buruu leaped into the air, pounding his wings furiously. He sailed up twenty feet, thirty, swooping around their heads, beak clamped tightly on the triumphant roar that threatened to spill over and alert the entire city.

DO YOU SEE, YUKIKO? DO YOU SEE?

Yukiko threw her arms around Kin's neck, planted a kiss on his metal cheek. "Kin-san, you did it!"

Again, the boy extricated himself from her arms, flipping a switch on his belt. The burning blue light of his cutting torch arced at his wrist.

"He's not free yet."

Buruu landed, claws sparking across stone, shaking his whole body like a soggy hound. The Guildsman bent down and began cutting at the two-inch-thick iron chain around the thunder tiger's throat. Molten steel spattered red-hot onto the flagstones, the smell of burning metal drifted thick in the air. The arashitora nudged the Guildsman with his cheek and purred, a subtle gesture of thanks that made Yukiko's heart swell.

We're nearly home, Buruu.

The sound of the gala hung faint in the distance under the rumble of the gathering storm. She thought of the flight to come, into the mouth of the tempest, leaving this stinking city far behind them. Free. At last.

She looked at Buruu's wings, pictured the small mechanical arashitora Kin had made for her, still sitting on her dresser.

"Aiya. I left the toy you made for me in my bedroom."

Kin made a sound, deep within his helm. A sneer.

"Perhaps Lord Hiro can fetch it for you."

AH.

"... What did you say?"

NOW I SEE.

Kin fixed her in his molten stare. She could see her face reflected in his single eye, illuminated blue-white by the cutting torch, brief joy dying in her eyes.

"You heard," Kin rasped. "Where is Lord Hiro? Shouldn't he be here 'protecting' you?"

She could feel Buruu in her head, the vaguely self-satisfied air of one who's finally found the missing piece to a troublesome puzzle. But the smugness was underscored with uncertainty about the danger Kin now posed.

HE KNOWS.

They descended two more flights of stairs, smooth stone beneath their feet, their breathing too loud in the humid dark. Michi led the way through the tunnels, past the rusting iron bars and cramped cells, the pitiful moaning scarecrows inside. She stopped at each cell with an occupant and unlocked the door, but the emaciated stick-men inside could barely raise their heads at the sound of freedom. At the sixth cage down, a rat twice the size of Aisha's dog raised its head from its feast and shrieked, bloody mouth open wide.

The rag-men reminded Michi of the children in her village: flesh draped like translucent cloth around their bones, all elbows and knuckles and hollow cheeks amidst the fat rice fields. Little boys and girls, starving to death, surrounded by so much food. Sometimes she still had nightmares about them; silent waifs standing in the burning village, watching her uncle's execution.

When all this was over, when the Guild and the Shōgun were nothing but a bad memory, she would write a book. A true history for Shima's children to read and feel and remember, that they would know the real price their country had paid for fuel and power. That they would know the names of those who stood in defiance of tyranny, who fought and died so that they might one day be free.

"The Lotus War."

She couldn't imagine a name more fitting.

They arrived at Masaru's cell. Kasumi knelt at the bars and stretched her hands toward him, voice wet with tears. The rice and dried fruit Michi had smuggled in had done him good; he looked stronger and sharper, the flesh on his bones wasn't so gray. But he was still weak, drunk on stinking heat and lack of sunlight, clothed in grime and tattered rags. She unlocked the cell, turned to Akihito.

"Can you carry him?"

The big man didn't answer, just shouldered past and picked up Masaru in a bear hug, a grin slapped onto his face to hide the anguish at his friend's condition. Kasumi held tight to Masaru's hand, kissed him on the lips. Michi wrinkled her nose at the thought of what he must taste like.

"We need to go," she hissed, eyeing the corridor.

"Indeed you do."

A match flared in the gloom, a bright hiss of sulfur illuminating a wrinkled face, hard, sunken eyes. Minister Hideo puffed at his pipe, flame pulsing between his fingers, light rippling across the banded armor of the bushimen surrounding him. Naked kodachi glittered in their hands; short, single-bladed swords ideal for close-quarter fighting. Though there were no Iron Samurai among the soldiers, the conspirators were still outnumbered by at least a dozen.

The sound of footsteps from the stairs made Michi's heart sink. More bushimen poured down from the entrance, cutting off their escape.

So many.

Too many.

"We are betrayed," she whispered.

K in, I'm sorry."

"Don't." The Guildsman held up one gauntlet, stabbed at the release clasp about his throat. His helmet peeled away in its tiny ballet and he tore it from his head, unplugging it from his skin before dashing it against the ground. Face gleaming with sweat, cheeks blotched with anger. "I feel enough of a fool already. Don't make it any worse."

"Kin, I wanted to tell you . . ."

"But you were afraid if you did, I wouldn't help you, right?"

"I suppose, but—"

"So you lied instead. Well, congratulations. You got your way. I hope you get everything you deserve."

"I didn't lie to you, Kin. I just didn't tell you the whole—"

BEWARE.

Yukiko frowned, the sounds of metal footfalls ringing at the edge of hearing.

What is it?

INSECTS. MANY. THEY ARE COMING.

The sound grew louder, Kin breaking his stare and glancing about as the din of ō-yoroi and chainkatana rose. Chattering steel and hissing chi.

"Oh no," Yukiko breathed.

Two dozen Iron Samurai charged into the arena from east and west: heavy, steel-shod footsteps, golden jin-haori, neo-daishō filling the air with the growl of serrated metal teeth. Yoritomo stalked at their rear, yards of red silk billowing behind him, one hand resting on the hilt of his katana. His face was torn, four long gouges running down his cheek to his throat. Spattered in blood, hands and face, eyes glazed white in a pale mask splashed with red. Another Iron Samurai walked by his side.

"Oh, Kin, no."

She turned to him, disbelief in her eyes.

"You told them?"

34

STORMDANCER

Rats screeched in the darkness, their cries echoing among the stink.

"Lay down your weapons," Hideo exhaled, the air swimming with cloying lotus smoke. "Or die here and now."

"Bastard whoreson," the big one spat. "I'll kill you and all your little girl-friends."

The giant set the Black Fox down on the cell floor, stepped into the corridor. Hideo noted with faint satisfaction that the fool had chosen his weapon poorly; the corridor was too narrow to swing the kusarigama's chain. Neither the sickle nor the woman's bo-staff would be a match for a cadre of bushimen with koda-chi. The girl with the tsurugi might prove problematic, however, and of all these traitors, Hideo wanted her alive to question. He had been trying to uncover the Kagé cell within Kigen for years, and suspected there might be more rats in the cellar. A few days in the torture cells, and her singing would put a nightin-gale to shame.

"There is no need for violence," the old man smiled. "Yield now and we will show you mercy."

"Like you showed at Daiyakawa?" the girl spat.

"Or to Captain Yamagata?" sneered the woman.

Hideo sighed, leaned on his walking stick. He was getting too old for this nonsense. All things being equal, he'd rather be taking a nice, cool bath. He turned to the bushiman captain, drawing slowly on his pipe as the man met his stare. The lotus in the tiger's mouth flared bright, reflected in tired, bloodshot eyes.

"Bring me the girl alive."

The dragon uncoiled upon his tongue.

"Kill the others."

T he Iron Samurai fanned out around the periphery of the arena floor, weapons drawn and ready, all growling teeth and rumbling motors. They glared out from behind their horned oni masks, the black enamel on their ō-yoroi gleaming a bloody scarlet in the light of the smothered sun. Buruu roared in warning, setting the iron plates squealing. The air was filled with static electricity, broken fingers of blue current running along the iridescent skeleton of his wings. He set his eyes on Kin, ready to end the boy for his betrayal.

"Kin, how could you do this to us?" Yukiko demanded.

"What?" A whisper.

"How could you tell them?"

". . . You think I betrayed you?"

"How else did they find out?"

"I gave you my word." Wounded eyes. Voice catching in his throat. "I gave Buruu his wings. I would never betray you, Yukiko. Never."

Yukiko blinked, breathing hard, searching that knife-bright stare and finding only truth. She glanced back at Buruu, ashamed of her suspicion, unable to look Kin in the face. At that moment, she realized the boy had risked everything for them. He had discovered the truth about Hiro, known that she had deceived him. Despite all of that, he had stayed true to his promise.

But if it wasn't Kin who betrayed them . . .

THE SISTER.

"Aisha?" Yukiko frowned at the Shōgun.

Yoritomo sneered, wiped one hand across the bloody gouges on his cheek.

"No, my sister refused to betray you. And still she dared beg for mercy." His eyes danced with the memory. "She found none."

Bloody fingers curled into a fist.

"Nor will you."

Yukiko swallowed.

"Then how did you know?"

The Iron Samurai standing next to Yoritomo reached into the folds of his jin-haori. He hurled a small, glittering object across the arena floor, bouncing and skidding to rest amidst the dirty straw. Kin's gift: the tiny, mechanical arashitora.

"Little escapes the attention of Minister Hideo," Yoritomo smiled. "Or his spies. Lord Hiro was most eager to make amends for his failure after your first round of treachery."

Yukiko narrowed her eyes, sucking in a long, trembling breath.

"Hiro?"

"So pretty on the outside." The Iron Samurai's voice sounded hollow and breathless within his oni helm. His eyes were green glass. Empty, flat mirrors. "But inside you're black and rotten. A liar and a whore. Kitsune trash."

She took a step back, as if he'd struck her.

Buruu growled and dug his claws into the floor, flagstones cracking to rubble. *GIVE HIM NOTHING. HE DESERVES EVEN LESS.*

"Kitsune trash is good enough for a Tora samurai to lay down with though, right? Good enough to sleep with to get what you need?" She shook her head, her voice a low hiss. "You're the whore, Hiro. Living your whole life on your knees, never once looking up from your master's shadow to see what's happening to the people around you. Serving a throne that fills its land with ashes and its children with cancer."

Yoritomo laughed, slapping Hiro on the broad, flat spaulder covering his shoulder.

"She still has some spirit, eh? Peasant fire?"

"And you?" Yukiko turned on the Shōgun. "You make a wasteland and call it an empire. You're a parasite. A leech, bloated with the blood of your people." She spat on the ground at his feet. "Baby killer."

Yoritomo's smile died on his lips. He slowly drew his katana from its scabbard: three feet of gleaming steel, patterns of light rippling across the metal like sunlight on rushing water. He leveled the blade at Yukiko's head.

"Leave the arashitora alive," he growled. "Kill the others."

Masaru could barely stand.

He slumped against the wall, breath rattling in his lungs, watching the shapes dance in the dark. Michi was a blur, a shadow melting from one spot to the next, tsurugi glinting in the glow of Hideo's pipe. She lashed out, catching one bushiman across the throat with her blade. The man spun like a top, clutching the red spray at his neck. The girl slid down into a split, kimono riding up around her hips, plunging her weapon into another soldier's crotch.

Akihito was bleeding from a slash across his shoulder, back to back with Kasumi as she struck out with her bo, sending a bushiman's blade clattering from nerveless fingers. She broke the man's leg and pushed his face in with two rapid-fire blows, sending him back into his fellows with a bloody gasp. Another two bushimen launched a savage riposte that she barely deflected, and three fingers from her left hand sailed off into the dark. She cried out, barely able to keep a grip on her staff, leaning back into Akihito. The floor was slick with blood, treacherous beneath their feet. Though the trio was making a brave fight of it, their foes were too many. It would only be moments before they were overrun.

There in the dark, with death a few breaths away, Masaru thought of his daughter. He thought of her arms wrapped around him as she gave him her forgiveness, here in this very cell. He thought of her as a little girl, running in the woods with her brother, pure as new snow, stretching out with the fresh, trembling gift toward the faint sparks of life that lingered in the dying bamboo.

The gift he had urged them to hide.

The gift he had passed to them both.

Yōkai blood.

Hunt Master. Black Fox of Shima. He had hidden it well, ever since he was a boy, even from his sensei. Even as he eclipsed his master and became the greatest hunter in the Empire. Rikkimaru had often joked that Masaru was gifted. If only the old man had known . . .

Naomi knew. She had loved him for it, thought of the Kenning as a blessing from the Gods. He still treasured the memory of the joy in her eyes when she told him he had passed it to their children. But by then, the "gift" had seemed a curse to him. A blessing he had squandered, used only to make himself a more efficient killer. Forcing the wolves into his pits, the foxes into his snares. The last eagle he had ever seen died on the tip of one of his arrows. At his command, the serpent children of the Naga Queen had turned and devoured each other in front of their own mother, the last of the Black Yōkai blinded by tears of grief as he ended her. The gods had not intended it to be so. Kitsune would have been ashamed of him.

And so when Naomi died, he drowned his grief and the Kenning both, in liquor, in the cloying stink of lotus smoke. To forget what he had become, his abuse of the gift he had turned to butchery. Like a prisoner, he closed it off in a dark room in his mind, hoping it would atrophy and fade, the memories of all the blood he had spilled along with it.

But the long hours of sweating de-tox in this pit had cleared the cobwebs from his skull. He could see the doorway clearly now, the one he had closed and locked so many years before.

He watched the steel dance in front of him, heard Michi cry out. He saw Akihito take a blade to the thigh, opening a gash that was almost bone-deep. A sword sank up to the hilt in Kasumi's gut, another into her chest, blood spraying from between her teeth. And Masaru walked down the long dusty corridor in his mind, and stood before that rusted iron door. Reaching out with shaking fingers, he turned the handle and opened it.

Off in the dark, the prison rats pricked up their ears, and listened.

The Iron Samurai charged.

The bloodlust swelled within Buruu, spilling over into Yukiko, minds instinctively reaching toward each other. Two sets of eyes, six feet planted on the earth, the strength of their wings knotted tight at their shoulder blades, tantō in their hand. They were in the Iishi again, Lady Izanami's Red Bone Warlord roaring in the rain, the taste of black blood on their tongue. She leaped up onto his back, slipped into his mind. They bared their teeth and screamed their challenge, a roar drowning out the growling swords, the hiss of armored death charging at them headlong.

Too many to defeat.

But not too many to fight.

Kin removed a brass cylinder from his belt and stabbed one end against his chest. There was a sharp cracking noise, a red light sprang to life at one end of the tube, and he hurled it at the oncoming samurai.

A soundless explosion, a white sphere of light, tinged at the edges with translucent, bloody red. The sphere expanded in the blink of an eye, catching four of the charging samurai in its arc. There was a sudden stench of evaporating chi, the sound of fuel lines expanding and bursting, a rush of blue-black vapor. The samurai collapsed under the dead weight of their ō-yoroi, chainkatana falling silent as their motors stalled.

Buruu and Yukiko charged at the gap in their circle, pouncing onto a samurai and disassembling him completely, the pieces flying apart like dry leaves in a storm. They leaped into the air, feeling the heat beneath their wings, soaring across the row of growling swords. Coming down behind the knot of warriors, swiping at their backs, metal shredding like paper. Blood spraying in the air, on their faces, scent filling their lungs. Eyes in front and behind, moving like water, severing arms and opening throats and leaping into the air again, wings a blur, roaring in defiance. Choking sounds. Wet bubbling writ upon broken stone.

A flash from Kin's second grenade burst in the middle of the samurai thicket, armor dying in the aftermath. Boiling clouds of blue-black rushed from the ruined ō-yoroi, the men inside howling in frustration as lifeless iron bore them to the ground.

Yukiko and Buruu flew up above the melee, leash snapping taut, groaning but holding fast. They swooped down again, the chain sweeping through the samurai like a scythe. They were a slingstone on a tether of metal, cutting through the assembled men, a hot blade through snow, all hissing steam and spraying blood. The sun glinted off the metal on their wings, the tantō in their fist, the murder painted on their skin.

They turned their eyes to the traitor, sea-green stare alight with rage, neo-daishō snarling in his hands. He dashed forward and kicked Kin in the chest, katana glancing off the Guildsman's armor, a rain of sparks against the brass. Kin deflected the blows with his forearms, staggering beneath the flurry. The loading crane on the Guildsman's back uncurled and snapped at Hiro's head, a hissing viper with iron jaws, catching the samurai's chainwakizashi and tearing it from his grip.

The Guildsmen of Shima were many things, but they were far from fools. They had gifted the Iron Samurai with weapons to cut through flesh and bone in the blink of an eye. To lay entire armies of meat to waste. But against a Guildsman's skin? Hiro's weapons were butter knives against a brick wall.

Still, the Iron Samurai was adept, honed by years of training that Kin had spent crouched over a workbench. And so the boy's feet were swept out from under him and he crashed to the floor amidst a burst of chi fumes. Blue sparks spilled from his armor, Hiro stomping up and down on his chest. The samurai raised one black enameled foot to crush Kin's unprotected head.

They roared, a boom of thunder across the arena floor, setting the plates of Hiro's armor squealing. He turned to face them, chainkatana in a double-handed grip, breath heaving in his lungs. He tore the helmet from his head so they could see his face, damp with sweat, fearless, fierce eyes, teeth clenched.

Yukiko's voice was a low, dangerous growl.

"You can't win this, Hiro."

He drummed his fingers across the hilt, spat on the ground.

"To wield the long and the short sword," he hissed, "and to die."

They bounded into the air, wings spread, blue lightning playing across the edges of their feathers. The hands that had held them in the night, that had sent goosebumps shivering down their spine, now swinging the growling sword toward them, an unrecognizable mask of hatred for a face.

Their flesh separated, what had been Yukiko springing from the back of what had been Buruu. They took Hiro's right arm off just below the shoulder, beak shearing through black iron in a shower of sparks and bright red. Their knife sank up to the hilt in the gap in his breastplate, just below his armpit. Sticky warmth flooded over their hands as they held him tight, lowering him to the ground in ruins.

"Goodbye, Hiro," they whispered.

Their breath rasped in their lungs, hearts thundering in their chests. They wiped their hand across their faces, smearing the blood across pale skin, and turned to face Yoritomo.

The Shōgun dropped his katana and ran.

A chittering horde, eyes of red, jagged teeth glittering in the dark. They scampered from the shadows, all thick tails and mottled fur and sharp claws, a fly-blown legion grown fat and fierce on corpse-meat. The vermin of Kigen's gutters, now rising to consume its best and brightest.

Minister Hideo screamed as a beefy black fellow with knives for teeth scampered up the folds of his sokutai robe and began tearing strips off his legs. Bushimen around him began crying out, sleek, mongrel shapes sinking little fangs into the unprotected flesh behind their knees, gnawing at their heels. Screams echoed down the black corridors, the sound of night-terrors and sweat, shrieking, childhood fear.

Michi lashed out with her tsurugi at the flailing soldiers, blade sinking up to the hilt, painting the walls. She swept away their feet, sending them crashing onto the ground, the skittering horde of black shapes and bright eyes washing over them like a seething, squealing tide. Sharp teeth sank into soft skin, exposed throats, eyelids, the floor awash with scarlet. It was a hard death to endure. Almost as hard as it was to watch.

Hideo sank to his knees, flailing as the black shapes poured over him, bright mouthfuls of pain tearing through the lotus haze. The bone pipe fell from his twitching fingers. Michi stood over him as he rolled about on the ground, screaming, thrashing, begging for the mercy of the bloody sword in her hand.

She looked down on him, eyes cold, and sheathed the weapon at her back.

"Remember Daiyakawa," she whispered.

Masaru dragged Kasumi away from the carnage, back into his cell. Akihito crawled in beside him, pale with grief and pain, tying a bloody rag around the gouge in his leg. Masaru tore Kasumi's uwagi, tried to staunch the blood flow from the wounds in her chest and gut. Kasumi coughed, blood on her lips, teeth gritted.

"Leave it," she gasped, pushing Masaru's hands away.

"No." He pressed harder at the bubbling wounds. "We're getting out of here."

"Masaru . . ." Kasumi winced, swallowed thickly. "If they knew our plan . . . t-they know Yukiko's too." She squeezed her eyes shut, doubled over for a moment. "The arena. The arashitora. All of it. You have to help her."

Masaru kissed her hand, smudging his lips with blood, unwilling to let go. Kasumi pressed his palm against her cheek. A thin red line spilled from the corner of her mouth.

"We have to go." Michi hovered by the cell door, spattered in gore. "The ship is waiting."

Masaru's eyes didn't leave Kasumi's as he spoke, "Yukiko is in danger."

"You can barely stand." Michi nodded to Akihito, "He can't stand at all."

"Get him to the ship," Masaru glanced back at her. "Get Akihito out of here."

"Masaru, you bastard, you're not leaving me again." Akihito tried to get to his feet, clutching his leg. "No chance in all the hells."

"You can't fight if you can't walk, brother."

"I'll bloody crawl if I have to."

Kasumi blinked at Akihito, the light dimming in her eyes.

"Go. There is no shame."

Akihito stared hard, jaw set, clenching and unclenching his fists. He glanced down at the wound in his thigh, the blood pooling on the floor at his feet, then back into her eyes.

"It's a scratch. I can fight."

"Fight another day, you big lump."

The big man's face crumpled and tears spilled down his cheeks.

"Kas' . . ."

She smiled up at him, pale lips smeared with red.

"Remember me, brother."

Akihito sat for a long, silent moment, holding his breath lest it emerge as a sob. Then he leaned in to kiss her brow, teeth gritted against the pain. Michi padded up beside him, offered one bloodstained hand. Struggling to his feet, the big man threw one arm over the girl's shoulder. Looking down at Masaru and Kasumi, he closed his eyes as if burning the picture into his mind. Then he hung his head and turned away.

Sparing one long, sad glance for the lovers on the bloody floor, Michi turned and began hobbling out of the cell, struggling under Akihito's weight. They became shadows, black shapes limping in the dark. Their footprints glistened on the stone behind them.

Masaru turned back to Kasumi, squeezing her hands tight.

"My beautiful lady," he whispered.

He remembered the touch of her lips, the feel of her skin, those sweet, desperate nights together beneath the stars. He'd been blind. He should have loved her as she deserved. He should have seen that punishing himself meant he was punishing her too.

I should have married you, love.

"I . . ." He swallowed. "I should have . . ."

"You should have." A faint smile. "But I knew it, Masaru. I knew."

She exhaled, drifting closer to that bottomless, colorless edge with every breath.

"I will miss you." She closed her eyes as she began to fall. "I love you."

He squeezed her hand, willing her away from the brink. He couldn't see her face for the tears in his eyes, the sting of his grief. He could only feel her, smell her, listening as her breath became shallow and frail in the dark, and then became nothing at all.

"Wait," he whispered.

But she didn't.

The beast roared, straining at the end of its metal leash, the chain unwilling to break. Yoritomo glanced over his shoulder as he fled out into the street, saw the Guildsman light a blue fire at his wrist and begin cutting the tether around the arashitora's throat. In seconds, it would be free, pursuing him on those accursed clockwork wings.

The Guild had betrayed him. Hachiman's chosen.

Out into the blinding heat, long red cloak billowing behind him as he fled down the broad cobbles of the arena district, into the alleys and squeezeways near the Market Square. The Shōgun screamed for his guards, for anyone, cries ringing off hollow stone. The streets were empty, not a soul to be seen. He could hear the sound of music and laughter drifting on the choking breeze. Breaking left, he dashed toward Spire Row and the gala at the base of the sky-spires. He tore off his cloak, threw it behind him. Lost in his fear, no pause for thought, flight instinct flooding his veins with adrenaline and pumping into trembling, taut muscle. Thunder rumbled to the north.

He heard a roar bouncing off the alley walls, his face twisting in fear.

It is behind me.

He screamed again, stumbling through the alley trash and out onto the Market Square, breath burning in his lungs. His muscles were tense with anticipated agony, the terror of dying beneath the beast's claws turning his gut to water. It screamed again behind him, a prelude to his bloody end.

A crowd of revellers paused mid-song, faces pale with astonishment as the Ninth Shōgun of the Kazumitsu Dynasty barrelled through them, scattering them on the flagstones. He pounded across the cobbles, stumbling and almost falling down the steps surrounding the Burning Stones. The blackened columns rose into the air about him, casting long shadows on the ground. A child cried out from across the way, several drunken men dropped to their knees in supplication. The unwashed masses, instinct forcing their foreheads into the dirt.

Why do they not run? Do they not fear the beast?

Yoritomo risked a wide-eyed glance behind him and saw only the girl. Not the gore-soaked thunder tiger that had torn his men to ribbons. Not the engine of beak and claw and lightning he feared was chasing him. Just one feeble little girl with a bloody knife in her hands.

He skidded to a halt in the pit, incredulous, ashes billowing around his ankles. His fingers closed about the textured grip of the iron-thrower in his obi, drawing it from its holster. The girl charged headlong toward him, snarling, knuckles white on the handle of her tantō. Her eyes were a demon's, alight with hatred.

The iron-thrower rose in slow motion. The muzzle flashed, bright as a second sun. A boom rang out like thunder as the bullet ricocheted off the stone at her feet.

The girl froze.

Masaru had only stopped long enough to tie the hakama of a fallen bushi-man around his waist, snatch up a pair of bloody goggles and a blood-stained kodachi blade from a gnawed, twitching hand. Dashing along dark sweating corridors, bounding up the prison stairs three at a time, past the open cells and slumped bodies of Michi's victims, up toward the sunlight. He sprinted out into the blinding glare, hand up to blot out the light as he strapped the lenses over his eyes. Pawing at the thick droplets of congealing scarlet on the glass, he bolted in the direction of the arena.

A group of drunken revellers took one look at the half-naked, blood-drenched, sword-wielding madman dashing down the street toward them and fled in the other direction as quickly as they could manage. Matted gray hair streaming behind him, fists clenched, bare, bloody feet pounding on broken cobbles, Masaru ran as fast as his body would take him, through the twisting maze of alleys past the chapterhouse, across a broad footbridge, east toward the arena. Breath dragging in his lungs, salt burning in his eyes, broken glass and cracked stone tearing at his heels. But the pain was nothing compared to the thought of his daughter fighting and falling alone; the fear of losing the only thing he had left in this world turned his gut to grease and shushed the meager concerns of his body away.

And so he ran, breath hissing between his teeth, heart lurching in his chest, flesh slick with a sheen of sweat. He could see the walls of the arena looming up over the jagged rooftops in the distance, the empty, snaggle-toothed faces of the Docktown tumbledowns. His grip on the hilt of the kodachi was a vice, the buildings around him nothing but a blur, running so fast he felt he might fly. He seized hold of a downspout as he rounded a corner, skidding to a stop as he heard a strange sound split the air.

A hollow boom, as of too-close thunder. The sound of a ricochet cracking off splintering stone. Not as deep as a dragon cannon. Louder than a kindling wheel.

Only one man he knew carried a weapon capable of making a sound like that.

He tilted his head, frowning, breath heaving in his lungs, listening to the fading report bouncing across cracking brick and crumbling mortar. Glancing at the streets around him, the sun above him, desperate to get his bearings. He cursed, torn with indecision, turning his head left and right. And with a whispered plea to Kitsune, he dashed off toward his best guess, hoping that, one last time, Fox would look after his own.

The distance between them had weakened the link, pulling them far enough apart that Buruu's bloodlust was momentarily overcome by Yukiko's fear of the iron-thrower. Alone among the Burning Stones, she could see Kin through Buruu's eyes, desperately cutting through the thunder tiger's tether, the arashitora near-mindless with impotent rage.

The iron chain melted, one droplet at a time.

The despoiler lord sneered as the killing fury inside her faded, the ugly, snub-nosed barrel aimed squarely at her head. His eyes glowered above the iron sight.

YUKIKO.

Buruu.

WAIT FOR ME.

A bead of sweat crept down her face, the taste of salt lingering at the corners of her mouth. She was out of breath from the chase, heart thumping in her chest, wisps of loose hair plastered to her cheeks. Yoritomo backed away to a safe distance on the other side of the pyre pit, eyes narrowed at the dust and lotus ash blowing down the Way, coiling among the blackened tinder at the foot of the stones. The wind-swept space between them was too wide for Yukiko to lunge across with her tantō; he'd end her with the iron-thrower before she even got close. His lips were twisted in a cold smile, finger on the trigger, the barrel a bottomless black hole.

"So now you see what you are," Yoritomo sneered. "One pathetic little girl. Nothing. Nothing at all."

A crowd had gathered around them, wide-eyed and awe-struck. A small boy in a festival uwagi carrying a bright red balloon recognized Yukiko, pointed to her with a cry.

"Arashi-no-ko!"

The cry echoed across the Market Square, repeated in a dozen different voices down the street, the name spreading out like ripples on still water. Yukiko could hear heavy footsteps ringing on the cobbles, glanced toward the sky-spires. A multitude of soldiers was rushing toward them up the Way, Iron Samurai and bushimen, chainkatana and naginata spears drawn, crying out in alarm. Dozens upon dozens. Too many even for Buruu.

They'd be here in moments.

She turned back to Yoritomo, fingers slick with sweat on the handle of her tantō, folded steel glinting in the light of the muted sun. She had bathed the blade in the blood of a dozen oni, cut demons from the deepest hell down to the bone. But the knife felt so tiny in her hands now; a fragile splinter of metal, far too short, far too small.

He's too far away to touch.

WAIT FOR ME.

Yoritomo followed her gaze down the Palace Way, smiling at his men's approach. The game was over. The girl had taken her chance, risked all in one final gambit. And the king still stood.

Checkmate.

"Your father is dead." His smile was lazy. Gluttonous. "He and his whore and that ignorant Fushicho thug. They all died in the bowels of the prison, cut to pieces by my men. A pity they are not alive to torture. I will have to make do with you."

Yukiko's heart sank, bitter tears welling in her eyes. Her father. Akihito and Kasumi. So it had all been for nothing. The thought that she would never see them again filled her, an anguish and rage almost too painful to bear.

How much more can this man take from me?

She glanced back at the approaching guards, picturing the little bamboo valley where she had grown up, her father and mother seated by the fireside, she and her brother lying with old Buruu in their laps; the brief summer days before the winter it had all begun to fall apart. And in the wake of that image, a bright spark of realization rose above the despair inside, the burning anger of her loss.

She remembered the wolf, the cold winter snow, Satoru and old Buruu by her side. She remembered her rage at the hound's death, reaching out across the Kenning to snuff out the wolf's life with her hatred. She remembered the shape of Satoru's mind, the pain of his death pushing her inside him as the venom took him away.

He's too far away to touch.

She glared at Yoritomo across the stones.

But I don't need to touch him to hurt him.

She reached out toward him, hands motionless, straining to her limits, her father's words ringing in her ears.

This is something worth sacrificing for. Something greater.

NO. WAIT FOR ME.

Her temples began to throb, eyes narrowed to paper cuts.

I AM COMING.

The bushimen were seconds away. Crossbows and needle-throwers. Naginata and nagamaki. Buruu wouldn't stand a chance.

They are too many.

WAIT FOR ME!

Help me, Buruu.

WAIT!

"I'm going to kill you, little girl," Yoritomo sneered. "Like I killed your whore mother."

Yukiko glanced at the young boy and his balloon. Fear and awe shone bright in the child's eyes.

"Let me show you what one little girl can do," she said.

Yoritomo frowned as the blood began dripping from her nose, bright, salty red spilling over her lips and mingling with the taste of her sweat. She felt the shape of him, the heat of him, stretching toward him and closing her fist about his mind. Somewhere far away, she could hear someone calling her name.

This is it. Our chance. Help me, brother.

"What are you—"

A gasp, eyes wide, mouth open in shock. Yoritomo moaned, pain registering at the base of his skull and spreading bloody fingers throughout his synapses.

The shape of his mind was slippery, alien, not at all like the mind of a beast. Yukiko felt it sliding away, her rage not hot enough to maintain her grip, a serpent slithering between her fingers. And then, someone was beside her, inside her, anger entwining with her own. A familiar warmth, a strength that lifted her up and carried her on his shoulders high above the ground, the whole world at her feet. Together they pressed down, using the hate, the rage, seizing hold and wrenching from side to side, gray matter running to pulp in their grip.

Yoritomo staggered away, a shapeless gurgle spilling from his lips as his ears started to bleed. He put one hand up to his brow, pawing at his temple, hemorrhaging turning the whites of his eyes a dark, cloudy scarlet. The iron-thrower wavered in his grip. He blinked. Gasped. Squeezed the trigger.

A muzzle flash. A burst of sound. A voice roaring her name. A hard shove, something heavy slamming into her from behind. A metallic breeze whispering past her cheek, so close she could feel its heat. Hear its hiss. She was falling. She was weightless.

The little boy cried out in horror.

The Shōgun collapsed on the ground, blood pouring from his nose and ears and eyes. He spasmed, spine arching, heels kicking at the stone. Fingernails clawing at the sky, lips peeling back from bloody teeth. They wrapped their hands together and strangled until nothing remained inside him, darkness fading away into a whimper as the Ninth Shōgun of the Kazumitsu Dynasty folded down upon himself and ended on the ash-covered stone.

Blinking, gasping, she came to her senses. The presence inside her head receded like an ebb-tide, leaving her hollow and empty in its wake. She reached out toward Buruu, felt him speeding closer, but still too far away.

Then who . . .

There was blood on the cobbles around her, blood on her skinned hands and knees. The smell of the shot hanging in the air. Someone had shoved her, pushed her out of the way. Someone . . .

She turned, saw him writhing on the stone, sticky red spilling from his mouth and the hole in his throat.

No.

She crawled toward him, a scream tearing loose and echoing across the square.

"Father!"

A roar from the skies, a typhoon wail. The soldiers looked up and cried out in fear, scattering as Buruu landed atop Yoritomo's corpse, smearing it across his claws and shattering the flagstones beneath. He spread his wings, lightning flashing on his feathers, electricity dancing across the manacles on the Burning Stones. White fur, black stripes and spatters of warm, fresh red. The bushimen fell back as he circled around Yukiko and Masaru, roaring again in warning.

The thunder echoed the beast's cry. Raijin was pleased.

Kin descended from the sky in a cloud of burning smoke, blue-white flame flaring at his back as the crowd scattered out of his path. Roaring at the soldiers to back away, he landed beside the arashitora, brass boots crunching on the cobbles. Anguish welled in knife-bright eyes as he caught sight of the girl kneeling over the bleeding body of her father. She looked up at him, eyes shining with tears, pale with grief.

"Kin." Her throat was raw, choking. "Help me with him."

Face drawn with sorrow, he helped Yukiko lift Masaru onto the thunder tiger's shoulders. A ribbon of blood spilled from the older man's mouth, spattered across the cobbles, smeared on the Guildsman's skin. A murmur rippled among the spectators, watching in amazement as Yukiko leaped on Buruu's back.

Fly, Buruu. Fly!

A collective gasp ran through the crowd as the beast leaped into the air. People pointed in wonder, eyes wide, blessed with a story to tell their children.

"Stormdancer," one whispered.

A gale swelled beneath Buruu's wings as the ground fell away below them. They spiraled upward on Kigen's thermals, up into the rumbling sky. The buildings became toys, and the people became ants: tiny dark figures gathered around the blackened pillars and a small spot of blood, staring skyward. The ocean stretched out to the south, red waters melting into deeper scarlet, the wind caressing their skin.

Yukiko cradled her father in her arms, rocking him back and forth. Her hands were soaking wet; dark, hot floods gushing from his neck as she pressed down on the wound.

"Father," she whispered. "No, please, no."

She clutched him, desperate, hot tears and blood smudged across her cheeks, her whole body shaking with the sobs. Masaru opened his mouth but no words would come, thick red bubbling and bursting on his lips. He clutched a handful of the arashitora's fur, white knuckles, trembling hands. He pressed his fingers to the beast's flesh, reached out for his warmth in the growing cold, the spark to keep the dark at bay.

Buruu tossed his head, narrowed his eyes.

I CAN FEEL YOU, OLD MAN. POKING AROUND INSIDE MY MIND.

Yes.

YOU CUT ME. YOU TOOK MY WINGS.

I am sorry.

WHAT DO YOU WANT?

There are things I would say. But the wound . . .

AND WHY WOULD I HELP YOU? AFTER WHAT YOU DID TO ME?
Because you love her too.

The sky around them was red as blood, dimming to black where the clouds reached down from the north. They flew toward the roiling storm; the great beast, the dying man and the weeping girl. And with a slow nod of his head, the arashitora closed his eyes, took hold of the man's fading thoughts and cupped them in his talons, carried them across the vast, empty gulf to the girl's waiting mind.

YUKIKO.
. . . Father? How?
THE KENNING WAS MINE BEFORE IT WAS YOURS.
You helped me. I felt you.
ARE YOU SAFE? IS IT OVER?
We're safe, can't you see? We're flying, father. We're flying.
I . . . I CAN'T LIFT MY HEAD.

She squeezed his hand, blinked away her tears.

Then use our eyes.

His lashes fluttered against his bloody cheeks. The island stretched out below them, swathes of brown and green, a swaying ocean of red blooms. The mountains loomed in the distance beyond the autumn storm, the dark shadow of the Iishi, shrouded in rolling mist. They could see the lightning, feel the wind on their skin. The hands of the tempest held them tight, ozone and thunder, willing them home.

I SEE, ICHIGO.
It's all so beautiful from up here.
IT IS.

Blood dripped from his fingertips, falling through the sky like soft rain. The song of thunder rolled around them. He thought of Naomi singing by the fireside, Satoru beside her. He thought of Kasumi stalking through long grass, wind playing in her hair. He pushed the pictures into her mind.

THEY ARE WAITING FOR ME.
No.
I LOVE YOU, YUKIKO.
No. Don't you dare say your goodbyes to me.

She shook her head, willing the darkness gone, flaring in his mind with stubborn, warm light. A scream welled up inside and spilled over her limits, a long wavering note of grief echoed by Buruu, the pair roaring in defiance together as if they could frighten the end away.

Stay with us.

I CAN'T.

Don't leave us alone.

LET ME GO.

No. All this is for nothing if you're gone.

THEN MAKE IT FOR SOMETHING.

Masaru closed his eyes, felt the wind on his face, the bleeding land rushing away beneath him, a final peal of thunder drifting off into blessed silence.

He smiled.

SOMETHING GREATER.

EPILOGUE

Sumiko prayed.

The procession wound its path down the Palace Way, a snaking line of beggar monks clad in death-white, shaved heads bowed low to the earth. Each held a funeral candle between outstretched fingers, flames guttering in the dawn light, a sluggish sun rearing its head over the black waters of Kigen Bay.

Forty-nine days since the Seii Taishōgun's death. Forty-nine monks to pray for his rebirth after forty-nine nights in the courts of Enma-ō. Tradition held that the souls of the dead were reborn in the Hour of the Phoenix, as daylight banished the deep of night. And so they marched toward sunrise to the beat of somber drums, the air thick with incense and mournful song, pretending it would make a difference. A throng had gathered to watch the procession, Sumiko among them, just one more beggar girl amidst the mob. Each spectator whispered their own prayers and hid their own thoughts and wondered what would come next.

The war with the gaijin was forgotten. The zaibatsu were poised to war with each other. Tiger and Phoenix, Dragon and Fox, all scrabbling for Shima's empty throne. The chapterhouses buzzed like hornets' nests kicked from their trees. The Guildsmen urged calm, watching as their creations were amassed across smoking fields of dead earth, poised to destroy each other.

Dangerous thoughts bloomed in Sumiko's head; thoughts that had taken root these past few weeks and refused to let her rest. Thoughts that there must be a better way than this.

At midnight they would gather around the almshouse radio, she and her friends, listening to the pirate broadcasts and wondering if the words they heard were true. The crackling, metallic voice spilling from the speakers at weeksend spoke of their enslavement to chi, to the men who controlled it. It said that the Guild had liquefied gaijin prisoners of war to make the inochi. That the very fuel on which their Empire had been built was made with blood; razored gears and metal teeth lubricated with the lives of innocent people. And though the Communications Ministry scoffed at the claim, none could help but notice how rapidly inochi supplies had dwindled once Shima's armies retreated from the fronts. How the price of the fertilizer had skyocketed once the slave fleets began flying home with growling, empty bellies.

Could it be true? Were we so blind?

People whispered in the long midnight hours, asking the same question, over and over.

Has all this been bought with innocent blood?

The riots after the inochi broadcast had been brief, brutally suppressed. And now an uneasy peace had settled over the clan metropolises, broken glass crunching underfoot, violence on hold until the official period of mourning came to an end. Forty-nine days of fragile, jagged silence. Forty-nine days spent waiting to be told who would rule, now that the Kazumitsu Dynasty had lost its only son.

Sumiko kept her eyes on the ground, lips moving in silent prayer. Not for Yoritomo, Seii Taishōgun of the Empire, but for the people he had murdered. The women, the children, the old and the weak. The prisoners who had been dragged up the hill into the chapterhouse, to die frightened and alone, a thousand miles from home. The soldiers who had perished on foreign soil, fighting in a war built on lies and the fear of empty fuel tanks. The starving beggars, the silenced dissenters. Even the great Black Fox of Shima. Every soul sent on its way for the sake of greed and hubris and madness.

It had been a small thing to begin with; just a few spirit tablets laid out to mark the place of the Black Fox's death near the Burning Stones. Nobody knew who had put them there. But then a few had grown into a dozen. And then a hundred. At first, the guards had tried removing the markers and paper flowers laid to honor the dead, but soon there were thousands of ihai laid out across the Market Square. A silent recrimination, a graveyard for the countless bodies with no grave to call their own.

Sumiko had made one herself. A simple tablet of stone, carved with her mother's name, as black as the blood she'd coughed at her ending.

A cry rang out among the crowd, picked up and carried by a dozen other voices, fingers pointed at the sky. A single word, rolling among the mob like breaking surf, awash with wonder and awe. Sumiko looked up and the prayer died on her lips.

"Arashitora."

A majestic black silhouette against the brightening, bloody sky, flying out of the north with the poison wind at its back. It soared overhead, above the gasps and cries of astonishment, heading up the Palace Way. The procession collapsed into bedlam, the solemn rows of monks and spectators dissolving into a throng of running feet, thousands of people breaking ranks and following the silhouette up the street.

Sumiko squinted behind her goggles in the grubby dawn light, one hand up to blot out the sun.

"Gods above," she breathed.

There was a rider on the thunder tiger's back.

The shape circled above the Burning Stones, splitting the air with rasping, beautiful cries, its wings making a sound like rolling thunder. It was the color of clean snow, black slashes across pristine white, lightning playing at the edges of its wings. Eyes flashing, cruel, hooked claws and beak, proud and fierce.

Sumiko had never seen anything more beautiful in all her life.

A metal frame sat over its wings, gleaming and iridescent, feathers made of hard bloodstained canvas. The beast circled lower, alighting on the cobblestones as the crowd gathered, surrounding them in a wide circle. The few Tora guards among the mob watched on fearfully, hands slack on their naginata.

The rider was a girl Sumiko recognized. Long hair, dark eyes, pale skin clad in mourning black. She was the girl they sang kabuki plays about in the Downside taverns. The girl the street children mimicked, running among the gutters and alleys, flapping their arms and hollering at the sky. The girl that had gifted her with a full purse and a sad smile in the shadow of the sky-docks.

Arashi-no-odoriko, Stormdancer, Slayer of Yoritomo-no-miya.

The girl dismounted, placed a circlet of fresh wildflowers on the ground. A rainbow of color woven into a beautiful wreath, the scent of jasmine and chrysanthemums, azalea and wisteria rising above the black lotus stink. She gently set an ihai among the others, dark stone, a single word carved deeply into its face.

Father.

The girl bowed her head, lips moving as if in prayer. She wore a short-sleeved uwagi, and Sumiko could see her left arm was horribly scarred; the flesh about her shoulder was a patchwork of new burns. An old-fashioned katana in a black lacquered scabbard was strapped across her back. Her face was a grim, pale mask, cold as stone as she lifted her eyes and stared at the sea of wondering expressions around her.

"People of Kigen," she called. "Hear me now."

The toxic wind howled in off the bay, bringing the stink of rot and lotus ash, coating the throats of the crowd, seeping into their pores. The girl's voice rose above it.

"For forty-nine days, we have mourned our lost; those we loved, and those who loved us." She swallowed. "Now the time for grief is over.

"For too long we have lived, fat and prosperous on the back of the machine, on the fuel that drives it. But there comes a time when the price grows too high, when the oil runs too red, when we begin building our lives on the shattered lives of others. And at the last, the machine we once controlled ends up controlling us.

"Some in this land would have you bleed for them now, to plant their flag where another's once flew. Others would have you light a fire, to make ashes of the endless fields, to reduce those five-sided slave pits on the hill to rubble. A few would have you do nothing at all. To remain meek and cowed, to bow your heads and accept what the machine hands you. They are not afraid of you. But they should be. The few should fear the many."

She held out her arms, showing the terrible scar where irezumi must once have been.

"I believe that when the engines that poison our land and choke our sky lie rusting in the earth, we will be free. Free to choose a new path. A path that will not end with our destruction, or the destruction of the world around us. I do not know what that new path will be. I only know that it will be better than this. That it is not too late."

She turned and vaulted onto the back of the waiting thunder tiger. The beast opened his beak and roared, and the sound of his wings was a breaking storm.

"Each of you must decide where you stand," she called. "All we ask is that you refuse to kneel. You are the people. You have the power. Open your eyes. Open your minds. Then close the fingers on your hand."

The arashitora leaped into the air, lightning crackling across the tips of its feathers. Up, up into the choking skies they soared, the sound of beating wings building like the storm to come. And with a fierce cry, they wheeled away and turned back to the north, to bring fire and smoke and the promise of a new day.

Sumiko watched them fly away, the scent of fresh flowers filling her lungs.

She looked around at the assembled people, young and old, man and woman and child, each face upturned and alight with wonder.

She nodded her head.

And into the poisoned air, she raised a fist.

GLOSSARY

GENERAL TERMS

Arashitora—literally "stormtiger." A mythical creature with the head, forelegs and wings of an eagle, and the hindquarters of a tiger. Thought to be long extinct, these beasts were traditionally used as flying mounts by the caste of legendary Shima heroes known as "Stormdancers." These beasts are also referred to as "thunder tigers."

Arashi-no-odoriko—literally "Stormdancer" (feminine). Legendary heroes of Shima's past, who rode arashitora into battle. The most well-known are Kitsune no Akira (who slew the great sea dragon Boukyaku) and Tora Take-hiko (who sacrificed his life to close Devil Gate and stop the Yomi hordes escaping into Shima).

Blood lotus—a toxic flowering plant cultivated by the people of Shima. Blood lotus poisons the soil in which it grows, rendering it incapable of sustaining life. The blood lotus plant is utilized in the production of teas, medicines, narcotics and fabrics. The seeds of the bloom are processed by the Lotus Guild to produce "chi," the fuel that drives the machines of the Shima Shōgunate.

Burakumin—a low-born citizen who does not belong to any of the four zai-batsu clans.

Bushido—literally "the Way of the Warrior." A code of conduct adhered to by the samurai caste. The tenets of Bushido are: rectitude, courage, benevolence, respect, honesty, honor and loyalty. The life of a Bushido follower is spent in constant preparation for death; to die with honor intact in the service of their Lord is their ultimate goal.

Bushiman—a common-born soldier who has sworn to follow the Way of Bushido.

Chan—a diminutive suffix applied to a person's name. It expresses that the speaker finds the person endearing. Usually reserved for children and young women.

Chi—literally "blood." The combustible fuel which drives the machines of the Shima Shōgunate. The fuel is derived from the seeds of the blood lotus plant.

Daimyo—a powerful territorial lord that rules one of the Shima zaibatsu. The title is usually passed on through heredity.

Fushicho—literally "Phoenix." One of the four zaibatsu clans of Shima. The Phoenix clan live on the island of Yotaku (Blessings) and venerate Amaterasu, Goddess of the Sun. Traditionally, the greatest artists and artisans in Shima come from the Phoenix clan. Also: the kami guardian of the same zaibatsu, an elemental force closely tied to the concepts of enlightenment, inspiration and creativity.

Gaijin—literally "foreigner." A person not of Shimanese descent. The Shima Shōgunate has been embroiled in a war of conquest in the gaijin country of Morcheba for over twenty years.

Hadanashi—literally "someone skinned alive." A derisive term used by Guildsmen to describe the rest of the Shima populace.

Inochi—literally "life." A fertilizer which, when applied to blood lotus fields, delays the onset of soil degradation caused by the plant's toxicity.

Irezumi—a tattoo, created by inserting ink beneath the skin with steel or bamboo needles. Members of all Shima clans wear the totem of their clan on their right shoulder. City dwellers will often mark their left shoulder with a symbol to denote their profession. The complexity of the design communicates the wealth of the bearer—larger, more elaborate designs can take months or even years to complete and cost many hundreds of kouka.

Kami—spirits, natural forces or universal essences. This word can refer to personified deities, such as Izanagi or Raijin, or broader elemental forces, such as fire or water. Each clan in Shima also has a guardian kami, from which the clan draws its name.

Kazumitsu Dynasty—the hereditary line of Shōgun that rule the Shima isles. Named for the first of the line to claim the title—Kazumitsu I—who led a successful revolt against the corrupt Tenma Emperors.

Kitsune—literally "Fox." One of the four zaibatsu clans of Shima, known for stealth and good fortune. The Kitsune clan live close to the haunted Iishi Mountains, and venerate Tsukiyomi, the God of the Moon. Also: the kami guardian of the same zaibatsu, said to bring good fortune to those who bear his mark. The saying "Kitsune looks after his own" is often used to account for inexplicable good luck.

Kouka—the currency of Shima. Coins are flat and rectangular, made of strips of plaited metal: more valuable iron, and less valuable copper. Coins are often cut into smaller pieces to conduct minor transactions. These small pieces are known as "bits." Ten copper kouka buys one iron kouka.

Lotus Guild—a cabal of zealots who oversee the production of chi and the distribution of inochi fertilizer in Shima. Referred to collectively as "Guildsmen," the Lotus Guild comprises three parts: rank-and-file "Lotusmen," the engineers of the "Artificer" sect and the religious arm known as "Purifiers."

Oni—a demon of the Yomi underworld, reputedly born to the Goddess Izanami after she was corrupted by the Land of the Dead. Old legends report that their legion is one thousand and one strong. They are a living embodiment of evil, delighting in slaughter and the misfortune of man.

Ronin—literally "wave-man." A samurai without a Lord or master, either due to the death of the Lord in question, or the loss of the Lord's favor. To remain ronin is a source of great shame—the samurai will typically either seek a new master, or commit seppuku to regain his honor.

Ryu—literally "Dragon." One of the four zaibatsu clans of Shima, renowned as great explorers and traders. In the early days before Empire, the Ryu were a seafaring clan of raiders who pillaged among the northern clans. They venerate Susano-ō, God of Storms. Also: the kami guardian of the same zaibatsu, a powerful spirit beast and elemental force associated with random destruction, bravery and mastery of the seas.

Sama—a suffix applied to a person's name. This is a far more respectful version of "san." Used to refer to one of much higher rank than the speaker.

Samurai—a member of the military nobility who adheres to the Bushido Code. Each samurai must be sworn to the service of a Lord—either a clan Daimyo, or the Shōgun himself. To die honorably in service to one's Lord is the greatest aspiration of any samurai's life. The most accomplished and wealthy among these warriors wear chi-powered suits of heavy armor called "ō-yoroi," earning them the name "Iron Samurai."

San—a suffix applied to a person's name. This is a common honorific, used to indicate respect to a peer, similar to "Mr." or "Mrs." Usually used when referring to males.

Seii Taishōgun—literally "great general who subdues eastern barbarians."

Sensei—a teacher.

Seppuku—a form of ritualized suicide in which the practitioner disembowels himself and is then beheaded by a kaishakunin (a "second," usually a close and trusted comrade). Death by seppuku is thought to alleviate loss of face, and can spare the family of the practitioner shame by association. An alternative version of seppuku, called "jumonji giri," is also practiced to atone for particularly shameful acts. The practitioner is not beheaded—instead he performs a second vertical cut in his belly and is left to bear his suffering quietly until dying from blood loss.

Shōgun—literally "Commander of a force." The title of the hereditary military dictator of the Shima Isles. The current line of rulers is descended from Tora Kazumitsu, an army commander who led a bloody uprising against Shima's former hereditary rulers, the Tenma Emperors.

Tora—literally "Tiger." The greatest of the four zaibatsu of Shima, and the clan from which the Kazumitsu Dynasty originates. The Tora are a warrior clan, who venerate Hachiman, the God of War. Also: the kami guardian of the same zaibatsu, closely associated with the concept of ferocity, hunger and physical desire.

Yōkai—a blanket term for preternatural creatures thought to originate in the spirit realms. These include arashitora, sea dragons and the dreaded oni.

Zaibatsu—literally "plutocrats." The four conglomerate clans of the Shima Isles. After the rebellion against the Tenma Emperors, Shōgun Kazumitsu rewarded his lieutenants with stewardship over vast territories. The clans to which the new Daimyo belonged (Tiger, Phoenix, Dragon and Fox) slowly consumed the clans of the surrounding territories through economic and military warfare, and became known as "zaibatsu."

CLOTHING

Furisode—a style of kimono robe, with long sleeves that reach to the floor.

Geta—sandals with elevated wooden soles.

Hakama—a divided skirt that resembles a wide-legged pair of trousers, tied tight into a narrow waist. Hakama have seven deep pleats—five in front, two at the back—to represent the seven virtues of Bushido. An undivided variant of hakama exists (i.e. a single leg, more like a skirt) intended for wear over a kimono.

Jin-haori—a kimono-style tabard worn by samurai.

Jûnihitoe—an extraordinarily complex and elegant style of kimono, worn by courtly ladies.

Kabuto—a helmet consisting of a hard dome to protect the crown, and a series of flange-shaped reticulated plates to protect the head and back of the neck. Kabuto are often decorated with a crest on the brow, typically horns or sickle-shaped blades.

Kimono—an ankle-length, T-shaped robe with long, wide sleeves, worn by both men and women. A younger woman's kimono will have longer sleeves, signifying that she is unmarried. The styles range from casual to extremely formal. Elaborate kimono designs can consist of more than twelve separate pieces and incorporate up to sixty square feet of cloth.

Mempō—a face mask, one component of the armor worn by samurai. Mempō are often crafted to resemble fantastical creatures, or made in twisted designs intended to strike fear into the enemy.

Obi—a sash, usually worn with kimono. Men's obi are usually narrow; no more than four inches wide. A formal woman's obi can measure a foot in width and up to twelve feet in length. Obi are worn in various elaborate styles and tied in decorative bows and knots.

Sokutai—a complex, multilayered robe worn by male aristocrats and courtiers.

Tabi—ankle-length socks with split toes. Boot-like, sturdier versions called jikatabi are commonly used in field work.

Uwagi—a kimono-like jacket that extends no lower than mid-thigh. Uwagi can have long, wide sleeves, or be cut in sleeveless fashion to display the wearer's irezumi.

WEAPONS

Bo—a staff, measuring between five and six feet in length, usually constructed of hardwood and shod with metal.

Daishō—a paired set of swords, consisting of a katana and wakizashi. The weapons will usually be constructed by the same artisan, and have matching designs on the blades, hilts and scabbards. The daishō is a status symbol, marking the wearer as a member of the samurai caste.

Katana—a sword with a single-edged, curved, slender blade over two feet in length, and a long hilt bound in criss-crossed cord, allowing for a double-handed grip. Katana are usually worn with shorter blades known as wakizashi.

Nagamaki—a pole weapon with a large and heavy blade. The handle measures close to three feet, with the blade measuring the same. It closely resembles a naginata, but the weapon's handle is bound in similar fashion to a katana hilt—cords wrapped in criss-crossed manner.

Naginata—a pole weapon, similar to a spear, with a curved, single-edged blade at the end. The haft typically measures between five and seven feet. The blade can be up to three feet long, and is similar to a katana.

Nunchaku—two short lengths of hardwood, joined at the end by a short length of chain or rope.

Ō-yoroi—suits of heavy samurai armor powered by chi-fueled engines. The armor augments the wearer's strength and is impenetrable to most conventional weaponry.

Tantō—a short, single- or double-edged dagger, between six and twelve inches in length. Women often carry tantō for self-defense, as the knife can easily be concealed inside an obi.

Tetsubo—a long war club, made of wood or solid iron, with iron spikes or studs at one end, used to crush armor, horses or other weapons in battle. The use of a tetsubo requires great balance and strength—a miss with the club can leave the wielder open to counterattack.

Tsurugi—a straight, double-edged sword over two feet in length.

Wakizashi—a sword with a single-edged, curved, slender blade between one and two feet in length, with a short, single-handed hilt bound in criss-crossed cord. It is usually worn with a longer blade, known as a katana.

RELIGION

Amaterasu—Goddess of the Sun. Daughter of Izanagi, she was born along with Tsukiyomi, God of the Moon, and Susano-ō, God of Storms, when her father returned from Yomi and washed to purify himself of Yomi's taint. She is a benevolent deity, a bringer of life, although in recent decades has been seen as a harsh and unforgiving goddess. She is not fond of either of her brothers, refusing to speak to Tsukiyomi, and constantly tormented by Susano-ō. She is patron of the Phoenix zaibatsu, and is also often venerated by women.

Enma-ō—one of the nine Yama Kings, and chief judge of all the hells. Enma-ō is the final arbiter of where a soul will reside after death, and how soon it will be allowed to rejoin the wheel of life.

Hachiman—the God of War. Originally a scholarly deity, thought of more as a tutor in the ways of war, Hachiman has become re-personified in recent decades to reflect the more violent warlike ways of the Shima government. He is now seen as the embodiment of war, often depicted with a weapon in one hand and a white dove in the other, signifying desire for peace, but readiness to act. He is patron of the Tiger zaibatsu.

The hells—a collective term for the nine planes of existence where a soul can be sent after death. Many of the hells are places where souls are sent temporarily to suffer for transgressions in life, before moving back to the cycle of rebirth. Before Lord Izanagi commanded the Yama kings to take stewardship over the souls of the damned in order to help usher them toward enlightenment, Shima had but a single hell—the dark, rotting pit of Yomi.

The Hungry Dead—the restless residents of the underworld. Spirits of wicked people consigned to hunger and thirst in Yomi's dark for all eternity.

Izanagi (Lord)—also called Izanagi-no-Mikoto, literally "He who Invites," the Maker God of Shima. He is a benevolent deity who, with his wife Izanami, is responsible for creating the Shima Isles, their pantheon of gods and all the life therein. After the death of his wife in childbirth, Izanagi traveled to Yomi to retrieve her soul, but failed to return her to the land of the living.

Izanami (Lady)—also called the Dark Mother, and the Endsinger, wife to Izanagi, the Maker God. Izanami died giving birth to the Shima Isles, and was consigned to dwell in the Yomi underworld. Izanagi sought to reclaim his wife, but she was corrupted by Yomi's dark power, becoming a malevolent force and hater of the living. She is mother to the thousand and one oni, a legion of demons who exist to plague the people of Shima.

Raijin—God of Thunder and Lightning, son of Susano-ō. Raijin is seen as a cruel god, fond of chaos and random destruction. He creates thunder by pounding his drums across the sky. He is the creator of arashitora, the thunder tigers.

Susano-ō—the God of Storms. Son of Izanagi, he was born along with Amaterasu, Goddess of the Sun, and Tsukiyomi, God of the Moon, when his father returned from Yomi and washed to purify himself of Yomi's taint. Susano-ō is generally seen as a benevolent god, but he constantly torments his sister, Amaterasu, Lady of the Sun, causing her to hide her face. He is father to the Thunder God, Raijin, the deity who created arashitora—the thunder tigers. He is patron of the Ryu zaibatsu.

Tsukiyomi—the God of the Moon. Son of Izanagi, he was born along with Amaterasu, Goddess of the Sun, and Susano-ō, God of Storms, when his father returned from Yomi and washed to purify himself of Yomi's taint. Tsukiyomi angered his sister, Amaterasu, when he slaughtered Uke Mochi, the Goddess of Food. Amaterasu has refused to speak to him since, which is why the Sun and Moon never share the same sky. He is a quiet god, fond of stillness and learning. He is the patron of the Kitsune zaibatsu.

Yomi—the deepest level of the hells, where the evil dead are sent to rot and suffer for all eternity. Home of demons, and the Dark Mother, Lady Izanami.

ACKNOWLEDGMENTS

Jay Kristoff would like to express heartfelt gratitude to the following outstanding human beings:

My brilliant and beautiful wife Amanda, for being my alpha, beta, most brutal critic, and above all, for indulging me in this absurd little dream.

Joe "Three-card" Monti and Jason Yarn, for kind words and encouragement during the throes of endless rejection.

Caitie Flum, for boundless generosity and sage advice, with no expectation of reward.

Lindsay "LT" Ribar, for plucking me from the slush in defiance of all muppetry.

Patrick Rothfuss, for taking precious time to talk to a stranger halfway around the world, and speak words both wise and true.

Matt Bialer, for holding my hand, shooting dead-straight and selling ice to eskimos.

Pete Wolverton and Julie Crisp, for making me polish until it gleamed, and indulging my prima donna histrionics with minimal mockery.

Lance Hewett, Narita Misaki, Sudayama Aki, Paul Cechner and Amber Hart, for making my shoddy Japanese *slightly* less shoddy.

Christopher Tovo, for the love in the alley behind Cherry Bar.

Jimmy Orr, for designing clan logos that are, without a doubt, completely orrsome.

Araki Miho, for calligraphy beautiful enough to wear for life.

Zack de la Rocha, Philip H. Anselmo, Serj Tankian, D. Randall Blythe, Mark Morton, Corey Taylor, Mike Patton, Maynard James Keenan, Billy Corgan, Chad Gray, Robb Flynn, Trent Reznor, Jerry Cantrell, Layne Stanley

(R.I.P.) and Peter Steele (R.I.P.), for poetry that has inspired and sustained me far more than simple written words ever could.

My fellow hellions around the Absolute Write Water Cooler, and all my beautiful bitchez in the Apocaladies.

My family, for unconditional love.

But most of all, to you, who hold these words now in your hand.

May it one day become a fist.